An Oracle's Deception

An Oracle's Deception

White Wood

KENNETH RIVERA

ISBN: 978-1-7336631-1-3

To those who believe in me.
Thank you!

To those who collaborated with me.
Thank you for not kicking me through the window.

To those reading this.
Enjoy.

It was a pleasure working with all of you.
Now let us roll the dice and see if this gamble pays off.
—K

Contents

Prologue

Deep within the bowels of Laberynthea, there is an oracle who has no known name. She is a maiden with silver hair, a reflection of moonlight in tangible form. Her red lips turn roses envious at her sight, and her eyes are a deep lavender that holds so much pain and misery. She wanders Laberynthea lost, longing for someone to find her or for those who left her to remember her. Even after countless years of loneliness, she recalls a great war as the catalyst for her imprisonment. Born with an incredible affinity for magic and a trusting heart, the oracle was manipulated, used as an instrument of war to foresee the plans of the ethereal beings known as *holies* and *daemons*. These are alien creatures to our world who invade our lives, mind, and free will for their end goal, whatever it may be. After the war ended, she became hunted by her own kind, who sought to use her powers for their own selfish gain. She was taken to Laberynthea, the City of Time, just to be abandoned by her closest companion. Now, eons later, she remains alone in a mossy stone ruin overtaken by time. Erased from history by those she aided and now a legend of old, she found solace in prayer to the gods. But even they decided she was too powerful of a tool for them to control; thus, they sank Laberynthea deep underground during a massive earthquake to keep the city that defies the gods hidden.

Abandoned by all, she trains her powers so that one day she can escape her prison and keep all the horrors in Laberynthea in check for the good of all.

Now, she dreams and foresees futures and events without the ability to tell another living being outside. The oracle had the same recurring dream throughout time, the same recurring whispers from the tapestry of fate. She can see and hear a simple nightmare about the end of existence, and it all begins in White Wood.

Luck Has It

I t never fails. Every time I sit down and roll the dice, I get the worst outcome, but I could be wrong this time. I pull out two six-sided dice from my bag, rolling them gently on the wooden seat on the merchant's cart.

"Snake eyes." With a sigh, I roll again. "A three. It could be the bumpy road. Let us try this one." I put the six-sided dice away, grabbing a metal twenty-sided dice. With a roll, it shows me what I expected. "A one. Really? This is silly now. One more time." I gently throw it, revealing a fifteen. "I'll take what I can get. Oh well, I should get back to work," I murmur as I put the dice away in my bag jumping off the cart onto the cobblestone road.

The bright yellow sun is high in the sky, a breeze is blowing fresh, crisp air, and the forest is alive with the noises of small animals, birds, and bugs. I take a deep breath and smile, for everything is going according to plan.

"Another beautiful day," says the old merchant, snapping me back into reality. "I have a feeling today will be a wonderful day, you know! The fortune teller in Ocean Front told me so."

"Really?" I say in a playful tone as I put my hood up on my head to shield my eyes from the sun. "Well, that is good news. The fortune teller told me that I was in danger and to make sure I keep both feet on the ground."

He chuckles. "Lady Luck is on our side, for the rest of my fortune was that I would get to River Front in one piece!"

I nod at him and think that this is the most comfortable mission I have had since I ranked up in my guild. Usually, I am tasked with some God-awful job, like protecting a flock of sheep from a troll at night during a storm. Or my last one, transporting a dozen chicken eggs that were actually basilisk eggs, which hatched while I was sleeping. I'm lucky enough that the newly hatched basilisks thought I was their mother and looked away from me.

With a sigh I snap out of my daydream, rubbing my watery eyes a bit too hard, making me see stars. I notice that the birds in the trees stopped chirping—quite odd—so I look around but see nothing out of the ordinary. This sudden silence worries me because I had heard stories of bandits migrating around this area. Hopefully, that is not the case, but I expect something since my luck is never on par.

A bird of prey must have spooked them, I think as I glance toward the sky, and behold, I see a condor circling above us. With a sigh of relief, my nerves start to calm down.

"There above us, look! It is such a rarity to see condors around this area, especially at this time of year." I pull out a small notebook and write down the sighting. "Hopefully, it is a good omen."

The horse that is pulling the cart with all the merchandise tells me a different tale as it begins to buck and whine. "By the Three!" the merchant shouts. "What has gotten into you!" he says, trying to calm her down.

Again, I look around with much more detail at the trees surrounding us. Animals have a more acute sense of danger, and seeing the horse buck and whine puts my nerves on edge again. As we move forward, I cannot help but feel that now I am being watched, hopefully by some friendly woodland creature and not by some beast or monster licking his lips. Nervously, the merchant stops walking and looks behind him. "There is a grim aura around here. Should we pick up the pace?"

I look behind towards him and give him a reassuring smile as I put my notebook on my back satchel. "It is just the sudden silence in the forest. Remember, there was a bird of prey flying above us. The birds might still be hiding, and your horse is a bit startled. I have my eye out for wolves or any pesky creature, don't worry." My job is to keep calm between us, to show him bravery and confidence, even though my hand is firmly on the hilt of my sword.

With a nod, he starts walking toward me. "Also, don't worry. Remember what the fortuneteller told you and what he told me! Just keep our feet on the ground, right? Seems pretty easy!" I pause to look at the road, reassuring myself of my own words.

I sigh and look toward the forest and see a small glimmer on the ground. I walk up to it and see it's a gold coin. "Huh, shiny! Lucky day for me, indeed!" I smirk as I run toward it, picking it up. Once the gold coin is in my hand, I hear a twig snap, and somehow, the world beneath my feet is upside down and under my head.

My stomach feels queasy while I'm pulled to what I think is up. I hit a few branches along with a bird's nest, covering my face in feathers and shame—an experience I have not had in a few days. I shake my head and mutter, "Ugh, what happened?" As I look around, I notice a noose on my leg, and I am hanging upside down on the top of an awfully tall cedar tree as the gold coin slips from my hand, falling down. I sigh in anger.

"Keep both feet on the ground. Right."

As I look up to the ground, I see a few bushes rustling,

and four figures come out of the shadow with weapons already drawn, walking toward the merchant.

"Oh no," I say softly.

Fearful for what is to come, the merchant stutters as he tries to get his words out, backing away slowly. "I mean you no threat or harm!"

One of the figures answers, "We know, old man. Now everything here belongs to us, even you."

"Oh no!" I mutter to myself again as I fumble to get free, thinking, I don't know what will kill me first, the sheer embarrassment of being caught in such an obvious trap that, might I add, the damn fortuneteller warned me about, or these bandits raiding the merchant I was supposed to be protecting! Thank you, sin of avarice, for pulling my strings. God, my brother is right. Pyrite can be gold at times.

As I try to untie the noose, I look back up to see three of the bandits harassing the merchant and having a jolly time, like how children bully the smallest of the group, but the last one carries a different air about him. He stares at me as if he has not eaten in a long time and I look tasty enough to nibble. I'm sure it's the blood rushing toward my head, but I could swear his eyes change color quickly. After a stare-off, he looks away toward the wagon.

I look back at my tied leg. *Easy enough,* I think. I will just cut the rope and attempt to fall back to the ground safely and defend this merchant before he gets killed. These bandits are just toying with him and hopefully will talk amongst themselves.

A scream erupts throughout the silence of the forest, followed by loud laughter. I quickly look back up and toward the group. To my luck, the merchant has a new stab wound courtesy of the bandit, and a few more coming his way.

Oh, good, he is getting killed in front of me. Great job, Ruffus.

How could I have been so careless! Damn it all—this was not supposed to happen!

I fumble to grab the lucky dagger that I have hidden in my boot. It's ten inches in length, with a wooden handle that has seen better days. The only reason it's lucky is that it was my father's, and it saved him from many close encounters with undead creatures and a carnivorous plant in his travels.

I grab hold of the dagger and start to cut the rope, only to notice that the branch holding me is about to snap under my weight. I have two choices. I can wait for the inevitable snapping or try to cut the rope, freeing myself, avoiding a long fall and hitting other branches.

"Lucky day, my ass! The last time I get my future told by a low-grade mage."

I take a short breath and swiftly cut the rope, attempting to land as quietly as I can. I twist in the air, so I fall feet first. I land on a thick branch, startling some birds that were hiding, causing a ruckus. I follow through by jumping off the thick branch to the next tree, stabbing my dagger into the bark so I will not slip off. I keep repeating the word "quietly" to myself as I start to descend from the top of the tree.

With the elegance of a dying bird, I make it to the base of the tree, and I give a quiet sigh of relief. That could have gone smoother.

I could hear the bandits on the other side of the tree rummaging through the cart and calling out their findings. I stand up quickly, putting away my dagger as I move to the edge of the tree to see only three of the bandits. I promptly turn around and see the edge of a sword a few inches away from my face. I grunt as a not-so-friendly man with a scar on his face grins at me with what I assume is delight.

"Quite the show, cutting the rope, jumping off the tree, and landing 'quietly' away from my servants. If you are trying to run away, you need to be silent." He keenly observes me like a prized steak cut. "Anyway, I have a plan for you."

I smile and reply mockingly, "A plan for me? But we just met, and honestly, I was hoping you would have ignored me. Much easier to escape unnoticed."

The man let out a low, malicious chuckle, muttering the word "unnoticed" and slowly moving the blade closer to me. "Unlucky you, now, move. It's no fun if my prey is cornered."

Our eyes are locked as I start to move away from the tree as his blade follows me.

Okay, time to get some distance. I think while calculating my next move.

I back away slowly and then feel as if I bumped into a rock, simultaneously noticing that the other three bandits in the cart scavenging went quiet. I already knew what was behind me. With a glance to each side, I decide to strafe left.

As I start to move, I feel myself trip on the root of a tree. Good thing, too, since a sword swing misses me from behind. I brace myself for the fall, rolling a few feet away, only to recover and turn to face them. All the bandits are in front of me, ready to stake me and use me as a pincushion. They are human, carrying well-crafted weapons and wearing dirty leather armor with a broken insignia on their chests. I know I have seen the symbol before, but I am too preoccupied to look at it in detail.

The scarred bandit nods and says, "Subdue him."

Two of the bandits start to move toward me, both with weapons at the ready, while the leader and the other stay behind them, observing how I react.

"Now, don't make this easy. I have not had my fun today yet," one of the bandits says to me as he licks his lips and runs toward me.

I feel my adrenaline rush hit me, my senses sharpen, and I know I cannot escape. I have no choice but to fight my way out. As the first bandit closes on me, I quickly reach inside my leather coat, picking out a few throwing knives.

My brown jacket has seen better days. It's tattered and dirty, with a few patches. For the most part it keeps me warm on a cold day, and it has so many glorious pockets for all my stuff. The knives I pull out are sharp enough to pierce through plate armor if I throw them hard enough. Lucky for me they don't cut through my coat.

I take aim and, with a flick of the wrist, let them fly. As luck would have it, the first bandit rushing me catches both. one in the chest, the other in the stomach. He stumbles down and falls face-first to the cold ground.

By no means am I the best knife thrower in this realm, but as of now, the gods are giving me a moment to shine. After celebrating this victory in my head, I see the second bandit quickly make his way to me, about to strike me down.

I dodge and jump in the nick of time, backstepping, letting loose another two knives at him. Sadly, only one makes contact in the thigh, but it buys me enough time to pull out my sword. As my opponent tries to recover from the volley, I rush toward him. I deliver a swift hit, knocking him out with the hilt of my sword and kicking him to the ground. The bandit groans painfully and stops moving after a few seconds, lying still on the grass. All I hear after finishing my second fight is a loud, slow clap. I look up and see the man with the scar smiling at me.

"Strong and agile. You will make a great minion. Do me the favor of submitting to my power."

His whole demeanor changes as he kneels and begins to chant something. To my demise, I quickly see his eyes changing color again to a milky white.

What in the gods' name is he doing? I grab two more throwing knives from my coat pocket with my right hand.

As he stands up, I feel an immense pressure on top of me, like someone tied a boulder with extra luggage on my shoulders without me noticing, and I drop my knives on the ground. I look at him directly in the eyes again, and for some reason, I start to remember old nightmares of monsters I had as a kid.

Panic starts to cloud my judgment, and for no reason, immense dread begins to consume me. I move my gaze away from the man with the scar and see that the third bandit has a horrified face and is on the ground whimpering, moving away from him.

He is just a human, a commoner, like me. Why can't I stop trembling in fear? Is it magic? If it is, I have not felt this type of magic before, I think to myself. *He is chanting a spell; I know it. Is this a new type of enhancement magic, making him appear more frightening than he is? I need to calm down. Don't look at his eyes. They are the gateway to one's spirit, revealing intent. Ruffus, move, you have to move! He has you petrified. Snap out of it!*

The third bandit breaks the silence. "What are you doing!" The man with the scar looks at his hands as if they are new to him. He then looks at me with milky white eyes. As he talks, it sounds as if another deep, low voice combined with his is talking to me.

He stretches and says in my language, which is commonly known throughout this continent, "Now, meat bag, I need you to die for a few seconds."

The bandit next to him gets off the ground and starts to run away as he yells for help.

The man with the scar bites his lips and says excitedly, "He dies first."

Maybe my eyes are slow, or I am not paying attention for

a second, but suddenly he appears to be standing in front of the bandit who was running away, and with one swift motion, decapitates him with his hand.

By the gods, I need to escape this fight! I have to buy some time, I think trying to calm myself to then say, "What type of magic is this?"

The man smiles as the body flops down, spraying blood out of the fell bandit. "Magic? Humans use magic, do they not?"

"Aren't you hu—"

"Speaking to buy time is a pitiful tactic. I am not done with you, meat bag." He looks at me, and his expression changes. "Your face is not one of full fear, and I see the wisdom in your eyes. You know what I am?"

I can say, without stammering, "I know you aren't human anymore and not a friend to my enemies." I look toward the puddle of blood and body twitching in front of him. Only a sharp sword or ax could have done such quick work, yet it was his hand. I look at him and see his features changed. He seems bestial like a rabid dog or even dare I say Daemon.

Mockingly, he throws the head next to me, making me flinch. "This will only take a second." As those words escape his lips, he runs toward me at blinding speed. He tries to hit me, but I snap out of my panicked state and dodge backward. It was only thanks to the sweet pain that I inflicted on myself with my knife on my thigh that I regained control. He keeps coming at me with full force, and I cannot attack back. As I keep avoiding his hits, the man hits the environment, knocking down three trees with ease and creating impact holes in the ground with his fists.

I jump off a rock, flipping in the air.

"Stop moving!" he yells at me, trying to land blow after blow. Ignoring his demands, I keep dodging backward, hiding behind trees and trying to block his attacks. I instantly grab a small pouch from my belt, spinning it like a sling. This pouch in particular contains some sand, volcanic ash, ground red pepper, and other goodies. I usually use this concoction to blind people and get away, but only as a last resort.

I throw the open bag of powder point-blank and hit my opponent on his face. I stop him dead in his tracks, and he howls in pain, which makes me feel slightly guilty. He also tells me what he thinks of my mother, which is not very nice—quite rude actually—and blind to the fact that his words are not valid. My mother is a lovely lady, and she does not work in a brothel. While he is distracted, I decide to end it. Taking a life has always been a hard decision, and who am I to do such an act? I will only do it in self-defense, and sadly, today, I will put another tally against my karma. I plunge my sword directly into his chest as he tries to lunge at me one final time. Not even a possessed man can stay standing after I stop his heart.

To my surprise, he grabs my sword by the blade, and with his one good eye, he glares at me. A strong surge of electricity hits me, and I get thrown a few feet, landing hard on my back.

As my eyes focus, I see he has pulled my sword out of his flesh and is now wielding it as he walks toward me. As I lie on the ground coughing, I notice smoke coming off me like a fresh roast out of the fire.

"You have ruined my body. Now, I will take yours!" He raises my sword, and sparks start to fly out of it, stopping him in his tracks. He looks at my weapon, worried. An explosion bursts from the blade, and he releases it with a scream, accompanied by my gasp. My sword flies toward an unconscious bandit, landing next to him.

I take this opportunity to throw the last knife I have on me straight at the scarred man, and it hits him in the chest, making him seize and fall abruptly on the ground as if he were a rag doll. I sigh weakly as I stand, limping toward him. He is still breathing and alive, to my surprise. As I get near him, I check his chest and see a scar where I impaled him. I pull my dagger out of him and see his wound quickly heal itself. I look at the blood on the blade to see it evaporate like ice in a desert.

"I impaled you. How are you not bleeding out or dead? Huh, curious. I bet the scholars and mages back at River Front would love to examine you, for a modest fee, of course," I whisper to him as I finish inspecting his person.

I walk away from the scarred man and make my way toward the cart, only to notice the merchant's body lying next to it. My heart sinks as I see the expression of fear on his pale face. I kneel and close his eyes, so he may obtain peace, and pray that his spirit finds his way to Elysium or wherever he believed he would go when he died.

Exhaustedly, I stand again after prayer and search for the merchant's horse; hopefully, it has not run away. I mean, I would have. Luckily, she is tied up to a tree nearby, looking spooked as ever. I saunter to her while humming a song my mother taught me when I was a child. I always thought singing calmed even the most potent and most fearful of beasts, and, like magic, it works. With little hesitation, the horse allows me to get near it, freeing it from the tree.

"There, there, you are a good girl. Now, let's tie you up on the cart. This nightmare is over," I assure her as I run my hand through her ragged mane. "Good thing these brigands tied you up. I can't have you get eaten by wolves or any other creature." I walk the horse to the cart and prepare for departure.

Before I leave, I search the cart for rope, and to my good fortune, I find a bunch of it, but as I get off, I hear a loud yelp and a small explosion again. I quickly look toward its direction and see the bandit I knocked out, steaming as if he was on fire a few seconds ago. He is on the ground at a weird angle that not even a contortionist would try while holding my sword. The horse starts bucking and whining, but I calm her down again, this time by shushing her and giving her honey I found in the cart. "Huh, note to self, be careful when I pick up Coal," I say as I inspect my surrounding area. "I guess no one else is getting up soon. Better bury the bodies and tie up my prisoners."

I was able to dig two shallow graves on the side of the road for the bandits, marking them with rocks and putting a small check on my map in my notebook to inform the authorities where I buried them. After cracking my back and throwing a makeshift pickaxe back to the cart, I go and tie up the scarred man, but as I get near him, my chest begins to burn from the pendant hanging around my neck. I rip it off to look at it. My father gave this pendant to me. He also told me that if it ever glows or burns, it means there is an evil spirit near me.

I look at it. "Well, you could have told me sooner." The fight is over! Damn thing must be broken. Useless trinket, good thing you are pretty.

As I tie him up, I can hear him murmur and mutter things. I become nervous and decide to tie up the pendant on his rope, in case he wakes up and wants to eat me or kill me. Even though I don't think a charm could stop him, it gives me peace of mind knowing it is on him. I tie the other bandit up once I see that he again was knocked out by some unknown force and throw him on the back of the cart.

I walk back to where my sword is and stare at it. The obsidian blade made by my mother, which is heavier than most one-handed swords, is lying on the forest floor. "Well, in all my years of owning you, never has this happened."

I grab a twig and throw it at the blade. Nothing happens. I

grab another stick and poke the sword. Again, nothing happens. I get closer to it, kneel in front of it, and tap it with my hand, and to my surprise, nothing happens.

I look at it closer and pick it up by the leather-bound hilt. "Huh, I'm not dead. That's good." I scrutinize the sword, and seeing the blood-stained rectangular blade, I gently clean it off on my jacket. With a strong swing, I expect it to explode on me, but nothing is happening. With a gentle flick, I put it inside its sheath, sighing in relief. "I should talk to my brother or mother about what happened."

After making sure the bandits are not stirring and are secure for this trip, I move to take care of the merchant's body. I rummage around and find some high-quality linens in the cart. Wrapping him up with them, I gently place him behind the conductor's seat.

I feel ashamed that I failed him. "I'm sorry, old man, and I shall get your body back to River Front in one piece."

I hit the reins, and the horse starts to move the cart. As we make our way, I again cannot help but feel as if I am being watched. I look toward my prisoners and see they're still out cold. I then look at my surroundings to see nothing out of the ordinary. Dusk is now upon me, I still have a way to go before I reach River Front, and I know these roads are not safe at all at night. Strange monsters and hungry werewolves roam these forests, although it's not a full moon tonight, and they usually do not attack the roads.

"To the City of Trade. Get me there fast and safe," I say to the horse as I hold my sword close to me.

Dusk begins to turn to night, and all I can do is look up at the stars that begin to appear in the darkening blue sky. The crisp winds chill me to the bones as the forest starts to make its evening noises.

The Grand City

Nighttime falls as I make it out of the woods safely with the bandits still unconscious. The city's sound breaks the cricket's musical ballads and the evening owl's hooting as I start to see the City of Trade, the center of the map, and the capital of this continent: the dwarven city, River Front.

The city is alive with lights and the sound of people. The tall buildings and the queen's castle shine brightly as if they are a beacon for travelers to find their way to the city. Even from a distance, I can see smoke billowing out of the Artisan District and strange lights coming out of the Mage Quarter. I have never felt so glad to be back.

River Front is the realm's trading post. All towns, villages, and even foreign kingdoms come here from far and wide to make a profit. River Front is also the only city in the known provinces where any school of magic can be practiced freely—in a safe and supervised environment, of course. Citizens don't want to wake up to another summoned archdaemon or archangelic figure, otherwise known as *daemons* and *holies,* causing destruction. Those were messy battles—it took eight days to kill them both as they almost ushered in the end of times.

River Front is also the central headquarters of the Arcadian Militia. Arcadia is a specialized branch of the city guard designed to train all manner of people in the arts of warfare.

The queen's bodyguards and a leading force of protection reside in this city and this kingdom's towns. They are the elite of the elite, and one day I'll be a part of them with my brother. That is, of course, if I don't die first.

I shuffle through my satchel to find my notebook with a River Front map. As I look at the map, I smile because of how symmetrical the city is. It drives me slightly crazy how well they built this place.

"River Front is round like a compass and has two rivers intersecting in its center, almost as if the cartographer drew a perfect *X* on my map. How did the dwarves build this so well? Never fails to impress," I murmur.

I skim the map and look at all the sections drawn out. The river successfully divides the city into four sections: the Mage Quarter, Traders' Berth, the Pavilion, and the King's Quarter. The Mage Quarter is where all manner of magic spells, items, artifacts, and odd trades happen. This town area is filled with towering buildings, magical wards, and shield spells, just in case an archdaemon escapes, or a giant fire occurs again. It also houses all of the primary schools of magic and their leader, holding the *Meister* title, which belongs to Helena Lotusrosé. She is a renowned eldar native to this city who discovered how to harness moonlight's power, creating a new magic school that only a selected few can attend. Her genius has been talked about for five hundred years. Still, she only just turned into a meister after her teacher, the previous meister, sacrificed himself to defeat an elder ice dragon that almost destroyed the city.

The mages there control the Halls of Knowledge, an immense college where anyone from children to old spirits goes to learn and practice magic. The Grande Library is the cherry on top of the district, and this public library is open to everyone.

I have learned so much from the bestiary books there that

I would confidently brag that I'm a bit of an expert in beasts and monsters. All recorded spells known to man, elf, and orc can be researched and learned from there. As a child, I always wanted to wield magic, but I didn't have a clear attunement, so I usually failed every time I attempted to perform a spell. No matter how much I read or practice, I just can't make it work.

Then there's Traders' Berth. As the name states, it's where the majority of commerce happens. There are shops upon shops there, and it is the busiest area in the whole city. The buildings and shops in this part of town run underground and connect with a railway system built by dwarves that leads to the Bank of the Kingdom and the Auction Plaza. The plaza houses the most expensive shops in an old, exhausted gold mine beneath Traders' Berth and stretches outside the city's wall. The Auction Plaza is where people can sell and haggle with pretty much everyone. All items can be found during the daytime, from animals to weapons to spells and scrolls.

Come nighttime, this area of town becomes one of the most heavily guarded. Due to the sheer number of illegal activities happening at any given time, it is also the best place to buy the rarest items if you don't get caught first by the guards.

The third section of this town, the Pavilion, is where most city residents live, from the nobles in High Peak to the slums where the less fortunate live next to the river. This area is the headquarters of most guilds. It includes the Architect Guild, Athletic Guild, and all-time favorite Knitting Guild. Those old ladies can kill a second-ranked daemon lord if they feel like it and knit a blanket simultaneously.

Finally, the area I'm heading to is the King's Quarter. It's where the Grande Cathedral, Castle Trujillo, Castle Town, and the Arcadian Militia reside. Of course, this area has grand buildings made by professional architects from the Architect

Guild and the Artisan Guild. King's Quarter is the only area of the whole city with a gate dividing it from the River Front. The Grande Cathedral is the brightest of all the structures inside King's Quarter. This place houses all thirteen of the deities that exist in lore from all religions of our continent. It was built after the First War, where thousands died in the name of their deities under the holies' and daemons' influence and, in my opinion, constant intrusion, separating people and killing innocents. It is said that the spark of war started in a place called Laberynthea, but no one knows if it's true or even if the site exists anymore since many of the books telling the tale were destroyed.

The king ordered this quarter of the city to be where all deities can be praised and respected. He thought that if all the religions were held as equals, the war would stop, and people would unite for a more significant cause. Though many don't agree and will always think their religion is better than others, this would help prevent another theology war, or so he hoped. As additional security, he established the Arcadian Militia to keep watch and maintain peace with its many branches. The Arcadian Militia is also where the elite soldiers are recruited through robust screening and trained to protect this kingdom, not of a single theology, but the people and country as a whole.

"Praise my luck, I made it to River Front before they raised the gates." I look toward the ramparts as the guard change begins.

I make my way from the outer wall of the city to one of the main gates. People living outside them are lining up to enter the gates, while others come out to go to the inns for a night of drinking. A few of the soldiers protecting the gates casually approach me as I draw near.

"Good evening, what is your business in the King's Quarter, and may I see your merchandise invoice?" one of the soldiers says in a bored tone.

"Evening, sir. I hold merchant goods and some bandits bound and gagged that murdered the owner of this cart." I fumble around in one of my pockets to find the invoice and my contract with my guild.

One of the soldiers inspects the cart and sees the bandits and the late merchant's wrapped-up body. He looks at the other two guards, nodding toward them. One of the soldiers runs up to him, and they both have a quiet conversation as the other guard checks my credentials with great interest. After the guards end their discussion, they nod toward each other and run inside the gates with great haste, leaving a small dust cloud behind them. The guard checking my credentials looks up at me and says, "I will get in contact with the Warrior Guild's liaison and verify your quest contract. As of now, please proceed to the King's Quarter with me to put your prisoners and yourself under surveillance."

I nod and move to the passenger's side of the cart, handing him my weapon. I pray my sword does not explode again, but nothing happens when he grabs it. The guard hops on the driver's seat and snaps on the reins, making the poor horse whine and move quickly, taking us through the gates to the King's Quarter. I sit back, relax, and enjoy the ride as I watch the scenery. It may be nighttime, but people are still buzzing around the city. I see a few drunken elves, a dwarf kissing a feline beastwoman, and a band of human and beastman street performers dancing with a funny-looking jester. I see beastmen gambling and others making music out of sticks and what looks like a crocodile's back and a dragon skull.

As I breathe in the air, I feel a sort of excited energy. This is a pretty nice city to live in. I am never bored here, but business before pleasure. I must get to the Grande Cathedral to talk to my brother and get this problem sorted out.

As we reach the cathedral grounds, I see clergymen and women igniting the streetlamps using their magic, as well as a few apprentices attempting to help, some ultimately failing at their practice, igniting their clothes.

That does not seem very safe to me.

The guard maneuvers the cart away from them as they practice. "I do not feel like being burned to ashes by some clumsy apprentices," says the guard in a mocking tone.

I smile and agree.

We find an open stable to put the horse and cart near the cathedral entrance as a crow with a small parchment attached to its leg lands on the guard's metal helmet. The crow takes the parchment from its leg with its sharp beak and taps on the helmet, hard.

The guard shakes his head violently, smacking the crow off. It slips and falls on his lap, dazed, letting the parchment go as it turns around and flies away, cawing as if it was mocking him. "Damn messenger bird, I'll make stew out of him one day," he mutters to himself as he opens the small scroll and reads the contents of the parchment, mouthing the words. He finishes reading and puts the note away. "Grab your weapon, Warrior. Your credentials check out. You are free to go in the cathedral if you wish, but do not leave this district until your liaison and our captain arrive to retrieve the bodies."

I jump off the cart and stretch, letting out a loud yawn as I scratch my head. I then grab my weapon and sheath it ever so carefully, praying no more shenanigans will happen. I walk to the back where the bandits are tied up to see that they're still knocked out, which is odd to me, as it has been hours since the fight, and neither of them has moved or woken up. But the guard walks up to them and inspects their bindings to see they're still tied up securely, putting my worry at ease.

"I have family in the cathedral. May I go retrieve him?" I ask the guard.

"Yes, make it fast though. My captain will be here soon, and he will want to ask you questions. Just so you are aware, you are being watched," the guard says as he looks at the contents of the cart. I nod and leave with a spin. As I make my way to the golden main doors of the Grande Cathedral, I can't help but take in their beauty. Both doors are as tall as oak trees, with imprints and carvings depicting the known world's history. All deities came from the same story. Though they branch off to different belief systems, everything came from the Three.

The Three are what I understand to be the original gods, while the deities are their children. As I look at the carvings of the world, a familiar voice whispers in my ear, "You are late, Ruffus."

I turn to see my friend, Clover Hearth, a common eldar or elf. She is beautiful, shorter than most female elves at five feet, five inches, pale as the stars, with golden hair that shines and reminds me of a full moon. Her eyes are a deep emerald green that stares right into your spirit, and she has a smile that can melt anyone's heart in a second. She is wearing comfortable-looking tight black pants and a silver tunic embossed with a few flowers on the bottom. She is a rarity of her kind, having been raised by humans. She has all the grace of her eldar ancestry but the mouth of a sailor.

"Damn elf, don't sneak up on me! What if I had stabbed you?"

"It would not be the first time you have attempted to harm me, human." She grins at me.

I sigh in annoyance, "First of all, it was an accident. How would I have known you wanted to surprise me with a masquerade party when I was coming back home drunk? Any rational person would have started throwing knives!"

"Who drinks at three in the afternoon during winter? But I digress. Why are you here and not checking in with the guild?"

I explain to her what happened on the road and to the merchant, in great detail. She listens to my story with great interest. "Well, that is unfortunate." She sighs. "I will go to the cart and see if I can recover the old man's body. I will show them my guild credentials so they know I am someone who matters."

"Hold that thought for a moment, Clover. Let me talk to my brother first to see what I can do about the odd bandit I told you about. Don't let the guards take any of the prisoners away."

"I will stall them, Ruffus."

She smiles at me, making my knees feel weak. Honestly, even though I'm not attracted to her anymore, she can still charm me with that smile.

I quickly look away and clear my thoughts. "Clover, you're lucky eldar folk have natural beauty. You know I can't resist your smile."

"I know, that is why I do it. Now meet your kin. I will be waiting for you both." With a wink, she turns around and starts to walk toward the carts.

I watch her, and I cannot help but smile. Once she is out of view, I look up to the starry night for a moment and shake my head.

"Damn elf. It should be a sin to be that attractive," I say as I begin making my way inside the Grande Cathedral. "How in Hell did she find me so quickly?"

A Will-o'-the-Wisp Tells Me a Story

Entering this building is like entering a new world. It feels as if all of my problems in the entire realm are suddenly gone.

I feel peace, tranquility, and harmony. Off in the background, I can hear hymns being sung to appease the Three, adding to this place's ambiance and serene feeling.

A female human monk approaches me and bows as if I am royalty. In a soft voice, she says, "May the resonating light of the Three be with you."

I return the gesture and ask if she could accompany me to the library to find my brother. With a warm smile, she nods and asks me to follow her through the building. Those who do not live or work in the cathedral always need an escort. This massive building is like a maze, and I have gotten lost quite a few times.

The Grande Cathedral is a magnificent structure. The inside walls and decoration are built with polished marble. The statues are made out of precious stones, and the hallways have powerful enchantments to aid meditation and holy magic, which houses healing magic and other types. The ceiling shines with floating orbs of light that change brightness every few minutes.

They remind me of the stars shimmering in the sky. The top also has a mural of how the Three created this realm, or so we think. Most of these murals are artists' depictions of what the history books say.

The cathedral itself is gigantic, with multiple churches inside on the main floor. The upper levels hold the main hospital of this city and the living area for most students, workers, and teachers, while its underground section is like a labyrinth since it contains many hallways leading places I have not even gone to and I'm too scared to explore since there are rumors of ethereal beings residing there. The catacombs, armory, classrooms, and library are also located there and are hopefully ghost-free. This area is also the most populated building since it is where the residents and townspeople learn about their religion, healing magic, and other things.

After walking a few minutes, we reach the main stairs that take us underground, where the library resides. I again feel as if things are staring at me, and when I look at the ceiling, I can see stone gargoyle statues gazing down upon me with their sapphire eyes in a scary way. I shudder as I think, *What if those creatures come to life?* We finally make it to an enormous set of double doors. The monk opens them up, revealing a magnificent-looking chamber.

"Wow, hard to believe this is so deep underground. Then again, this is a dwarven-built city, and all they do is dig," I murmur to myself as we enter.

Books upon books line the shelves, reaching all the way to the ceiling. There is an immense levitating orb in the center of the room where the librarian's counter resides, and encased inside is a great white flame that fills the entire library with vibrant, warm light. Archaeologists and most mages call it the Light of Knowledge, which burns bright if there is the will to learn. Around the room, small will-o'-the-wisps pop out of the orb and begin to float around lazily. They bump into people, put books away, and whisper secrets of texts long forgotten to those who seek their knowledge. As a child, I always wanted to eat a will-o'-the-wisp because they reminded me of powdered sugar. As one lands on my head, I grab it gently while it warms my hands. I control the urge to squeeze it as it floats away toward another person.

We make our way to the librarian's counter, where the appointed head of the library, known as the master librarian, resides, whose sole duty is to guard this place. The redundant title is only given to anyone who is exceptionally gifted with magic and can control the Light of Knowledge's immense, overflowing power. He is appointed to ensure the library here in the Grande Cathedral and the Mage Quarter are in check and working order. He also keeps restricted powerful tomes and artifacts under surveillance to make sure no one accidentally gets a book or a magic wand and summons an archdaemon again. From what Clover and my brother have told me, the master librarian mostly spends his time doing the thing he loves: reading books and teaching.

We make it to the counter and see a tall, slender, hooded male eldar standing behind the counter, gathering will-o'-the-wisps and returning them to the Light of Knowledge. He is wearing a white robe with a golden accent and what looks like obsidian glasses.

"Fascinating little creatures, are they not?" asks the tall elf as he turns around, greeting me with a smile. "He is under my supervision. Nora, go with peace, and may knowledge guide your way," he says in a soothing but stern voice.

In turn, my escort bows and walks away as a small wisp bumps into her. The elf faces me and looks at me with his bright, analytical orange eyes. He knows exactly what I want, and he already knows where it is and how to get it. Seven wisps pop out of the floating orb behind him as he mutters something in an odd language that is not elven. The wisps change color to a light green and disperse in a blink of an eye in a different direction. "Ruffus, my dear child, welcome back. How may I aid you? There is a new beast manual in stock, or are you here for a daemonology manual?"

"Oh," I murmur not surprised. "Good evening, Master Librarian. I seek my brother, Jura. Is he here in the library?" I ask as politely as I can. Last time I interacted with him, he caught me sleeping while researching wood nymphs, drooling on the pages. In my defense, someone had to have charmed the book for me to fall asleep precisely in the anatomy section.

He looks at me as a new wisp pops out of the orb and floats away. In a flash, it returns, whispering something into the librarian's pointy ear. "Your brother has been informed of your arrival, as well as your predicament with your bandits."

I stop breathing for a second, wondering how he could know, and then I remember these particular will-o'-the-wisps in the library are knowledge incarnate. Thoughts that are in one's mind meld with the fire when you are near. Any relevant information is shared through the library. In other words, if you have a secret and you want to keep it that way, you should not come here.

"So not to worry, my child of light. Nothing personal is ever retrieved here," he says in a reassuring voice as he senses my worries. "I have instructed my wisps to retrieve all relevant books on daemonology, summoning, and known spirits to aid Exorcist Juratan and yourself in identifying what is wrong with Kellel."

Puzzled, I ask, "Who?"

"Kellel is a missing Arcadian soldier who turned rogue and the bandit you had a skirmish with."

At that moment, the seven wisps return with a few books and scrolls. The librarian grabs one of the wisps out of the air gently. It quickly changes color and floats up to his ear, and a worrisome look comes about him. "In fact, he used to be a cadet in the Arcadian Militia recon division. Arcadia lost contact with him after he was sent to White Wood Forest for a routine mission." The Librarian grabs the wisp near his ear and hands it to me. "Place it carefully near your ear and listen. A memory will unfold in your mind that might have taken one hundred years to complete, but only a mere second to view."

I grab the wisp reluctantly. It weighs nothing, and it radiates warmth. I feel as if I am holding mist, and it takes all my willpower not to squish it. I let it float a few inches away from my ear, and suddenly I hear a faint whisper. I close my eyes and concentrate on it.

Its whispers sound like a small child, and it says to me, "Learn from me!"

Instantly, I feel a rush of heat flow into my ear, and I allow the feeling to engulf my mind. I open my eyes and see the Arcadian bulletin board, with flyers for missing personnel next to the duty roster added four weeks ago. More than one person has gone missing. The rest are either deceased or have become wanted men. My vision changes quickly, and I see the flyer for Kellel come into view, dated two weeks ago—a member of Arcadia's recon group, one of the most influential and prestigious militia branches.

Weird, soldiers from Arcadian Militia are loyal to a fault— that's why they're chosen. This can't be the same man. I can feel the memory fade.

I slowly open my eyes again as I feel a hand on my shoulder.

I focus my sight and turn to see who it is, and in front of me is my big brother, Juratan, smiling at me. He looks the same as I remember, light tan skin like me, and taller than me by three inches. He is five feet, nine inches tall and built to fight, and he has the scars on his face to prove it. His long black hair is tied up in a knot and has dark blue streaks throughout it, just like Mom's, accompanied by Dad's blue eyes. He was always any girl's first choice, as he is handsome and has nobles asking him to marry their daughters daily—so much power, but he never takes advantage of that.

He is wearing his exorcist robes, consisting of a black leather coat hiding his combat gear, gilded in silver finishing and badges from the training he acquired. He wears the Three's crest on his chest, an upside-down triangle with a tree in the middle, representing the Soul Tree. The Soul Tree is an old legend of the goddess Ann and the creator of balance, commonly practiced by exorcists.

"Well, Ruffus, I'm surprised no one accidentally came up to you thinking you and I were the same person, like last time!" He takes a good look at me and scoffs. "Mother will murder you if she sees you like this! Your duster is dirty and missing pieces of leather, your hood is torn, and I'd never guess you had brown hair since it's stained with blood, and your blue streaks of royalty are purple, tsk, tsk. At least you did not damage your eyes! Full moon yellow iris, just like Mom's."

"Examining me for intruders through my eyes, Jura?"

"With the adventures you have, I must make sure I'm talking to my Ruff. But then again, who would want to possess or even share a body with you?"

He pauses for a second to hug me. "Ruff!" Jura says in a welcoming voice. "You look like fifty horses ran over you!"

"With the day I had, it feels like a hundred."

Jura makes a fist and places it on my cheek, moving my head to the side. "Glad to see you alive, but now to business. The wisps have informed me of your situation. I have grabbed all my gear to tackle this problem."

I look to his side to see he is not carrying his sword. "Hey, Jura, where is Quartz? I think this is the first time I've seen you without your sword?"

"Oh, right, it is currently receiving a blessing by the hierophant of the Three after the battle against another archdaemon in the Mage Quarter," Jura says as he scratches his face. "Fun fight—lucky I had the trinket father gave me. It did absolutely nothing to help." Jura pulls out a small silver figure of what we decided looks like an owl.

Both of us have small silver charms that our father brought back from his trip to an archaeology site that people thought would be where Laberynthea would reside. He brought them to a priest to get them blessed, but it backfired since the charms seem to be enchanted with a more powerful spell of an unknown factor. Yet he gave them to us as presents.

I grab a blank scroll from a wisp. "We should ask for help with this bandit."

"I have already informed a few friends of mine from Arcadia to assist me," Jura says as he turns to the librarian. "Thank you so much for your help, Master Librarian."

He nods at both of us as he pulls out a new wisp from the orb.

Jura grabs some books the wisps brought and looks at me. "Get ready for a show. I will meet you outside. I need to go grab Quartz."

At that moment, four wisps come to view, carrying a blanket by each corner. Resting within the silk veil is a beautiful blade. The silver center of the blade is shining brightly. Engraved in the middle with gold are the words "Mother's Protection." The blade's edges are crafted out of pink quartz, and the silver embossed handle has leather straps tied to the grip.

"Oh, speak of the devil slayer. The hierophant must have finished with his blessing," Jura says as he grabs the sword. "Please send my thanks to him," he tells the wisps.

I look at his sword, and I still remember when he got it, back in our small village by the mountains. In the town of Bern, it was rare for anyone to get chosen to become part of the Arcadian Militia, but Jura showed a lot of promise and demonstrated that he had the core values needed. As a present, my mother, the village blacksmith and head of the Merchants Guild there, made him Quartz.

She combined the rare pieces of moon ore, silver, and rose quartz, and it took five days to complete her masterpiece. When she finished forging the weapon, she set the blade on the village shrine and prayed to the Three to protect Jura on his quest to become an initiate and any other future endeavors.

Being his younger brother by four years, I was naturally jealous of him. At the age of fifteen, he got such a fine gift, such a great opportunity, and I still had to practice with wooden weapons and help around the house. Eventually, I got over it and worked hard to become better than him.

That was fifteen years ago. Once I got my sword, I joined the Warriors Guild, and now I'm here. It's not bad at all, and I do have high hopes that I will become part of Arcadia soon. I just have to keep working.

Jura looks at me. "Ruff, would you like your sword blessed?" I shrug, and Jura smiles, sheathing Quartz.

"Let's go, then," he says. "Can't keep the guards waiting." With that, we walk out of the library, headed to the cart, followed by a few wisps.

Two for the Price of One

As we reach the golden doors of the cathedral, we can hear screaming and yelling from the outside.

"Did a fight break out?" Jura murmurs to himself.

"Do you think?" I ask as I look at Jura, and in unison, we both say, "The bandits!"

We drop the books and scrolls as we run toward the cathedral's already open doors, and we can see a crowd of people already gathering to see what the commotion is. Once we reach the courtyard, Jura starts moving people out of our way to get to the cart faster. Once we make it, we can see multiple guards detaining the runaway soldier Kellel a few feet away from the cart. It appears he is in another frenzy and somehow broke out of his bonds.

The man looks worse than when I fought him. His clothes are burnt, his face has an extended cut through his cheek, and, overall, he is smoking as if he was just on fire. The city guards have him circled and are ready to attack.

"What happened to him?" Jura asks as we walk toward the guards.

"Oh no, Clover was watching over him. Where is she?" I say in a slight panic as I look around to find her. I spot her through the crowd to see that she is sitting on the cart, being attended by two clergymen. I leave Jura's side and quickly push through the crowd to her.

"Clover, are you okay? What happened?" I notice the bruises on her face and small bloodstains on her tunic.

"Ruffus, he killed the other man, the one that was tied up, and almost did the guard in!" she mutters, shuddering. "He was muttering something, I got closer to listen if he was okay, and he then tackled me to the ground. I was able to push him away, but when he got up, I saw that my attack did nothing to him. He rushed toward the guard, knocking him out. I tried burning him, but he used the fire to get his hands unbound. He then jumped and tried to strike me. I was able to repel him, pushing him to the cart. I felt dread, fear. I imagined my own death."

I do not ask any more questions, as it's unlike her to lose a fight or even shed a tear in any situation. She uses elemental magic as her fighting style, and her story checks out since there is a substantial burn mark on the floor where she says she was tackled. It is incredible Kellel is still alive and not turned into ashes. Clover is one of the strongest magic users I know. She is renowned in the Warriors Guild for her bravery, and she is a scholar in the College of Magic.

Even when she uses magic, she does not suffer from its side effects. Anyone using too much fire magic would die of hypothermia, as casting a fire spell uses the body's internal heat. If they used a water spell, they could die of dehydration. This is why magic is dangerous—its side effects can kill the caster.

I shift my view to the bandit. He is now bound by seven guards pinning him down on the ground while four others have their weapons drawn. Multiple clergy members have already started to create a circle of white ash around the guards on Jura's command. Jura also instructs the civilians observing to clear away and leads the clergymen on which symbols they must etch on the ground. This is Jura's specialty, removing foreign spirits from people or items. As an exorcist, Jura has learned how to use holy magic as a weapon to help him fight against chaotic creatures. Using too much of this magic will exhaust his energy and can corrupt his mind. I have always told Jura that using too much of this magic would turn him into a pessimist. He disagrees but then complains when his water cup is half empty.

After all the symbols are placed, a few more guards appear to cordon off the area. Jura sits down in front of the circle facing Kellel and starts to mutter a prayer of some sort and meditate. The clergymen follow Jura's actions and encircle the outside of the white ash, imitating Jura.

The white ash forming the circle begins to glow brightly, and without warning, a light shoots up from it to the sky. It grows as tall as an oak tree, and the top eventually seals, creating a pillar of white transparent glow, a sort of light prison.

A raspy voice suddenly yells from the cathedral doors, "Hold the barrier! Grand Master Sermon and I will assist!"

It comes from an old pale human man that reminds me of a chubby gerbil holding a golden staff. He is wearing blood-red robes with a funny-looking short hat that looks like a paper-crafted boat. By the looks of his staff, I know he must be a high-ranking priest of some sort. He is accompanied by a tall, bald, moss-colored orc female whose presence intimidates me. Orcs are known to be fearsome, ruthless people when it comes to battle.

This race was accepted as "civilized" by humans during the religious war when they sided with them to defeat the elven radicals that almost eradicated the beastman race for their supposedly heretical beliefs. Soon after, humans and orcs became allies. I have known multiple male orcs, and they all say the same thing: female orcs are as rare as diamonds and ruthless as a landslide. If a seven-foot orc tells me their six-foot-one female counterparts are scary, I believe them.

Her attire is unique, red and yellow cloth robes. Her fists are wrapped up in clean bandages, and she is wearing giant beads on her neck made from simple wood with strange markings etched on them. Oddly enough, she has no shoes on, and her belt carries a small waterskin.

With the raspy voice, the gerbil-looking man commands, "Soldiers of Arcadia, release him and escape the barriers!"

In a flash, all the soldiers pinning Kellel jump back through the cylinder barrier, landing gracefully on one knee. I can see and hear the awe from the crowd as they see the Arcadian soldiers move as one. Then the four soldiers guarding the escapee jump out of the barrier. In that instant, Kellel jumps to his feet and, with full force, charges toward my brother, punching the wall of light, creating a hollow sound on impact as his fist bounces off the barrier. I notice that he no longer looks human. His face structure is the same, but I can see an image surrounding his face as if he had a transparent mask.

With a terrifying cry, he says to me and points, "You! You brought me into this place! I will spill all your blood and feast on all of your children!"

"Silence, spirit!" the orc woman shouts, gaining everyone's attention.

"Sermon, let us bring this to an end," the man in red robes says in a soft voice as he glances at me.

After the gaze, I can see he is searching for something in his robes as he fumbles into his pockets and sleeves to pull out an assortment of strange items, and with a low "Aha," he picks out a small misty crystal that looks like a chunk of quartz.

He looks at Sermon and nods at her. She nods back and walks to one of the circles' ends while he stands on the exact opposite side of the ring. He throws the crystal into the barrier, and as it passes through the light, a low hum begins vibrating in my ears. It never lands on the ground, but it levitates several feet in the center of the barrier, spinning violently.

Sermon raises her hand, and the crystal remains in place, motionless. Kellel starts to wail in pain immediately, screaming death threats to everyone, scratching his face as he begins to punch the barrier harder and harder. Seconds later, he falls on the ground, convulsing, and starts to steam as if he were burning alive. The crowd gasps as out of his mouth a black mist erupts, shooting to the top of the pillar.

The man in red starts to chant loudly in a language I do not recognize as Sermon closes her eyes, moving her hands as if she is weaving something between her fingers. Her hands start to move faster and faster, and then both make eye contact and raise their left hands toward the crystal, simultaneously yelling, "Ter' Kal," which means "seal" or "imprison" in Elvish. The black mist instantly begins flowing into the crystal, making a hair-raising sound like a million bees flying around us, turning it an obsidian color.

As soon as the crystal changes color, my brother yells, "Now! Encase the Signet Crystal!"

I watch in amazement, as I have only heard of a Signet Crystal once before but never seen one. They are used to capture holies or daemons that possess people.

All the clergymen and women in the area raise their left hands and, in unison, thrust their hands toward the cylinder barrier. Jura stands up and, with both his hands, physically pushes the cylinder barrier toward the floating crystal. The barrier's light engulfs the crystal, making it shine in a blinding light.

Jura is glaring at the crystal as if he is expecting it to

shatter. Once the light starts to dim down, the new obsidian-colored crystal slowly descends to the ground. Silence looms in the courtyard, and the knights cautiously begin to walk toward Kellel, whose skin is pale and full of cuts. It appears that he is not breathing. The crystal falls from its slow descent and lands next to Kellel. It sounds as if a heavy piece of metal fell on the stone street as it hits the ground.

The guards make way for Sermon to walk up to the crystal. She carefully observes it and, with a sigh of relief, pulls out a piece of cloth from her pockets and picks up the crystal cautiously. She glances at the man in red and starts to walk toward the cathedral's entrance as if nothing new has happened. A small formation of soldiers guard her and push people out of her way as they approach the golden doors.

The man in red lets out a bored sigh and says, "Excellent work, Exorcist. Fantastic work, knights of the Arcadia, and superb work, children of the clergy." He says this with great praise toward the clergymen as he walks toward the cathedral with a few guards following him.

The guards, clergy, and Jura bow their heads in response, but I can't help feeling annoyed about how calm that man was over what just happened. I turn my gaze toward Kellel to see a few soldiers grab him and carry him away toward a medical cart. After he is strapped in, the cart starts moving toward the Arcadian fortress's main gates.

I walk up to my brother to see him standing proudly but drenched in sweat, heaving in exhaustion. He looks as if he has been running away from a rolling boulder down a hill in the summer.

I quickly pull a handkerchief out of my pocket. "You okay, Jura?" I ask as I wipe the sweat off his forehead. "This trick of yours is going to kill you. As amazing as it is that you can conjure a wall of light, you can't put your body through that much stress yet. You're still brand new to the exorcist spells, and with what you told me, these spells will drain you of your mental fortitude, life, and energy if you are not careful. All magic has its consequence."

"They are known as miracles, Ruff," he says as he coughs. "Bah, a miracle is an unexplained phenomenon, while magic is something without scientific explanation! Both are extremely dangerous," I scold him.

Jura looks at me and smiles weakly. "Careful, you'll be branded a heretic and won't be allowed in the cathedral anymore."

"Hah," I laugh loudly. "King's law protects my theological view!"

He lets a small laugh out and says, "It's good training, regardless. This miracle took much of me though." He sighs. "If I am to become the best, I must practice. Can't let anyone down, you know?"

My heart sinks as I finish drying him off. "Juratan, stop blaming yourself for—"

"Ruff, I'll be fine. Just help me get to my room. I might be standing, but I fear that if I move, I will fall. The captains and my colleagues are here, and I can't let them see me in this weakened state. Let's go quickly."

"Tsk, fine." I put his arm around my neck, grabbing his belt to keep him stable. I take a quick look around and find Clover, who is walking toward me.

She is writing something on a piece of parchment, and once she gets near me, I say, "Hey, Clover, do I have to tell the guild dispatcher what happened? And if so, can it wait? I have a pressing matter to attend to."

"Ruffus, I will write the report for you and deliver it to

the dispatcher. Know that the old man's body has been taken away by the proper authorities, and they have confiscated the merchant's goods." She glances at Jura for a second and looks at me. "Take care of your sibling, but please send me a wisp or a messenger raven concerning anything else that happened on this mission today. I will be waiting."

"You are my stars, Clover!" I smile at her.

She smiles back and shakes her head. With that, I turn back around, and we start to head toward the cathedral. Once we make it into the main building, I can see quite a few wisps flying frantically, bumping on people and candles. The master librarian's helpers are trying to catch them and send them off back into the library, but to no avail. Around the corners, soldiers are running as if they're ready to attack someone, and the muses that were singing are silent. The feeling of peace this place had is gone for the moment.

"Wow, I never thought this place would feel so unwelcoming," I murmur to myself.

"I blame you, Ruff," Jura says jokingly. "You brought an unknown spirit into the city. Even the Grande Cardinal and the Zen Grand Master came out to see what was happening."

"I wonder how much trouble I am in. It can't be that much, or I would have been arrested on the spot," I say, wondering.

"I'm sure Clover saved you on that. She is a highly respected person in this city."

"I know. She developed new magic spells and helped the meister defend the Mage Quarter when the summoned archdaemon attacked," I say in a bored tone.

"You sound jealous, Ruff, but anyway, take a left here—the living quarters are this way. I got changed to the upper levels," Jura says weakly.

"I know, I remember. I have been here before!"

"Your other left, Ruffus," Jura says, annoyed.

"Right, sorry."

After a few minutes and a painful set of stairs, we make it to the cathedral's housing quarters. The structures here seem to be made of pure white stone and marble. Unlike downstairs, these have a more home-like feeling than grandeur, and the row of doors is made from yew and dark oak. The walls here have etched drawings of all the gods and some protective wards.

"Made it. Here is your hole-in-the-wall, Jura," I say to him as I search his pockets for keys.

"Ruff, where is your key?"

"Somewhere on the bottom of my bag, which I left on the merchant's cart. I hope Clover finds it," I say, worried. "I have my favorite book in there!"

I find Jura's key and unlock his enormous door carved out of yew. Above the door, there is a plaque that reads, "Apprentice Exorcist Juratan from Bern." As we walk in, I can smell the scent of good soup cooking. Jura has a beautiful place. It has one master bedroom and a hearth in the middle of the kitchen with his cooking pot. He has his private washroom with working water pipes and a nice living room filled with pictures of our family and a few mounted weapons.

I help my brother sit on a chair closest to the unlit hearth. He thanks me, and, with a snap of his finger, a tiny flame sparks on top of the wood, turning on the hearth.

"I should practice my magic one of these days," I say, somewhat impressed. "If I tried that, I would most likely combust into flames." I leave Jura's side and walk toward the washroom. "Jura, I'm fixing you a quick bath. You smell of ash, burnt wood, and salt. After you're done here, we'll go get some food," I yell as I try to remember how water pipes work.

After I finish prepping his bath, I walk out to the kitchen

to see him fast asleep on the chair. This last spell must have drained him completely.

I walk up to him and douse the flame with some sand next to the hearth. I sigh and take off his armor and weaponry and place it next to the chair. I summon all my strength to move him from the chair to the bedroom, which is easier said than done.

"By the gods, he has gotten heavy! The life of a man of the church makes you gain weight!" I murmur to myself.

After putting him to bed, I can finish changing him and put covers on him. I leave the bedroom, take off my armor hidden by my duster, and place my weapons in the living room. I decide to take a quick dip in the tub and relax. Since I haven't cleaned myself for about a week, I must smell horrible.

As I scrub, I can see the water turning a disgusting color. It makes me shiver, thinking of all the sicknesses I could get if I do not shower regularly. After washing and rinsing the tub of all the grime and dirt I left, I dry off with a long piece of cloth I find in the washroom. I can see the white linen piece is now a few different shades of gray and brown.

"I should throw this away," I say, disturbed.

I take a second cloth and wrap it around my waist as I take the dirty one to an empty bucket next to the door. Now that I am clean and relaxed, I take the opportunity to see and walk around Jura's apartment.

I smile, seeing he kept his wooden sword we made as children together. We used to play pirates and soldiers. I look at the paintings of our family and us. Mom at her workshop, looking happy with her hammer and the blazing fire from the furnace behind her. Around the rim of the furnace, a tiny fire gecko is looking toward her. The next painting is our dad, trying to look impressive with his compass. He is next to his books and maps, with a few artifacts on the floor. Beside that is a painting of our old pet dog and me. The animal was as big as me back then, and I can fondly remember the painter was angry at me because I moved too much.

I stop once I see her painting: our sister, Yubia. I sigh quietly and touch her portrait. She was a beautiful young girl with a light complexion, ocean-blue eyes, and blond hair. She was born with the ability to communicate with the dead and talk to spirits. The church called her a *medium*. They knew how rare she was, so they offered to teach her how to use her powers. She would help people and send wayward spirits to the afterlife. Such powers had their drawback though. Daemons tried possessing her many times while holies wanted to manipulate her. Phantoms and specters haunted her daily. In the end, a powerful necromancer turned to a lich, tricked her, and killed her while trying to send a daemon back to the underworld. She was able to exorcise the daemon from Jura, but in turn, the lich took her life, adding to his own. They never found the undead mage, but Jura swore he would find him and avenge Yubia's death.

Not a good memory before going to sleep,

I look away and sluggishly move on to see the rest of his house. I find myself exhausted and grab a pillow from the couch that our mother made for him. After finding extra covers, I look at all the candles, concentrating on each one, willing them to turn off with a snap of my finger. I expect at least one to turn off, but they still burn brightly. Disappointed, I turn off the wax candles lighting his house and bedroom manually.

The only light source left is a half-cracked window with the moon shining brightly through it. I set myself on the foot of Jura's bed like back when we were children, but before I lie down, my eye catches a small drawing on Jura's nightstand. It's one of both of us fishing back in Bern. I grab the framed picture and kiss it because it reminds me of a simpler time and a happier moment in my life.

Feeling comfortable and clean, I place my makeshift bed on the floor, and once my head hits the pillow, I realize how exhausted I am. I look to the ceiling to see small gems embedded in the top and walls. They look like stars in the night, shining, and the pattern they make reminds me of the night sky back home in Bern. With a long yawn and the memory of the night sky, I drift off to sleep only to dream about soup.

Down the Drain

I awake to the smell of coffee and toast, and as I stretch, I feel loose, well-rested, and annoyed that there is a ray of sunshine right on my face. I slowly get up off my blankets to entirely shut the bedroom window that was left semi-open, and I notice as I walk that, somehow, Jura is up before me.

The window will not close completely. I rattle it and end up opening it again. "I guess it is time to wake up, then," I say as I rub my eyes and sniff the air.

I sit back down to notice all my clothes folded, my boots shined, my leather coat cleaned, and a new pair of undergarments.

"Mhmm, clean clothes," I say in a happy sigh as I adjust myself and walk out of the bedroom, half dressed.

Out in the kitchen, Jura is wearing an apron and short pants, cooking food. Whatever he is cooking smells like mom's cooking.

He smiles, noticing me, and sits in a chair in front of the small pot on the hearth. "Good morning, lazy. How'd you sleep?"

I stretch and yawn again. "Great, actually. Did you clean my stuff?"

He smirks as he stirs the pot. "Actually, no, we have monks that help out with the chores. The grande and great cardinals sent them as a thank-you for the hard work."

"Yeah, they even polished Coal and took all the bloodstains out of my gear," I say as I sit down next to Jura, surprised Coal did not explode.

Jura frowns and replies, "Which I am curious about—how you let yourself become so dirty. Mother would have killed you if she knew the state you were in!"

"Well, you know me, I get in trouble too much and forget the basics of hygiene."

"So I figured. You smelled!"

"Hey, I took a bath last night!" I say as I smell under my armpits.

"I know, my favorite drying linen has an ecosystem growing out of it."

Then we both start laughing. I missed that. I missed my big brother. I visit him every time I'm in town, but we only say hi, before he leaves to go on a mission or I get a new job right away from the guild.

Jura stands up and hands me a plate of food. It has egg drop soup and bacon, my favorites. After he passes me the plate, he takes off his apron and throws it toward the bedroom. I notice he has a scar on his chest that goes from the left breast to his stomach.

"Damn, what did you piss off, Jura? This scar is huge." I put my food aside and stand up, reaching out, feeling his scar. "It's new skin. This had to be weeks ago!"

"Oh, that." He looks depressed for a second as he feels it also, but he quickly recovers. "Ha, the last woman thought I was unfaithful with two others. I tell you, elven women are ridiculous—never date them!"

I know he is lying, he does not have the time to court a woman, and the scar looks as if a claw slashed him, but I play his game. "We all know you are a heartthrob. All women want you, must be so hard for you to be good!" I say mockingly as I fall into his arms and attempt to be as dramatic as I can be. He flinched as he caught me telling me that the wound was deep, and it took magic to heal. If I did not know better the muscle was sliced.

I can see a smile and a little spark in his eye as he holds me. "Why, yes, Ruffus, I am quite faithful! I am also a smart man in my relationships, unlike someone I know, who was an idiot in his last relationship."

I smirk and glare at him. "Oh, pulling out the Clover card?"

"One of the most desirable bachelorettes in River Front and you fumbled."

As quick as a cat, I grip Jura and jump off him, away from my food and the kitchen area. I land ready to fight, but I cannot see Jura anywhere.

"Psst, behind you."

"C'mon, as if I have never fought with you before. If I were you, I'd check where my hand is." I smile.

I know Jura will go directly behind me in a fight—he does it all the time when we spar—but now I am ready. I had grabbed my wooden spoon from my plate when I stood up to mock Jura, and it is aimed at his stomach.

"Smart. If that were a dagger, you would have won. But my hands are free for your neck now, and all I need for you is to surrender, or I'll choke you out."

"I don't surrender that easily." With a quick jerk, I try flipping to the side, but Jura's left leg meets me in the air, and with a swift kick to my rib cage, he knocks me down.

"Why do you always dodge left?" Jura says as his bare foot is on my chest.

"Because your right leg is your weak one," I say painfully. "And your left is defenseless."

With my elbow, I hit his right knee, knocking him down on top of me. We both look at each other and laugh even harder as we try to sit up.

"Next time," I huff, "I swear I will knock you out." I rub my rib cage.

"Next time, little brother, I will show you less mercy and choke you out until you can see Elysium," Jura says, rubbing his knee.

I smile and punch the side of his shoulder as a loud knock at the door startle us. I grab a blanket and throw a shirt at Jura so we can both be somewhat decent to our unknown guest.

An all-familiar girly voice shouts from the other side of the door, "Open up, sleepyheads!"

I gasp. "Crap its Clover. Do not touch that doorknob."

Sadly, Jura had made it to the entrance and turned the handle. To his luck, the door then slams open, catching Jura square on the face.

"Good morning! Took you long enough to answer, Juratan. It is not polite to keep guests waiting!" Clover walks in, carrying a basket. She is wearing her field scout gear, consisting of a green cape hood, brown combat robes, and a flower in her ear.

Huh, it looks like she is about to head out on a mission.

She looks at Juratan, who is on the floor, holding his bloody nose. "Oh, Juratan, whatever happened to you?"

Jura just glares at her and runs toward the washroom.

"Jura, you're leaving a trail of blood. Oh, that will stain the wooden floor." Clover walks up to me and places the basket in front of me.

"What's this?" I ask.

"It is your payment from the quest. Did the door hit you on the head too?"

I glare at her.

"Oh, a glare, so intimidating, Ruffus. Regardless, you were awarded fifty gold for the escort and six hundred gold for the live capture of the bandits that have been plaguing the roads and the capture of a live, lesser daemon," Clover says as she looks around in the apartment.

My jaw drops. "Six hundred?"

"Correct," Clover says.

"All for me? By the gods!"

"Correct," Clover repeats, slightly annoyed.

"By the Three, this is more than I make in a season!" I quickly fumble to grab the basket.

"I know, and that is with all of your deductions taken away," she says as she searches her pockets.

"What deductions?"

Clover gives me an evil smile. "Well, the simple fact that you failed the mission since the merchant died. That alone cost the guild one hundred gold for the funeral arrangements. Also, you lost the guild's reputation by failing, which cost you a huge deduction."

"Oh, right." I hold the basket full of money closer to me.

"Let us not forget about the permits you do not have! Since the merchant died, you became the wagon's owner under the guild contract, and you didn't have a merchant's permit or an export and import permit when you entered the town. You delivered your goods late, and there are a few broken items that were meant for some of the nobles in town. The Merchants Guild is pretty upset with you at the moment for also squandering their name."

"Oh, right," I say in a quiet voice.

She pulls out a notepad from her pockets and starts to read. "Can't forget the services and materials used to extract the daemon that man was possessed by. Those were pretty expensive. And, yes, the Grande Cardinal billed the guild. Plus, the guild fee, lodging, food, and repairs for your gear in Water Front last time you quested there. The inn you stayed at told us that an IOU stamped on the back of a lady of negligible virtue is not a form of payment in the city of Water Front."

I remain silent.

"It all added to seven thousand three hundred and fifty gold in debt you owed the Warrior Guild. This quest was the beginning of your debt payment. Technically, you were about to start working for free," she says as she walks up to Jura's breakfast and grabs a piece of toast.

I put my face on the basket and sigh.

She takes a bite of Jura's toast. "All in all, the daemon was your saving grace, and he, she, they were worth so much gold. After you captured it, you were technically rich. Do you know how many scholars wanted it? But alas, all debts must be paid off with gold, right, or so the dwarves in this town would say." She pauses and stares at me. "Why is your face on the basket, Ruff?"

My mother once told me men should not cry over silly things like money or items, but that did not stop me from tearing up. After regaining my composure, I lift my head and see Clover sitting comfortably on Jura's rocking chair, still eating his toast. I ask her to turn while I change my gear.

In turn, she laughs. "It's not like I have not seen it before, Ruffus."

"First of all, I'm not naked, Clover. I'm shirtless. Second, I'm just polite, so close your eyes," I say as I walk to the bedroom. I can hear her giggle and munch on the piece of toast. I grab my shirt that is next to my makeshift bed and put it on. The smell of lavender on it makes me happy. "Mhmm, clean shirt, just like Dad used to do them!"

I walk back out to see Clover grabbing seconds and reading a small pamphlet. From where I am standing, it looks like her pamphlet is a mission slip. These small pamphlets contain requests, missions, or jobs the guild gives out.

"What you got there, Clover? A job for me?" I ask as I walk to her.

"Nothing for your eyes, Ruffus," she says as she folds the pamphlet and sticks it in her pocket.

From the washroom, I can hear Jura yelling in pain for a second. He then walks out without his shirt on and still with a bloody nose. "Ugh, my favorite shirt is now stained with blood." He glares at Clover as he walks up to her. "You are still here and eating my breakfast."

Clover giggles and takes a bigger bite of toast. "Youf fsholf offef foof tof yourf." She swallows. "Guests."

"I would have offered food, but you went ahead and ate it, Clover. For an eldar, you sure do not act like one. All others of your kind I have met are considerably more courteous, well-spoken, and well-mannered."

She smiles. "Happens when humans raise an infant eldar. I learned these manners from your kin. Of course, I would never act this way in front of my elders or brethren. They would think I have gone mad."

Jura takes his plate from her. "We humans aren't all ill-mannered, my grace."

"True!" she replies. "But you're the one indecent and dirty in front of a lady."

Jura tries to fight back, but nothing comes out of his mouth. With his plate, he walks away to the washroom again, grumbling under his breath, "It's my damn room, and you ate my toast."

"Instigator," I say to Clover.

After finishing my breakfast, I grab the basket that Clover

brought and quickly count the rolls of coins. The washroom door opens, and Jura walks toward me with a clean shirt.

"Here, Jura." I throw six rolls of coins to him, and he catches them all elegantly.

"What are these for?" he asks as he counts them.

"Well, you did most of the job after the soldier tried to escape again. What was his name?"

Clover spoke up. "Knight of Arcadia, Kellel."

"Yes, Kellel, that guy. I still wonder how a knight of Arcadia got possessed. Aren't you all immune?" I ask Jura.

"No one is immune to possession. We are trained to resist and avoid possession. A strong entity must have been present to aid in the possession, but I was not there, so I don't know." Jura puts the rolls of coins on a small table. "On a happier note, let us go to dinner together with this gold. We can go to the restaurants near the castle and eat like nobles!"

"Which restaurant are we going to? I know a great dwarven cuisine place in Castle Town!" Clover says as she jumps to her feet.

"Not us as in you, me, and Ruff. Us as in Ruff and I," Jura says dryly.

"Hmmp!" Clover pouts as she searches for something in her pockets. "Before I forget, Ruff, this is for you." Clover hands me a letter sealed with blood-red wax.

"Who is this from?" I ask as I take the letter.

She shrugs. "I think it is a summons from the Warrior Guild's leader."

"Pass it here, Ruff," Jura says as I hand him the letter. In a surprised voice, he says, "This is what the high council uses to write their letters! I had no idea your boss was part of the council."

I shrug and say, looking at the paper, "Neither did I. The council is made up of the leaders of different groups that help the royalty rule?"

Jura bites his lower lip. "Well, it's more complicated than that, but, yes. The council is made up of guild leaders and discusses affairs concerning River Front. Regardless, you better head out there now. No sense in keeping him waiting."

I nod and look in Clover's direction, but she has vanished. I walk toward Jura's bedroom, pick up the rest of my gear, and finish getting dressed.

"Jura, I'm off," I tell him as I walk up to the door.

He walks up to me, hugs me, and tells me to be safe and not be late for dinner. I nod and leave his room hastily. As I make my way out of the maze known as the Grande Cathedral, I see the Master Librarian talking to a female elf. She is wearing an elegant white dress and a tiara. She glances at me with bright violet eyes, and I fall immediately in love and am at a loss for words. Her beauty is almost godlike.

She smiles at me and looks back to the master librarian, who also stops examining her and analyzes me instead. I snap away from Cupid's arrow and feel as if I am still under surveillance. Quickly, I pick up the pace and open the golden doors to leave the cathedral. Outside, I can see many Arcadian soldiers standing at attention and a crowd of people in awe at someone, but I am too far away to see who it is.

Guess someone important just left or is arriving.

A band of royal guards marches in front of me. Curiously, I look in the direction that they are headed. The gates of Castle Town are wide open, and an elegant carriage drives up the road toward the castle.

I shrug and walk in the opposite direction, only to see monks and soldiers staring at me and whispering to each other. Noticing this, I pick up the pace and leave before I gain too much unwanted attention.

HQ Warriors Guild

As I cross the bridge that divides this area of town, I remember why I like this magnificent city.

River Front is buzzing with life. Everywhere you look, something is happening, from a street fight to a sale of werewolf blood to old ladies knitting while discussing the best way to slay an elder dragon. Nothing seems to trouble people here at all, and by the sounds of it, they are happy.

I take the alleyways to the heart of the Living Quarters once I get off the bridge. It's not as safe as the main road, but it's much quicker. Gamblers, unique shops, and strange-looking people roam these alleyways. As I walk through, sellers pop out of the woodwork, offering me items I would not want to be caught with, although they're cheaper here than in the underground market. A few harlots whistle toward me to catch my attention, but I quickly look down, hoping they will not recognize me. Luckily, I make my way to the guild's front door without any problems and with a new type of poison I acquired from a vendor.

The doors are gigantic, made of ruku wood, one of the most robust natural materials known to man, on which a massive battle-ax is lodged in the top of the door. Rumor has it that our last guild leader threw the ax at our current leader as a reminder that no weapon can break what he built.

As I go through the open doorway, a large chamber opens before me. Hundreds of people are sitting, chatting, drinking, and eating at the central pavilion tables.

There is a giant notice board with missions, requests, and escorts for the guild to fulfill to my left. Attending this board is a dwarf woman posting new assignments for anyone who wants to take them and chat up a storm. To my right, there is the way to the underground arena, where warriors, mages, and such people go to fight and prove they're the best. Directly in front of me is the guild's main counter, where most guild attendants work. They offer lodging, food, and drinks for the right price.

I take a deep breath and make my way up to the counter, shoving various drunken elves, beastmen, dwarves, orcs, and humans to the side so I can pass. Before I can reach the counter, a hand grabs the back of my coat and drags me backward. I am about to strike back when I find myself in a warm but strong hug.

"My cub!" says the booming voice behind me.

The smell of strong ale, the grip of his hug, and the fact that I was called a "cub"—I know exactly who is hugging me. I try to turn, but this beastman picks me off the ground with one hand and squeezes a tad bit harder, and I can feel him sniffing me all over.

"I can't breathe, Erol!" I say, gasping.

With a roaring laugh, he puts me down and says, "Welcome back, Ruffus. I have missed you!"

I turn around after he lets me go and hug him back. "I have missed you too, Erol. I'm glad you are safe!"

Erol is a tall bipedal tiger beastman from the savanna region called the Wilds. His yellow fur shines in the sunlight, and his black stripes give him a distinct pattern from other feline beastmen. Tall as a mountain, he is around six feet, seven inches. He is also built to destroy mountains, and no one would be foolish enough to pick a fight with him, for their hands might break when they hit his muscles.

His intimidating demeanor would make anyone think twice about approaching him with a grievance. His most distinguishing feature is his eyes. The iris has a red tint like a ruby that fell into crystal-clear water. He is shirtless, only wearing a harness that he uses to attach pieces of armor quickly if he needs to. His trousers are worn and black, and his boots have seen better days, and if I had the money, which I now do, I would buy him a newer pair of boots.

Erol comes from an area that overall lacks what humans and elves call "standard education". But never underestimate him, he is smart. He is more attuned to natural knowledge, survivability, and the history and tradition of his race only, and his people rarely delve into magic. This fact causes people to think he is uneducated, even though he is fluent in orcish, feline beast, and typical human, though his language barrier makes it a bit difficult to understand. His thick accent doesn't help his cause. Whenever he talks, it sounds as if he is harsh and mean, while in truth, he might just be trying to be sweet.

Erol kneels to look at me eye to eye. "My cub, you seem to have fought a strong foe and won! That deserves strong drink!"

"A quick one, Erol. I have business to attend to," I say as I grab his mug from his hands. After I take a few sips from his drink and cough, realizing how strong it is, I ask, "How was your mission to the Sacred Mesa out by the desert region? Last time I heard, golems, thunderbirds, and wyverns were plaguing the small settlements."

He smiles and stands up. "It was good, but I finish early. I destroyed great sword I crafted, trying to cut golem in half. Had to finish the monster with fists."

I grab one of his hands and look at his knuckles. "Not a scratch on them. Those monsters are no match for you."

"None are, my precious cub. Now, where are you off to? This business you speak of, where is it?" he asks as he pushes a tall, drunken elf out of a chair and offers it to me.

I take a bigger sip of his drink and pull out the summons from my pocket.

With a light chuckle, he says, "Good drink, is it not? Here, sit down, let me see the paper, and drink the rest."

I hand both items to him as I sit on the stool that he so kindly vacated for me. The drunken elf sees me on the chair and begins to babble at me, waving his arms. With a long sigh, I look at the elf and gesture for him to go away, making him turn red with anger.

"Hold this, please," Erol says to me as he hands me his mug. With a quick swoop, Erol picks the elf up by his head and growls. His hand covers the poor drunken elf's whole face.

"Now, now, Erol, let the poor guy down. We did take his chair," I say, calming him down and getting off the stool.

Erol grins at me and lowers the elf down slowly on the stool. I apologize to him and promise I will buy him a drink, but the poor elf is shaken and sits down quietly on the floor. I can hear Erol chuckle, and he grabs me by the shirt, making me come close to him. I don't resist and put my head on his chest as he hiccups and reads by mouthing words on the letter.

"Last I know, the guild leader was battling in the arena. He should be there. Let me grab more drinks, and we shall head down there together," Erol says as he sniffs the air.

I nod at him and take his mug. I offer it to the elf, only to see him asleep on the floor. I glance at Erol to see him walking away to the bar. With a scoff, I follow him. I have known Erol for around nine years now. I met him during a hunting mission back near my hometown of Bern. He was a freelancer back then. A wyvern—a small, dragon-like creature—was plaguing the trade routes, and this guild hired a team of four consisting of Clover, Erol, a warrior named Lue, and me to take it down. Lue, an odd elf who overthought, got eaten and killed after he rushed in to fight it on its own, and only the three of us remained. Thanks to him, the wyvern could not fly away quickly, leaving us the chance to fight and capture it. With a mighty roar and caution, Erol went head-on with pure strength to slay the beast as Clover and I backed him up.

His raw power knocked the beast into submission, but when we thought we had won the battle, the wyvern got ready to spout fire, and Erol was unaware of this. I ran up and jumped on him with a fire ward Clover crafted for me. I broke the small glass ward, impaling my hand with shards, but I was able to create a dome that covered both Erol and me from the hellish flames. After the fire died out, both of us were sizzling. We had minor burn marks on our bodies and faces, but we were, in the end, safe. I apologized to Erol for abruptly jumping on him, praying that he would not beat me to a pulp. All he did was move me off him, stand up, and pick me up, bumping both our foreheads together.

A small tear came to his eye, and he softly spoke. "No one has ever shown me this type of kindness. Thank you. Anyone else would have seen me die before this. Thank you for giving me a chance to live."

In all honesty, I reacted to save him because earlier, he said that if we won the battle, he would pay for food, and I had not eaten well in three days, although I will never tell him that. Since then, we have had many missions together, and our friendship has grown. I would trust this beast with my life and spirit if I had to, but not my beer.

"Beautiful dwarven maiden, I need drinks!" Erol yells as he makes his way up to the counter.

"And I desire payment, beastman," the dwarf server says as she pours a new drink.

"Put it on his tab!" Erol points at me. "My cub will pay for it later!" he says as he grabs his drink and smiles at me.

I glare and shake my head at Erol. "Let's just go and find the guild leader." I look toward the bar maiden. "I'll come back and pay for it when I'm finished here."

"I do not accept IOUs, Ruffus. Remember what happened last time?" she says as she serves another drink to an orc.

"Yeah, I remember. Let's go, Erol," I say as I start to walk away.

We make our way through the bar to the arena's entrance. The doors are old and uncared for, with chips missing from the front. Erol gets in front of me and pushes the door open. Immediately after, I feel the intense heat and the smell of smoke. "It's like a furnace in there," I say as I walk past the entrance, heading to the stairwell.

"The smell of smoke reminds me of my tribe's shamans. On this day, mages fight in the arena," Erol says as he takes a drink. "Das is good mead."

We descend to an underground pavilion that reminds me of a cave entrance at the bottom of the stairs. Our footsteps echo as we walk into the enormous circular pavilion. A few feet in front of us, an elven guild maiden sits on a chair reading a book the size of the table it was set on and giggling with a small drink in her hand.

We reach the table, and I clear my throat.

She looks up and smiles at both of us, and in Elvish, she says, "Greetings, fellow guild members. Do you wish to seek glory in the fighting pits? Prove your strength in a trial, or spectate?"

I speak back in Elvish, "I seek the head of our guild. He has summoned me. Where might he be?"

"Our master is tending the beast cages. Please go through those doors." She points to a set of broken-looking doors.

I nod at her and thank her for the information. "Let's go, Erol. Fate awaits me, and I feel pretty lucky about this!"

Erol takes one last gulp, emptying his mug. With a slight hiccup, he licks his lips and places the cup on the maiden's table, running after me.

I reach the doors and forcibly push on them as Erol catches up to me. The doors open to a dimly lit room filled with rusty cages, and they all seem to be empty. As we walk in, I feel a piercing gaze upon me and hear skittering feet.

I slowly grab my knife but feel Erol hold my weapon hand. "My cub, it's just a rat. Calm yourself."

I nod and slowly release my grip on my knife. "This place has always been creepy to me. The last time I did not pay the tab, I had to clean a few cages here. The rats are the size of cats down here, and they attack in packs. I swear I saw one walk on its hind legs."

We both continue to walk, looking for the other exit doors in this room, hoping to find the guild leader and leave.

Erol stops me abruptly and smells the air. "This area of the room smells of odd beasts, none I have fought before. There, through those doors, the smell is coming from."

Erol points at an archway that connects to a dark room. I walk to the doorway and notice a plaque written in Elvish: "Fighting Pits."

"Your sense of smell is keen, beastman," a low voice says behind us as it breaks the silence.

I quickly jump in fear and turn around. I look at Erol, who keeps sniffing the air and is uninterested in the new voice. I can see the silhouette walk toward us, and as it gets near with a lantern, I can see him: a tall, buff, sage-green orc, standing proud with a grin on his face. He carries battle scars on his chest, arms, and thighs. His black hair melds with the darkness in the room, and his smile shows his lower fangs are somewhat chipped and covered in a gold plate. Like Erol, he wears a leather harness on his chest. In the middle of the harness, an emblem of a dragon stares at me as if it were alive. His boots and shorts are gilded with silver, and a badge of a fist and two axes are attached to his belt. The symbol is the Warriors Guild. He stops as he gets near Erol and spits inside a cage.

"Welcome, Ruffus!" he says as he looks at Erol. "Well, turn around and let me see all of you. I have heard of you, and I, for some reason, imagined you smaller, like a human." He is still looking at Erol.

I wave my hand slowly from a distance and quietly say, "Sir, umm, I'm Ruffus."

I feel the orc's eyes pierce through me as he walks past Erol and comes closer to me. "My mistake, human, but I guess I imagined you right."

I could see his hazel eyes examine me as if I was a weapon. "Go on, give me a spin, and let me see what I'm working with here." I spin quickly, expecting him to laugh.

"Hmm, well, it can't be helped!" he says, disappointed, and looks toward the doors. "So, Ruffus, I have a mission for you." His eyes meet mine, and I feel a chill run down my spine and immediately feel intimidated. "Through these doors, you will be fighting a monster. Lucky for you, I won't tell you what type it is, but the high council wants to be entertained, and since you failed your last mission"—he grins at me—"you must kill it if you choose to accept. If not, you will be demoted back to initiate, and you will have new duties with the guild, starting with cleaning this place up. Oddly enough, I have not seen the last initiate I sent down here a few days ago. Although the rats have gotten fatter, for some reason." He scoffs, "Funny, I could have sworn I even saw a rat walking on its hind legs here too."

I felt that my life was ending, one way or the other. Either I fight an unknown monster and possibly die, or I get eaten by rats. The worst part is that I lose all the hard work I have put into this guild. My honor will be gone, and nowhere else will accept me, not even the brothels. Not that I mind.

I gather the remaining courage I have, stand tall and proud, and say, "I accept the mission, sir!"

He glances at Erol. "If you want, Ruffus, you can ask for three more companions. This is a standard mission and posted as a priority on the guild's board."

"Guild leader, I will be ready in an hour for this battle. I just need to check my gear," I say nervously.

With a nod, the guild leader walks up to the doors and kicks them wide open. The roar of the crowd and applause begins as he walks to the center of the arena. With a booming voice, he says, "The challenge of the day has been accepted. Ruffus has agreed to fight the daemon!"

A chant and cheer for fighting break out in unison around the stands from the crowd. I stand in shock and fall to my butt. I cannot believe I have to fight a daemon in front of people. It takes at least a squadron of seven to take one down.

Nausea begins to set in, and my head feels lightheaded until I feel a hand on my shoulder. I look and see Erol wipe the dust off my shoulder. With confidence and fire in his eyes, he looks at me and says, "I will fight with you. Now, my cub, let us have a glorious battle."

Erol's eyes are full of conviction and a desire to fight, but I quickly look toward the cage, pondering if this fight is worth it until I see a rat the size of a gnome with a fork in its tiny paws eyeing me with great care.

I look back to Erol, who is looking toward the open door, listening to the cheers, and think to myself, *Oh gods.*

Preparations

fter the announcement of my fight, a few guild maidens come to me and escort us to the arena's staging area. This room is an armory with an alchemist's desk. It also contains an anvil and smithing tools that, to my surprise, are well-maintained, unlike the beast pens. The maidens explain that I can use all the materials to fix, create, and craft gear until it is my time to fight.

"Fighters, we shall all leave you to your demise! Know that we have guards outside the doors, and also, escape from this staging area is impossible! This is where we locked the Shadow Thief, the leader of the band of thieves that used to plague River Front, when she was finally caught. Not even her lockpicking ability helped her escape, and that was her forte!" she says as she walks out and shuts the door behind her.

A loud locking noise comes soon afterward.

I take a deep breath and sit down on the floor as Erol explores the room. "My cub! There are thrown weapons here for you. Look. knives, axes, spears, darts, and bastard swords!" I get off the floor and clean the dirt off my pants. "I should have taken a few more detours before I came here. I mean, I left Jura in the morning and arrived at the guild at sunset. I did not get supper yet."

Erol turns around, carrying a few weapons in his hand and

a basket filled with odd materials in another. "What are you speaking?"

I cover my face with both my hands. "I'm sorry, Erol, and I'm babbling. I talk too much when I'm nervous." I shake my head and growl under my breath, "By the Three, how are we going to kill a damn daemon? Honestly, with all the accidents that happen in this city, you would think they would not allow one to fight freely."

"Well, we fight and kill it, cub! It's simple!" Erol chirps. "Maim it until no more maim. Then eat if we can."

I sigh and compose myself. "We don't know what type of daemon it is. And we don't eat daemonic beings. Or I hope we don't."

"They are all the same, cub," Erol says as he grabs a sturdy-looking pole made of black wood and a sharp-looking ax headpiece, along with a few other items.

I walk up to Erol and observe what he's doing. "Is it a minion? A low-tier daemon that follows orders of stronger beings? Or could it be a named daemon, an ascended minion, a daemon that becomes conscious of its power? They stop being referred to as an 'it' then! Named daemons gain new powers unknown to them, making them a danger to themselves and whatever surrounds them. Or worse, an archdaemon, you know, what almost destroyed the Mage Quarter a few months ago in this city!"

Erol starts heating the forge and begins working on his craft. "You are babbling, my cub. I have never fought a named daemon you speak about. It will be a great challenge. I have killed many minions, so we will be victorious if our opponent is one."

"How are you so calm, and what are you making?" I ask as I massage my eyebrow with my index finger.

"A bar'fau, cub. It is my favorite weapon," Erol says as he licks his lips.

"It looks like a halberd combined with a fauchard. Will the wood be able to support the weight of the blade and hammer?" I ask Erol as he hammers down his unfinished weapon.

"The pole is ruku wood, won't break even if an elder dragon stands on it," Erol says as he heats the metal.

"You should go see my mother one day so she can induct you into the Crafters Guild. They get the best materials from the Merchant's Association," I say as I take out my sword and inspect it.

"The matriarch of your line is superior to me! Her craft created the beautiful weapon you carry. I cannot stand in the same room as her with my crafting. I want to be better to impress her."

"You jest. You have crafted a new weapon quickly and effortlessly—you are at a master's level! Heh, after you're done, you should sharpen my sword as I get us armor," I say to Erol as I pat his back.

With a warm smile, Erol winks at me and says, "It was quick for the only reason that this is a dwarven forge, and all the materials were ready to assemble and are already sharp and with the right shape. Enough of me—tell me the story again of how you got your blade. It inspires."

"Well." I look at my sword and smile. "I got this by accident."

I look around the room for the armor bench. "When Jura left for Arcadia, my mother was tasked by our village elder to create a sword for our shrine. As thanks to the Three for bestowing good fortune on my family, it took her three months to design it. She crafted it out of silver, stardust, and copper. It was a beautiful ceremonial blade; her love, creativity, and proficiency were forged into that blade. Its silhouette was odd and uncommon. It was more diamond-shaped than anything, and, of course, the sword's materials made it impractical for a fight with such soft metals. After my mom superheated the finished blade with dragon's fire, she got into an argument with my father. In a rage, she threw the first item she got her hands on at him, and with her hulking strength, she flung the sword out the window, right into the coal mines below our house. The sword impaled itself in the wall and became stuck there."

"Your father was a fool to anger her!" Erol says as he cools off his weapon.

"Trust me, you don't want to anger Mother. Anyway, I was practicing magic inside the mines because I thought it was a good idea and accidentally set fire to a burrow of rats. As I was running away from these beasts, which were the size of small dogs, I might add, I stumbled upon the impaled sword. I tried pulling it out of the wall, but the damn thing was stuck in there good, so I used the only thing I could at the moment: magic. I was able to pull out the sword using earth magic, specifically by shifting the wall.

"Since I was new to the spell, I used a bit too much power, exhausting myself. The sword flew out of the wall with a chunk of coal embedded in it, successfully squishing two rats when it landed. I had no idea it was a sword since it looked just like a club when I pulled it off the wall. To my luck, I created a cave-in, killing the rest of the rats but trapping myself in," I say as I find metal armor the size of Erol.

"As a mere child, you killed creatures just like me. I'm proud!"

"Well, in the end, I was stuck in the cave for one day until my mother punched the rocks out of the way to save me. When the search party found me, I was unconscious from the lack of air, but I had the sword clutched in my hand. Afterward, my mother tried to separate the coal from the sword, but it had fused with it. In the end, she shaved the big chunks of coal from it, destroying the diamond shape it once had, making it more rectangular. She left a thin coat of coal. That's why my sword has an odd shape, and it's heavier than a normal sword. She thought the sword was lucky and gave it to me as a present. She also told me never to practice magic again, or she would kick me. Of course, just like Jura's sword, she blessed it and wrote in gold 'Mother Protection' in the middle of the sword. Good thing, too—I'm sure I'd be dead if it were not for her blessing. Oh, and here, Erol, I found steel armor for you," I say as I walk with the chest piece.

Erol grabs the sword that I left next to him and glances at me. "My cub, this sword shall lead you to victory! I shall try to bless it with my luck to give to you. You only need my blessing and your matriarch's!"

Somehow, that makes me feel better. "Thank you, Erol. Now, here is your chest piece. The rest of the armor is over by the table. I have seen you fight with armor before, and I can say it makes me jealous of how agile you are with it."

"I shall finish this weapon in a few minutes and put on my armor," Erol says as he dips the heated metal in the oil.

Time goes by, and as we finish gearing up, we hear a gong break the silence. I stand ready and prepared. I glance back at him, who just finished his last piece of steel armor. I walk over to the whetstone and my sharpened sword while Erol walks next to me and gives a final inspection of his weapons.

"Stand back, cub. I need to give one swing and make sure the blade head won't slide off."

I do as I'm told as Erol walks up to a few training dummies. With a strong swing, Erol decapitates six of the ten figures effortlessly.

"We face before us a mighty foe, and I mean to slay it," he says, clenching his fist.

I run toward Erol and use his shoulder to jump off and close the gap between me and my target. With a full swing, I take off its straw head. I land next to the freshly decapitated mannequin, sheathing my sword. "After we kill this monster, I'll buy us a drink. Deal?"

"You know how to make this fighter happy! My cub does care about me!" Erol says as he runs to me and picks me up in a firm hug.

A loud gong goes off, interrupting the death grip that Erol calls a hug.

"We are ready," Erol says with conviction as he puts me down while I gasp for breath.

"Till the death?" I ask Erol.

"Till the death," he replies.

"Oh, and, Erol, before I forget, take this." I hand him a pouch filled with potion vials and balms.

Erol looks in the pouch and takes a small inventory. "Around ten pointers, burn ointments, and water in a container."

"I was able to get syringes for us just in case we get injured. Remember, these potions don't cure broken bones—they just numb the pain," I say as I open the staging area door.

"Ever think what might be in these potions?" Erol asks. "Nope, better to not know what they are and just feel the effect!" I say, walking out.

As I make my way to the arena doors, I shake off my fears and get ready for the fight.

I hear the cling and clang noise of Erol's armor coming up behind me, and in a soft voice, he says, "Thank you for the medicine, cub."

As the double doors open, I feel Erol staring at me, and I turn to look at him. We both nod and enter the roaring arena filled with cheers, boos, and the all-too-comfortable chant, "Kill."

Unwelcomed News

As Erol and I walk to the center of the arena to present ourselves to the lords and the crowd, I cannot help but notice how gory the stadium was left. It is covered in ash and chunks of flesh with fresh blood on it, and there is what looks like a needle with yarn on the furthest corner.

"What a terrific fight!" the booming voice of a wolf beastman announces. "The Knitting Guild has defeated a hellhound, and in only five minutes, without breaking a sweat! Never have I seen such gore and carnage! How in God's name did they create a web of lines so quickly?"

The crowd above roars in pure excitement, chanting the name "Mrs. Beth" repeatedly.

"Now for the main event! These two warriors from our guild will fight a lower-tier daemon, also known as a minion. But don't be fooled! This minion killed and took over an Arcadian soldier without a sweat!"

The crowd breaks into boos and insults the Arcadian society with glee.

The announcer cheers, "Our warriors of the night are Erol of the Wilds!"

The crowd goes wild and starts singing a song about beer and how Erol stole a guild maiden and took her back to the barracks.

I look at Erol, who is not fazed by the song. "You never told me you were this popular. And what is this business about a guild maiden?"

Erol looks back at me, confused. "I have only slain dragons, a few giants, and a few other monsters. I have done nothing of great importance, my cub! I am not known, I promise, and as for the beer elf, someone stepped on her leg, breaking her. She could not walk, so I took her to the barracks and mended her leg. Do not be jealous, my cub. Nothing happened, I swear!" he says to me, embarrassed and nervous.

Before I can answer back, the announcer starts talking again. "And his companion for this quest is Rummus! From a town near Bern!"

The crowd goes silent, except for the drunken patrons, who all yell, "Woo, I love rum!"

Erol's eyes glow brightly in happiness. "They give you the silence respectful of warrior's entrance! I had no idea my cub was so honored!"

At that moment, I gently put both my hands on my face and sigh deeply. "I hope my brother is not here to see this embarrassment."

Erol taps on my shoulder and points up to the crowd. "My cub, look, your sibling came to see you be victorious!"

I look up to see Jura talking to Clover in a worried manner. Next to them, I can see the beautiful elf next to my guild leader and the Grande Cardinal from yesterday. A black lion beastman approaches Jura and instructs him on something, making Jura snap to a position of attention and walk away, taking Clover with him to the lower stands. After the lion beastman arrives at the stand, I notice that all of them turn to stare at me.

By the Three, they are all looking at me, I think to myself.

"It is my pleasure as the announcer of the night to introduce to you all the special guests tonight! From the Grande Cathedral, Grande Cardinal Ludwig, the man responsible for catching this vile creature!"

Cheers and applause erupt as Cardinal Ludwig waves in a bored manner.

"Next is the meister of magic, the queen's magic specialist, and strongest and most beautiful elven sorcerer of this land: Meister Helena, director of the Mage Quarter!"

The crowd cheers louder, and a few patrons let out a whistle and a few other catcalls as Meister Helena stands and bows elegantly.

"Next up is Commander Leto from the Arcadian Army," the announcer says, uninterested.

The crowd just applauds, and a few patrons yell a few profanities at him as Commander Leto stands and looks disgusted at us.

The announcer yells with great praise and energy, "And last but not least, give it up for the king of the arena, the impaler of the horde of succubi, the killer of the dreaded dragon Frost, and your leader and mine, Berserker Alan of Spire Tundra, the strongest fighter of all the realm!"

The crowd goes wild. The cheers, praise, and sheer amount of energy that just his name brings makes the arena rumble.

Why are they all here? And staring at me? And am I fighting the same daemon? I think to myself as I look back at them.

Erol notices me staring off. "Cub, are you okay? You have not said anything in the past minute. I worry."

"Erol, we are fighting the same daemon that I defeated once. It knows me," I tell him as the announcer talks about a brief history of the Warriors Guild.

"Is that bad?" he asks.

"If it bears anger at me and it gains power, it will be stronger than normal. A grudge makes minions stronger—they feed on the fear and anger they hold. Or that's what Jura told me once, and what books say!" I explain.

"Now! It is time for the battle! Warriors at the stand, please throw your handicap toward our combatants!" the announcer asks.

Nothing was thrown into the arena by them, and the announcer starts to talk again. "Patrons and viewers, throw your handicaps in!"

From the higher crowd where the nobles sit, satchels, beer mugs, an old arrow, and a sewing set are thrown down to the arena.

I hear Jura yell my name out of the crowd, and I see him throw a big bag toward me.

I catch the bag with decent elegance and open it. A tiny violet wisp escapes the bag and bumps into my forehead, and in a deep voice, it whispers in my head, "Share this memory!"

I feel as if I am breathing steam in from a hot spring, calming and comforting. I can hear Jura's voice in my head, speaking to me. "Brother, fate does not fortune you," he says, panting. "Someone sent me this wisp about what was discussed on the council, and it contains grave news. Now think of me and see what I have seen!"

I close my eyes, my mind is filled with images, and a vision comes to play. I see Cardinal Ludwig and the rest of the lords sitting around a round table. They all speak over each other, except for a beautiful elven maiden sitting and drinking from her cup.

"Enough! By the Three, we need order!" Cardinal Ludwig slams his staff on the floor, creating a loud echo, and lights up the room in brilliant colors.

The chamber goes quiet, and it is established that Cardinal Ludwig is in control of the room for the moment.

"I have asked for this meeting because now we have a minion possessing General Moss's soldiers!" He waves his hand above the table, and a map of Haidyenten, the continent we live on, appears. It shows multiple locations, and in the center, River Front. "We all know these heathens, monsters, and daemons are coming from that damned kingdom of White Wood! We need to eradicate it with holy fire to purify the u—"

"I will not provoke a war with White Wood!" A black lion beastman rises from his seat, interrupting Cardinal Ludwig. He is wearing beautifully crafted armor that stands apart from the rest. It is gilded with a silver finish. On his breastplate is a symbol of a sword facing down, with wings coming out of the blade with a sun in the background. The emblem that my brother wears as one of his badges—the symbol of Arcadia.

"We cannot eradicate one of our oldest allies without proof that they, in fact, are summoning these creatures. Ludwig, as one of the cardinals from the Grande Cathedral, you should be asking to send aid, not requesting a war plan. You know better. The pope and the hierophant are the only ones to incite a holy war with the consent of the Five." The beastman glares at Ludwig.

"Commander Leto, you are a failed protégé of General Moss and the youngest member of this council. If I were you, I'd bite my lesser tongue before you are relinquished of the duties!" Ludwig answers with nasty scorn.

The room goes deathly silent. I can see Leto's hand shaking in fury as the other hand hovers on the map.

Leto licks his lips as he creates five flags on the map. "Cardinal, I am the second-in-command of the Arcadian forces, an honor bestowed by the queen and General Moss. I know strategy, and I recommend this." Leto moves the flags onto a point on the map that is surrounded by woods. "We send five soldiers to assure that nothing is wrong with our ally kingdom."

"You mean to spy?" asks a male dwarf wearing a dirty apron, half-moon glasses, and an odd-shaped hat with a contraption on his head that reminds me of a magnifying glass.

Leto looks in his direction. "I have sent envoys that never came back, Magnus."

He stands up on his chair in an uproar. "And when were you going to tell us this bit of information? Trade is being disrupted, and the flow of money into this kingdom has stopped! My investors in various guilds depend on White Wood trade goods. This problem must come to an end!"

With anger in his voice, Leto says, "You are only informed when it is necessary. You are not part of the militia, a need-to-know basis like the cardinal here. Now we will execute this plan to restore—"

An all-too-familiar orc throws a dagger toward the center of the table, making his presence known. With a light chuckle, he stands and smiles at Leto. "You seem to forget, we are all equals here, not your pampered soldiers of Arcadia. We do not take orders from you."

A slight growl escapes Leto's lips. "As long as General Moss is gone on his campaign, I command River Front's law enforcement, military envoys, and war room. I will not be sending untrained brigands to do a soldier's job, Berserker Alan. Know your place. The only use we have for a Warriors Guild is to complete the mundane tasks that we do not deem a threat."

Alan makes a fist and looks livid, changing his green hue to a darker, almost violet tone. In a threatening voice, he speaks in Orcish, which makes Leto grab the hilt of his sword and Magnus laugh uncontrollably.

He speaks in the Common language again and says, "Your weak soldiers can't even do a successful mission. The only reason we know of the trouble of what is happening is that my warrior brought him to us!"

"Peace be with both your raging spirits. This argument gets us nowhere. Let me speak and resolve this issue," the elegant elven maiden says in her native tongue as she stands to look at Alan and Leto. "Time is running short. My mages have informed me that the woods surrounding the town have grown in magic exponentially. We all know what can happen when wild magic is unchecked, and accounting for the history of that location, we would not want another break-in rift of spirits."

The room agreed.

What are they talking about? Rifts? Spirits? White Wood? And I know I have seen her before, talking to the Master Librarian. She is pretty. Clover could take a few pointers from her.

"Lady Helena is right," Leto says, avoiding eye contact with her and putting his guard down.

Alan breaks eye contact with her, sits down, and pulls out a book from a bag underneath the table. "I will look at my roster of warriors and see who is the strongest, other than me, to send on the mission that Commander Leto suggested."

"Thank you, Berserker, for your support. I will muster my captains and see who of all of them is fit to lead this venture." Leto sits down, nodding at Helena.

Ludwig sighs in discontent. "Meister Helena, I will send an enforcer to make sure no chaos ensues between the commander's men and the berserkers' warriors," he says as he waves his hand on the map, making it disappear.

Helena ponders for a few seconds. "I'll have a field mage keep surveying the forest and contact White Wood. Knowledge is key at this moment, do you not agree?"

Ludwig nods.

Helena waves her hand, and a new map appears, showing a dense forest. In the middle, there is an area labeled White Wood. "What I know of this place is what you all know and the history that my sibling has taught me. I also have felt an influx of magic coming from that direction for some time, as I know all attuned in the ways have felt also." She puts her index and middle finger in her temple. "I can sense a strong magic presence, but I am unsure of what it is. This means that it is strong enough to summon daemons and holies. This poses a great danger to all surrounding kingdoms. A war between contrasting spirits will consume all living beings in the area. The oddity is that the magic is coming from both spiritual ends, holy and daemonic."

"Holies give order to this world, and daemons will destroy us all," Ludwig grunts.

"Regardless of how you view the spiritual entities anyone here follows, we all know these entities do not belong in our realm," Helena says dryly to Ludwig. "Now, I have asked my sibling to give us his point of view on this matter." She makes an elegant hand movement, and a water-like orb materializes in the air, glowing faintly in an aquamarine hue. In Elvish, she speaks toward the flying globe that floats around the table, "Have you found more information about our guest that our soldiers and warriors captured?"

The orb glows brighter, and an echoing voice reverberates from it, speaking in Common. "No, Meister, but we could release the creature and interrogate it to make sure that it came from White Wood. If the creature did, we could gather information if it were summoned to our realm or if it came from a magical rift. We can also extract all its memory if it repossessed someone, a much easier and less time-consuming task. Know that its memory could be seized if the creature dies, but it will have exponential gaps in knowledge."

"Grand, a fight! Just pin him against a prisoner," Alan spoke up.

"Thank you, Master Librarian," Helena says as she waves her hand, dissipating the orb.

Ludwig mutters, fetching something in his pocket. "A fight, Alan?" He pulls out a crystal and slams it on the table. "This is no mere opponent!"

The room goes deathly quiet as Helena closes her eyes and takes a deep breath, muttering as she exhales. "I feel it is a lesser daemon, a minion. The first possession gave it enough power to ascend soon." She opens her eyes and looks at Leto. "Did your soldier survive the possession?"

"Of course he survived. No such creature can kill my soldiers." Leto smirks.

"True, they may not die, but my warrior defeated a possessed Arcadian soldier and brought the daemon to our attention," Alan retorts as he spins a dagger in his hand.

Leto bares his teeth.

Ludwig speaks up. "Seems you are right about that, Alan. We shall send the same warrior to fight it again."

Everyone in the room turns to look at Ludwig with surprise. "If the warrior fails, he becomes possessed, and it will be easy to interrogate."

"I will not send him to certain death! A minion on its own is a challenging task to kill, and he has proven his mettle—he deserves a rest. I will fight it!" Alan stands, putting the dagger on the table.

Magnus sighs and says, "This is not a matter which you or any of us can fix by ourselves. By your guild's rules, the warrior who fails a mission must go through an evaluation by the leader and a panel of individuals to see if he is a fit for your guild. As of now, we are your panel. Let us not forget that he also let a man die under his protection, a crime of its own. Your guild's prestige fell when the nobles got the news. Thus, your patrons, the ones who keep the guild funded, are considering withdrawing their investment. They want collateral, the warrior, or the daemon. We chose the daemon, and your warrior will have to fight it to prove your organization is not a waste of coins. What guarantee do the investors have that the old guild leader has chosen the correct successor? Let us not forget, he brought a daemon, although unwillingly, without knowledge to this city that has suffered attacks by its kind." He darts a look toward Helena.

All the members of the council nod except Alan, who is at a loss for words.

Leto sits down and smiles at Alan. "Your brigands are a dime a dozen. If one dies, another will take his place. The report the elf brought us clearly states that he failed his mission. Are you afraid that we will all see what a pitiful warrior he is, making your guild look bad overall?"

You really do not hide anything, do you, Clover? It's not her fault—she is truthful in her paperwork. Ugh, I cannot hold a grudge against her, but, Damn, I think as the vision continues.

Alan's glare toward Leto could rival a basilisk.

Leto continues, "And anyhow, if I know right, you challenge a warrior from your guild, they will not back down. Pride gets in their way. If he ends up winning, your guild will get the recognition you want, the patrons you need, and be as worthy as Arcadia. Within reason, of course."

"Alan," Helena speaks softly, "I must agree with sending your warrior to battle, and the daemon knows him. It has a greater chance of attempting a vengeance possession, giving us the edge of information to fix this problem. If we challenge this creature, it may commit suicide and damage the information we need."

Alan puts his hand on his face and slowly massages his eyebrows. "Damn it, you are right. This is for information and the guild. Know I am against this, but I see reason."

"He will survive, Alan," Helena reassures him.

"If not, I will get the executioner's chair ready for a possessed man," Leto says mockingly.

Alan takes a deep breath. "After he wins, Leto, I expect a few private words with you. I see too many teeth in your mouth."

"Then it is decided. Ready your warrior. We will see him fight tonight in your arena," Ludwig says with finality.

The whole room, in unison, says, "Agreed."

As the vision fades away, reality comes back to me.

"My cub, are you okay?" Erol asks. "You have been silent for a few seconds since that puff of smoke came out!"

The only words that escape my mouth now are, "Oh shit, oh boy."

Lightning Strikes in the Oddest Places

"What, boy? There is none here. Yes, the arena is messy and the watchers will throw stuff to aid us in our victory soon, but no one has thrown a boy," Erol says, looking around, "except for your kin. He threw an item sooner than he had to, surprising both of us." He chuckles lightly. "No wonder he's single."

I roll my eyes and grab the wisp floating in front of me. "Here, genius, know what I know."

Erol grabs the wisp out of my hand and puts it on his forehead. A few seconds later, he takes a deep breath and hands me the wisp. "So, you are bait, a rabbit, and we have to kill this creature so you don't get killed. I will help you survive, cub. You do not have to worry," he says as he puts his hand on my shoulder.

"Fighters!" the announcer says with energy. "Are you ready?"

Both of us nod and draw our weapons out. The crowd cheers loudly for both of us. Around the arena, white light is forming, and the cheers seem to dampen out. I suddenly remember the barrier that was created to capture the daemon. I look around and see clergymen and my brother muttering something and glowing slightly brighter than the barrier.

"The protective barrier around the stands has been created! Now, lords, throw your handicaps in!" the wolfman announces.

"He keeps saying handicap." I look at Erol.

"Yes, I forget this is your first time in the arena. A handicap is like I said. Sometimes the crowd throws items at us to help us, or, like what happened last time to me, they threw a smoke bomb. Still killed the harpy in a few minutes," he answers in a slight yawn.

I walk around and inspect the items on the floor. I find a few broken arrows, tomatoes, broken syringes, and a needle and thread. Inside the bag Jura threw, I see ten vials that glow with white light.

Holy water.

The arena begins to rumble as we both notice a levitating crystal floating on the top, changing colors quickly. I run back to Erol, still looking at the crystal, and get ready for the fight. It lets out crackles of black lightning, and a monstrous roar echoes around the arena. In a blinding flash, it shatters with a loud explosion, shaking the ground. As I open my eyes, I see it, a creature forming from the smoke.

If I went to the Grande Library and looked up the definition of terrifying or horrifying, I would see a picture of this creature, not because of its appearance but of the aura it lets out, and I would also pick up a book on how to make better life choices. This creature stands around eight feet tall, with maroon fur covering his body except for his back. Down through his spine, his fur color is black as the night. His muscles rival even that of our guild leader, and as the creature stretches, I can see every muscle fiber move on his command.

Its claws can quickly rend flesh with a single sweep, and

its elbows have spikes sticking out that I can see tiny sparks of lightning escape every few seconds. Its head reminds me of a lion combined with a bat, and attached to its forehead, there is a white horn with strange markings. Its lower half is similar to a feral dog attempting to walk on its two legs for fun. It stomps the ground with its feet, moving the sand with its three toes as if it is marking its territory.

As it finishes stretching out its hands, it yawns, showing everyone in the room its enormous fangs. It lets out a bellow and says, "I am imprisoned no more."

Erol and I stand a few feet away, ready to attack, but neither of us moves an inch.

The creature opens its eyes, revealing it to be milky white. I feel that its gaze pierces like a knife. "Feeding me my first captor is a good way of getting on my good side," the creature says with a growl. "What a marvelous offering!"

"Erol, have you fought anything resembling the creature in front of us before?" I ask dryly.

"Not like this one, it's different. Feels stronger," he says as he grips his weapon harder.

I try not to show fear since I'm facing a powerful being in front of my bosses, who expect me to fail, and a crowd of bloodthirsty people who want to see a great fight.

"Paralyzed with fear so soon? I have not even started! Don't you worry, I will finish you soon, but as Father always taught me, play with your food first!" Quickly, it raises its hands and slams them fist-first to the ground, creating a fissure that explodes, knocking me back a few feet.

Erol wipes the dust off his shoulder and roars a command, charging toward the creature. I bounce back onto my feet and charge behind Erol, moving to flank. I still have the beast's attention, but I do not care because Erol is upon him.

He uses a rock to jump off and is in the air, ready to impale it square in the chest.

"You should have died when we first met, you sack of flesh!" The daemon roars as it opens its mouth, and a flash of light erupts from it.

The attack's sound is deafening, as if someone had taken a million metal shrapnel and decided to make them clang against each other. I throw myself out of the blast's way, but I feel a pulse hit my leg, and suddenly I start to convulse. My skin feels as if a surge is running up and down my body, not allowing me to move and inflicting a tremendous amount of pain. My body twitches without my permission, and a feeling of nausea sets in. As I fall on my side and attempt to regain my mobility, I hear the creature roar in pain. Struggling to move my head, I can make out that Erol's attack worked. He impaled the beast in the chest with his polearm and with a solid punch to the face made it fall on one knee.

The daemon quickly blocks a second blow Erol is trying to deliver. With a swat, it knocks Erol off itself and sends him flying a few feet away.

It stands up with a grunt as it removes the polearm from its chest and begins to walk toward me. "Your companion is troublesome, but my electricity should have stunned him just enough to see your demise." It licks its lips as it gets closer. "I want you. I want to be inside your deepest memories and distort them and slowly destroy everything you hold near and dear."

I regain control of my hands and quickly grab a syringe out of my pocket. I remove the cap that protects the needle and stab my thigh. In a few seconds, I regain control of my body and I can move.

"What is that? What did you use on yourself?"

It charges at me once it sees I'm mobile again. It rears its hand back and throws the polearm directly at me, but I saw that coming. I do a backflip, dodging, and with all my strength, I push off the ground with my hand, giving me enough mobility to grab a pair of throwing knives from my side pockets and throw them at the daemon with great accuracy. As my blades land on the beast, I can hear the crowd cheering, giving me a slight boost of morale as I land.

The daemon takes a knife to the stomach, and another embeds itself in his chest. Regretfully, I was aiming at its eyes, but it seems I do not have complete control of my movements just yet. As the beast flinches, I take the opportunity to grab a vial of holy water, courtesy of Jura, and soak my following two knives. I sprint to flank the beast, but I feel static pop all over me. I drop my knives as I get a strong shock.

"YOU WILL DIE!" the beast roars as the lightning comes pouring out of him.

"Oh shit, let's not do that!" I say to myself as I ditch my current plan and run toward Erol, who is twitching and trying to get up.

Lightning is hitting the barrier and striking at the oddest places. Quickly, I grab a new knife from my side pocket and throw it at a random location so the lightning has a target.

I slide next to Erol. My heart skips a beat when I see how injured he is from just a hit from the daemon. I try to grab him, but I shock myself by touching his armor. "Stupid question of the day, big guy, but are you okay?"

With a cough, he says, "Yes, just got blindsided. I shall make him pay for your pain and mine."

Another terrifying howl comes from behind us, and we turn to see the daemon morphing into a new being. A blinding light with an explosion right after knocks both of us back a few more feet. The arena rumbles, cracking the barriers my brother and other clerics had put up.

An echoed laughter resonates in the arena. "I who have no name ascended from a mere underling to a new powerful being. I am no one's dog anymore. I am my own master."

"My cub, you must get my polearm back. The wood will allow me to withstand the electricity!" Erol orders.

"We're out of luck. The damn daemon is naming itself. We must end this now somehow! Get your armor off if you can and stab yourself with this. You will gain full control back with this potion. The adrenaline that it packs will heal you and help!" I quickly hand him a syringe and run off to grab the polearm, which, to my luck, was on the other side of the arena next to the beast.

As I run toward the polearm, I dodge lightning strikes and jump over the broken floor and stone unearthed by the battle. I notice some of the handicapped items on the floor as I run. "There has to be something useful around here to use!" I growl to myself.

"My name is Valke, the son of the archdaemon Vet!" he roars.

I hear the announcer quickly yell out, "The son of Vet! One of the oldest beings in every religious scripture! The daemon has named itself! It has ascended, and it is aware of its power and existence. Warriors survive as the guild decides the next course of action!"

"Ruffus, move!" Jura yells loudly enough for me to hear.

"Die!" Valke yells.

I look above and see Valke about to land on me. I roll out of the way, giving me a few inches of movement before our named friend starts a frenzy of attacks on me. All I can do is dodge as quickly as I can and attempt to counter.

Valke punches the ground with a smile, transferring electricity to the area I was standing on, successfully stunning me, making me dizzy. With a loud bang and a hit from the back of the daemon's hand, I get sent flying to the edge of the arena. I slowly move my head to look at Valke as I begin to stand.

His transformation changed his fur from maroon to a gray hue, and he grew a new set of tails that move quickly, creating a static noise as he walks.

"How does it feel, Ruffus? How does it feel to feel death's grip on you?" he asks as a small chuckle escapes him. "I can feel your body shutting down. I can see your desperation trying to move you away, but you can't. Do not fret. I will release you from this mortal coil, and with your body, I will ascend once again." I can hear the crackling of electricity get louder, and his muscles tense up. With a war cry, he yells, "YOU BELONG TO ME!" and starts charging at me.

What fantastic speed. But this time, I am prepared. Once he is upon me, ready to finish me off, I quickly throw the vial of holy water I am holding inside his open mouth. Valke's eyes widen as he loses his footing, but he is going too fast to stop abruptly.

I am not quick enough to move, and Valke tackles me to the wall of the arena. I feel a snap inside of me, and a sharp pain shoots up my chest, making it hard to breathe. I fall on my butt, leaning against the wall, smiling as I see Valke squirm in pain, yelling curses in an odd language that I do not care for.

I can taste blood in my mouth, and the room begins to get dark. Damn it all. I can't breathe well. A potion will numb my pain, but I can't overdose. Okay, I got this, I think to myself. I cough blood as I say to Valke, "What's wrong? Bite your tongue?"

The vial went right inside his mouth, and the glass broke. He gets down on one knee and coughs up a silver-like substance that is his blood and glass onto the floor. With a heave, he says, "It stings, it burns. What was it?"

By this time, Erol has already grabbed his weapon. With a mighty roar, he charges with full force again. His polearm is already cocked back and ready with a swing. The daemon looks at him, and I'm pretty sure I hear him mutter, "Shit."

With all his might, Erol swings his weapon, hitting the daemon square in the face. Even though I'm sitting on the ground, I feel the pressure of the impact. Valke is sent flying back across the arena, making the crowd roar in excitement.

I cannot move. My body is numb, and a slight cough escapes my lips. I'm lucky the potion I gave Erol worked so well on him. He is standing tall and looks uninjured with a cocky smile on his face. Unlucky for me, a syringe will not cure a broken rib, but it will let me power through the pain until this fight is over.

Erol looks back to Valke. "Hurry, my cub! The creature is down. We can finish this!" He looks at me and puts on a worried face. "Oh no. Here, cub, take this poker and move with me!" Erol grabs one of his potions, runs to my side, and stabs me square in my chest, making me yelp and gasp for breath.

Instantly I feel a tremendous amount of energy rush through me, and my pain becomes tolerable. I wipe the blood off my mouth as Erol pats me on the shoulder.

I glare at Valke, who is regaining his ground, and say to Erol, "Keep knocking him down. I'll make sure he can't move." We both sprint to him with all the speed we can muster.

The daemon stands up, but Erol says in his native language, "Tacch' en!" which means, "Too late!"

Erol lets out a flurry of combos, making the daemon counter and dodge him as I sneak from behind, and with a swift cut, I sever his tendon, making Valke cry in pain. The beast's tail shocks me mildly and makes me jump back as Erol tries to deliver a decisive blow. Valke catches the polearm with both his hands, surprising us, and if a glare could kill, Valke would have murdered Erol right then and there. I hear sparks come out of the polearm, and the top of the wooden handle starts sparking flames.

"You annoy me, beastman. Now see the underworld!" Valke opens his mouth, and a bright beam of light shoots out of it, shocking Erol worse than when he attacked me. Erol roars in pain as he flies back a few feet, landing hard on the ground, twitching uncontrollably.

The crowd gasps in disbelief.

I snap to action quickly and open a vial, dowsing my knives in holy water. I jump on Valke's back and stab him once in his back, and I impale his eye with the other blade. I use the knife in his eye to move his head and beam away from Erol.

Valke starts to flail in pain and releases the grip on Erol's polearm. I see both his hands try to grab me, but I jump off his head and throw one more knife at him. As I land and roll next to Erol, I thank the Three that I do not feel pain because I'm sure all my movements would make me give up and let myself be killed by Valke.

"Erol, get up!" I say as I shake Erol. I quickly check his pulse and sigh in relief, knowing he is still alive but unconscious.

From behind us, I hear a loud bellow saying, "Enough!" Lightning flies out of him, pushing us back.

"You have lived long enough!" he shouts. He starts to chant in an odd language, and I began to feel fear like never before.

He starts glowing brighter, electricity is jumping all over his body, and little pieces of debris begin to float around the arena. I grab one of the few throwing knives I have left, and I receive a static shock. I quickly turn to see little crackles of electricity flying out of Erol's fur and armor.

"Ruffus, no spells, no vials of magic water, nothing can save you now," he says as he walks toward me. "Can't you smell it? Your companion's life is weak. I can taste his spirit on my lips," he taunts.

Valke disappears and appears next to me and whispers, "Let's play, puppet."

He backhands me, knocking me a few feet away. I land hard and struggle to get up since the potion's numbing agent is starting to wear off. I look in his direction and see him grabbing Erol by the chest plate.

"Get away from him, Valke. It's me you want!" I yell with rage.

He looks at me and drops him. "You are brave, little human, but correct. I don't need this waste of meat."

I notice next to me a long needle and an odd-looking roll of thread. I shuffle and grab both items and feel the thread is coarse. It feels more like wire than wool. I quickly look up at the stands and see my brother being held back by a few soldiers, but they promptly meet the end of his fist. Our eyes connect, and he touches the wall of light and begins to chant.

"My savior," I murmur to myself as I make sure the needle and thread are tied strongly to one of my last knives. I stand, hiding my weapon from Valke, who is cracking his knuckles as he nonchalantly walks to me.

"Can you give me a second, Valke? I'm thirsty," I say as I pull out a vial of holy water and take a drink. As I put the vial down, I can't see him anymore.

"Have you had enough respite?" Valke whispers to me from behind. I turn quickly and, in surprise, spit my water all over his chest as he kneels in front of me.

With a mocking smile, he says, "Your holy water has no more effect on me. It seems you have lost all faith. Do not fret.

I now will end it," he says as he grabs my shirt, raising me a few feet in the air.

"Actually, I was thirsty, and think of the water as a target I just painted on you." I smile at him.

Valke gives me an annoyed look and then raises his other hand, ready to impale me. Before he can strike, a volley of what looks like bright arrows stab him in the back. He drops me and turns to shield himself from the rest of the volley.

I pull out my sword from my sheath, and with force, I vertically slash him. He lets out a loud, painful howl and hunches his back. I use my momentum and slash upward, allowing me to jump higher. Once I am in the air, I slash his neck, but Valke moves his hand quickly to cover from my attack. I cut a deep gash on the back of his hand, puncturing the long needle in his wound, and land back on the ground.

With a roar, he screams, "DIE," and I can see the hand start to glow. The thread is attached to my knife, which I chose to throw away from all of us and is lying on the ground. I see the thread light up as the electricity runs through it toward the wayward knife, which explodes a few seconds before it reaches it.

Right then, I can see the daemon heaving heavily, and I know the battle is almost at its end, either for him or me, thanks to my brother.

I See Myself

*T*ime to be positive and think of nice things. Dogs, beaches, rivers, and dodging this bolt of lightning being hurled at me! I roll to the side. *It could be worse. I mean, I could be trapped, fighting against a daemon—oh, wait. I need more positive thoughts.* I duck behind debris created by the battle. *If I make it through this fight, I will definitely be ranked up.* I jump and dodge an incoming slash to then somersault, grab a rock on the floor, and hurl it toward the daemon's face. *What else is good? Ah, yes, Jura will treat me to dinner, and I'll get to buy Erol a few drinks.*

The rock hits Valke's face, causing him to get even more enraged. "A rock? I'll return the favor!" he says as he grabs a gargantuan boulder and throws it toward me.

Cub, cub, cub. Erol will repeat that same word like a mimic bird. Then he will sniff me all over. Oh, I need to dodge this rock. I slide under the boulder, missing my head by a few inches. *Okay, it missed Erol. All is well. I should fight away from him. I don't want him killed. What's that noise?* I look toward Valke, who has his mouth open and is producing a blinding light. *Oh, he's charging his beam, crap.*

"I WILL EAT YOUR CHARRED FLESH!" he barks at me as he shoots an ear-shattering beam.

Oh, right, I need to survive first. Okay, I actually have to think and stop having an internal monologue. I look at the beam and whisper to myself, "Oh shit."

I throw a knife that I picked up off the ground through his beam of electricity, diverting the shot to hit near Valke, and with a grand explosion, it knocks him off his feet.

After the dust settles, Valke walks toward me, bleeding in different places and cracking his neck in annoyance. "You have bored me long enough."

I cough weakly as I swipe away the dust in the air and say, "You sure talk a lot, Valke. How about we—"

Valke's voice comes from behind me. "Your consciousness is mine, meat bag."

I feel my head being squeezed by Valke's claw-like hand as he picks me up a few feet off the ground. I try shaking off his grip, but I am stuck tight.

"I can sense your fear and thoughts right now. You're weak enough now for me to possess. Thank you, now I can kill both our brothers," he says, seeming content.

In an instant, I feel the heat of his breath, and an immense surge of electricity runs through my body. For a brief moment, everything in the world stands still—no noise, just the sound of my heartbeat. Then I begin to feel as if it is engulfed in flames. I cry for help, but I have no voice, and suddenly, I am standing alone.

All I see is my surroundings turn to white marble, the floor, the people, the ceiling. His thoughts go into my head as if a spider is burrowing through my ear. I feel him reading all my thoughts, trying to peer into my deepest secrets, trying to push me out. I try to move, but like a fly I am caught in a spider web made of needles piercing through my skin.

I want to give up, and I fall to my knees. Nothing in this world is worth the pain. I should just submit and give up. I look to the floor as my vision darkens.

Suddenly, I hear a familiar voice echoing directed toward me. I look up, and all I see is myself, as if I am looking into a mirror. He has my sword drawn and a look of determination in his eyes. Behind me is another person looking directly at me, but I cannot recognize who it is. As quickly as I notice the silhouette, it evaporates in a puff of smoke. I turn to face myself, or what I think is a copy of myself, rushing toward me.

My body starts to move on its own, and I see that I have the daemon's claws, and I feel them charging up with energy. I try to control the hands, but it is futile as my claws aim and shoot a bolt of red energy. My doppelgänger dodges gracefully, getting closer with each passing second. My other claw closes and makes a fist, aiming to impale him straight through the belly. "Don't come near me. I can't control my body!" I try to yell toward him, but the only sound that comes from my mouth is an angry roar.

The doppelgänger jumps, elegantly swinging my sword, ready to impale me with Coal. I don't know what to do. I don't want to attack him, but I don't want to die. There is a primal urge inside me that needs to be the only one alive. I charge up one last time to end him, but a calm, peaceful voice asks me to stop. Such a sweet, familiar tone of love—I forgot how it felt. The voice asks me to let go while a dim light lowers my arm, allowing me to put my claw down, letting the doppelgänger stab Coal deep into my chest. Oddly enough, I feel no pain. I fall back while the doppelgänger falls on top of me as we bounce slightly to the ground.

The floor is cold yet comforting, but I do feel the warmth of my blood as it pools around me. The doppelgänger looks at me with a sympathetic smile as he gets closer to me and whispers something that I cannot quite understand. I move my hand to caress his face, and as I bring my arm up, I see I don't have the daemon's claws anymore. As I touch him, I experience an odd sense of protection, a familiarity. He then grabs my hand and closes his eyes as he gets near me, kissing me on the forehead. Tears run down the side of my face, and as he opens his eyes, the room starts to shine brightly. We lock eyes one last time only for the world to explode into a million colors, and I slowly lose vision.

"Release him," I hear a familiar voice echo as I feel like I'm freefalling back into my mind.

I slowly open my eyes, and my senses start coming back to me.

Everything around me looks blurry and in sluggish motion. As I turn my head, I clearly see Valke flying slowly back away from me, as if I pushed him away. I get up off my knees and look around. I do not feel any pain as I touch my side with the broken ribs, and I know I should at least feel a sting. I look up to the stands and see my brother jumping into the arena, still falling midair with his sword drawn. I start to focus better and notice a few Arcadian soldiers moving like snails into the arena with their weapons drawn. I quickly turn to Erol, and there he is, also moving slowly as he runs toward me.

I turn back to face Valke and hear a low whisper telling me, "Go forth," accompanied by other words I cannot understand. I decide this is my one chance. I run back to the daemon and raise my sword, ready to attack. I notice Coal is glowing in a black aura as I get near Valke. I have never seen this happen. *Should this worry me?*

I shake the thought and dodge a bolt of energy Valke throws at me. I jump, ready to stab the daemon and finally end this. As I jump, I see that Valke will impale me with his claw, but it seems like something is holding him back. A strong sense of déjà vu rushes through me as I stab Valke and fall on top of his chest.

A pulse of force erupts out of the sword, pushing me away, but I hold on to the blade like an anchor on a rock. I look directly into the daemon's eyes, and he is looking back into mine.

As our eyes lock, I can hear random whispers around us praising me, praising Valke, and warning both of us of something in an odd language that somehow, I understand. I notice that Valke's eyes widen, and for a fraction of a second, he has the same color iris as me. My heart sinks as a rush of feelings comes over me. I can feel his pain, his misery, and his woe.

I feel that his life was forced to become what it is, and I feel pity for him. I caress his face and whisper, "I'm here. You are released. Be at peace."

The creature touches my neck, and I kiss his forehead, and I notice that he begins to shed a tear. I grab his hand, and I feel baffled, for I never knew daemons could cry. A strong pull from my sword takes my attention away from Valke. I look at the hilt of the blade and see it glow faintly, and from the wounds of the daemon, I can see bits of light coming out and melding with my sword. I turn to him as a light from his eyes leaves through a tear and floats up toward the ceiling.

With one last long sigh, Valke lies dead.

I notice a muffling noise in the background starting to clear up and getting louder and louder. I turn to see Jura and Erol sprinting toward me as the crowd goes wild with cheers and excitement, and a few of them even throw coins.

I roll off the body, falling onto my back next to Valke, reminding me of my injuries as my whole body starts to ache. As I look up, I see the small glimmer of light that escaped Valke's eye dissipate into the air.

"Huh, I guess luck is on my side," I murmur as the room starts to grow dark and the noise begins to muffle itself again.

Aftermath

The darkness around me feels heavy. I think I'm dead. It's dark, really dark, my eyes are open, and I can't see a thing. Hmm, should I panic? Well, dead people don't panic. Something smells like good soup though. I'm sure I can hear something shuffling around me. Oh gods, am I possessed? Okay, okay, relax. Just try moving your arms—they feel like boulders are sitting on them. By the Three, please, please let me not be dead or, worse, in a coffin, alive. Okay, I can't move my arms. Let's use my legs. Oh gods, I can't move them either. At least I can wiggle my toes. Ah! Something grabbed my big toe! Oh, something is touching the side of my face. Maybe I can talk, I think, and quickly attempt to speak. "Mhemhmllow?"

I can hear a louder, muffled voice, and now I know someone is talking to me. I feel like something is helping me sit up. Was I lying down? Slowly I feel something relieving the pressure on my face and gradually see the light coming to my eyes.

Oh gods, it's bright. Wait, my eyes can see the light! Am I at the end of the tunnel? As my vision starts to focus, I see someone very close to my face, looking at me and moving around. I gently shake my head. I see a beautiful blonde woman wearing a pair of black-tinted glasses, but I could see the bright eyes through the tint. I move my head back and notice pointy ears. She moves her face away from mine. She has a silver tiara with four colored gemstones that change every few seconds.

I notice she is staring through me instead of looking at me. Then our eyes lock, and her shiny colored eyes are staring at me as if she is looking into my mind. She points her index finger at me, causing me to flinch back, and it starts to glow a golden light. She proceeds to gently tap my forehead, somehow fixing my sight, allowing me to see normally without focusing or straining. "Well, welcome back to us, Ruffus," she says in a calm voice.

I try to move my arms and see that both are bandaged up, along with my legs and the rest of my body.

I let out a weak cough. "Where am I?"

"Ah, I see you can speak again. You are in the Grande Cathedral nursing station, child." She replies as her other hand starts to glow in a golden light, rubbing my arms gently.

I feel the life coming back into me, and I now can wiggle my fingers and move my arm freely. "What happened to me?" I ask as I stretch my fingers.

A deep voice growls behind me, "You were severely injured in your battle against the daemon. You have been unconscious for three days. Meister Helena has been personally nursing you back to health."

I turn my head slightly to see a black lion beastman staring at me like a hawk, examining me from head to bandaged toe. He has a fresh-looking scar on his nose and forehead. By the looks of it, the scar was made by a knife or sword of some kind. "Commander Leto is right. Thanks to your endeavors, we were able to extract information from the body of the daemon, and we have learned a fair amount," she says as she checks my other arm.

I look down.

"Do not fret. You saved the daemon. You were able to release its tormented spirit. The vessel left behind received a proper burial, according to the law of this land—well, once we got what we needed," she says as she rubs my chest gently, making me sigh in relief.

"If it died during my battle, how were you able to extract information from it?" I ask as I practice making fists with both my hands.

With a devious smile, she stops rubbing my chest and grabs a vase of water, serving me a drink. "A story for when I know you won't feel sick to your stomach with the details," she says as she walks out of the room, followed by two other elven people who blended with the wall.

I scoff as I look and move my shoulders. "That answered nothing."

A familiar voice speaks. "You don't want to know!"

My guild leader walks in with a fresh batch of scars on his arms and a limping right leg. "Meister Helena does not have to explain how she did it. But let's say she has a weird way with the brain and be glad she did not do it to you—ugh, all that gray matter." He sits down on the bed beside me. "Excellent job, Ruff. You have made me and this guild proud. Expect a rank-up. Not many people can say they defeated a minion, which ascended during the battle, I might add!" He then proceeds to shift a glare at the lion beastman. "Leto, I thought I smelled shame and blood. How's the nose?"

I feel a glare and a sense of death coming from Leto as he says, "As good as your leg, Alan. I will take my leave now." As he walks out, he says, "Ruffus, you are no Arcadian, but you did defeat a daemon. You have my praise." He proceeds to walk out of the room.

Alan starts to laugh. "Well done, boy, you made Leto the Mighty proud!"

I look around the room. "Where is Erol?"

"Ah, yes, your companion. Know that he is safe and fully

healed from his wounds. The last time I saw him, he was talking about food and something about a cub. Alas, he has been beside you every day since the battle, trying to feed you. He really must like you! You know how beastmen are, loyal to the end—well, if they like you, that is." Alan stretches and gets off the bed. "Your brother should be up here soon. He took your equipment, and we are using our resources to repair what was damaged. Think of it as a present from all of us to you, for almost getting you killed. Oh, that reminds me—give thanks to your kin."

I look at him with a puzzled look.

"The exorcist broke the rules of the arena to save you. But do not worry—he will not be punished for interfering in your battle. It is almost impossible for two people to defeat a daemon of that category." Alan massages his thigh, which had a bandage and a bit of blood on it. "Actually, Meister Helena ordered the fight to be terminated twice, but the damn cardinal interfered. Also, her advisors have never seen a metamorphosis like that happen ever on a battlefield, so the mages wanted to see what would happen next."

"I am glad to have helped their morbid research. What happens now?" I ask.

Alan looks out to the window in my room. "What happens now is that I leave you alone to rest. I'm sure Meister Helena will be back soon to care for you for a while longer before she retires back to her studies at the university." Alan turns and gives me a gentle look, which I would have never guessed he could do since he looks either too excited or pissed off. "Rest, kid. I will have a mission for you soon."

I nod and thank him for visiting me. Alan leaves the room, and all I can hear is silence as I lay my head on my pillow. I did not notice how tired I was, and with a long sigh, I close my eyes and drift off to sleep once again, hoping I do not wake up fully bandaged again.

The Figure

I dream about my battle, and my mind keeps replaying the possession. I can see Valke in front of me, glaring and smiling with pure gusto. Beside him, I see another creature. It looks exactly like Valke, but there is a different air to him. They are both looking at me and walking toward me. I try to turn to run away, but my feet are glued to the ground. I then feel a hand on my shoulder, and I turn to see a familiar face, but I cannot recognize it. As I try to talk, I see both creatures grab me and drag me to the darkness.

I wake up gasping to a different dimly lit room. I must've gotten moved as I slept, and most of my bandages have been removed. I slowly sit up and glance out and see I have a bigger window, and a beautiful crescent moon shines directly inside, providing more light. I can hear the wind lightly rattle the window and the leaves of the tall trees rustling outside. I yawn, looking around the room, and see a new set of clothes folded neatly on top of a chair next to the bed. On the floor, I see shining new boots and boxes wrapped in fine linen, and they all have an *R* stamped on the top.

I check my nightstand for a jug of water but see a vase of flowers blooming and a card standing against it. The cover is elegant, and drawn on the envelope is a clover. I pick up the card and open it gently using the light of the moon to read the contents.

Ruffus of Bern,

Thank the goddess that you survived the encounter with the daemon. Just so you are aware, I bet on you winning the fight, and the odds were 1:1000. Thanks to you, I made a small fortune and purchased a new apartment in the nicer part of town with my winnings! Also, know that you and Erol are now part of the Hall of Fame in the Warriors Guild, and your name has been written down in the Grande Library's Achievements book as "Luckiest Fight of the Era."

Truth be told, I was worried about your safety and prayed for you during the fight, as short as it was. After you collapsed, Meister Helena ordered you to be taken to the city's best medical facility. I know you will be well. One of the most powerful sorcerers in the city is with you. Whenever you wake up, please send me a message, and I will visit you.

Clover

I smile and put the card away where I found it. At the side of the bed, I see Erol sitting in a chair, using his hands as pillows at the foot of my bed. Next to him, I can see a children's storybook opened under his face, catching his drool. I'm guessing he was reading me a story or attempting to. I move and touch the side of his face and wipe his cheek. Poor guy does not know how to read well in Common, but he tries.

I grab the book and see what story he was on: "The Prince of the Oasis." I look at Erol and wonder why he was reading a story of an exiled prince who saved his kingdom by finding an oasis lost in the desert. I try to read what part Erol left off, but the moon got covered by clouds, and the dim light faded away.

I mark the book and gently close it as I put it on my nightstand next to my card and vase. I close my eyes and hear a slight noise from the door that bothered me enough to open my eyes again. I glance at the room entrance to see a silhouette of a man sleeping on what looks like a rocking chair, with his feet propped up on a small wooden stool. As the light of the moon enters the room, I see Jura wearing his exorcist gear, and Quartz is out of its sheath, glowing faintly.

I have never seen it glow like that before, but Jura gets his weapon enchanted and re-enchanted all the time, and without thinking about it, I conclude that it must be an after-effect of all the magic the sword has gotten. I lie back down, and my head hits the pillow again. As I look at the ceiling, I see a small glowing piece of parchment. I focus my eyes and make out a few etched symbols that I don't recognize now, and as I try to focus more on them, my head starts to pulse in discomfort.

I give up looking at the ceiling and turn to look at my vase of flowers again, just to notice another dim glowing piece of paper on it. I get back up, grab the vase, and examine it.

"Is this a ward?" I murmur to myself. I quickly look all around the room and see the same piece of paper stuck to the walls, door, window, and bed frame and see they're scattered around the room.

I remember my father teaching me about these wards. They're meant to keep chaotic and inherently evil spirits away or suppress chaotic magic and black magic. The symbols etched on them are from an old school of magic that the holy used to combat daemons once upon a time. Also, these wards are used to power up healing alongside order and law magic. Oddly, different schools of magic are created to counter each other and come from two separate roots. In daemon, magic is made to destroy, while holy is made to restore. It is also seen that holy was created to control, while daemonic magic was created to free the controlled. The only neutral type of magic that exists is elemental since fire can both create and destroy, water can drown or revive, and earthen can sustain life and bury it. In this case, these wards create a controlled healing environment, or so I hope.

Calm down. You're okay, Ruff. These must be used to enhance healing magic. There is no daemon after you anymore. You killed him.

A flicker of light suddenly illuminates the room. Surprised by it, I remain still and see where it's coming from. I muster all my strength and get up off the bed. I slightly groan, as my body is still weak, but I manage to stroll on the cold, damp floor to the window. I quickly look at myself to see the dry blood on the bandages and notice I am wearing a robe that reminds me of a sleeping gown.

As I look out the window, I see that I am on one of the cathedral's tallest towers and can view the whole city from here. Again, a bright light flickers, and I pinpoint it to a rooftop of a mansion near the city walls. A small figure is dancing and jumping, throwing what looks like a bolt of white energy toward the cathedral, dimming itself before it even reaches the building. Every time it jumps to a new roof, it throws a little bolt of light toward the cathedral as if it were taunting.

I am too far away to determine what it is. It reminds me of a thin-looking scarecrow. But as quickly as it came, it dashed away toward the gates and disappeared into the river. I rub my head and wonder if I'm hallucinating.

The room's silence breaks when I hear a whisper come from behind me. I slowly turn and see Jura and Erol still asleep. Curiosity moves me as I shake my head and follow the whisper. It sounds like an adult hissing toward me, speaking in an odd language that I cannot understand, but it reminds me of the language Valke spoke when casting a spell. I make it to the location where the whisper gets louder and notice it's my sword. I can see Coal is also glowing faintly in a violet light. My gaze goes directly to Quartz, and I see it glowing brighter.

I then turn to look at Coal. I slowly extend my hand, reaching for the hilt. Before my fingertips make contact, I steel myself for an explosion or a horrible event to unfold. A tiny spark comes out, lightly shocking me. As I grasp the hilt of Coal, I feel nothing—no new energy, no new feelings, nothing. I stand and move the sword around, expecting something else to happen, but nothing does. The whispers that call my attention become silent, and I can only hear my heart beating. "Very curious," I say in a low voice.

"Ruffus?" Jura's voice breaks the silence.

In a scare, I jump and turn to Jura. He is holding Quartz in his hand, and the sword is not glowing either.

I can hear a small amount of fear in his voice. "Ruff, is . . . that you?"

"Yes, Jura, it's me. Who else would I be?" I whisper quickly as I put Coal back in his sheath and rest him against the wall. Jura sighs in relief and puts Quartz back in his sheath, walking to me. In a quick move, he hugs me, and I can feel him trembling.

"I thought I lost you too," he speaks in a sad tone. "I'm sorry I could not help you sooner." He wipes his face with his arm. "After the daemon put his hand on your head, I jumped to the arena to kill him." He looks at me and wipes a tear off his face. "After you blacked out, some knights were taking you away by the cardinal's order, but the meister stopped them and ordered for you to be taken to the hospital. That asshole wanted to burn you with holy fire to make sure you weren't possessed."

I wipe another tear away from his face and say, "Well, I'm

me. No second creature here." I tap on my head, giving myself a slight headache.

He smiles and laughs as he sees my pained demeanor. "Yes, this is you. Only an idiot would tap on his head when he has a concussion. Now, here, let's get you back to bed."

I scoff. "Well, what if I'm a big, bad monster?"

"Well, in that case, Meister Helena would have seen the creature inside you, and you would have been stripped naked and burned by boiling holy water, and then you would have gotten some brand-new tattoos on your skin," Jura said evilly.

"By the Three, I'm joking. I'm me, don't burn me at the stake," I say. "Jura, pull out your sword for me," I ask as he helps me get in the bed.

"Odd request. Why?" he says as he puts the blankets on me.

"Your sword was glowing just a few moments ago, before you woke up. Am I hallucinating?"

Jura does not respond and freezes in place.

"There was something bad near us, wasn't there?"

"It detects spirits and glows quite a lot in this area. Wisps make it glow, and remember, there are spirits in the catacombs of the cathedral," Jura says calmly as he fluffs my pillow.

"So, how did I do?"

"What, in the arena fight? Well, you fought a daemon that named himself and ascended to a stronger being. You lived, so I say you did somewhat well. I sent Mother and Father a letter telling them of this achievement. They are both proud, and Mother has a gift for you when we visit home this winter," Jura whispers.

I rub my head and grunt quietly, "This damn headache hasn't left me."

Jura takes off one of his gloves and places his hand on my forehead. "You still have a small fever, it seems. You might be dehydrated. I will fetch a pitcher of water. I will be right back," he says as he starts to walk out. "Oh, and, Ruff, do not attempt to leave this room. There are wards placed everywhere, and they will alarm everyone on this floor if you leave."

Annoyed, I say back, "So I am trapped in here?"

"Technically, yes. Remember, you were almost possessed. The monks here are making sure your spirit is fully restored and healed. Even though the meister checked on you, Cardinal Ludwig does not trust your well-being."

I nod.

"I will be back."

Jura walks out of the room, and I lay my head on the pillow. I close my eyes to lower my headache and feel something grab my hand.

"I am sorry, cub, I could not protect you," Erol whispers.

I look toward where Erol is, and I can see his eyes have changed from his usual red hue to aquamarine blue in the dark. Because of this, he can see in the dark better than most people.

I grab his hand back. "You are fine, and I'm alive. You are alive and well. Now our names are in the Hall of Fame. I'm sure you will get all the maidens and the gold you deserve now."

I can see him give me a weak smile. "I do not need them, and I will take you to a feast, you and me. But for now, know I am here guarding you. I shall make you dinner tomorrow and tell you more of the prince who has been written about in the book I got."

"What part did you stop reading at, Erol?" I ask as I grab the book from the nightstand.

"He was lost in the desert after he fought with a thief who stole his dagger," Erol says proudly.

I smile and return the book to him. "You have read a lot to me, thank you."

Erol's grip on my hand gets stronger, and I feel him shake a bit.

"Here, take one of my pillows."

He nods, grabs the smallest pillow, and lays it on the bed as Jura walks back into the room.

"Here, Ruff, take this glass of water and drink this small vial. It will cure your headache and help you fall asleep," Jura whispers to me as he glances over Erol.

Erol looks at Jura with jealous eyes and glances back at me, murmuring something in his native tongue.

I grab the concoction with my free hand and take a big gulp of water and medicine, letting out a slight cough.

"Thank you, Jura," I say as I feel the immediate effects of the medicine.

"Sleep, Ruff. I will be back. I have to write a brief report. But I will be right outside this door. If you need anything, just say my name," Jura says to me as he tucks me into the bed and shoots a glance at Erol.

"Okay, Jura, and don't worry about me. I've got Erol here keeping an eye out for me," I say as the room starts to spin.

Jura scoffs, and I can hear him say under his breath as he walks toward the door, "Damn beast can't even keep you safe." I turn to look at Erol, who is looking down with his eyes filled with shame. I put my bandaged hand on his cheek and tell him, "You saved my ass. Thank you."

Erol takes a long sigh and grabs my hand, saying, "Sleep, my cub. I will watch over you and make sure you are safe from now on."

The sweet-tasting potion is making me drowsy, and I hallucinate lights in the room. Erol lays my head down on my pillow and opens the book again. He starts to read slowly, and I cannot help but close my eyes and drift off into a deep slumber.

A Normal Day

A few more days pass, and morning comes with the cool wind of autumn. All I can smell is the horrid stench of burnt food. As I get out of bed, I see Erol next to the makeshift hearth he made, attempting to cook, and Jura smacking him over the head with a rolled-up piece of parchment.

"What in God's name are you doing, you alley cat!" he yells.

"Stand aside, subordinate. I am cooking for Ruffus," Erol says firmly.

"No you are not, flea for brains! You are putting oil on bread and setting it on fire! And how on this earth did you start a fire?" Jura asks as he continues to hit him with the rolled-up parchment.

"Fire cooks food. For an Arcadian, you would not survive a day in the Wilds," Erol huffs.

"You cook meat on an open flame, not bread! Look, there is a small oven right over there!"

I get out of bed and walk toward the window, ignoring the smell of smoke and burning wood. My body has a few aches and bruises, but I feel immensely better. I am free today.

As I look outside, I see that it is another beautiful day in the city. I sigh and tap on the window.

"Ruff! Good morning." Jura walks up to me. "How are you feeling today?"

"Won't lie, I'm in a bit of pain," I say in a monotone voice, still looking out the window.

Jura smiles and says, "Count your blessings. You have healed quickly. Anyone else would still be bandaged up, drinking out of a hollow tube." Jura searches in his pocket, pulls out a small bag, and shows it to me. "This here is a special powder that I found in the infirmary made with alchemy stuff. They call it healing powder. The man who sold it to me told me the ingredients, but I threw money at him. He said it will soothe you and relax your muscles." Jura opens the bag. "Smells of jasmine! Now I'll draw you a bath and mix this in there so you can feel as good as new."

Erol laughs loudly and says, "You truly are inferior. My cub is fine. All his bruises will flee his body when he eats more of my food!"

Erol turns around, and I see blood on his furry chest. In his hand, I see what I think is a heart and a liver, and a cleaver in the other.

"You vicious cat! He needs real food, not some organs! Ruffus, what has he been feeding you these past days?" Jura barks at both of us.

"See what I mean? I disbelieve he is your kin. You are smart and willing. He is dumb and closed-minded. He knows nothing of nature and the world. I blame brainwashed books! And organs are real food from real beasts that I killed myself!" Erol says proudly.

"I am open-minded, you uncultured swine!"

"I am no pig. I'm a warrior!" Erol hisses back.

As they keep bickering, I snatch the bag from Jura's hand and shuffle my way to a nightstand to grab a piece of bread Clover had sent up for me. As I walk into the washroom, I take off my robe and look at my body in the mirror.

I can still hear them outside, bickering like an old couple

over how a heart can make me more robust, and chicken soup is food for toddlers.

I fill up the tub and gently remove some of my bandages. I look at the washroom and think, If I had money, I would build something like this. I also need a home. Ugh, I hate living in the guild barracks.

As the tub gets full, I put the powder in and see it sizzle and bubble up. I dip a finger.

Well, it's not acid. Time to jump in! As I get in and sink myself in the water, I let out a sigh of pure ecstasy. "By the Three, this must be what Elysium feels like!"

The bickering gets louder and turns more violent. For a second, everything becomes silent, and I start to worry, but as expected, I hear my brother yell, and the sound of a chair or a table crashing comes a few seconds afterward.

The door to the washroom slams open to reveal Erol with a bloody nose and a cut to the face, carrying a plate of cooked meats. "Cub! I have made you more food of my people. Here, the heart of a stone dragon for healing your bones!"

I sit up and use the remaining bubbles to cover myself as I sigh. I do not feel like fighting with him, so I take the plate. "Thank you, Erol, but I am in the middle of a bath."

"Yes, my cub, I can see that, but no time. You must eat my food so we can go drinking before we leave on our mission!" he says happily.

"Can I have some privacy, Erol?" I ask in annoyance.

He seems confused. "Ah, I understand, my cub is shy! I forgot. If you want, I could unclothe so we are the same and you won't be embarrassed!" he says as he starts unbuttoning his trousers.

"Wait, no! Erol!" I get out of the tub. "Damn you, cat, you will pay for—" Jura storms into the room and sees Erol naked with me, trying to grab his clothes from the floor.

Erol glares and stands proudly at Jura. "You want second round?"

In turn, Jura closes his eyes as he turns around and leaves the washroom, shuddering.

"He fears the sight of me, as he should," Erol says happily as he looks at me.

"Yeah, sure, he fears you," I say as I throw his pants to his face. I finish drying off and putting a clean pair of socks and undergarments on. I explain to Erol why getting naked in a non-public washroom is wrong, and I kick him out as I put new bandages on.

As I walk out, I see Erol dressed and munching happily on something that I'm pretty sure was a face once. On the other side of the room, I see Jura with a bandage over his head, inspecting my new gear.

I walk up to him, and he turns to greet me with a confident face. "Ah, Ruff, good to see you somewhat dressed and not near that cat," he says, glaring at Erol and rubbing his forehead. "Oh! Before I forget, this is your brand-new gear!" He hands me a new set of clothes and armor.

My long old leather jacket was torn in the fight, so Jura gives me a new one. It is the same style as my last one, but the material is soft to the touch and surprisingly lightweight. The inside is black, with streaks of red fur running up through the spine of the coat. It also has multiple hidden pockets to hide all my throwing knives and any other goodies I might want to carry without adding an odd shape. The exterior color is gray with silver trimmings, and on the backside, there is a white streak of fur running down the spine.

"This is soft. What type of leather is this?" I ask while I turn the coat inside out to notice it can be used either way.

"Blessed daemon leather. It will keep you warm in the winter and cool in the summer. As a bonus, it will also insulate you from electricity and shield you from fire. As you have noticed, it can be worn on whichever side you desire—black as night for blending in or white as snow for winter coverage. Perfect for a guild scout or the queen's spy!" he says as he fixes the collar.

"Heh, I do not think I will ever be part of the royal guard. Is this from Valke?" I scoff as I check the seams and the pockets of the jacket.

"Yes, daemon and holy hide are extremely rare, and the artisan guild managed to make a lot of great gear for you. The knitting guild also helped," he says as he helps put the coat on me.

I smile with joy. "This is a great fit, and it will be perfect to wear armor underneath! Oh, and what about the remains of the daemon?"

"Meister Helena made sure the law was followed and gave the bones a proper burial," Jura reminds me as he hands me the rest of my gear.

"Yet I will be wearing him, kind of insulting, good."

Jura shows me my new pair of boots made of the same leather but in a dark brown hue and gilded with silver. They are comfortable to wear and fit snugly on my feet. He then hands me a pair of gloves that feel like a second skin. Solid and durable, they are the same as my jacket and can change between colors. After I inspect the gloves, Jura hands me a new gray linen tunic that smells of jasmine. He also gives me lightweight chainmail armor. It's embedded with leather and cloth, which creates a comfortable, lightweight hoodie I can wear under my tunic. Finally, I get a new set of pants, nicely woven and stretchy, made with the same leather and linen as the rest of my armor.

"Your new armor can withstand cuts because of the hide. Be

careful, though—a sharp, blessed blade can still cut through, but that's why we wear chainmail. The Artisan Guild leader, Magnus, also told me that the gloves could be used to cast beginner spells and simple protective wards easily, and knowing your affinity with magic, it will come in handy. You can even cast a spell now. Also, the boots are made and tempered in such a way that they make little to no noise when walking or running if you know how to walk stealthily," Jura informs me as he helps me get dressed.

"What a bounty! Hey, Erol, did you get any new armor?"

"Of course he did, but he can explain to you what he got since I was not paying attention to his stuff." Jura smirks as he looks at Erol.

I can see Erol's tail wag side to side, eyeing Jura as he lets out a low grunt.

"This is perfect. I feel right as rain and ready to leave this place!" I grab my satchel and Coal, but as my hand touches Coal's hilt, I feel a strong jolt of energy but play it off like I'm excited to hold my sword again. That's new and unexpected, stop it.

"Well, I agree. I see no reason why I should keep you here any longer, Ruff!" Jura says, and with a snap of his finger, I feel a weight lift off my shoulder. "There, you can leave the room without setting off an alarm," Jura says as he looks out the window.

"My cub, I will meet you at the guild. I have already been briefed on our mission," Erol says, still munching on what I think is a crab claw.

"Do not overstay your welcome, cat. The hospital might need this room for someone else." Jura glances at Erol.

He just keeps munching on his food, looks at me, and winks. I walk up to Erol, take a piece of meat from his plate that does not look burned to a crisp, and thank him for the food. With a smile, Erol nods at me, and I walk out of the room with Jura.

"I honestly don't know what you see in that beast!"

"Well, Erol thinks you're annoying, so I guess it's mutual." Jura looks away with anger.

We both walk for a few minutes through corridors and staircases, reaching the exit of the cathedral. Jura turns to me and says, "Well, Ruff, I will remain here and look for more information on the mission that was given to me. If I find anything of relevance, I will send a wisp your way." Jura hugs me. "Be safe, and if you can stay the night in town still, find me, and we will go out and eat. I owe you that much."

I nod and head out of the cathedral. As I walk out the doors, I feel the sunshine hit my face and the wind run through my hair.

"Feels good to be free!"

Mission

I make it to the Warriors Guild with no problems, but traversing through the damn place is a problem. Since I defeated such a strong enemy, I have become somewhat of a celebrity amongst guild members. People come up to me to congratulate me, and others buy me mugs with drinks or even food.

A few of them even started singing songs about how I almost got roasted and Erol saved me.

I ignore the songs and thank the patrons for the drinks as I make my way up to the guild's main counter by pushing drunks out of my way. Two elven guild maidens salute me and ask me to follow them, which is a first. Usually, they want me to keep my distance.

They take me through a new part of the guild I have never been in. It is where high-ranking members eat, talk, and stay away from the ordinary guild members. This area had paintings of past leaders hung up on the wall, and the prettier butlers and maidens worked here. As we traverse through the room, we make it to a double set of doors that have dry blood on them and a hole that could fit my face through easily. I steel myself while knocking on the door, only for it to open by itself slowly. I finish opening it, excusing myself, half expecting to be attacked by something.

I peek my head inside to see the guild leader's office. The office itself is oval-shaped, and it contains trophy cases, ranging from big ones to the stand-alone pedestal holding a beautiful dagger. The room has a map of the realm on the back wall with darts sticking out of it. Next to the map, there are swords, axes, halberds, and heads of creatures making funny faces mounted next to each other.

I notice a second floor that holds a bookcase and what looks like barrels that remind me of alcohol kegs. A few loosely dressed human guild maidens appear on the second floor and look down on me in a tired manner.

Alan calls for me to come in and approach him, driving all my attention to him. He is sitting with his legs propped up on a barrel, facing the map of the continent.

One of my escorts approaches Alan and bows. "Berserker Alan, shall we leave Ruffus here?"

In turn, he stands and smiles at the maiden. "Thank you, beautiful. You are dismissed. Return to your duties."

She bows and leaves the room, closing the door behind them. I sigh, turning to look at the second floor again and noticing the women upstairs have vanished.

Alan speaks up. "Come here, boy."

With slight hesitation, I near him, taking a quick glance at my surroundings. My eye darts to a scroll on his desk trimmed in gold with the queen's seal on it. I have rarely seen the seal since it was only used for high-level missions. I look up at Alan, who is grinning at me while he throws two darts in the air, catching them in a playful manner.

He puts his hand on my shoulder and says, "So, Ruff, I have a new mission for you. Simple and easy. That is why I did not place it on the mission board. I was saving it just for you and your companion." He squeezes my shoulder a bit harder as he says this. "You will go to the kingdom hidden in the western part of this continent, deep in a forest where druids commune, White Wood, on a supply run. Carts will be handed to you at the gate of the city with our emblem. Of course, the beastman known as Erol of the Wilds will join you as a bodyguard to you and the supplies." He plays with his darts with one hand.

"Once you reach White Wood safely, report to the cathedral there. More instructions will be given to you. Oh, and before I forget. This cargo we're handing to you is of vital importance." He gives me a severe look. "Do not lose it. You will receive three carts with the same gear, just in case you get raided by bandits on the roads. At least one of these carts must make it to White Wood. Alongside to help you, I have requested ten horses, two for each cart, and four extras just in case."

I look at the map behind Alan. "Just in case what?"

Alan lets go of me and walks to his desk, grabbing the elegant-looking scroll, and in a low voice, he says, "Just in case."

With a wrist movement, Alan throws the scroll to me with a bit of heft. "Good luck, Ruffus. May your sword bring your enemies down. You are dismissed," he says as he turns to face the map again, throwing his two darts, which land on a location called White Wood.

I bow and walk out of the office as quietly as I can, closing the doors and turning my back to the broken wooden frame only to notice the high-ranking guild members observing me as I quickly stand tall and walk away from the guild leader's office. I pick up the pace when I see a few of them grab their weapons casually, and as I get to the doors, a tall, bulky human blocks my way. His tan eyes pierce right through me as if he has already thought of ten different ways of killing me. His face is full of scars, and his bald head is filled with tattoos of orcish and beastmen origins. He is dressed in heavy armor stained with washed-off blood and dents. He is holding a broad sword that is my height and tipping it toward me.

I give the man a fake smile and walk by him, and once I'm out of the room, I sigh in relief, "Whoa, I thought I was about to pick a fight!"

As I make my way out of the guild, a poster catches my attention. The man that blocked my path was the current champion of the arena. The second-strongest warrior in the guild, and if something happens to Berserker Alan, he will take his place.

I shake the feeling of fear away and make my way to the exit doors of the hidden guild area. I can feel people looking at me now as I walk through the room and even catch a few whispers saying, "Looks like the berserker has a new dog."

The door slams behind me, and to my relief, no one looks my way. I feel as if I have had enough attention for one day from my guild, but sadly, it doesn't end there. I attempt to make my way through the pavilion toward the exit, when I'm stopped a few times by the new members to answer questions on what strategy I used to kill the daemon.

I tell them all the same thing. "What strategy?"

Finally, I make it out of the guild, and the city is starting to wake up now. More people are in the street, and the clock tower's bell rings ten o'clock. Lucky me, it's still morning. The shops should be opening, I think as I check my satchel—potions, medicine, bandages, flint, tinder, dry meats, and a new waterskin. I desperately need to restock! Once I finish creating a list in my head, I make my way to the market area for my last-minute preparation.

Time goes by quickly as I finish my shopping. I end up with more things than I needed, but then again, who doesn't need a waterskin filled with the best wine to celebrate? I sit down on a bench near the fountain where all the outdoor shops are stationed to organize my bag. I take a moment to take in the sights and clear my head before I continue arranging my bag and pockets. I see tourists walking around with their maps out, new adventurers running around doing guild errands, and children playing in the fountain before a mage finds them and sends them back to school. I listen to the chatter of people haggling over food and asking where the merchants found the items they are selling. I hear the conversations of nobles talking about the latest gossip and hear the town crier saying news about the weather, the happenings on the other islands, and the war occurring on the north of our sister continent.

This kingdom of River Front seems so innocent to me. There are no significant crises other than the accidental summoning of a powerful creature. The people are not all bad. There has been no major war since the theological one that ended up creating the Grande Cathedral. In the end, the food is cheap, the beer is plentiful, the shops are always stocked, and the water in the canal is drinkable. All is well here. I wonder if White Wood is the same.

A few hours go by as I make my way to the city gate where my carts are stationed. I almost get trampled by a rider with his beautiful stallion, and as I jump out of the way, I notice the rider is the champion from the Warriors Guild. He delivers a package to a guild maiden and rides off out of the city. I pick up the pace and see a few people from my guild walking around, talking about their missions. I notice a row of simple wooden carts with River Front's crest guarded by a few Arcadian soldiers.

I am approached by a happy-looking old female dwarf who has her silver hair tied like a bun with the Warriors Guild's badge on her lapel. With a gentle voice, she says to me, "Ah, dear me, you must be Ruffus of Bern! My old eyes have not failed yet," she says in contentment. "Your bodyguard is finishing reading and signing for the contents of the cart. It is only two pages long, but he has been sitting reading the list for almost forty-five minutes!" She laughs.

Poor Erol, at least he's trying to read. "Yeah, he's just making sure he memorizes what we have!" I search my pouch for my scroll and hand it to her.

She puts on an enormous pair of glasses, making her eyes look ten times as big as they usually are. She mutters what she reads on the paper. "Ah yes, yes, your credentials. Please follow me," she says as we slowly walk. "The carts have weapons, medicine, food, a spell crate, and a mystery crate created by the College of Magic. Do not open that one—I was told it would explode."

"Excellent. Does the ledger that my bodyguard has contain the exact amount and type of item in each crate?" I ask her.

"No, just what I said. That list is here with me, only to be given to you. Oh dear, before I forget, congratulations! I'm here to inform you also of your new rank in the guild. By the style of weaponry you use and your combat style, you are now known as a scout class, subdivision Swords Master. Congratulations, dear!"

I thank the old dwarf lady and think, *Yes, I got out of the lower-tier ranking. Still silly that I need a label. What if I wanted to be a jester or a knife thrower. I blame Arcadia for having to give a title to everything.*

She bows. "May your sword bring down your enemies! Now, run along, you have work to do, and I must go to my knitting meeting." She laughs. "Oh my, knitting meeting, that rhymes."

I stare at her blankly, trying to ignore what I just heard. "My cub, you are early!"

I turn my head to see Erol walking toward me. He carries

a shiny new polearm and a new leather harness that seems to be made from the same material as mine. He also has a set of new baggy pants, which look incredibly comfortable, and on his shoulder, he has a pretty worn-out-looking rucksack, which I'm guessing is carrying his things for the mission.

"Erol, glad to see you made it." I wave at him.

"I would not miss it for the world. Now, come here." Erol picks me up and sets me on his free shoulder, walking toward the cart.

"So, cub, how long till we reach White Wood after we depart from here?" he asks me in a cheerful voice.

"Well, it's a few days' travels. If we have no stops and push on through, we should make it by the third day at nightfall," I say, and look at the clock tower.

He nods and sets me on the leading cart. "Would you like me to travel with you in the head of the caravan or secure the back?"

"Stay up here with me. The horses are tied to each cart, and I'm sure they're trained to follow us. It's a long ride to White Wood, and I do not want to be bored talking to myself," I say while getting a bag of dice from my satchel. "We can gamble!"

"As you wish," he says as he throws his bag on the back of the cart.

"Oh, I almost forgot. I got you something."

Erol's ears perk up. "A gift? Well, what is it?"

"I got you a new charm for your weapon. A tiger beastman was selling it. It's from your area. See, it has writing from the Wilds, and you told me you hailed from the savanna region," I say as I pull out from my left inner jacket pocket a feathered charm with a few bones attached to the base of the string. "Something to remind you of home! After getting our asses handed out to us, I thought we might need a bit more luck on our side. It almost looks like my charm, which I'm grateful Clover brought back to me while I was in the hospital."

Erol grabs the charm, examines it, and sniffs it. "It smells of home. Thank you, I will treasure this." He smirks at me. "I want to command the horses!"

I move to the side, stretching and yawning as I look at the big blue sky and say, "Truly, a beautiful day."

Erol jumps in beside me, snapping the reins, making the horses move. I look behind us and see the other horses starting to follow us.

I grab a few bottles I had in my satchel and open them with my teeth. I look at Erol and say, "Well, here is for an easy mission and a hard day of work!"

Erol grabs both bottles and takes a big gulp. "Mhmm, this is not water, cub!"

"Yeah, that was my drink. Now hand it back!" I say as I try to grab my bottle.

"One of us needs to be responsible, and I choose you, cub," Erol says as he takes another gulp.

I shake my head and grab a small ceramic bowl, an acquisition from some gamblers in the marketplace, out of my bag. "Here, I'm using your tail to anchor this bowl so we can play dice."

"What are we betting?" Erol asks as he guides the horses out of the city.

"My drink. I want it back," I say slyly.

"This is acceptable, but if you lose, I get your drinks, and you buy me more drinks. And once you have no more gold, I take your shirt," Erol says, sounding confident.

"We both know you won't win. Now roll."

With his free hand, he rolls a six and a one. "I have a seven, your turn."

I laugh and say, "Oh, my drink will taste so good after I roll!" I throw the dice and go silent.

Erol looks at the bowl and smiles. Moving closer to me, he whispers in my ear, "Snake eyes."

Chilly Welcome to Town

The days go by slowly and peacefully. We stop in a few different towns to resupply on alcohol, food, and sweets.

In the taverns, we hear odd rumors about White Wood, about how monsters have been seen roaming close to its kingdom and how the town is closed. White Wood soldiers have not been keeping their roads safe, and trade stopped a few weeks ago. As we ride, I cannot help but speculate that the king might have gone mad, or there is a power struggle in the kingdom of White Wood.

"Hey, Erol, what do you think of all the rumors we heard in the taverns we visited?"

"I do not believe in rumors. Humans and elves spin yarn when they are drunk."

"Guess you are right, but keep an eye out. I have not seen any guardsmen or soldiers throughout the roads. With my luck, we are due for a bandit raid."

Erol scoffs and says, "Let them come. I need a good fight."

In the end, no bandit raids and no monsters try to eat us, just birds flying around us and a beautiful view of the countryside. The leaves are starting to change into a lovely orange tint as summer is slowly ending. The wind is crisp and cool, but the sun keeps us warm. The only off part is that my partner is snoring loudly and now is the owner of my shirt and socks, courtesy of my great luck with dice, cards, and guessing games. Whenever he wakes up, we gamble and play card games to see if I can win back my property. Sadly, I end up losing twenty pieces of gold and my favorite knife, and now I owe Erol an all-expenses-paid trip to any hot spring he chooses with all the alcohol he wants.

I never was good at dice. Next time, I'll bring a book. After we play, we talk about our past missions, how much Jura is a subordinate, and how I should be the pride and joy of my clan. I'll never understand why Erol dislikes him or thinks that I live in a clan. I conclude that that's how Erol was raised since I have never traveled to his home.

Time passes by, the sun begins to set, and the night creatures come out, hooting and howling. The crows start to sing the song of the evening. We make it to the edge of the forest of White Wood as mist starts to roll out of the woods, giving it an unwelcoming feeling. A faint smell of smoke blows toward us, making me nervous. A forest fire is no joke, and we could die if we are trapped. For that matter, the sound of birds, or any other animal in the forest of White Wood, is also missing.

"Not long now, cub."

I look on the map. "The kingdom of White Wood lies deep in this forest."

"Hey, Erol, why is it called White Wood?" I ask as I look to my sides.

"Well, my cub, look at the trees. The bark is pale white. I read in a thick book that this is where the druid folk commune with the spirits. It must be true since I also heard one of my kin talk about it at one of the taverns."

I nod. "I have never been here before, nor have I heard anyone talk about this place. I only know it as a little star on the map. It's odd to see all these trees, and they don't have many leaves on them. Sort of creepy, if you ask me," I say, looking around as we go into the forest, the natural boundary line of White Wood kingdom. "Heh, I feel dumb asking such an obvious question. I should have read about this place before heading out."

"The book also says that this area is holy ground for nomads and some legend about a monster that sucks blood, but I could not finish reading to find out why there was a mast ecodus," Erol says as if he's trying to sound smart.

"Mast ecodus?"

Erol nods. Did he mean mass exodus?

As we go further into the forest, the horses start to pick up the pace and begin to whine and buck uncontrollably.

Erol calms them down by singing low and saying, "Calm, beast, keep your courage."

"These are Arcadian horses. They do not get frightened easily. Erol, can you smell or see anything?" I ask as I look around the endless darkening forest on either side of us.

Erol sniffs the air and growls low, making me nervous.

"Everything okay, big guy?" I say, looking behind, making sure we have all our carts.

He pauses and looks at me, saying, "There is a smell of fresh soil, smoke, pestilence, and something I cannot identify."

"Let's keep our eyes open. All these stories and the sheer lack of patrols on these roads can only indicate that something bad is around the corner."

As we make our way deeper into the forest, I can feel a sense of dread and fear. I can see Erol still controlling our horses with growls and low humming. Darkness creeps toward us as the last rays of light begin to fade, and as I look up, I can see one of the moons starting to show through the tall trees, but the canopy is not letting the light permeate down. As we plunge deeper into the forest, I can hear whispers speaking to me, coming from my sides, and little puffs of white light appear and disappear in the corner of my eye.

Erol brushes his tail on me, startling me. He chuckles and moves closer to me, hitting me again playfully with his tail. I look at him and see a sly smile on his face. I smile back and shake my head, grabbing his tail and playing with the fur. I calm down and feel better knowing he's here with me. I know he will protect me, and I will return the favor if he needs it.

The whispers in the forest turn to low chanting, breaking the silence.

"Hey," I whisper, "can you hear that?"

"Yes, my cub, it sounds like the language of druids."

"Are they friendly?" I ask as I look toward the darkness to our sides.

"No druid I know would commune in this forest anymore, my cub. They say it's been tainted for a while. Rumors have also been spoken in the taverns in our guild for the past months about this place being cursed and dangerous. Sadly, I can't get my favorite ale anymore since no one gathers in these woods or near these woods," he says in a scary voice, trying to frighten me by showing me his teeth.

"Tsk, here I thought you don't believe in rumors you hear in the taverns and you only think of drinking," I say, puffing his tail.

He pulls out a water skin that smells of my wine. "I don't know what you're speaking about, cub!" He takes a drink.

A few hours pass, and an unholy darkness consumes the forest, making it impossible for me to see well.

"Hey, Erol, I'm jumping on the back and grabbing a lantern. I can't see my hand in front of my face," I say as I turn around and carefully avoid the shifting boxes. "We should have turned on a light sooner, but I don't want any attention drawn toward us."

"It's there, my cub. Trust me, I can see it!" Erol says playfully. I feel around and find a brand-new oil lantern. I open the glass case and snap my fingers, creating a small flame on my pointer finger. I feel proud that I can finally cast a spell without it completely backfiring on me. Doing this reminds me of the rules of magic. if I use fire magic, my temperature will drop, and in the worst case, I could suffer hypothermia. Magic will always have horrific consequences if used to an extreme. I shake the thought off my head and turn on the lantern.

"Little thing packs a punch!" I say to myself as I hang the lantern on the side of the cart, facing it to the front.

The bright light beams in front of us, allowing me to see the road. After a few seconds, I use the lens on it to point it toward the back carts. I can barely see the back cart because there is a fog following us that consumes the last carriage, but I conclude that we have all our horses since I can hear their footsteps on the stone road.

I turn to the front, and an ungodly chill goes down my spine. I quickly inhale, grabbing my sides, shivering. I see my breath clearly and wonder if my use of fire magic is why the temperature dropped so fast in my body. I turn to look at the carts behind us, and on the last carriage, I see through the fog a glowing, white, thin figure that looks like a scarecrow sitting in the driver's seat.

I stare at it, and whatever it is, its staring back at me.

All the horses from all the carts start to buck and whine, and I can hear Erol attempting to calm them down again by speaking loudly, creating an eerie echo. My eyes are locked on this thing, and then I notice the extra four horses are missing. "Is everything all right?" Erol asks as he tries to keep the horses calm.

I stay silent and slowly reach for my knives with my

trembling hands. I had always had a fear of anything that could be or that resembles the undead, ever since I saw a ghost when I went to visit my sister at her grave. Jura saved me from joining their ranks when I was attacked by the phantom that was in the graveyard. The bestiary book that I own states, "The unruly creatures don't just kill you, but they try to absorb a living person's essence to try and become whole again." This has only solidified my fear of them.

The glowing white figure stands up, spinning once in place, creating what looks like two spears in each thin sticklike-looking hand. It jumps and spins again, throwing the spears, hitting the connector to the last cart. The last two horses are freed and start to panic.

"Cub, what is going on back there?" Erol yells at me.

"Erol, go faster!" I bark at him, not losing sight of the thin creature.

"Cub! What—"

I turn to see his glowing blue eyes. "Erol, go!" I yell, quickly turning my head back.

Only one horse remains from the last cart still following us, and the white figure is on top of its back. It jumps straight up, dropping something on the horse, almost causing the poor creature to lose its footing. The thin figure lands on the head of the horse and quickly taps its forehead. The horse looks like it almost falls again, and something in the air immediately starts to smell like rotten flesh.

I cover my mouth and nose to shield myself from the smell and hide my panic. With the bit of light we have, I still see the horse losing part of its flesh on its face and the color of its skin change from brown to a sickly pale white or an almost glowing green. One of its eyes falls out, leaving a socket that has a red light emanating from it.

Every step the horse takes, it seems to be losing chunks of flesh, and it starts to whine in a shrill, high-pitched voice as if it's being slaughtered in front of my eyes. The white creature sits down on the horse, and it looks as if it is disappearing entirely on it. A few seconds later, a figure erupts from the back of the horse, forming what appears to be a decomposing human skeleton, and releases a loud screech, making me cover my ears.

"Erol, GO!" I yell as I shake the fear off me, quickly grabbing another glass oil lantern, and promptly turn it on so I can see around my area.

With a snap of the reins and a threatening roar, the horses start to sprint faster. I hear horses whine on our side of our cart, and out of the woods, two horses that look as if they have been dead for weeks start running next to us on each side of the cart.

"Speak! Talk to me!" Erol yells at me, looking to his side. "Some creature killed four of our horses and took one of the carts!" I say as I throw a knife toward the dead-looking horse next to our cart, making it slow down.

One of the horses that erupted out of the tree line jumps and bites down on the neck of a horse in the second cart. The other tries to bite but misses. The reins release the horse and make the second cart tumble and break. The free horse runs out of the road into the woods. I watch it disappear, and a loud death cry comes a few seconds afterward.

"We have lost two carts and eight horses in a matter of seconds!"

"Can we fight this creature? Hold on, sharp turn!" Erol yells back.

I hold onto the sides, dodging the moving crates trying to squish me. "I have no idea where it went, and the horses disappeared. Quite frankly, I don't think we are fighting a living creature!" I say as I look around.

"Something is coming from my left! Prepare yourself, cub!" Erol yells.

I grab a throwing knife, turn to his left and see a glowing figure in the forest, but I cannot make out what it is, and as it gets closer, I gasp in horror. A black undead stallion is galloping twenty feet away from us. The creature is approximately fourteen feet in height and the width of two horses. The stallion's face is still whole, with a metal plate covering its forehead. Its eyes are glowing red spheres that haunt me to my very core.

Every time its hooves hit the ground, sparks fly out, causing it to leave tiny embers in its wake. Its backside is armored with rusted-looking iron plating, and its long tail has chains with dimly lit lanterns hanging off them. The chains create a deafening noise, causing our horses to panic even more. Around the area, wisps are floating, dashing in and out, changing from their pale hue to a low, glowing green, giving them light.

There is a body lying motionless on top of the horse. It looks like a giant version of a human or an elf. It's too dark to see clearly. The corpse has an enormous spear stuck through its back, impaling it to the horse. An object appears to be contracting and expanding in a slow and steady beat on the spear. Unexpectedly, we hear laughter as a glowing white figure erupts from the corpse, taking the shape of a decomposed human.

I stand in awe, trying to understand what I'm observing. The physical body is impaled on this enormous horse, but the spirit body is attached at the hip and continues to gain shape and fill up space. The spirit body is shirtless, and the skull has a mouth full of sharp, fang-looking teeth, and it shifts its look toward me. The spirit begins to laugh and screech as if it has awoken from a slumber, and around its head, a crown forms, looking like a bunch of tree roots connected.

The spirit's glowing green eyes focus directly on me, giving me a sick feeling in my stomach. I react by throwing my knives at it, but they pass through its ethereal body as if they are nothing. The spirit loses its interest in me and raises its hand toward the sky. With a crack of lightning, a gargantuan, two-handed sword forms in its hand. After a few seconds, it swings it with ease, and its sights go to me and the cart again.

A low whisper inside my head tells me, "He comes for you. We will take you into the abyss. What joy!"

"Here he comes, all hail the king!" a child's voice joins.

"Let the madness rule over you and show your true colors!" an old man's voice whispers after.

Voices start to flood my mind, making me cover my ears and yell, "Get out of my head!"

"My cub, concentrate! These voices haunt me too—stay strong!" Erol's voice breaks the madness that sets in me.

The last whisper came from the undead horse in a deep, bellowing voice, saying, "Kill him, kill them all, feast, feast!"

"Hold on, another sharp turn!" Erol yells at me again.

Erol turns the cart onto a smooth road, losing the monster next to us. Strong gusts of wind are making the trees dance, and between them, I can see lights flicker on and off that remind me of what came out of Valke when I killed him, but bigger and brighter.

I shake my head and muster my courage. "Enough! I'm done with this nightmare! Erol, keep this cart as steady as you can. When these things come around, I'm going to fight back!"

"Do not be rash, cub! There is a bow back there—shoot it!" Erol says as he tries to control the horses.

I look at the shifted cargo and find the weapons crate. With my lucky knife, I crack it open, revealing a medley of new weapons. I quickly find a strung bow and a quiver filled with arrows. I equip it to my hip and nock an arrow in place. I can hear more whispers telling me to die and give up, slowly growing louder. I take a deep breath, close my eyes, and concentrate.

As I exhale and inhale, I find peace and perceive that something is coming. As I open my eyes, I can make out an odd shadow in the woods creeping toward us. I take aim and shoot my arrow. A loud ping accompanied by a whining of pain follows a few seconds later. From the direction I shot, the monster bursts out of the woods, knocking a few trees down, accompanied by a horde of what looks like our dead horses.

"You have got to be kidding me!" I yell out loud as I keep shooting arrows at our enemy.

I hit a few of the horses, knocking them down, hopefully taking them out of the fight.

"Hold on, another sharp turn!" Erol shouts at me with a sense of urgency.

I brace myself, and the cart slides off the road for a second. "Why are the roads not made in a straight line? By the Three, Erol, get us back on the road!"

"Djinn's flame! Cub, look to the front!" Erol shouts back.

I turn to look at the front and exhale in an annoyed manner to see White Wood on the horizon, lit in flames. The town also seems to be entrapped by a dome, not allowing the smoke to leave. I turn again to face my enemy, and all I see is a glowing blade about to decapitate me. I duck quickly, smacking my head on a crate and losing a few inches of my hair in the process as the blade's edge misses my head.

I recover and ready an arrow, aiming at the exposed flesh on the horse's armor. Once I find my mark, I let the arrow fly. The horse does not stumble, but it lets out a loud bellow that makes me flinch and lose my balance, falling on the cart's wooden floor.

I shake off the disorientation and grab the side of the cart to see the spirit miss by an inch, hitting the cart's wheel.

Erol yells at me, "Hold on! People block the gates!" He pauses for a second, then says in a panic, "What is this? Those are not people!"

"Run them through, Erol!" I say as I shoot a few more arrows toward the monster.

As I run out of arrows, I look out of the corner of my eye and see Erol seize his weapon. "Reach for my hand and brace yourself!" Before I can even move to grab Erol's hand, I black out. When I awake, I'm not quite sure if I am in the air flying or falling, but I'm definitely not touching the ground. The world is spinning around me, and I can't get a grip in any direction. I land hard on the ground, rolling and hitting something or someone in the way.

As I come to a stop, I try to move and recover my sense of direction. I stand, shaking and feeling as if I were hit by a moving cart filled with rocks. Looking around, I see houses on fire and the ruins of what looks like a farmhouse. I cannot see Erol, and I start yelling for him in a panic. All around me are bodies on the ground, some decapitated, others missing limbs. Some are children, and others are adults from every race. In the distance, I hear people crying for help and the roars of strange creatures echoing through the town. The pungent smell of fire, pestilence, and sulfur engulfs the air, leaving me nauseated and gagging every single time I breathe. I wipe the blood running down my forehead and turn to see our cart smashed into a building. Out of sheer luck, the building isn't on fire, and the cart doesn't look wholly damaged.

To my surprise, I do not see the monster that attacked us anywhere, which makes me happy that I do not have to worry about that at this exact moment. I start to run to the cart, only to feel immense pain in my sides. I fall to one knee, gasping in pain. I grit my teeth and let out a weak "ow" as I stand again, now limping toward the cart. I search for my satchel and remember I took it off on the ride here.

Ngh, no potions for me, it seems. No matter, I think as I keep limping toward the cart.

I'm sure I'm not delusional because of the pain and the horrid smell, but some of the dead bodies on the ground appear to be twitching and moving. For my sake, I choose to ignore that as I keep moving forward. Once I reach the cart, I see the horses are dead inside the building, and I start to worry, thinking I'm the only survivor.

As I panic, I hear moaning beside me, and I quickly turn to see a bunch of rubble moving on the ground. I make my way there, praying that it's not a monster, but once I reach the pile of rubble, I see a yellow tail drenched in blood.

"Oh no," I whisper.

I get on my knees and move the rubble as best as I can without injuring myself, and there, I see him, my best friend, impaled by a piece of wood through the rib and as bloody as me. His wounds are severe, and if he doesn't get treated soon, the blood loss and infection will take his life.

"Hold on, Erol," I groan to him as I limp back to the cart to find the medicine crate. My satchel is on the floor near the wreckage, next to my sword. I look up to the sky and thank the gods in happiness when I open my satchel. None of my medicines have broken, a miracle in itself. I hurry and grab a syringe just to see the needle is broken. I curse under my breath and decide to just drink the concoction. The taste is horrible, and I almost throw it up, but I stomach it and press on. The effect of the potion is not immediate, but it's better than nothing. With my newfound strength, I move the heavier rocks off Erol and force him to be comfortable. "Is this my end, cub?"

I smirk at him and shake my head no as I open the vial.

He gives a weak smile and says, "Good, I'm not leaving my cub in such a smelly place." He scans and looks behind me, and his expression changes quickly from a weak smile to a troubled face. I look behind me, and all my fears come true. Corpses are walking toward us.

I feed the drink to Erol, who doesn't seem fazed by the taste, and say, "Get up, big guy, get up. I do not want to join their ranks just yet!"

He nods as he swallows his drink and stands with my help as I put his arm around my neck to support him the best I can. He tries to play it calm, but I can see real pain and agony on his face still. Good thing the potion will numb him up in a few seconds and help him get some of his energy back.

I glance behind us again and see that the corpses are shambling toward us at an alarming pace. As we walk toward a nearby door, Erol lets out a growl of pain. I look down and see his leg isn't moving correctly, and his foot is at a new angle.

"I am fine, cub, just need to sleep on it."

I don't answer since all my energy is going toward helping him move to the door. As we limp, I see the windows are entirely barred from inside. A few wards have been placed on the top of the window. The door has dents, pieces of wood missing. It looks like it was almost breached once. We go in front of the door, and I tell Erol to hold on. I try to kick the door open with my right leg but end up hearing a loud snap that sadly comes from me.

Erol's eyes widen as he looks at me, trying to say something, but I just look away and say, "I'm okay, just made out of glass, it seems." I hold back a tear. "Thank the gods for the numbing effect of the potion."

From inside, I hear a low growl and a child screaming, "Go away!"

I knock on the door loudly and say, "Please let us in. We're in danger, and my friend is severely injured!" There is silence, and I knock again. "Please! We have supplies from River Front. I seek sanctuary for him!"

Silence looms from inside the house.

I keep knocking, and as I look behind me, I see the corpses are only about twelve feet away. My leg gives out, and both of us fall to the ground. I panic and remember my brother once gave me holy ash, the essential component to making barriers. I can remember Jura once told me it could hold back daemons, undead, and creatures created by chaotic magic.

I search my person and find the little bag of ash. It's not enough for a circle, but it would be enough to create half a ring if I use the house walls. The ash smells strongly of sage, salt, and other plants that I can't identify, and as the corpses get near us, I'm able to make the half-circle cover both of us. I close my eyes and remember the instructions for how to make this spell work. I pray to a deity and concentrate, imagining a wall building up. I believe the wall is there and have faith it will hold. I am not the best with magic, but I will try my damn best, and with the help of these gloves, it should be easier to channel.

All I can think of is Erol and his safety. I pray to the gods to just save him, to let him live. I pray to the Three to keep us, to send me some luck, and to help me survive for another day so I can fight with my brother and friends. I open my eyes to see a fragile and dim-looking wall of light. The corpses reach the wall and put their hands on it as if they're trying to push it away or push through it.

I feel the energy leave my body, and sweat drenches my forehead. I have never attempted a spell like this after my accident in the mines when I was a child. Everything around me starts going dark quickly, and I begin to breathe heavily, but I push on. I'm exerting too much energy, and a migraine begins to set in, but I keep the barrier up and pray that it is strong.

A corpse hand passes through the wall. I bite my lower lip and try to concentrate harder, but the pain in my leg and sides makes the task even more difficult. The taste of my blood reminds me of how hopeless this endeavor is. My will is breaking, and fear of failure is dominating my emotions every second. I let out a slight cough and turn to look to my side. Erol is staring at me with tired eyes. He gets closer to me, puts my hands down, and turns me to face him. Unexpectedly, he gives me a gentle hug, putting my face on his chest and wiping my bloody nose and lips with his free hand. I tremble as I try to break away, but I feel his bleeding wound and begin to tear up.

He whispers, "I am here," and holds me tight.

Tears start to run down my face. "I'm sorry, Erol. I tried. I can—"

He shushes me and caresses my face, and as our eyes meet, I hug him back.

I can hear the wall of light cracking and the monsters' loud moan on the other side.

"We fought till the end, my cub. Now rest," he whispers, and kisses the top of my head.

Anger surges in me, and I look at Erol. "No, not yet!" I see a slight smile on his face as I turn around and grab a knife out of my coat. I try to stand, but at that time, the wall erupts, knocking me back down again, stabbing the blade into my leg. I hear yelling and what sounds like a roar, but it was not Erol's roar.

I feel an intense heat around me and several hands pushing me and pulling me away. I break free and try to fight, but what looks like a hammer meets my face, knocking me out.

White Wood

I feel no pain as I regain consciousness. *It's odd, since I should be dead or inside some creature's belly, being digested for nutrients. I hope I taste bad.* I slowly open my eyes only to meet a bright light, and I start to shuffle around, grunting in discomfort. Once my eyes focus, all I see is my sister looking down at me, smiling.

Shit, this again? No, really, am I made out of paper?

I hear a muffled noise on my sides and see two shadows forming in the light. I close my eyes and sigh, putting my hand on my face and massaging my eyebrows. This time, I see a woman and a little girl staring down at me with concerned looks on their faces. The woman raises her hand above my head, and it starts to glow a faint turquoise color. She hovers it over my face and down to my chest, placing her hand gently over my heart. I take a deep breath and sigh in pure comfort as I start to feel like my usual self.

The woman removes her hand from my chest and scans the rest of my naked body with it. Sternly, she says, "Well, you are healed now and soon be back to peak performance." She grabs a wet towel from a bucket near her and places it over my forehead. "You only had five fractured bones, including a rib snapped in two and a broken wrist, six torn muscles, a hairline fracture on your skull, and a shard of bone poking out of your leg. It is a miracle you were even able to move before we saved you. I can tell you left a hospital about three days ago. The bones are not fully healed."

I slowly sit up and look at myself, seeing that I look like a mummy wrapped up in bloody bandages. My gaze goes back to the woman who healed me. She is of medium height, a human brunette with light blue eyes, wearing a pair of round glasses that have seen better days. Her hair is tied up in a ponytail with a big dirt-stained white bow holding it in place. Her skin is lightly tanned and full of fresh burn marks all over her hands and arms. She has a unique side bag with a caduceus imprinted on it and what looks like a worn-down and cut-up doctor's cloak with bits of blood spatter everywhere.

I groan and finish sitting up. "Is that all? I feel like I'm under-healing these past few days."

"Don't be a smart ass. You are lucky you had medical supplies in that cart of yours and that your body had a small trace of high-grade medicine in it! If it were not for your friend shielding you, I would not be conversing with you. Be quiet if you don't have anything to say, and be grateful that he saved you and that we helped." She points at Erol.

He is on a big table, also bandaged up. He is missing small chunks of fur on his face and arms. I can see his clothing is ripped, and his bandages are stained with his blood. Attached to his hand is a small string-like tube connected to a bottle of violet-looking liquid hanging from a coat rack. This is the first time I have seen such a simple contraption.

I turn to the woman, who is cleaning her hands on a cracked silver bowl, and say, "Will he be okay?"

She walks up to him and, drying her hands on a piece of linen, flicks the glass bottle. "Yes, he will be just fine, but the medicine will take a few hours to work effectively. Both of you had an infection from those monsters we call *revenants* scratching you. Luckily, this is a top-grade antibiotic and metabolic regenerative concoction with morphine added to it— not my recipe, and I would not combine those compounds, but they effectively worked this time."

I stare blankly at her, and she sighs. "It's a combination of your red-tinted potion or healing serum with more medicine, as most people and untrained holy magic users call it. Goodness, you don't even know what's in the medicine you so freely take?"

"Magic?" I give a pained smirk.

She glares. "No magic, just good old-fashioned alchemy." She fixes her glasses and says, "I mean, it takes three weeks for the blood flower to actually bloom and the chemical compounds to make sure it's stable and not poisonous for use and to—"

I groan. "Okay, I get it, you're smart. Your big words hurt my head," I interrupt. "The only thing I know about alchemy is how to boil water in a pot."

"The pain you feel might be your concussion, but what do I know, right?" She sighs and looks at Erol. She raises her hand, and it starts to glow again. She closes her eyes and begins muttering an incantation, placing her hand on his forehead. He begins to twitch and groan in discomfort.

I look down in shame. "I am sorry, Healer, and I did not mean to be a wiseass." I look at her and ask in an interested tone, "What are you doing to Erol?"

A child's voice answers me: "Laura is mending his lung."

I look to my side to see a small, blue-eyed, skinny, blonde human girl no older than five, I would guess. She is holding a worn-out stuffed dog with deep red eyes. Her clothes look like a mage apprentice uniform, but they are tattered and dirty. Her face is white as porcelain with minor dirt marks here and there.

She looks dehydrated, and her hands and arms are full of old and new cuts.

Laura looks at me and gives me a stern, annoyed look. "I'm a healer trained by the Holy Church, besides being an alchemist and a doctor. I use magic to mend flesh and repair bones quickly. I use alchemy to make medicine for the rest that I cannot cure, like infections, diseases, and pestilence. Now, please rest. You are in good hands. The revenants have now come out in hordes, covering the entrance to the town. Escape has now become impossible for us." She turns her gaze to the small girl and says, "Lynnet, please be a dear and hand our friend that light pink vial on the top of the crate with the hexagon imprinted on it."

The small girl walks to the crate and flicks her hand, moving the potion to her hand. She walks back to me with the vial and hands it to me gently. I look at her, nodding and thanking her. I see her hazel-green eyes, when I swear they were blue just moments ago.

I look at Laura, who is gently rubbing Erol's stomach. Her gaze turns to me, and she says, "It's a compound containing—" She stops talking, adjusts her glasses with her shoulder, and says, "It's a sleeping aid."

I mutter, "Oh," and look around the room once more before drinking the potion. The doors have a ward covering them, and all the windows are barred with wood and broken-looking furniture. A sofa in the den seems to have been chewed on by something with big teeth, and a few tables look burned to a crisp. I see one crate of medicine inside the house with us and my weapon propped next to it. On the side of the crate, there is a small end table with a picture of two adults smiling with Lynnet in the middle holding a flower. They all are wearing mage's robes.

"Lie down for me, please," Laura says as she walks toward me. "I will put you to sleep for around two hours. That should be enough for me to finish repairing your bones, and for the fever to subside." She places her fingertips on my forehead as she drinks a small vial.

I lie down and sigh as her hand touches my forehead. "What happened in this town?"

She looks grim as she feeds me the potion, examines my eyes with great interest, and says, "I promise to tell you everything once you are fully recovered. Now, close your eyes."

I do as I'm told and ask, "What is in the potion again?"

"Liquid courage," she replies.

"So much for learning the ingredients," I smirk.

"Do you always talk this much?" she scoffs.

I try to reply, but the potion has quickly taken its effect, and I am out like a log.

It feels like a few seconds pass by, and I gasp myself awake. Next to me, I see Erol cuddling on me and lightly snoring. He smells cleaner than usual and does not look like a mummy, which is an improvement. I move away from him and stand next to the bed, stretching, listening to all my bones snap, crackle, pop, and it feels fantastic.

I extend my muscles and tousle my hair. As I walk to a broken mirror and see if I have new scars, I'm in my undergarments with no bloody rags or linens on me. My body has no new scars or bruises and is surprisingly clean. Overall, I feel strong, healthy, and hungry.

It's like I never got almost killed! I wonder why it took four days for me to heal in the hospital. Oh yeah, they thought I was possessed.

I look around the room and see all my stuff on the side of the bed with some new stitching and an attempt to remove the fabric's bloodstains. As I get dressed, I can hear yelling in the distance, as well as odd cries echoing outside. I slowly walk toward the window and look through the small cracks in the barrier. All I see is the town still in flames and smoke covering the sky. I turn to finish gearing up and see Erol barely covered by a blanket, napping like a baby, lightly snoring and drooling all over the straw pillow.

I smile and hold my laughter. "How did we get into this mess, and why do I keep waking up next to a naked beastman? The gods have an odd sense of humor."

Out of the corner of my eye, I notice a ladder going downstairs, and the incredible aroma of food hits me like a brick. My stomach growls loudly, and my feet start to move by themselves toward the smell of food.

Laura notices me come down and fixes her glasses. "How did you rest?"

I sit down in front of the dimly lit hearth next to Lynnet, who's petting the stuffed dog while eating a piece of toast. "Pretty good. How long was I out?"

"I told you, two hours. I gave the medicine enough time to finish working. I had finished washing both of you of the dirt and dried blood when the beastman woke up in a fit. It took me half an hour to explain to him what I was doing and that I was not washing you to be sacrificed to a monster. After he calmed down, he picked you up and took you upstairs, thanking me and asking if I had dragon marrow to cook," she says while handing me a plate of beans and a loaf of bread.

I shudder at the thought of dragon marrow and what Erol would have done to me if he had some. I shake off the thought and ask, "So what happened here, or is there another potion I need to drink?"

Lynnet stops eating and holds her stuffed dog closer to her. Laura puts her plate down and looks up, sighing. "I don't know, honestly."

I look at her and Lynnet and say, "There must be something wrong. I mean, the welcoming party I met was not friendly. Aside from almost getting killed by what I can only assume is a ghost rider and a whole bunch of undead, I think I deserve a better explanation other than this place is haunted or cursed or the famous, 'I don't know.' I mean, I assume you live here."

Laura looks down. "All I can tell you is that for the past few months, there have been odd disappearances here, after the prince left the castle to the woods. His father, my king, led a party to find him but never returned. Then a few weeks ago or so, soldiers of Arcadia were sent here to provide extra protection from the monsters in the woods, but they all went mad. They caused havoc in the town and ran back into the woods as if they were animals." She pulls a scroll out of her bag. "The town crier vanished, so the king's jester—a mad elf, if you ask me—handed out these scrolls stating that the city would be closing soon. It said to pray for the prince and that all holy activity must cease."

I finish eating my beans and walk to the nearest window. "That doesn't fully explain why there are undead roaming the streets," I say as I look outside.

"Yes, I know." She puts her plate down, walks toward me, and looks through the cracks of the window. "I fear we might have an undocumented necromancer in this town or a corrupted druid." She massages her forehead with her hand. "It didn't help that before all of this happened, there was an outbreak of a plague, which closed trading to other places around three weeks ago. Again, we were told to stay home and to use only alchemical remedies to cure ourselves."

"There was an outbreak?" I ask as I move away from the window.

Laura looks at me. "No worries, you are not infected. I made sure." She fixes her glasses and says, "Most doctors and alchemists left for the woods to contain it by order of the royal family. I did not go since I thought it would be ludicrous to leave a whole kingdom without doctors. I understand that holy magic is healing magic, but magic does not cure a disease. Sure, it makes the body withstand the disease, and the body will eventually cure itself, but the process can take weeks, even months, to happen fully. Alchemy is the only effective way to eradicate sickness quickly."

"Those painful needles do come in handy. And you say kingdom, as in White Wood is a kingdom, but it is so small," I say as I walk back and sit by the hearth.

"Yes, White Wood is a kingdom, and it takes up the whole forest and mountains. It's quite enormous. All the towns are located inside the forest and well hidden compared to River Front. Which reminds me, do not overdose on your healing potions—too much of a good thing will kill you, and taking four of those will kill you," Laura says as she checks the integrity of the barricade on the door.

"Going back to this mess of a kingdom, necromancers are not all bad. I know a few mages that have delved into the arts, and they have saved many people. Terrifyingly, of course." I fix a plate of food and put it to the side for Erol as I keep talking. "Other than a necromancer, how can a druid be the source of this? I know they commune with the spirits, and they might be odd, but not evil. It must be the plague. Why else would I be sent here with a crate full of medicine?"

"Yes, well, there have been cases where a disease can reanimate a dead body. But I can assure you that the malady is all but contained. There is something else raising the dead and bringing creatures from the forest to attack us. The only thing that can control the animals in the forest is a druid," Laura says as if convinced.

"Necromancers do not control living animals. They can only reanimate the dead with a corrupted spirit. So, you are right, and druids are peaceful and would never order an attack from local wildlife," I say as I rub my chest, feeling a tiny scar.

"Yes, yes, I know, and a necromancer can control the remains, bending them to his or her will," Laura says as she walks up to me. "I honestly do not know what is going on. As you can see, we are speculating, but all I know is that we must get out of here. This is the last of our food, and we could only bring in the medicine crate before more of the undead came to attack."

"I am amazed you both have survived this long out here. How did you do it?" I ask, looking at the child.

Before Laura can answer, a loud, bellowing noise shatters the peace we had in the house. I stand quickly as Laura runs to the door and braces it. A light quake knocks me down on the ground and makes a few glass containers shatter on the floor. It lasts for a few seconds before the ground stops shaking.

"Is everyone okay?" I ask as I stand.

"The magic has gotten stronger," Lynnet says, running to Laura, who is still bracing the door.

Laura grabs Lynnet and hugs her, "Do not worry, child. We will get out of here."

I run to the window to see no corpses, monsters, or terrifying creatures outside. I look at Laura and say, "The coast seems to be clear. Grab the essentials—we are leaving now."

"Where would we go?"

"To the only haven in this town, the cathedral," I respond, giving her a reassuring smile.

"How do you know it's safe to go there? We just came from

that part of town. I think the smart thing to do is leave through the main gates."

"I know for a fact that out there in the woods there is a monster that we cannot beat, at least, not now. And I was sent here to take these supplies to the cathedral and provide aid. So, my mission is to make sure that cart out there makes it to its destination and to save people on the way." I walk to the staircase and say, "Oh, before I forget! I am the best at escorting people to a destination!"

Lynnet and Laura look at each other, then quickly look at me and nod their heads. I smirk and wink at them, but as I go up the stairs, I feel like I will throw up in fear and uncertainty.

Wind, Lightning, and Fire

I wake up Erol and tell him to get ready to move out. In turn, he smiles and grabs me, pulling me into the bed with him. "My cub, can we nap here instead? See, we are warm and comfy!"

"I will eat your food if you do not move from this bed, Erol," I say, pushing him away.

He lets me go, jumping out of bed as he stretches happily. I glance at his body and see that all his wounds are fully recovered, and he only has a chunk of fur missing and a mark where he got impaled by the accident.

Erol notices and starts to flex his muscles in front of me. "I impress you, do I not? Touch my body and see how I have no injuries! All because of dragon marrow, and as you slept, I fed you some so you could be as strong as me!" he exclaims as he turns to flex even more.

I throw his undergarments and pants to his face as I walk away from him and climb down the ladder, unimpressed. As I leave, I can hear him whisper to himself, "My cub is impressed. I do good."

I reach the bottom of the ladder and see Laura and Lynnet packing some vials that have an eerie glow to them, a few scraps of food, a small cauldron, and what looks like a few plants and clothes. Erol walks down a few minutes later, dressed, with a cocky look on his face. He nods his head at the girls and, with a glimpse at me, winks and smiles. I raise my eyebrow at him and stare blankly, thinking what I might throw at him that would hurt. "Are you done?"

He keeps smiling and walks to the door.

"Are both of you pretty ladies packed up already?" I ask as I check my pockets.

"Yes, I managed to salvage all the medical supplies we have here and the ones in the crate," Laura says as she puts a few vials in her bag and Lynnet's backpack.

I see Erol look out through the barred window. He takes a long sniff and walks to the door, slowly opening it.

"Mhmm, thunder clouds, the rain might quench the fire in this town," Erol says to me as he walks outside. After a few seconds, he returns and informs all of us that the coast is clear.

I walk out to the darkness of the outside, which reminds me of twilight. When the sun is almost entirely set, the burning houses' light gives enough illumination for me to see. I turn to the cart, which is still a few feet away from the house, dented and stained with blood. The landscape is filled with destroyed houses, while others are engulfed in flames. The bodies that once surrounded the houses are gone without leaving a single trace. The smell of smoke and pestilence burn my nose as I breathe, making me nauseous, but I shake the feeling and walk to the cart.

Upon reaching it, I examine it with great care to see that it, miraculously, is not thoroughly damaged. There are a few dents and broken railings, but the frame is still intact. All it needs is a wheel changed, and there is a spare under the cart. I tap on the wood, pulling myself onto the cart while doing a front flip.

"No monsters here," I murmur as I move a bit of debris on the back to check the rest of the broken boxes. All the weapons, magic, armor, and food crates are still there and unopened. A few medical containers are gone but accounted for. Laura and Lynnet somehow must've gotten them inside after they saved us. I wonder how they moved them. These boxes are heavy enough to make a grown man think twice about lifting them.

I examine the site and walk toward the crashed horse to see our horse mangled and half eaten. I close my eyes and shudder at the thought that if Laura had not saved us, we would be dead, or worse.

"Cub! Look, we are in luck. A wheel under the cart, and it is in rolling shape still."

Lynnet walks up to the cart and creates a small orb that follows her above her shoulder, providing light. Then she jumps up on the back and begins to rummage around. "Miss Laura! There are boxes of books here and scrolls. Teacher Olm taught me how to read these!" she says excitedly as she looks in the magic boxes.

Laura follows her and says, "Be careful! There might be other items in there that can harm you! Please get down. Mr. Erol is trying to fix the cart."

"It is easy. My strength holds even a dragon!" Erol says as he deadlifts the cart.

I scoff at his confidence and find a wooden beam to put underneath it. With a grunt, Erol places the cart on the beam and claps his hands clean.

"Are you okay, big guy?" I ask as I move away, looking at his bandaged hands and neck.

"Of course!" Erol says as he squats to grab the new wheel underneath.

As he gets to work, I look to the dark sky, thinking about what else we might encounter, and I can't help but wonder if it's still nighttime.

Erol and I arrived early in the night, but some time has passed. As the smoke shifts above us, I see a low, gray light that reminds me of a barrier trapping the smoke, clouding any outside light source. I sigh quietly, lie down on the ground, place my ear to the broken cobblestone road, and concentrate.

I can hear Erol's movement clearly, and Laura is pacing back and forth. I take a deep breath and close my eyes. Other than hearing Erol and Laura, I can feel a faint tremor getting stronger and stronger. The vibration has an odd pattern as if it is being made by more than one entity, and then I hear a loud rumble and vibration that make me open my eyes and get on my feet.

I walk up to Erol and ask, "How quickly can you change the wheel?"

He turns to me with a few screws in his hand and a few nails in his mouth and smiles, saying, without dropping one, "With my recovered strength? In no time! Now go fetch me a drink. I thirst for fun times." He gets back to changing the wheel.

I keep looking in all directions, worried about how calm it is. I pull Coal out of its sheath to see if it has any visible damage, but my mother's craftsmanship is second to none. After inspecting my sword, I check my gear and bag once more. I murmur what I have: extra throwing knives, flint and tinder, a few small unbroken syringes filled with anti-venom, a small round container that has aloe extract, a few vials of the ever-helpful potion that can numb even a broken leg in a few seconds and an empty syringe attached next to it, rations that I can make last for around three days if needed, thin Knitting Guild–grade rope (about ten feet of it), cloth and a sewing kit, and, last but not least, a strong hook that, with enough force, can attach itself to any surface and help me climb with ease.

I finish looking at the contents of my bag and glance at my

surroundings again. Erol is finishing up setting the wheel on as Lynnet and Laura check the magical crate's content with great interest, naming a few of the items as they come across them. I pull my notebook out, and a map falls out of the pages. I quickly open it and see a topographical map of White Wood as I pull my compass out. If my calculations are correct, we are close to the cathedral, which is downhill from us.

Everything seems to be going smoothly, and all I can think of is, the faster we make it to the cathedral, hopefully, the safer we will be.

Suddenly, a bright crack of lightning, followed by a deafening thunderclap, makes all of us flinch and cover our ears.

"Loud!" Erol says as he sniffs the air. "Cub, how will we move this? I can push, but the ground is wet, and I might slip!"

Before I answer, Laura comes up to him and says, "Erol, can we turn the cart in that direction?" Laura points toward a downhill path that goes deeper into the city. "The cathedral is in the middle of the city, and it's a direct path downhill from here. If we can control the speed, we won't need a steed to move."

Erol seems worried but agrees to the idea and says, "There is a braking speed stick in the cart. We can use it to slow the two back wheels down."

Laura puts a quizzical face and says, "Braking speed stick?"

"It's called a brake, Laura. Imagine a clamp on a wheel." I jump on the cart and point it out to Laura. "It closes on the back of the wheel, slowing the rotation of the wheel to a full stop if we want to."

"Ingenious," Laura says as if fascinated by the concept.

Lynnet pulls out a lantern and gives it to Laura. "Do we need light?"

I jump off the cart and say, "I don't think it is a good idea.

We do not want to attract any unwanted attention." I look up to the smoky sky.

"Won't we be blind in the dark?" Laura asks as she puts the lantern down.

"Erol here can see well in the night. Anyway, there is an ominous light that the fire in this city provides, and I can see around twelve feet in front of us. We should be fine."

A strong gust of wind hits us, the smoke clouds above us start to churn malevolently, and the weather seems to be turning worse with each passing second. We all flinch as lightning strikes a house, and it combusts around fifty feet away. As we all shake off the scare, I turn to look at the newly burning building and fall deathly silent. A figure stands where the lightning hits, glowing bright orange with a yellow aura, moving erratically. Its body seems to be made of stone debris and connected by the bright light itself. It is as if a stone statue erupted and was glued back together.

Laura gasps loudly and screams, "It's a storm elemental! How is that possible?"

Both Erol and I snap into action and start to push the cart toward the slope to take us to the cathedral. The cart is heavy, and even though the wheels work, they're lightly damaged, making it harder to push. I turn to look in the elemental's direction, only to see it has vanished, but in its stead, I can see a few walking corpses shambling their way toward us. The sound of Laura's yelling must have called them out.

I remember reading about elemental beings at the library. They only appear in a location when there is a shift in magic, allowing massive amounts of energy to create a consciousness of their own. For them to happen in nature is extremely rare. Then again, after witnessing the monsters here, I should not be surprised. They can also be made with a magic user trapping unstable energies and restoring a consciousness for them, usually used to serve the said person.

"We have incoming, Erol!"

Lynnet points in a panic and says in a shrill voice, "What is that!"

Erol's ears move to pick up all the noises, and with a grunt, he quickly says, "Flapping wings! Coming our way!"

Lynnet screams in fear, and Laura yells at us urgently, "Look out!"

Erol and I turn to see a volley of javelins lit in flame, headed straight toward us. Without thinking, we both move out of the way, evading the incoming projectile. Both Laura and Lynnet hide under some boxes, the boxes just barely getting hit by them.

"What in the gods' names is attacking us now?" I growl loudly.

"My cub, it looks like flying lizards! Fan out a second volley!" Erol yells as he throws a box to the cart, missing the girls.

Before we can react to the incoming hail of javelins, an enormous stone wall blocks the attack.

Laura starts to laugh loudly and shakes her fists in triumph. She then says, "By the gods, we lucked out! This magic box is full of protection scrolls!"

Both Erol and I look at each other and then turn our gaze toward her.

She continues, "Geotectonic scrolls, made from elemental magic, and—"

"Is there anything in there that can help us move this damn cart?" I yell as the wall starts to crumble.

Laura nods and quickly searches for more scrolls. "Oh, yes, yes, let's see."

The stone wall is close enough for me to use my body to push the cart, but of course it will not budge.

"Did you glue the wheel to the damn floor?" I ask Erol in a huff, only for him to growl and bite the wood of the cart. I turn my attention to the wings flapping closer as more projectiles keep hitting the wall. These creatures' cries remind me of an eagle screeching into a funnel, making it more profound and somewhat terrifying.

"Why aren't we moving?" Lynnet says hurriedly as she tugs on Laura.

"My child, I do not know. Now, help me find something to move this cart, a zephyr scroll or an explosion scroll!" Laura says as her hands tremble in a panic, sifting through boxes.

Lynnet moves around with her stuffed animal, helping Laura. She tries to move a box, but seeing that it's too heavy and that there is a vertical stick in the corner impeding her from moving the box, she says to Laura, "This stick! Is this the brake?"

Laura glances and tries to move it. Lynnet stops suddenly. "Miss Laura, it smells different," she says as she looks at the sky. "It smelled like when daddy took me to the summit of the mountain, and the lights in the sky seemed to be swimming."

Laura struggles to move the brake and says, "By the gods, why is this stuck here?" Not paying attention to Lynnet, she takes a closer look. "It's stuck!" She stops abruptly. "It smells odd, and my ears popped." She turns and shocks herself when she puts her hand on a metal plating covering a box next to her. Her attention goes to Lynnet, who is looking up at the sky. She glances up and gasps in horror, "Lynnet, get down! Erol, Ruffus! Brace yourselves!"

I look at Erol, who is pushing the cart, and suddenly, a loud, thunderous roar explodes behind the stone wall, throwing us clear to the front of the cart. The impact makes Laura hit the brake with her back, making it move a few degrees down. A click is felt in the cart, prompting it to roll down the declining road.

I shake my head and see the cart rolling toward me, about to flatten me, but I quickly move out of the way. The storm elemental pulverizes the stone wall and starts to release small bolts of lightning around its vicinity.

"The brake!" Erol says as he gets up, panting. "I forgot to release the brake! My cub, I know now why the cart moves with difficulty!"

I roll away from the elemental and start to run toward the cart that is slowly but surely picking up speed. Erol catches up to me and says, "Did you hear, my cub?"

I pant as I sprint. "Remind me to"—I keep panting—"kill you when we get to the"—the cart is five feet away from me—"damn cart, you stupid—"

I can't finish my angry, colorful sentence since both my feet are not on the ground anymore. It feels as if a gust of wind has picked me up, or the shockwave of an explosion right behind me has thrown me in the air.

With a dizzy trip and a painful landing, I roll, hitting a ceramic roof and chimney of a house, while Erol somehow lands in the front seat of the cart, making it move faster downhill with the newly added momentum.

I groan and quickly get up to the top of the roof and think, *Oh, I'm in so much trouble. Why am I always the one to be in immediate danger?*

Behind me, there are flying creatures throwing things at me. Below me, there is an undead wanting a bite of me, and nowhere to be seen is a storm elemental, who for some reason has a personal vendetta against us.

"How can this possibly get worse?"

A roar pierces the dark sky, coming from a row of houses, shaking the roof I'm on.

"By the Three, I should not have gotten out of bed and listened to Erol." I look around and see the next house is a jump away. I grit my teeth, and with all my might, I run and jump, making it to the next roof. "Okay, easy now, let's make it to the cathedral."

Jumping roof to roof, I do front flips, run on walls, use metal bars and wooden beams to cross gaps, and swing around to the following houses, utilizing a clothesline. I keep running, dodging javelins, rocks, debris, and anything that stands in my way.

I make it to a tall building and climb it to see the cart, the cathedral, and the surrounding area. It is a horrible sight. The whole city is, in fact, aflame, with many of the buildings destroyed. I can make out the castle in the far distance. I can see lights moving and odd monsters flying around it. My gaze goes to the cart again, and I see it getting smaller and smaller in the distance. To my surprise, I see a creature following it that resembles a dog that is the cart's size.

A spear lands next to me, snapping me back to reality, inciting me to start running again, faster and faster. Before I lose sight of the cart, I can see balls of fire and glittering movement in the cart and conclude that they are also fighting for their survival. I jump off a roof, rolling toward a clock tower scaffolding to climb it. The height might give me a new perspective on what would be the quickest path to the cathedral. While I climb, I look behind, noticing that the flying creatures are now breaking formation, moving away from me toward the castle's dancing lights.

"One thing less to worry about!" I say cheerfully.

The clouds above me start to churn, and the wind begins to pick up speed. I shiver as a slight drizzle starts to feel like tiny cold needles hitting my face. I make it to the top of the clock tower, and a strong tremor and heart-stopping thunderclap almost knocks me off the roof. The clouds in the sky begin to funnel down as if a tornado is forming. Lightning is dancing above me in the clouds, and I begin to think my idea was not the best.

I bring my attention to a familiar creature sharing the pointy roof with me. The bright silhouette of the elemental begins to move slowly, and I draw my sword out of its sheath quietly. The creature, for some reason, is not paying attention to me, and I conclude that I must be behind it or that I just mastered the skill of stealth. The creature raises what resembles an arm to the sky, and lightning hits it with full force, but it is unfazed. It moves its arm like a tendril in a flash, and a bolt of lightning shoots down, creating a loud explosion.

I don't know if this creature is shooting at the cathedral or the moving cart with my friends, but I won't take a chance.

I quickly charge toward it and aim to cut the rocky part of its arm. Without effort, I slice it with one clean sweep.

A loud boom of thunder comes out of the creature, knocking me back and almost pushing me off the roof of the tower. Lightning starts to escape its body, shooting back up to the sky. The elemental turns around, and to my horror, I see a stone face, and it starts to glow brighter, which gives me the impression that I angered it. The creature points its other arm at me and lets out a flash of lightning that hits me square in the chest. I feel jolts of pain all over my body as I try to stand. To my surprise, it speaks to me in the Elvish language. Its voice sounds as if someone is scratching nails on a piece of glass.

"How are you still alive, human?"

I slowly try to get up, but I find it hard, as my body does not want to obey me, and I keep twitching on the ground.

The elemental raises its hand, creating a ball of crackling energy, and says, "As my master created me to find a human, I will deliver you unto him."

Before it finishes powering up, a giant creature that resembles a grizzly-looking wolf swipes its enormous paw, knocking the elemental down. The beast opens its mouth, releasing an inferno of fire upon the elemental. I regain control of my body and curl up in a ball, covering myself with my jacket, hoping I will not be burned into a cinder. Although I know my jacket will protect me from fire and lightning, I can still feel the heat and pain as if I'm being burned alive.

After the blast, the elemental falls off the roof, screeching on its way down. When I uncover myself, I look toward the beast just to see it staring back at me with enormous, murderous, red glittering eyes. It is, in fact, a wolf, as black as night. It is big enough for only its top half to be on the roof. Its paws are the size of my whole body, while its teeth are as big as a sword and stained with what looks like oil or blood. Out of its nose comes steam, warming the immediate area.

I lie back down on the floor, thinking, This is my end.

I Ride a Mutt to Victory

What I'm looking at is a full-fledged hellhound, one of the most savage beasts ever to walk the land of the living.

The bestiary that I once read said, "Hellhounds are top-tier daemons amongst lesser daemons, an embodiment of rage and conquest. Protectors of archdaemons and great guard dogs for them. Capable of horrible deeds with no resentment, and their weaknesses, other than holy magic, are unknown." That's only a part of the introduction paragraph to a thick chapter of the bestiary book dedicated to them.

The hellhound places his gaze on me and examines my weapons, garments, and panicked face. I feel its hungry eyes looking at me as if I'm a fly on his path, easily shredded. Its sniff is remarkably strong, pulling me with every inhale and pushing me away on the exhale. I slowly start to crawl away when it lets out a howl that makes the tower shake.

I stop moving and lie down again, waiting for my end, when a deep voice that reminds me of Valke's speaks directly to me.

"Look at me," it says in a low growl. "Look me in the eyes, human."

"Y-you can talk?"

"Yes, I talk. Now turn."

I muster all my strength and struggle to stand up. I face

him, glaring at his ruby eyes, holding Coal as if I am ready to defend myself.

"Is it courage in those eyes? Is it fear of death that made you hold your weapon?" The hellhound licks his lips in delight. "Those yellow eyes of yours, they have a type of familiarity to me."

I remain quiet and ready to strike.

It shakes its wet fur, pelting me with the water and making the tower sway. "Well." He moves his head and looks to his side. "I was ordered to bring a human safely to the cathedral." He turns to face me again. "He answers to the name of Ruffus. Might that be you?"

I lower my guard and put my weapon away. "Who sent you, hellhound?"

It speaks in a bored tone. "A human sent for you. A bestlia asked her to recover his 'cub.' Although, to my knowledge, bestlia do not have human children."

"Take me to them, then. Take me to the bestlia named Erol and the human that sent for me, or may my gods smite you, daemon," I order the hellhound, attempting to sound brave and important enough. Little does it know, I'm about to piss myself.

It lets out a malicious laugh. "There is no god here to pray to, human. I made sure of that." It gets its nose closer to me and pushes me defiantly.

I point my sword toward it with a slight tremble.

Its ruby eyes glow a tad bit brighter. "You dare strike your savior? I can smell fear on you, and I can see your hand tremble."

"I got shocked twice by an elemental. I have a bit of a shake," I lie.

The hound's malicious smile is unnerving. "Move, human. My time is precious to me, and you are wasting it."

The hellhound opens its mouth, revealing a snakelike

appendage underneath its tongue, and in a quick motion, it wraps around me, trapping me, and throws me up to the sky. With a gasp, I turn around to see where I might fall, only to meet the hellhound's black fur in my face.

Rattled, I look up to see I have landed on the head of the creature, sliding down to its collar, feeling nauseated. Its fur is oddly soft and warm to the touch, and it's quite pleasant to be on. I take a closer look and see a blue ribbon wrapped around its neck. All I can think is how out of place this is and then grab the fur looking behind to see the rest of the body of the creature. Its hind legs are stable on the tower walls, and the tail is wrapped around what looks like a burnt body.

"Hold on, human. This will be a ride you will never forget."

I see his legs tense up. I feel an urge to grab onto its fur for dear life and whisper to myself, "Please, be gentle."

It lets out a small chuckle, turning its head to tell me, "Not a chance in hell."

The hellhound drops and lands on a few houses, destroying them in the process. With ease, it jumps back onto the tower to the top. Once there, it leaps to the dark sky. The force of the jump makes me feel as if a boulder is on my back, squishing me to the soft fur of the hellhound. At the peak of its leap, the weight of the metaphorical boulder dissolves, and I take a glance to see where we are.

I can't see much, for the smoke is blocking my view, except dim lights below me. The hound moves its whole body in joy and lets out a loud howl that shakes me to my core. I start to feel nauseated again as we slowly begin to descend.

"Going down all the way. Freedom never felt so good," the hound says in a satisfied tone. "Well, for now."

We start to fall fast, and the feeling of freefall makes my feet tingle as I slam my head on the fur, letting out a muffled scream.

I can hear the hound laughing maniacally at me, relishing my fear. With a loud crash, we land on another row of houses, flattening anything below us. Then I instantly feel the world shake as it starts to run.

"Hold on, I'm racing against it!" it says, as if content.

I take out my face from the scruff and ask, "Who's 'it'?"

I turn my head to see the storm elemental, broken and missing chunks from its body but right on our tail, throwing bolts of lightning at us.

"Take out that sword, human. Entrap it within!" the hound commands me as he flips in the air, dodging lightning bolts and other attacks from the elemental.

Still holding on for dear life, I yell at it, "What do you mean?"

Picking up speed, the hound says, "I smell blood on that sword. You have slain one of us with it. Now it is an artifact of unholy proportions. Use your powers to trap it!"

I pull out my sword, looking at it quizzically. I do not feel any power in it or new magic. I look back and yell, "I don't understand what you're talking about!"

The hound jumps onto a row of houses, flipping again in the air, dodging bolts of lighting and revenants on the ground. "No time to teach you."

I can feel anger in his tone as he squishes a revenant. "This ends now," the hound says as he turns around to face the elemental. With a roar, he opens his mouth, releasing a hellish flame that consumes all in its area, even the elemental.

A loud explosion comes from the direction the elemental is in. I look around the daemon's head to see the magical creature on the floor sparking weakly, yelling obscenities in Elvish toward us.

The hound hops on top of it and licks his lips in delight. With a victorious howl, he begins to devour the fallen foe. The sound of crunching stone against teeth and the elemental's screeches echo around us, and in a matter of seconds, I hear a low roll of thunder, and everything goes quiet as the elemental comes to an abrupt silence. After he tilts his head and swallows, the hound's hair becomes prickly like tiny needles as they stand up, releasing a slight crackle of electricity jumping around his hair.

"I grow with power. Lightning is now mine to command!" he yells potently. "The shackles that bind me grow weak, but I cannot name myself yet—no, not until I'm released." The hellhound sits and scratches close to where I was sitting. "Time to complete my contract."

The hound stretches and begins to run toward the cathedral at a quick pace.

As we make our way, I muster the courage to say, "Who is your master, daemon?"

He remains quiet.

"Is it Lynnet? She has a toy with red eyes."

"Only by my will does she own me. Now, my snack, I command you to remove the ribbon that is tied to me!" he says as he steps on a revenant in what almost seems like a joyous manner.

I look at the ribbon, and I can feel strong magic on it. "I do not think I can nor should remove it."

The hound scoffs as he keeps running through monsters as if he's not surprised by my answer.

A loud crashing noise grabs both of our attention, coming from behind us, making the hound stop in his tracks in curiosity. I gasp as I hear the hound growl at my old friend, the undead rider. His enormous horse just knocked down a house and charges with great speed toward us. With a swift slash of his sword, he smashes the hound to the side, throwing me off him.

"Undead king, I will devour you!" the hound yells as he recovers and takes a bite out of him.

With another swift slash, the rider cuts the hellhound deep and is thrown to the side, yelping in pain.

The hound coughs up silver blood and lets out a hellish flame, covering the rider, yelling at our new opponent, "You will pay for that!" He lets a war cry out as he charges toward the rider to attack it.

Both monsters are fighting each other with incredible power, but it is a one-sided battle as the rider keeps landing hits on the hellhound over and over.

Awestruck by the fight, I don't notice a revenant creeping up on me until its attack hits me in the back. I turn, and with a hard kick to its chest and a mortal blow to its head, I put the revenant down. I quickly notice that the cathedral is exceptionally close, and if I run for it, I will make it to the doors. As luck has it, there is an army of undead between me and my destination, and all of them look hungry enough to eat me.

I squeeze Coal's handle and decide to make the run. I pull out my sword and smile nervously, thinking about how this will make an unbelievable story if I survive. I start hacking and slashing my way through, dodging claws, grabs, and projectile vomit. Halfway through cutting through my path, a loud yelp comes from behind me, and the hellhound is thrown directly in front of me, blocking my path and bleeding profusely. Our eyes meet just for a second before his roll behind his head and he sighs loudly. I run to my only ally by kicking a revenant's head clear off and making sure I am safe before I feel if the hellhound is still breathing.

"C'mon, get up, you damned dog!" I urge him, but to no avail—the creature is knocked out cold.

The sound of horse hooves slowly making their way closer to me makes me realize how deep in trouble I am at this moment. I turn to face the rider, who is gradually making his way toward me, swinging the massive sword, clearing everything in his way. I start to panic slightly but hold my ground and get in a defensive fighting stance.

"You might be bigger than me and stronger," I say as the rider raises his sword to strike me down. "But know I will not falter." I walk backward and start kicking the daemon, hoping that will wake him up.

The hellhound moves slowly and says to me, "Kick me again, and I will tear off your limb."

"Noted," I say to him as I jump with all my strength and flip backward in the air to land on the hellhound, dodging the rider's sword.

The hound takes a deep breath and opens his mouth, spouting out a hellish flame more potent than before.

I hear the rider cackle in pleasure and his horse whine loudly in pain, ultimately making it back off from us and escape the torrent of fire the hound let loose.

"The smell of charred monster"—the hound coughs— "always whets my appetite." He gives a weak smile and says proudly, "I win this one."

I stare at the giant fireball of a monster running away from us, and I cannot help but think that this was an easy victory. It is an oddity for me to come out of a fight barely injured. I turn to the hound, who is licking his wounds and swaying left and right as he starts to walk toward the cathedral. I huff as I turn around again and look toward the sky, only to notice a thin white figure atop the nearest tower. "Hound, on top of the tower!" I yell as I put my sword away. The hound looks toward me with an exhausted expression and looks toward where I pointed. With an annoyed sigh, he says, "An overstayed guest, a rakefire. There is no end to this torment, is there?"

The thin figure that reminds me of a skinny scarecrow

shoots a bright bolt of light toward the blazing fireball that is the rider, quenching it completely.

"You have to be kidding," I say as the rider turns the horse around, making it charge at us.

"Why must you show me these things and ruin my victory, snack? I have half a mind to let it kill you and break my oath," the hound growls at me.

"Stop referring to me as a snack and look at the rider!" I yell.

Once the hellhound notices the rider, his eyes begin to glow bright red in a fury. "The king returns for thee," he says softly. I jump higher on the hound's back, and, in a huff, the hound leaps out of the rider's way and makes a break for the cathedral at full speed.

"We should be there in a minute!" I say, eager to end this battle.

"I feel that I'm growing weaker. The summoning must be almost up. Damn that child! That mage has forsaken my freedom!" he roars in anger.

"Watch your left!" I yell at the hound as a spear almost impales us.

The rider is a few feet behind us and catching up quickly. I can see the hound trying to be faster, but to no avail. I can tell he is exhausted and injured.

"Got any last tricks on you, snack?"

I turn to see the rider is right behind us, and an idea surges into me. I grab a throwing knife, aim carefully toward the horse's eyes, and say, "Shoot lightning toward my knife when I throw it! If I can hit his flesh and you shock him, that might buy us enough time to escape!"

I jump to stand on the hound, grabbing his hair as my anchor, and, with all my strength, I yell and throw my knife at the rider's horse. The knife's impact pierces through the armor into the flesh of the horse on its front. Simultaneously, the hound jumps, flips in the air, and throws a bolt of lightning that hits the horse and my dagger. The rider comes to an abrupt stop as the horse's leg stops moving, making them fall to the ground.

I hold tightly to the hound's fur as he does his somersault and attacks. I let out a small cheer as I see the lighting connect, immobilizing the horse. The hound lands on the last row of houses next to the cathedral, releasing a loud, victorious howl. "Who knew lightning would stop him?" the hound says aloud.

I look at the rider, who is struggling to get up, and say, "I did not. I hoped it did since if lightning immobilized me, it should do the same to the horse."

The hound laughs. "You put your faith in hope?"

"It worked for us. Now, let's finish him," I say as I pull out my sword.

A bright explosion blinds us both, and I can hear low whispers again, but I can't understand what they are saying. As my eyes focus again, I can see the bright scarecrow creature in front of the rider bowing at us. It spins in the air and shoots a ray of light on the floor, blinding us again.

I hear a small cackle around me, and as I focus again, the rider and the bright creature disappear.

The hound speaks in a low, tense tone, "I will."

The Crew

Never again will I ride this creature. We are less than four hundred feet away from the cathedral, and this hound decides to do flips in the air on purpose so I will fall or throw up, which I do.

"Still conscious, human?" he asks happily.

I glare at the back of his neck and slide off the beast.

He laughs and says, "I'm doing my job correctly, it seems." I ignore him and walk toward the cart Erol and the girls rode down here. As expected, it is empty. It has new burn marks, a few javelins, and arrows sticking out of it.

The hound comes from behind me and pushes me to the ground. I land on my face and quickly roll away from him, holding my bleeding nose.

"Jerk," I mumble as I turn to face him.

The hound sits in front of me and stares at me with his big, glowing ruby-red eyes. "This is the cathedral, human. Your friends and my master are inside. Know that you owe me a favor, and I will ask for it soon."

All the fear I had for this creature is now gone. I raise my eyebrow and say, "What if I refuse?" I stare with anger and wipe my bloody nose on my duster.

He lowers his head so I can feel the heat of his mouth when he talks. "Then I will personally escape from my entrapment and kill your family as you watch, as I did to the little bitch." He looks toward the door, lets out a slight growl, and smiles. "I will be in touch."

With one last howl, he melts into the ground, creating a shadow that tries to slide into mine. I avoid it and see it move toward the cathedral entrance, where Erol and the girls come out to greet me. The shadow moves erratically and fuses with Lynn's own shadow. A small stuffed animal materializes on the floor, and with a sad sigh, she picks it up and holds it tight by the neck.

Erol quickly runs to me. "My cub, you are safe! Thank the gods."

I look at him and see new burn marks on his face and hands. "I'm fine, just shaken up. What about you?"

He whispers to me as he glances back at Lynn and Laura, "The small one is powerful. Be wary."

Laura reaches us and moves Erol away to hug me. "By the gods' grace, I'm glad to see you safe, Ruffus." She takes a quick look at me and gasps softly. "Here, come with me inside. I need to assess your health and see to those burn marks."

We walk toward the cathedral entrance, and I can see Lynn still choking the stuffed animal with teary eyes. She then proceeds to wipe her face off with her sleeves, walking into the building first.

As we enter, I can see two heavily armored guards pushing the doors to a close when we go in. Their armor is of Arcadia, and it looks like it has seen better days. The soldiers look as if they have not rested for days. Inside the cathedral, all the chairs, tables, and statues are now moved to the walls and windows to provide reinforcement.

There are a lot of refugees in this cathedral, most of them bandaged up with old dirty clothes. Some are missing limbs and have no hope left on their faces. Some people of the clergy are singing and trying to lift the spirits, but to little avail. A bishop is giving a sermon and reminding the people not to lose hope and that together as a family, they will prevail, and the royal family will come to aid them.

The cathedral is a mess. The walls are battle-worn, and the ceiling has holes in it, destroying the art that it once held. There is rubble on the floor, and blood splattered everywhere. Each step I take inside feels more like a madhouse where people are just waiting to die rather than a sanctuary.

As we cut the corner, I see bodies stacked next to each other, covered with the nicest linen they could gather. A few refugees are praying next to them as an injured-looking bishop is humming a hymn for the dead. We stop and pay our respects to the departed before we move on to the infirmary.

The bishop comes to us, looking at Laura, saying to her in a low voice, "We lost another soldier. Please come back with me to the infirmary."

Laura excuses herself and, with haste, leaves our side.

Erol nods and says to me, "I will go help the men at the doors. I will be back, cub." He moves away from me as he grabs a wooden beam and makes his way to the front of the cathedral. I look his way and see him relieving one of the guards as he slams the beam onto the door, creating a loud echo.

A handsome young man is kneeling, praying to a statue at the center of the deceased bodies. He looks up at us once he hears the echo of the wooden beam. He seems as if he has just woken up from a nap with drowsy-looking almond-shaped eyes. With a long stretch of his arms, he stands up and approaches us with great interest.

He is dressed in dirty, battle-worn white robes and carrying a book on his worn silver belt. He is almost as tall as me, with a few bruises on his arm and a broken ring on his index finger.

He stares at me with his black eyes with compassion, looking directly at mine as if he has seen something that caught his attention. He quickly runs his hand through his long, jet-black hair to straighten it out and bows toward us, saying, "I see the light as you see mine."

His voice is soft, like a nurturing friend's, which calms me down. I bow back and say, "Likewise, priest."

He looks at me with an exhausted expression on his face and says, "I am your contact from the guild. I was also sent here with supplies by Grande Cardinal Ludwig to aid these people. My name is Michael Ravenholme, at your service."

I put my hand out in greeting and give him a weak smile. "I am Ruffus of Bern, Erol's companion, sent here by Berserker Alan of the Warriors Guild."

He nods and shakes my hand, impressing me with his firm grip. "Yes, your brother-at-arms told me what happened on the road here. We are blessed that you were even able to bring any of your supplies." He looks behind him. "Most of these refugees died because of the lack of supplies I brought, but we have yours, so we should be able to hold on for a day or two. The rations and medicine you brought have saved lives, and for that, I thank you."

A familiar voice speaks up behind me. "And our archmages would have failed to keep the barrier intact if it weren't for you." I turn around to see Clover. A rush of happiness surges through me when I see her, although I can see she has been through hell and back. Her robes are torn, and her face is dirty.

I smile and hug her.

She hugs me back, kissing my cheek, and says, "I am glad to see you live, Ruffus."

We separate, and I say jokingly, "Oh, this? This is a walk in the park. We only almost died twice."

She shakes her head with a small smile and says, "Only twice, huh? Let's hope we all survive the night." Out of her pockets, she pulls out a scroll that is stained with blood. She looks at me and says, "I was sent here by Meister Helena to help on this mission. Now I can try to report back to her that you have made it alive with a supply cart."

I sigh and look at Michael and back to Clover and ask, "What is really going on here?"

A new voice answers my question. "Our sources say necromancy at its finest."

I turn to see a tall soldier wearing a majestic helmet covering her whole face, with an Arcadian's badge on the breastplate. The armor is battle-worn, with many dents from top to bottom. The silver-colored cape is stained in mud and blood and torn in many places. The style of armor tells me that this soldier was a renowned captain of the Arcadian army.

"Good, we are all here," the soldier says in a muffled voice. She takes off her helmet to reveal an elegant, brown-faced woman with wild, frizzy hair. Her hazel eyes glimmer with the light, and her face has turquoise-colored tattoos that remind me of royalty. Her presence alone indicates that she is a natural-born leader with a powerful and somewhat intimidating demeanor. Her voice is commanding, firm but gentle. "I am captain of Arcadian Militia Division Seven. Trist Jasmine Range from the Dunes of Malermont. I was given charge of this mission by the Vice Commander of Arcadia, Leto."

As she talks, I notice that she has a slight accent. Her pronunciation of the letter *a* sounds more like an *o* to me, telling me that she isn't speaking her native language.

I look at her and nod. "Hello, Captain, I'm Ruffus. It is an honor to meet you."

Clover's eyes shift toward me, and I can see the surprise in them at how well-mannered I am toward an Arcadian soldier other than my brother. I have been known to be rude and uncooperative toward them in the past since they declined my application to Academia, the Arcadian school.

"I have heard of you. The tale of your victory over an ascending daemon is quite the story," she says, as if impressed.

I smile and shrug.

Clover rolls her eyes. She interrupts and says, "Necromancy? Captain, we already discussed this."

Trist shakes her head and says, "Yes, but we have new reports and reason to believe a rogue mage has turned to necromancy."

Clover shakes her head and says to Trist, "There is no definite proof yet. We have only seen him once through our scrying."

"Even so, with the facts we do have, it's leading us to believe the latter," Trist adds.

Clover breaks eye contact with her and looks at me. "Thanks to the delivery of your supplies, we can now establish a means of communication to River Front and see what our next course of action is. I will get in touch with the Meister." Clover bows her head and leaves.

Michael looks at me. "Ruffus, you should go get your burns checked. We cannot have you injured on our new mission. Please head down this corridor and down the stairs to the catacombs. Healers are expecting you." He points toward a dimly lit corridor.

"Thank you and excuse me." I nod at both Michael and Trist.

"You are welcome. May you keep the light within you. We will reconvene in an hour or so," Michael says as he turns to leave.

"Rest up," Trist tells me as she heads toward the doors of the cathedral.

As I make my way to the stairs, Lynn runs up to me, grabbing my hand. I look at her, surprised, for when she caught me, a slight static cling zapped both of us. She looks up at me and says, "I am sorry for the puppy. I hope he did not hurt you." Her eyes begin to tear up. "I told him to save you, I promise!"

"Lynnet—may I call you Lynn?" I ask quietly. "Why is there a hellhound listening to and obeying you? Did you summon him?"

She looks forward as we go down the stairs. "When the holes in the sky opened, a lot of monsters came out. Daddy took me out of school and tried to take Mommy and me here to the church." She closes her eyes and holds my hand tighter. "But the puppy was waiting by the gates. He was eating people trying to run."

I stop moving. "Did you name the daemon puppy?" She shakes her head.

We remain still, and I kneel in front of her, looking at her. "What happened next?"

She sniffles and wipes her nose. "When the puppy looked at us, it tried to jump on me, but Mommy—" she whimpers quietly "—Mommy made a wall of light and stopped him. She told me not to be afraid and to only look at her. Daddy said some spells and tied the puppy up, but he got out of it." She chokes on her words.

I caress her face and hug her, shushing her slightly. "Thank you for the story, but if it hurts to remember, you don't have to tell me."

"No, I have to tell you." She shakes her head, choking the stuffed animal. "He ate Daddy," she says quietly.

I keep silent and sit down on the staircase with her.

"Mommy cried and shouted a forbidden spell. Chains of light came out of her and trapped her and the puppy. She took my blue ribbon from my hair and made it longer. She tied it to the puppy and told me his name is 'Puppy,' a baby dog. He yelled at Mommy, cursing her and wishing her to die. Then she kissed me and asked me to cut my hand. She put a drop of my blood on the ribbon and told me to hide until she was done."

I look at her hand and see a scar. My gaze then turns to the stuffed animal, whose eyes glow dimly.

Lynn continues, "That is when the man came out of the ground wearing a black cloak and hit her. She fell to the ground." She wipes her face and stands up, still holding my hand. "The man bit her neck and stabbed her with a dagger, turning her to stone. Puppy's chains disappeared, and he stomped on her."

I stand up and walk down the stairs with her.

"The man disappeared, and the puppy started to walk toward me. He yelled at me to take the ribbon off of him, and I said no. He tried to hurt me but could not get near me. I told him to go away, and he went away."

We make it to the infirmary, and I can see Laura walking up to us with vials in her hands.

"Now, whenever I'm scared or in danger, the puppy comes to me and eats the monsters. I told him not to leave me, so he turned into this." She hands me her stuffed animal.

I take it and observe it. I feel hate, a temptation to kill, a type of primal surge. I shake my head, handing it back down to her.

"That is when I found her," Laura says as Lynn walks away to a chair. "That child saved me from a horde of undead with that thing. But every time the daemon escapes, her hands get burned." She sighs. "I can feel her energy and spirit weaken every time she summons it."

Laura applies ointment on my face and hands and walks me to a sectioned-off area with linen hanging on the ceiling to create a makeshift room. "It's fascinating she opened up to you. She is timid. I only had seen her a few times in school when I taught my advanced alchemy class."

I look at Lynn, who is now walking toward a cot. "Why does she keep it? Why doesn't she destroy it?"

Laura looks up and says, "Maybe it's the only thing left in this world that reminds her of her parents. Her mother was head of the Church of Light across town, and her father was the headmaster of the College of Magic. Both of these places are burnt to a cinder, and I do not know where her house is."

"She is too young to have already suffered so much," I say as I remove my shirt and armor.

Laura's hand glows blue and begins to inspect my chest, and she nods. "People are suffering. It's our job to help them and to try to save them. Now, please lie on that cot. I need to make sure you have no broken bones or torn muscles, again." She looks at Lynn and says, "Honey, please give Mr. Ruffus some privacy. Go help Bishop Dustin with the new medical crate."

Lynn gets up and leaves the makeshift room without saying a word, abandoning the stuffed animal.

"You would not know this, but you look like him."

"Hmm?"

She fixes her glasses only to grab my face gently. "You look like her teacher with those yellow irises. The way you carry yourself, although aloof, reminds me of him also."

"Laura," I say abruptly.

I gaze at the stuffed animal and say, "How can a hellhound enter a holy location without being detected?"

She freezes in place and looks toward the stuffed animal. We both remain quiet as its ruby-red eyes glow ominously.

The Plan

After pondering how the puppy can be inside this holy building, Laura tells me not to worry about it after she heals me. I know she will talk to Lynn to see if she put a spell on the doll to allow him to enter this cathedral undetected.

It takes a few minutes after Laura starts for me to feel better physically, but I don't think she can calm my mind. With a gentle pat to my forehead, she asks me to rest. It feels as if I only sleep for a few seconds, but I hear the morning bell on the tower ring as I wake. It is six in the morning. We survived the night with no casualties. The echo of the bells makes the walls shake in the catacombs, making dust fall into my eyes. I look to my side to see Laura asleep in a chair with Lynn in her lap, holding her gently.

I get up off the cot and button my shirt, putting my armor back on as quickly and quietly as possible so I can give them some privacy. As I go upstairs, I smell a faint scent of food and hear the clinks and rattling of silverware on plates. Once I reach the end of the stairs, I look out the barred window and see how dark it still is, even though I know it's morning. I make my way to the cathedral center, passing refugees praying while others eat beans and bread.

I see the archmages sitting in a circle in the cathedral center, emanating a green light that shoots up to the ceiling. Out of this light, four wisps shoot out, hitting the ground, bouncing like a rubber ball, hitting one of the archmages in the face. I pick up the pace to reach them and see Michael, Clover, and Trist, observing the light and the new wisps that appeared. Michael and Clover both sigh in relief and smile at each other when the wisps begin to float again with bright emerald colors.

Trist walks toward one of the floating puff balls and picks it up gently, but in return, it seems agitated and tries to get out of her grip. In the end, the wisp gets free of her hand, and, with a sizzle, it dissipates and drops a piece of parchment on the ground.

She looks at Clover and Michael and asks, "Why did it do that?"

Clover giggles and shakes her head at her. She picks up another gently, and it floats energetically on her hand. It shakes, and with a poof, it dissipates and drops a piece of parchment on her hand. She looks at Trist and says, "You were not gentle."

Trist huffs and says, "It is a wisp. It's magic, not a lifeform."

"Can you prove that, Captain?" Clover asks her quizzically.

Michael interrupts Trist, who looks like she is about to give a speech. "There is no proof that they are alive or dead. We and magic create them. Who's to say that wisps are creatures or just inanimate objects?"

I walk to them and say, "I always thought they were puffs of sugar."

They all turn to greet me.

"Actually, these are mule wisps. They can transport small items through portals or just hold items in place if needed. We created a new spell to produce these creatures," Clover says as she inspects the parchment the wisp dropped in her hand.

"Mages are not gods. You cannot create life," Trist says to Clover sternly.

Clover ignores her and examines the parchment closer. "These seem to be a type of purifying spell scroll, used to ward off chaotic magic and creatures."

Michael walks up to Clover and looks at her parchment with great interest, saying, "These parchments seem to be written with paper from the bark of one of the saplings from the Sanctuary of the Hierophant, a holy place only high-ranking members of the church may enter. See how it glows faintly, and the markings on the corners," he says as he points at it. "This is a treasure on its own. And, yes, Mrs. Hearth, these are potent miracles written and imbued on this parchment against chaos. This miracle reads . . . 'Shield, protection, and null chaos of the one.'"

Michael gently grabs the parchment from Clover. "As the text states, they are fantastic wards against chaos. How incredible. This is the same practice we use to contain spirits, corrupted souls, and daemonic creatures."

"Don't we need priests to activate these miracles?" Clover asks.

"No, that's the beauty of it! Usually, we would need holy ash and attuned people to cast wardings or shields, but even someone with no practice or ability can cast this mighty miracle. The pope must have created these. Only a man with such divine attunement can even attempt such a wondrous feat!"

I walk up to a wisp that is lazily floating in the air and gently grab it. The warm feeling in my hand gives me goosebumps. The wisp calmly shakes and, in a puff of smoke, drops a parchment on my hand. Clover and Trist observe me as I turn the parchment around. A small map of White Wood is etched on the back with four small Xs scratched around.

I walk up to Clover and Michael. "Look at this."

Clover takes my parchment and observes it. Both Michael

and Trist turn their parchment around and see that they have a similar map.

Trist speaks up and says, "Well, it seems obvious what our mission is." She looks at us. "A simple delivery to these locations and activating the parchment."

"Agreed, and I have an idea!" Clover says as she grabs the rest of Michael and Trist's parchments and the last wisp. "Michael, help me with a small miracle."

He nods, facing Clover. "Ready, Mrs. Hearth?"

They both close their eyes, and a circle of light appears underneath Clover and blows a gust of calm wind in every direction. The voice of Bishop Dustin echoes around the room, saying, "Muses and priests, pray for hope!"

The cathedral instantly becomes brighter, the statues glow in low blue light, and a rush of hope and faith floods my senses, making me feel safe as if all my problems are once again gone. The sensation of peace engulfs the cathedral.

Both Michael and Clover gasp loudly and open their eyes, now milky white. One last gust hits me, and I instinctively put my arms out to catch Clover, who falls into them as if on cue.

Trist rushes to Michael and catches him before he hits the floor.

Clover opens her eyes again, showing me her emerald iris with a hint of gray, a new color for her. She stands on her feet again, thanking me for catching her. I nod and look at Michael, who seems to be saying the same to Trist.

With an exhausted sigh, Clover says, "We have warded this cathedral, and it is now the central location for these parchments. When activated, the magic will bounce back here, providing a safe path for refugees to travel to the activated parchment areas. Simply put, imagine we made a big bubble around this cathedral. As the other parchments are placed in the respected areas, the protection 'bubble' will widen and become stronger."

Clover hands the parchments to Michael, who looks unfazed by what happened, and puts them in his pocket.

"Mrs. Hearth, this means I need you to remain here from now on until we finish this mission, understood?" Michael says as he puts his hand on her shoulder.

Clover nods, breathing heavily.

"The archmages, knights of Arcadia, holy men and women, will protect you. I know they will," Michael assures her.

I look at Clover. "What is he talking about?"

Michael says, "I mean that everyone in here, especially Clover, became a prime target to whoever wants to destroy White Wood. If Clover and the priests die, the hope and faith charging this parchment will become null or, worse, expand uncontrollably."

"Wait, what?"

"I became bound to this magic or miracle, Ruff. If the parchments get destroyed, I will feel the magic backlash. I would be the new host of the spell, and I would be able to displace it with the help of the holy men here to avoid a divine rift or holy rift. If a rift opens here, it would ironically be chaos because a holy would likely enter and would purge this town— and we could not stop it. We need necromancers, warlocks, and moth knights for that."

Erol walks up next to me. "Holy? As in the adversary of a daemon?"

"Yes. Believe me when I say holies are as bad as daemons. Just because they are creatures of light and taught a man how to perform miracles does not mean they are not dangerous. They might be more inclined to help us, but these creatures think we are tainted, so we will also be in danger if one is let loose."

Clover nods. "Trust me. I will be fine. The only reason I did the binding is that Meister Helena specifically trained me for this type of magic absorption. Even a bishop, if not properly trained, would be inadequate to control the influx of magic if a pamphlet is destroyed. Also, she knows I will not go mad with power if I somehow take the full brunt of energy. If I somehow do, the men of the clergy, the soldiers, and the archmages here have full permission to put me down. If worse comes to worst and we get attacked in here, which is highly unlikely now, these same people will be here to protect me."

I stay quiet and nod toward Clover.

"Well," Trist says, "we have spent enough time on this matter. We have to leave now to contain this situation in White Wood before it gets worse. We have three days before River Front's army arrives. If the situation is not under control, well, let's hope it is." She looks at me, passes her gaze to Erol, and finishes by looking at Michael. "Ruffus, Erol, Michael," she says commandingly, "get your gear and bags ready. We leave in half an hour from now. Ensure you all have everything you might need because we are not returning until we have placed all the wards. Understood?"

Michael nods as Erol cracks his knuckles. "It starts, then," I say.

Behind the Scenes

As we disperse to get ready, I pull Clover to the side and ask, "Hey, I feel as if I'm uninformed. I mean, why White Wood? There are other smaller places where an apocalyptic event such as this might make more sense, not that I wish it on another place. And how did a necromancer get this power to overtake a city as big as White Wood? Not even the Meister of Magic could do this, could she?"

Clover makes a funny face, and I can see her thinking. She sighs and says, "You are correct, Ruffus. Not even Lady Helena is powerful enough to do this. It's the forest. It holds untapped power that not even our researchers and scholars fully understand."

She pulls a small notebook from her bag, opens it, and says, "I gathered this information from the library. Here, let us sit on a bench so I can recount this story."

I nod as I pull out my notebook.

"First off, you have to know the forest known as White Wood—not to be confused with the name of this kingdom also—has always been a magical place, according to history. This extensive forest was created by the Goddess Ann, one of the three daughters of the Three. She forged this place in the Era of Creation as a sanctuary for wayward spirits. This same goddess also created the Ancient Woodland Elder, who became the forest guardian, a shepherd to the lost spirits in these woods, to help find their way back to Elysium, the paradise of the gods, through a spiritual conduit called the Soul Tree. The Ancient Woodland Elder obeyed their goddess well, without fault, and, for centuries, the woodland eldar kept this land safe. Of course, this is all according to sacred texts and documents that were written after the fact. Remember, most of this history was orally told, so the accuracy is questionable.

"The forest was bountiful with fauna and flora, which attracted new forms of life that the other gods had created. As more sentient beings came to the woods and feral humans, orcs, and lost races established themselves, territory here became scarce. The loss of habitat made some creatures go on a rampage, killing each other for a food source. The Goddess Ann was saddened to see her creations die, so she asked a few chosen eldars to make the ultimate sacrifice for her, and she turned them into pale white trees, making them part of the forest and new conduits for the spirits to return to Elysium. This sacrifice also diminished the woodland eldars' consumption of resources and restored a small piece of balance to the forest.

"But the forest's resources began to be exploited more by new invasive species, so, in turn, Ann unleashed her pure wrath on the intruders, for she had sacrificed most of her people to fix the balance. She created new, mythical, dangerous creatures to hunt invaders while the remaining eldar attempted to reclaim the land. Her latest creation did their job well and hunted, but these new creatures turned on the eldars, killing the remaining few, to her surprise. The eldars prayed for Ann to control her creations, but she could not take free will away. There was slaughter and carnage for decades to come. The deaths created corrupted spirits seeking revenge on the living and the goddess. The energy from these spirits created the first daemonic rifts to open, releasing daemons into the forest. This created more chaos and the introduction of magic to this continent."

She turns her page, only to sigh.

"One day, a lonely woodland eldar child sat down next to a pond to pray to the goddess for forgiveness, for the invaders, and for peace in the land because her clan was close to extinction. The child became saddened by the silence. She stopped praying to her and devoted her time to easing the spirits in the forest. Her discovery allowed her to turn the enraged spirits into seeds, giving them a new life, calming them. She became quite skilled at managing them and revitalizing the forest. The shift of magic she created attracted animals to her, and with the help of the spirits in the woods, she was able to understand all manners of creatures. She developed the ability to communicate with the white trees, which taught her about souls' and spirits' power.

"The spirits one day whispered to her of the old, potent magic of creation only practiced by the gods. She began to practice this magic with the help of flora and fauna, who sacrificed their lives to increase her power, making her the first to practice druidism in this continent."

"She became a druid?"

Clover nods and continues, "She had the ability to directly commune with the forest, create nature, heal diseased trees and animals, and transform into different creatures to cross the forest easily. With her new powers, she made new prey adapted to survive against predators, changing their behavior and hunting patterns. This created the balance that was missing in the forest, a balance in life and death. Thanks to her, the remaining eldar launched a strong campaign and started recolonizing and restoring what was destroyed.

"Ann became outraged because her creation, the woodland eldar, forgot about her and now revered a mortal. The goddess created new, more fierce creatures to kill the child, but the druid was clever, and for each creature created by the goddess, she created a prey or a new predator to counteract it and keep the balance in the forest.

"As old age crept up on her, she decided to teach animals, eldars, and other species about druidism so the forest would be forever protected and they could help reforest lost areas of the continent. In the end, time was the one to take the druid's life. When Death was sent to collect her, the Three did not allow her to be taken. The Three decided to meld her body into the enormous pale tree known as the Soul Tree, and, as her body decomposed, it created a new layer of bark known as Druid's Roots, located deep in the forest where only chosen druids would find it. I sadly cannot prove or disprove the existence of the location, so as of now we will believe it folklore. This tree became immensely empowered and is now a beacon of life that helps wayward spirits and the corrupted find their way home with more efficiency. This tree also charges the forest with an immense amount of magic, making it enchanted with life, calming the goddess. Now, she is remembered for creating the race that created druidism.

"For centuries, White Wood Forest became a playground for magic users. The free flow of magic helped students practice and hone their craft more easily. This attracted other kingdoms to try to conquer it and make its magic theirs."

"Was that the reason I was able to produce a barrier against the revenants?" I say as I look at my gloves.

Clover looks at me and grabs my hands. "These gloves assist with simple spells, and due to the wild magic in the air, even you were able to create something that would take years to master." I snap my fingers, making a small fire spark on the tip my index finger and middle finger. "I won't be able to do this when I leave?"

She shrugs. "I would hope your body remembers the ability, but let's continue.

"War broke out in the continents, and the Age of Conquering began. Kings ordered mages into the forest to drain it of its magic, and so they created destructive spells powerful enough to level entire cities. Druids in the forest fought back to save as much as they could, but it was for naught. Most druids were killed or captured in the war. Because of this, the spirits that died could not find their way back home. Holy magic was then used to dampen other types of magic, rendering the druids' power useless. This created a shift of balance in the forest. Unstable chaos started again, allowing more rifts to open and more daemons to enter the world. The forest then learned and adapted, using holy magic to counteract the chaos. This action accidentally created even more holy rifts, allowing angelic beings to enter our world, causing an apocalyptic event in the woods as these ethereal beings fought. After years of fighting, the last remaining druids found Druid's Roots and prayed to the first druid to restore balance. The first druid answered their prayer, and the tree bore a single fruit."

"How did holy magic dampen natural magic?" I ask.

"The purpose of that school of magic is to nullify all other schools of magic. It's a potent suppressor."

She continued, "The druids, overwhelmed with happiness, thanked the goddess and the first druid as they shared the fruit. This gave them a boost of strength, made them faster, and gave them the edge to save the forest and drive the war out. Such power allowed them to be corrupted by daemons and holies, for now, the druids wanted to restore other forests by killing their inhabitants and opening more rifts. They once again found Druid's Roots and prayed for more power to aid their new allies. The tree bore one last fruit, causing the druids to fight for it in bloody carnage. When the last druid left standing ate the fruit, he became sick and transformed into a hideous creature that could not see the light of day as a punishment for their lack of respect to their fellow druid.

"Hundreds of years later, nomads moved to the forest and created a small settlement at its edge. The impure spirits and the lone surviving druid began to prey on the new colony. He lured children deep into the forest, where he would feast on their blood and flesh, for all other creatures adapted to the abomination and were too quick to be hunted. One child was able to escape this beast but was mortally wounded by the druid. Running away from him, the child stumbled upon a Druid's Root and felt its warming embrace. He prayed to the tree not to save him but to save his tribe from the monster. As the child finished praying, he lay under the shadow of the tree, passing away in peace. Touched by the child's innocence, Ann resurrected him as the new predator to hunt the corrupted druid."

"Ann? Not the goddess, but the druid?"

"Yes, I found that odd too. In other scriptures, she had no name until now. Sadly, that's what happens with oral tradition. Anyway, the small child hunted the druid, killing him by draining his blood from his body, making sure he consumed his tainted blood. The child, now tainted, was able to find the Druid's Roots and asked for forgiveness for killing her creation, but there was no answer. Sadly, as the child returned to his village, he found all of his kinsmen dead by the druid's hand. The child, saddened, went back to the forest to live the rest of his life out as a guardian of the Druid's Roots, making sure no one would abuse its power ever again and ensuring the tragedy that happened to him never happens to anyone else."

As Clover comes to a stop in the story, Trist walks up to us, saying, "I'm sorry to interrupt, but we have to get going soon, Ruffus." Trist hands me a flask filled with an odd-tinted liquid. "The alchemist wants us to take this potion to help us guard against disease and the pestilence outside."

I thank Trist and look back toward Clover.

She nods at Trist and tells me, "There is more to this story, Ruff. I will finish it later. Please be safe out there."

I nod and put my notebook away. "If I find monsters I don't know or recognize, I will catalog them and later ask you about them. Might provide more clues on what is attacking the city." I look at the silver liquid in the vial and drink it all in one go. The horrid taste of bitter berries makes me dizzy as I sit back down again.

Welcoming Party

I feel the cold cobblestone floor on my face, and I can smell moss mixed with the iron from my blood next to me. I am face-down on the floor, although I don't remember why, and as I try to move, I feel an immense amount of pain shoot up and down my torso. I slowly move my head to my side, only to see Erol lying down, bleeding out of his mouth and body, with lifeless eyes. His armor is completely broken, with cracks and holes all over, as if Erol was shot multiple times with thick arrows.

I close my eyes and move my head to the front, only to see a tall, glowing, slender figure a few feet away from me, holding Michael by the neck a few feet off the ground. I cannot see what it is, for its body glows brightly, and it blinds me if I stare at it directly.

The figure's voice echoes as if multiple people are talking at the same time. It speaks in a softly raspy voice, "The light you hold has failed you."

The figure squeezes Michael's neck harder, engulfing him in black flames. Wailing in pain, he kicks the figure to let it go as hard as he can. Out of the corner of my eyes, I see Trist charging toward the creature with full force, smashing into it with her shield, only to meet an unmovable force. With a slight chuckle, the figure picks Trist up by the neck with its long free hand as if she weighs nothing. In a flash, fire combusts on Trist's body as if she's made of oil, consuming her completely. She only screams for a few seconds before her body stops moving. Seeing this, I again try to stand up but fail miserably at the attempt. I look again at Trist and the monster who's examining its fresh kill, tossing her aside.

"A valiant attempt made by her, but I only need you and the other two," it says to Michael, who is pale as snow and moving sluggishly.

The creature walks in my direction with a severe limp. I feel my skin burning as it gets near me. I try to crawl away, but my body has become as heavy as lead.

"You," the creature says to me as he kicks Erol's body away. "I need you to tell me where the others are, and then"—the beast picks me up by the back neck—"I will save all of you."

My body catches fire out of nowhere, searing my skin.

I look into this creature's eyes, only to see two empty sockets staring back at me as my world goes dark.

I gasp myself awake, clutching my sword in my hand, jumping off the bench I fell asleep on. I quickly look around my surroundings to see that I am still in the cathedral. People around me are watching me closely with weapons in hand, murmuring. Erol walks up to me with a smile on his face, followed by Michael, who has his eyebrows raised at me, and Trist, who has a stern look on her face.

"You wake! Tell me, did you win the battle in your dreams, cub? You were groaning and swinging your weapon!" Erol says as if he is proud of me for fighting in my dreams.

I wipe the sweat off my face and sheath my sword back in place. With a light huff, I sit back down. "Yeah, I won," I lie. "Last time I take a potion-induced nap in this place. Gave me a nightmare." I reach down to my belt and open one of my pockets, retrieving the small charm my father gave me. It glows dimly, warming my glove. I whisper to myself as I look at the trinket, putting it away in the pocket again, "Daemons."

Clover walks quickly toward us from the back and says, "Everyone is here and awake, good. Well, the archmages have created these hoop earrings for all of you." She hands all of us a pair of earrings. "As you can see, they are made out of pure copper with two small gems, moonstone and apatite. These enchanted pieces of jewelry are connected so you can communicate if you get lost or separated, and the closer you are, the clearer the communication will be. To use them, all you have to do is talk normally and touch them." Clover moves her hair with her hand and shows us the earring she has on. She proceeds to grab it with her index finger and thumb on the back of the earring. "I will be here in the cathedral giving you readings and scrying to help you on your journey. Also, if you meet a monster that you are not familiar with, describe it to me the best you can so I can record the finding and help find a weakness. If you have any other questions, the archmages and I will be here to give you a swift answer."

"Thank you, Mrs. Hearth. Were you able to establish a better link of communication with River Front?" Michael asks as he pierces a hole in his earlobe with a small needle.

"Yes, we were successful by using the supplies Ruffus brought. And as a bonus, we were lucky enough to make enough weapons and items to defend ourselves in case of an assault on this cathedral," she assures us.

Michael holds both his hands and whispers, "Thank you, and the Three, for your blessings."

"Praise them indeed, priest," Trist says as she replaces her earrings with the new ones. "The guards are ready to open the doors. Let's get moving."

Clover looks at me. "The first location you will be heading to is the Castle Town District of von Klausen, north of this location. Take this compass—it will help guide you." She pulls out a map from her pockets and opens it. "This is where all of you will enter the royal castle and place any of the wards you have in the throne room. Once activated by any of you, it should provide us access to any refugee and important figures left alive to come here safely. Remember, if you see any refugees, send them our way and we will help them. If they are unable to travel here, Michael will mark the location with tracking miracle so we can send a rescue party once the ward is active."

"Got it." I nod.

Clover hugs me. "Now, Ruff, go with them and come back alive."

I hug her back and say, "Be safe, you smelly elf."

She smiles. "I will, you disgusting swine."

The cathedral gates open, and our party of four walks out. Trist takes the lead, followed by Michael, who stares up to the sky, looking uncomfortable. I catch up to Erol, who is waiting for me, and we start walking closely behind Michael.

Erol gets close to me and whispers, "We can trust them, right?"

"I would think so. They're both here for the same mission as us," I whisper back.

As we head north toward our destination, we do not encounter monsters, daemons, or scary riders. The only constant is the sound of Trist's armor clanging and our footsteps on the bloody cobblestone road. Once in a while, we hear yelling from far away and the sound of roaring monsters. We stop and check our surrounding area, but nothing meets us.

The sky above is covered in smoke clouds, creating an unsettling smog. Our only light sources are the burning houses around our area, a giant green pillar coming from the cathedral that is shooting up to the sky, and a tiny oil lantern that Michael carries on his hip. As I look back toward the cathedral, I see faintly glowing, small wisps floating around lazily.

Trist pulls out the ward she was carrying and looks toward the front. She ponders for a quick second as I walk up next to her, handing her my compass. In return, she gives me a quick nod and takes off her helmet to see better. She stops abruptly, looking around, beckoning all of us to get closer. She murmurs something to herself and then speaks in a low tone to us. "According to the map, we should be getting near our first checkpoint. We are around nine klicks from von Klausen, yet the mist is not letting me see the castle that should be right in front of us."

Michael looks around also. "Is it odd that we have not encountered anything yet?"

I shift my gaze at Erol. "Do you smell anything new?"

Erol sniffs the air. Giving a slight cough, he wipes his nose on his shoulder and says, "Nothing new, my cub. Only the smells of smoke and decay."

"Well, then, let's change that. I would not want us to become sick because of this pestilence," Michael says as he fumbles with one of his belt pockets. He pulls out a small, round, silver object with a long, thin string that reminds me of a spider's web, opening it up to quickly close it again. "This should do," he says as he points at the silver object. With a brief chant, a small spark of flame erupts from his fingertips.

The small orb starts puffing out smoke. "What is that?" I ask.

He looks at me, surprised, and says, "It is some medical incense, from a compound of antidotes and immune-boosting plants. Alchemist Lauralee Rye gave me some just for this occasion." Michael starts to gently shake the incense holder, allowing more smoke to start pouring out of it.

Erol walks up to Michael and sniffs the air around him. With a contented sigh, he says, "It smells of jasmine and lavender combined. This is good trinket."

With an approving nod, Michael ties the small incense burner to his belt, letting it hang loose as its mist surrounds us with its sweetness.

Trist abruptly shushes us. "Do you feel that, Priest?"

He looks around and closes his eyes. "Captain, I do not feel anything. We are all alone."

She turns to look at him. "Exactly. I cannot feel your presence, nor our companions'."

Michael opens his eyes, looks around the area again, and says, "You are right. If there is any type of camouflage spell, I can get rid of it."

Trist shrugs. "I would not mind if you were to disenchant all magic around the area. You are the only one who can use magic freely. I can only do a few simple spells, and I doubt I will need them right now."

I walk up to Trist. "Do you think that is a good idea? A spell like that might give our position away, and I, for one, do not feel like fighting a horde of undead."

"I understand your concerns, and do not worry—a disenchant only lasts for a few seconds." She looks around again. "We all know that this place should be overrun, yet here we are, with no foe in sight. I know it's a risk to do such a powerful spell, but we have to make sure we are not being hoodwinked by any concealment charm or, worse, an illusion."

Michael beckons us as he stands next to Erol. "For this disenchantment to work, I need all of us to clear our minds. It will only take a second." He opens an old book that he has hanging on his belt. Quickly, he rushes through the pages to find the correct one. He closes his eyes, and, with a low mutter, he says, "Gone."

A bright aura surrounds him while a wave of light passes through us, heading in all directions. Trist puts her helmet on quickly, then holds her mace and shield out, ready to pounce. Erol and I turn to see if there is anything new in the area. Nothing has changed—no monsters, no invisible ambush. The only difference is that Michael is glowing white and looks confused.

Erol and I walk to Trist, who is still on high alert. I ask, "Are you okay?"

She stands straight and puts her weapons away. "Odd, I cannot feel anyone's aura. It must be an irrational paranoia setting in."

"It's fine. We are all high-strung right now." I put my hand on her shoulder.

She sighs and looks at me. "I apologize for panicking. My training usually never fails me." She looks behind us, and I see her eyes widening inside her helmet. "Where is Michael?"

I turn, and I don't see our bright friend behind us. We suddenly hear loud laughter, followed by a screech. We all take out our weapons as a strong gust of wind blows from the road ahead.

"We need to find Michael!" Trist yells.

The screeching gets louder and louder with each passing second.

Erol yells at Trist while pushing me away. "Move!"

I look behind Trist and see a giant humanoid with bulky iron armor, wearing a fresh skull necklace, running toward us with a gigantic ax in its hands. Its armor rattles every time it steps near us, creating a slight tremor. It raises his ax, spinning it above its head, swiftly crashing it into the ground, creating a small fissure. Out of this hole, little creatures quickly begin to crawl out with various weapons in their tiny claws, mostly daggers.

The undead bestiary calls them *nihldrens*. They're undead creatures around one foot tall, resembling small children with tiny little horns on their foreheads, with eyes as black as night. Bright-colored and fast, they are not the most fearsome creatures, but they can overwhelm anyone who isn't paying attention. These creatures can only be summoned by any magic user who knows the spell and has the will to cause harm.

"Erol!" I yell while pulling a throwing knife out of my jacket.

"I know, my cub! Watch your flanks. They are attacking in groups!" he replies.

The creatures jump toward us in rapid succession. I swing Coal, easily slashing them out of the air, a few of them turning them to dust, returning to the fissure from where they came. I turn to see how Erol is doing, only to see him decapitate a few of his foes in a single swing.

A few nihldrens jump at him, but Erol is quick enough to grab one by the neck, snapping it in a cold, deathly stare.

"My cub! They will keep coming until we plug that hole in the floor," Erol yells as he steps on another one, making it squeak and pop.

I see two of the little pests about to jump on Erol with really sharp-looking spoons. With luck in my hand and cockiness in my throw, I make sure I kill them with my knives. Erol looks at me as he sees what I did, smirking, only to go back to his fight.

I murmur to myself, "You owe me a pint."

To my luck, a small creature jumps on me, squeaking and screeching as he pulls my hood down, effectively blinding me. I flail and knock it off me, only to see my knife on its tiny body before it disintegrates. I turn toward Erol again and see him smiling as he smashes another one as he throws a knife, the blade landing next to my feet.

I scoff and look toward Trist. Gracefully she jumps, spinning in the air, smashing her mace on the giant monster helmet, successfully disarming it. The helmet flies right off, revealing a mountain troll. They are usually around eight feet tall, idiotically strong, but not the smartest of creatures.

"How did a mountain troll summon nihldrens? They can't use magic," I say as I run toward the fissure.

I see a smaller-than-usual nihldren climb out with a fork stuck to its hand. I run toward it, and once I get close enough, I jump off its tiny little head to help me make the fissure gap. While I am midair, I can see the bottom of the chasm, only to see that it is shallow, and Michael is on the bottom, fighting for his life against a horde of nihldrens attacking him. With a bright spell, he is able to eradicate a handful of them to then glance up, and our eyes meet.

A shattered plate of metal flies over my head and lands on the other side as a loud groan quickly follows from the troll. Trist is making short work of her opponents while she has two nihldrens attempting to stab at her feet as one hangs for dear life on her back. She doesn't seem even to notice the minor inconvenience of the little monsters.

Attempting to finish off her opponent, Trist jumps toward the troll with the intent to kill, only to meet the back of its hand, sending her flying. After pushing her away, the troll bellows in anger, making the ax's head glow a faint green hue. It picks it up and begins to slash at the air, leaving streaks of green all around. With one final slash, the sound of ripping paper echoes in the area, creating a jagged, hollow hole midair, where more nihldrens start to pour out.

"The ax!" I yell as I slash a few nihldrens out of the air.

To my surprise, I see Michael through the hole, smiting and kicking a few of the monsters.

"A portal?" I say aloud as I punt a small beast.

Trist blocks a heavy boulder and a slash of the ax from the troll, yelling in anger mixed with pain. In a grunt, she cries toward me, "Ruffus! It's the ax! Get the ax!" She falls to one knee, blocking with her shield. "Disable him!"

I start running toward them when a nihldren jumps on my back and stabs me on the shoulder with what looks like one of my daggers. With a jerking motion, I grab the creature and throw him to the floor, stepping on his tiny head. I look toward Trist, who yells to me for help while shattering the troll's right knee with her mace.

Closing the distance between us, I yell at her, "Brace yourself!"

I pull out a handful of my blinding powder from one of my pockets and get ready to deliver a punch that will hopefully blind this creature.

She steels herself, putting an arm on the floor and straightening her back. I jump on her back, and with her aid, I thrust myself with force toward the troll's face. With a loud yell, I punch the troll hard with a fist full of blinding powder.

With a deafening roar, the troll falls, giving me enough leeway for me to jump off his head, avoiding my own powder's residue. I tug and roll out of the way, squishing a few nihldrens in the process.

Trist smacks the troll's loose grip on his ax with her mace, completely disarming her opponent, and quickly puts her weapon and shield away to then pick up the enormous ax as if it weighs as much as a feather, cocking it back.

"Ruffus, duck!" Trist yells at me urgently.

She swings the weapon and releases it with a force that would rival Erol's swings. The ax flies directly toward the troll and impales it on the head. Both the troll and ax glow a faint green light and then explode, turning into ash. At that moment, the portals created by the weapon begin to disrupt, making the nihldrens run wild and retreat.

She turns to me and says, "Are you okay, Ruffus?"

I check myself and fix my hair. "Better than ever."

She rolls her eyes and says, "We need to find Michael."

"He is in the fissure over there. He is trapped with the little creeps." I point and start to run.

Trist nods and runs behind me as the nihldrens scatter and evaporate. On the other side of the fissure, we see small black clouds forming every few seconds and can hear Erol laughing loudly while he yells for a new challenge from the creatures as he jumps and spins his polearm. I feel him relishing this battle.

Trist reaches the edge of the fissure and kneels in front of it, making sure she does not fall in. Inside, Michael huffs and puffs in exhaustion as he executes some of the creatures around him. Trist reaches down into one of her belt pockets and pulls out a small silver scroll tied in a golden lace.

She yells at Michael, "Hold on!"

The scroll erupts, and a thin silver chain flies downward toward Michael, killing a few monsters on its way down. He quickly looks up toward the chain, sighing in relief. His hand starts to glow brightly, and with a hopeful yell, he puts his glowing hand up in the air, making the spell erupt in a blinding light, instantly disintegrating a few nihldrens while knocking others down. He grabs the thin silver chain with a strong jump. Trist, on her end, pulls him up with the force of a mule kick, launching Michael quite a few feet above the fissure.

He looks down and yells, "Gates to the underworld, I seal you in the name of the Three!"

He points his already glowing hand down as a beam of red light escapes his fingertips, covering the whole fissure. The earth rumbles and the area starts to close. Michael falls back down, but Erol jumps and catches him with a mighty leap. As they tumble toward the ground, a small echoing shriek of death comes from the hole, and all goes back to silence.

Erol and Michael land, and as they separate, Michael's face is fixed toward the sky's darkness with an enraged look. He pulls his book back out and yells, "Don't falter! The skirmish isn't over! There is a mage summoning these abominations. He can open portals and small daemonic rifts!"

A distorted voice echoes in the area, making us look in all directions. "Guess I do not need an introduction!" Laughter reverberates in my ears. "I will make you all dance on top of your graves!"

Michael and Ruffus Throw Rocks

The echoing voice brings a strong quake, making all of us lose our footing. Buildings near us fall, killing a few revenants and whoever else is taking refuge in the structures. Michael attempts to use a counterspell but cannot keep his footing, making him fall flat on his back. The ground cracks violently around our feet, shifting its elevation and creating new sinkholes. I yell out for Erol, but the sound of the crashing buildings and rocks muffles my voice.

I panic and yell to whoever can hear me to stop the mage from moving the ground. Memories from my childhood begin to flood my mind of the time the coal mine caved in, almost killing me. Fear engulfs me as a few fissures open next to me, and I feel an immense tug to fall into them. To my surprise, Michael grabs my leg and pulls me to him. I try to speak, but nothing but whimpers come out.

He quickly slaps me. "Get a grip!"

He then shows me a tall building ready to collapse, and, with my luck, we are in its landing path.

We both help each other stand straight, but a stone smashes into my back, knocking Michael and me toward the fissure next to us. As we both fall into the hole, I hold Michael as tightly as I can and close my eyes, hoping the fall will not be painful and will be deep enough to kill us both on impact.

The feeling of freefalling comes to a stop as I feel a hard crash and the sting of freezing water on my body. I open my mouth to take a deep breath, only to suck in a putrid-tasting liquid. I flail and somehow find myself drowning in five-inch-deep water only to quickly get up, coughing and throwing up the water I sucked in. I rub my eyes to see the same darkness around me with the small amount of illumination from fire and the cathedral's light.

Calming down and regaining my senses, I feel a strong tug on my back and fall back down in the water. Michael is flailing and drowning in the shallow water, attempting to grab anything to help him up. We use each other to stand, coughing violently while we check ourselves for injuries.

"By the gods, where are we now?" Michael says as he puts his hand on his chest, trying to calm his breathing.

I look up and see a broken stone statue. "I think this used to be a fountain."

"Oh dear gods, I swallowed some of the water. I hope no one used this as a washroom," Michael says in disgust.

I keep quiet and remember when I was homeless and used the city's water fountains to clean up.

"Ruffus, are you okay?"

"Yeah, just in shock, that's all. I thought we were dead." I walk to the edge of the fountain and jump off. "What happened?"

Michael follows me closely. "This forsaken town is full of surprises. To tell you the truth, I think we were warped to another area of White Wood." Michael squeezes his robes to get the excess water off.

"Where are Erol and Trist?"

He looks to inspect me. "Oh, Ruffus, you have a deep cut on your forehead. Let me—" Michael places his hand on my forehead and mutters an incantation, ignoring my question.

I gently grab his hand and say, "Don't worry about me. Just help me find the other two."

He nods and pulls back. "By the gods, I hope they are alive and well. Let's count our blessings that we are not dead."

I feel my forehead and run my hand to my ear, feeling my earring. "Clover, I need your help."

In a hazy voice, I hear in my head, "Ruffus! Thank the goddess. What happened? Where are you?"

I quickly explain the situation as Michael uses his magic to dry us off and patch up our injuries.

"I am relieved to hear you both are well. The scryers are informing me that the tremor we all felt was a geomancer in your area. The magic in the forest must have empowered him, but this mage might be one of the reasons for the catastrophe plaguing White Wood."

"Lucky for us, he found us so quickly, then, but how can he create portals? I thought only skilled arcanists could, not an earth elementals mage."

"I cannot answer that, Ruffus. We sadly do not have enough information here to tell you. After the archmages recover from keeping the building stable, we will rescan the area for more magic anomalies. Your mission still takes priority. Find this mage and stop him by any means necessary. Hopefully, that will stop us from using the wards. After you stop him, we can focus on search and rescue."

My earring vibrates, indicating that she disconnected our link.

Michael puts his hand on my shoulder. "Ruffus, do not

worry. I can still feel Trist and Erol. It's faint, but they are still alive. Now, let us continue. I do not know if we are safe here."

I agree and notice we are in the market area. There are vendor stalls, small shops, and blankets with goods scattered around the floor, along with a multitude of dead bodies. Some stalls are destroyed, and others are on fire. Some of the carpets have bloodstains, while others have bodies on them. Michael walks toward a woman's body to see that she is pale and has odd bite marks on her arms and neck. He gulps and shivers as he pulls out a silver necklace and looks at me, fearful.

I kneel next to him and see the marks on her body. "Are these fang marks from—"

"It could be several creatures. Some revenants drain the blood of their victims to try to become whole. The alps from the forest prey on women, and some fairies steal blood to make food. Or aswangs—although rare, they do exist."

"I think it's time we moved from here, Michael," I say nervously as I rub my neck and make sure my sword is near me, but I can't find it on the holster.

I frantically run back to the fountain and see the glimmer of Coal in the water. Trying not to get wet, I reach for it and grab it, thanking the gods that nothing came at me from the water and my sword was near me.

Michael smiles at me and quickly taps his forehead. "Okay, let's think. We are in what appears to be the marketplace of the lower and middle class," he says as he pulls his ward out.

"How do you know that?"

"The marketplace for the wealthy doesn't allow traveling salesman in the area. It's one of the commerce laws put in by our king that was quickly adopted by all other kingdoms."

"That seems unfair, if you ask me."

Michael looks at the little map in the ward and says, "Sadly, many of these merchants are from other continents and tribes that do not believe in the guilds' way, but they can still sell goods. Ironically, some of their goods are extremely valuable and rare. Okay, I think we are here, and our ward location is not that far."

"Think the mage will be there?"

"Half of me hopes so, and the other does not. I'd prefer to purge the evil from this location rather than repress it."

He starts walking, and I quickly catch up to him. "Purge seems like a powerful word."

Michael sighs. "Yes, and it was reinforced by the fact that this geomancer is using chaos from the city and forest to grow in power. Look around you—all these lost spirits and souls we cannot provide a proper burial for. The spiritual energy is lingering and easily tainted, or worse, consumed."

"Still, the word seems too strong for me."

"My job as a priest is to heal spirits, try to mend flesh, and keep order in this world. Although some might cause harm, all living things have a right to live—it's the undead that should not walk on this earth. They have had their time. They need peace so they can reach Elysium or the Soul Tree. I want to provide an environment for good to grow and prosper. All this death and decay is—" he stops as if to think of his next words as he sees a little girl's body "—a shameful waste of potential. That child there on the floor could have been a hero, or that man over there could have—"

The ground begins to shake slightly, silencing Michael in an instant. A familiar roar in the distance makes me gasp in hope and fear.

In unison, we both say "Erol," and we begin a sprint toward the noise. The ground starts to shake more frequently, but we both steel on until I fall face-first on the floor.

I groan loudly and my nose gushes blood. I ready myself and snap it back into place. As I try to get up off the ground, I feel a tight grip on my leg. Quickly, I turn to see a hand made from small stones grasping my leg. Confused, I pull my leg, but nothing happens.

"Michael?" I say as I turn to face him.

He is being held around four feet up in the air by a giant hand made out of stone. The hard part is moving and squeezing Michael, making him groan in pain.

"That can't be good," I say as I look around and notice the bodies on the floor twitching and moving. "This is definitely not good."

Michael lets out a slight hiss that sounds like, "It's worse."

We hear loud laughter coming from somewhere in front of us. As the dust settles, I see an eldar walking toward us. Unlike the common woodland eldar or water eldar, this one has pale grey skin, almost blending in with the darkness, and around him, stones are floating, encircling him. He is wearing a funny-looking costume that reminds me of a jester, but it is stained in blood. The closer he gets, the better I can see that he is wearing makeup, and his costume has a sense of royalty to it. He takes every step as if he's bouncing comically, and even starts whistling as he gets closer.

He laughs coldly and says, "You seem to be in a bit of a bind, Priest!" He circles us, kicking a rock toward my face. "I mean, it is amusing, even for me! You escaped my first trap, which I made just for you! Silly me, to not expect a priest to know necromancy! I mean, c'mon, how would I know a priest from the Grande Cathedral would know how to use the energy of a soul?" He cackles loudly as he again kicks a rock to my face. "I mean, it is genius. You harvested the energy of a dying man, trapped his spirit, let it taint, grabbed a soul, and used the rebound energy to use my portal to reappear in your original spot! Now, that's what I call a reappearing act! Good thing my enchanted ax was stronger and you only partially succeeded." His voice becomes serious. "You killed all of my nihldrens. All those kidnapped children now wasted. You know how difficult it was to trick a child?" He starts to giggle. "Not that hard. They are a dime a dozen if you offer them something good, like toys and candy."

The eldar stops in front of Michael and raises his arm, making a fist. This makes the rock hand squeeze Michael tighter. "I was supposed to kill you one by one, but then again, I love an audience. I mean, I was the late king's jester."

Michael struggles to break free and says with a grunt, "Why are you doing this?"

"For the sake of entertainment! Now it's curtains down for you!" He laughs maniacally and starts shaking his fists, making Michael scream loudly in pain.

I finally grab a knife out of my coat and throw it at the elf 's face. Before the blade makes contact, a stone floating near his face expands and creates a thin rock armor layer. The jester still flinches, and I feel the bind on my leg weaken. I pull away rolling left, and when I get up, I throw two more knives and a small ceramic cup I've picked up from the floor.

The jester jumps back recovering from my volley, raising his palm in the air, creating a wall of stone and dust, deflecting my knives and cup.

Quickly, I use the hilt of my sword and whack the arm that is holding Michael. The earth rumbles beneath my feet and launches me back a few feet, but I'm able to twist my body to land feet-first. I wipe the dust off my face, only to jump away again as small stalagmites jut out of the cobbled floor. The jester starts to laugh, and I can see him point at the ground and raise his finger, creating another one. I am only a few seconds quicker than the stalagmites, and more keep appearing around me.

The jester applauds and laughs excitedly. "My, my! Look at you skip, hop, and jump like a frog! More, I want to see more!" As if he's playing piano, his hands make more and more stalagmites erupt from the ground, and fatigue slowly creeps up on me.

A loud crack, followed by a boom, catches our attention as Michael creates a small implosion, destroying his bind. He falls to the ground, landing skillfully, looking angrier than I have ever seen him. He places his hands on the floor and yells a chant. Time slows, and I feel my legs get a boost of power. I dodge the last attack with a fantastic backflip toward Michael.

He slowly turns to look up at me, "Do you like how fast you moved?"

"Enhancement magic, a speed spell!"

He nods.

The jester creates a pillar around ten feet tall to stand on. Raising his hands, making more stones move around him, hovering.

I ask Michael, "Ready?"

Before he finishes nodding, I run toward the jester, recovered and refreshed with energy. Meanwhile, Michael chants, creating three small light orbs that shoot needle-like projectiles toward the jester.

Amused, he jumps on floating stones, dodging the needle-like projectiles easily, but what he doesn't know is that I am almost in range to attack him. Michael doesn't notice a wall of debris next to him that the jester formed while he was dodging his attacks.

"Priest! After a good show, it is polite for you to clap!"

The jester makes a clapping motion, and the wall of debris hit Michael hard enough to knock him down.

"Michael!" I yell as time starts to catch up to me and my jumps become less potent.

"That's enough entertainment from you now. You have been on for long enough." The jester jumps to one last floating rock as he loudly claps. The rocks blanketing Michael squeeze and compress.

"You are mine!" I yell.

The jester seems surprised about how quickly I make it to him. I have enough momentum to slash him twice on the chest and kick him down off the rock while in the air.

As he falls, he throws a volley of sharp rocks that I'm able to deflect as I fall right behind him. With a thrust, the jester sends a boulder my way, hitting me and making me land next to the pile of rocks Michael is under.

"Enough with this game of rock throwing!" Michael says, miffed.

He again erupts from the ground, making two javelins out of light. With determination, he stabs me with one and throws the other toward the enemy. Shocked, I expect pain, but on the contrary, I feel good, like I got a burst of energy, and I feel time slow down again. I get up and quickly catch up to the other javelin that I have a feeling I shouldn't touch. I pass the light-forged weapon and reach the geomancer, who has a panicked face. Without hesitation, I hit all the vital spots to subdue him. As he slowly falls toward the ground, I sidestep the projectile and let him suffer it. The jester starts to convulse.

Time catches up to me, and Michael makes his way to us. "What was in that?" I ask.

"A speed spell for you and a dazing spell for him."

"What if I touched the other one?"

"I'm sure you'd be convulsing on the ground like our friend here."

"Yikes, remind me never to get you angry, Michael."

He smirks and looks up to the sky with a sigh.

A bright light catches both our attention as the jester teleports away. Michael heaves as he wipes blood off his face.

"How?" I say.

"Impossible," Michael gasps.

"You both have put on a hell of a show for me. Again, you really impress me, Priest. Using the swordsman as your weapon is a smart idea! But this is act two of our play, and it is time for you to die. I will not fail my master. You see, he needs me, and I will bring him all the joy and chaos in this world!" Two red orbs appear on top of his palm and explode, releasing a red liquid around the area.

All the dead bodies start to twitch violently. "I, Malek, command and order thee to rise!"

"For the gods' sake," I say as I turn to see all the bodies moving.

Screaming for Glory

As Malek finishes casting his spells, a gust of ominous wind befalls our immediate area with a grim aura. The stench of decay and ash makes my eyes water and incites a violent cough as if the air itself is poisoning us. Michael quickly claps his hands, attempting to make a light dome around us, protecting us from the environment. Sadly, he's unable to concentrate as a revenant grabs his leg. The corpses around us twitch and stand, walking toward both of us, moaning and dripping ooze. With my right hand, I grab Michael and kick the undead, grasping him, while with my left hand, I swing my sword, wildly cutting away any reanimated body getting too close.

Michael quickly grabs his incense holder, flicking it, causing it to glow brightly, almost blinding me, but it dispels the smell almost instantly. I take a deep gasp of air and cough up brown mucus on the floor, clearing my head, allowing me to focus. Michael has the same response as I do, but before he finishes expelling the decay, he throws the small incense holder up, making it erupt in an even brighter golden light. Now, the undead fall where they stand.

With a weak cough, Michael says to me, "Slice and dice!"

I nod and begin to quickly decapitate whatever undead are still moving in our immediate surroundings.

Malek sees our actions and, with fury, yells and summons more red orbs, shattering them to create more and more undead around him. The ground around him begins to shake as he coughs more blood onto the floor.

"Your plan has failed, jester. Surrender and, by the will of the Three, stop this madness!" Michael says as he walks up to me.

"No! Never! The show must go on! I was given this body to possess, and I will not let you peasants destroy what I have worked for with his royal majesty!"

"Enough!" Michael interrupts.

Malek punches the ground with force, creating a fissure separating him from us. "I will not be silenced! I just need more power, a stronger summons. I will make you dance for me!"

Malek takes out a jagged dagger that makes Michael gasp, and with his blade, he slices his arm deep enough that an immense amount of blood gushes out. With a pained grunt, he says, "Rise."

A horde of nihldrens come out, followed by some creatures that look human but are fast, running on their arms and legs, their faces covered with sacks.

"Ruffus, run back with me. We need to gain distance between them!" Michael says in a panic.

I do as I'm told and ask, "What are those things?"

"Hunters!" he says as he pulls out a small, thin stick. "Do not let them grab you!"

"Why?" I say as I cut one out of the air as it tries to pounce on me.

"Cut more, talk less!" Michael yells, aggravated, as he blasts one with a burst of light.

One of the hunters throws a nihldren at me, forcing me to dodge, and with a fell swoop of its arm, it grabs my sword, letting out a nightmarish scream that makes me drop my sword, stunned.

My heart beats incredibly quickly. Nothing matters to me more than running. Horrid thoughts of death and fear engulf my mind. I think, *Leave Michael to his doom. His life is not worth more than mine. I must save myself! Screw these people. Their fate is sealed!* These thoughts are alien to me, as if they were being pushed onto me. By no means am I a coward, but this creature is forcing all these deep thoughts to surface.

The creature removes the sack on its head, revealing a brown, decayed face. It has no eyes, just empty sockets and a mouth filled with jagged teeth. It slowly unhinges its jaw, revealing a long, needle-like tongue. It lunges at me but gets pushed off by a bright light that snaps me back. All my fears melt and I can move again. I slap my face hard and pick up my sword to slash another hunter out of the air.

I look back at Michael to see him on his knees, struggling against a flock of nihldrens that ambushed him. I run to him quickly and turn the little monsters into dust. Michael nods and thanks me as he blasts another hunter out of the air.

"Ruffus, quick, think of love, think of hope!" Michael says as he puts the palm of his hand on my heart.

"How?"

A few hunters and nihldrens surround us, ready to attack. "Think of Erol!" Michael says, oddly calm.

I close my eyes and do as I'm told. I think of Erol. My mind begins to fill up with memories of him drinking at the tavern with me. His bravery against any foe he meets, all the times I had to stop him from peeking inside the girls' bath in the guild and the city public baths. A small chuckle comes out as I remember that he was there in the hospital waiting for me to wake up after the arena's fight.

I feel a click in my head, and Michael scoffs and thunders with pride and conviction, "Argumentarer!"

A strong pulse comes out of our heads, pushing all of the monsters away. Some fly twenty-five feet in the air, landing with loud cracks and dying instantly.

Even Malek gasps in pure pain, but he recovers and says, "It is too late—the finale is here."

I open my eyes and turn to face Malek. All of the monsters around us are dead, and a few puffs of black smoke land softly on the ground.

Malek screams, creating one final orb that is crimson red and smashing it to the ground.

"A tainted soul," Michael says dryly. "Be ready for the fight upon us. Gods know what he invoked, damn possessed elf. I knew no mortal holds so much power and evil."

"If those red orbs are tainted souls, how does he keep using them?"

"The forest's unstable magic. Magical artifacts like a piece of quartz can store souls. Or he is incredibly skilled and can take souls from the nether." He puts his hands together and makes strange hand signs. "But looking at him and how unskilled he is at magic, he must be a recently ascended daemon."

I look at Malek and think that would have been my fate if I had lost the fight at the arena, a puppet controlled by another. I box the thought to reopen later and see that Michael is building up energy for the last attack.

Malek growls at the comment. "Do not mock me, Priest!"

"I thought you were a jester, Malek," I say playfully to bide my time. "You need to lighten up and take a joke!" I elegantly swing my sword, mocking him.

Malek raises both his hands to the air with a scream as two wooden coffins erupt from the ground vertically. The new-looking caskets open, dropping two bodies on the floor, but only one begins to move.

A revenant shambles his way toward them but meets its fate as the corpses spring into action, consuming it. The new undead wears all-black, regal-looking dress, out of place compared to the other undead that usually run around naked or in scrappy clothing.

Summoning two more red orbs containing corrupted souls, Malek shatters them, and the red liquid fuses with the elegantly dressed body. The corpse stands and turns to face us, surprising both of us, as it is a woman who looks fresh, as if she died only a few days ago. Her pale skin and curly hair would have been beautiful if she were alive, but the eyes glow red, with malice behind them.

She turns to Malek and says, "Why have you brought me back? You were the one that killed me when I lived. Why can't I find peace in death?" Her voice starts to get louder, "Why do you forsake me, daemon?"

Malek smiles gleefully. "Ms. Holten, first chambermaid to Princess Alexandra." He sighs with passion. "As beautiful as you were living, you look great in death. Sad I could not possess you also."

"Swine, you tricked me!"

"Poisoning her majesty's wine and blaming you was in poor taste, I know, but you drank all the wine after her, so you must have liked it!" he says, playfully but with a hint of pain. "And if I'm frank, that idea was not mine; it was this person's who was your friend. Hate and jealousy are such a juicy drink for me."

She shrieks at him.

As they fight, Michael and I move farther away from them and whisper to each other.

"Did he forget about us?" I ask, but Michael seems panicked.

"He has no control of the undead. This will turn bad. We have to kill them both."

Before I move to cut them down, Michael grabs my hand and tells me to wait. He seems fascinated by what is happening. Ms. Holten shrieks, attracting our attention again. Malek impales her with the jagged dagger and says, "Now you are a prisoner to my will, your body is mine to use, and I command you to kill."

Holten grabs Malek by the neck and says louder, "My body is yours, but my spirit is not." With her other hand, she grabs the dagger and screams in Malek's face.

The hairs on my body stand up as I cover my ears to escape the horrible noise coming out of her. Michael is on his knees, covering his ears, screaming in pain, trying to recover.

Once the screeching stops, we both look at Malek's bloodied, pale, twisted face. He lies still on the ground as Holten's body lumps on top of him, her eyes hollow and her facial expression that of a screaming woman.

Disoriented, I touch my ears and feel blood coming out of them. Michael tries to talk to me, but all I can hear is ringing, accompanied by a painful migraine. He then puts both his hands on my ears, and immediately, I feel better. He again tries to speak to me, and this time, I can understand.

"Ruffus, can you hear me?" he says as he covers his ears with his glowing hands.

"Michael, what in the gods' name happened?" I say as I fall on my butt, looking in Malek's direction.

My hearing gradually gets better as Michael says, "Gods, I think his magic backfired." He sits next to me, sweating and heaving heavily.

"Are you okay?" I say as I massage my temples.

"Healing takes copious amounts of energy, and we have

been fighting nonstop. On a normal day, this would not happen, but the magic here, it's intoxicating," he says. "It's a sweet drink, as if I breathed in energy." He puts his hand on his ears. "My ears, they still hurt."

"My ears are killing me also. I swear I can still hear sobbing," I joke.

Michael laughs and shakes his head. "I know, me too."

We both look at the bodies and immediately stop laughing, for above Holten's corpse hovers a silver mist with red eyes staring right at us.

"Michael, is that . . . ?"

The mist forms itself into an ethereal woman with ragged hair and thin hands that look like claws. She floats two feet above the pile of bodies, letting out a loud sob. Her mouth unhinges every time she opens it. It looks at her body and begins to cry even louder, to the point that it's deafening again. We cover our ears, standing up quickly. Michael rips a page from his book, throwing it in front of us before the creature can cry out again. The page creates a wall of light, barely shielding us from its screams.

"Banshee!" Michael yells, but it sounds like a whisper. "Grab that dagger in her body!"

"Got it! What about Malek?"

"Not even a possessed man can survive a banshee's screech in close quarters. I will use the last of my magic to shield your whole body and haste you!" he says as he reaches his hand to me. "Grab the dagger and decapitate the head of her physical body! I will finish her off once you do!"

Once I grab his hand, I feel a jolt of adrenaline as my body shakes violently. I can see small drops of sweat falling slowly off of Michael's chin.

I let go of his hand, feeling elevated, strong, and hyper,

as if I could run to the ocean and back in a few seconds. The ground beneath my feet feels soft as I sprint toward the bodies and the banshee. As I make it to the fissure, I jump, clearing it with ease, and while I am in the air, I ready Coal. I land softly, slicing Malek's body to ribbons, and decapitate Holten's head from her body. I take the dagger off her corpse and face the banshee. The dagger starts to vibrate violently, sending waves of electricity to my body, almost impeding me from stabbing the creature. The banshee wails directly at me, sweeping me off my feet and pushing me away. Her scream shakes my bones and paralyzes me instantly.

Michael, seeing this, yells an incantation, and a gold shell surrounds my body, hitting the banshee, dematerializing her on the spot. I land on my back next to the fissure, nauseous and exhausted, waiting for another stroke of bad luck. The world catches up to me as I let a gasp of air out, pain wracking my body.

Michael runs to me, grabbing whatever part of my body is easily accessible, pulling me away from the bodies and the fissure, and with a last heave, he falls next to me, gasping for air.

"You are heavy, Ruffus," he says in between breaths.

I close my eyes and say, "Everything hurts."

"Rest easy, we won," he says as he relaxes his breathing. "And there are no immediate threats to us."

"My eyes are too heavy to open, Michael," I say, exasperated.

"So are mine, Ruffus."

"Would it be okay if we sleep? I promise that I am a good cuddler," I say, coughing.

"On the ground? Seems very boorish, and as tempting as that sounds, I have never cuddled, and I don't want you to be my first," he says in a slightly degrading tone.

"Clearly, you are missing out."

We both laugh and groan in pain at the same time.

"You are not a normal, boring, self-righteous priest, are you?"

He laughs. "I have learned that being human and personable attracts the flocks to my sermon." Michael grabs my hand. "Ruffus, we have to get up. We can rest once we activate the ward."

I open my eyes and freeze in place.

"Ruffus, why are you shaking?"

My mouth turns dry, and I say, "Can you bless me?"

Michael groans and sits up, looking at me. "Of course.

Once I give the final rights to this necromancer and grab a vial of his blood, I will bless both of us, for our luck has been a blessing by itself!"

I slowly sit up. "I'm sorry, I feel like I am hallucinating." My eyes fix on a familiar face.

Michael helps me up, noticing my fearful expression. "Ruffus, are you okay?"

I lie. "Yes, just take the dagger out of my hand, please. It makes me feel dirty."

"You did not let go of it?"

I shake my head.

Michael grabs it out of my right hand and says, "Odd, I feel no energy in this. The summoning must have depleted it."

To my eyes, Valke walks next to Michael, laying a hand on his shoulder, looking straight at me.

Michael shivers and looks toward his shoulder. He quickly nods it off and puts the dagger on his bag. "Ruffus, let me do my ritual, and we can be off to find the others."

I quickly nod, staring directly at Valke's eyes.

"Only you can hear me, only you can feel me, only you can see me," Valke's voice hisses in my head. "What violent power that dagger held, only to transfer to you and open your mind's eye." He appears next to me, making me stumble down.

Meanwhile, Michael nods at the corpses as he sprinkles salt over them, murmuring, "May the gods forgive you." He turns to face me, seeing I am on the floor again. "Ruffus." He walks up to me and helps me up, looking around us. "What vexes you? What is wrong?"

Valke is behind Michael, licking his lips, whispering, "What vexes you? Tell him, let it all out."

I stare at Michael and say, "Nothing, just starving and slightly annoyed that you did not want to cuddle or give me any food."

Michael looks at me in relief. "Ah, now I understand why you suddenly started to act differently. You must not get rejected a lot."

I scoff as we start to walk. "Some healer you are. Can't even mend my hungry stomach or lonely spirit."

He smirks. "Lady Hearth warned me about how inappropriate you are, but I appreciate the compliment, you heathen," he says as we both leave the marketplace, heading in the direction from where we heard Erol's roar.

To my fear, the hallucination I am suffering feels real. It may be the effects of the wild magic of the forest, or maybe the dagger cursed me. For now, I need to keep my sanity in check and not let anyone know of this malicious vision.

Three Is a Crowd

B ut why is Valke haunting me again? I mean, I killed him, my sword ran deep into his chest, and yet I see him. I look to my sides and grind my teeth. Where is he now? By the gods, am I hallucinating?

Michael breaks the silence as he looks at the ward he pulled out of his pocket. "We heard Erol when we fought the possessed jester, but I cannot sense him or Trist. The energy of this town is hindering my senses." He touches his earring and sighs. "Even our link of communication seems to be broken at this moment." I pay little attention to Michael and rethink our last fight.

Malek made portals, used magical items, and was also a geomancer. Then we learned he was possessed, allowing him to use other types of powers. He did mention that Michael was a necromancer also. I look at Michael, who notices and gives me a weak smile.

He says, "What's on your mind, Ruffus?"

"Well, Malek is dead, yet I have a feeling the undead are still roaming around."

He looks up to the sky and says, "I have a feeling you're right."

"Also—" I stop and think about how to approach the matter of him being a necromancer.

"He called me a necromancer. Is that what you are pondering?" Michael says calmly.

I look surprised and nod.

"Yes, I dabbled in black magic in my youth. You see, I tried to bring back to life my friend."

I let out a small "oh" and look forward.

"When I started my school healing, I thought I could save everyone. I was cocky."

He fixes his hair nervously. "There is a fine line between holy magic and necromancy. A person can only be revived two minutes after their death, and the spell needed to cast such a miracle takes around a minute and thirty seconds." He sighs. "I tried reviving him after his death and turned his spirit tainted. He came back as a violent undead. I was curious about the magic of it, not knowing I had committed a crime against nature. But enough of this story. We must keep hope if we are to survive this."

"You will have to finish telling me after we are done here, Michael. I will buy you a pint to make you feel better."

He chuckles. "I rarely drink alcohol due to it being taboo for clergymen, but I have drank wine before at church."

"Well, now you will work with me since you owe me for saving your life. Also, church wine is weak. I'll get us the good stuff. We can be sinful."

Michael smiles and shakes his head.

"Since we are on the subject of magic, Malek used the dagger to bring back people from death, but how?"

Michael pulls the dagger out of his bag and examines it. Well, necromancy is complex magic in the first place. It's on a sacrificial basis, as in a necromancer must kill to obtain a spirit. From that, he can wait until the spirit is tainted or loses its memory and becomes a soul."

"There is a difference?" I ask.

"Think of a soul as a blank canvas of pure energy. It can be distorted or molded into a living creature by the gods or powerful magic users. Once a soul gains the ability to retain a memory, it becomes a spirit no matter how short it might be. A tainted spirit only retains negative memories and emotions, like fear, anger, envy, and regret, making it more susceptible to chaos. Most daemons are tainted spirits," Michael says as he looks at the hilt of the dagger.

"May I have a look?" I ask. But Michael seems hesitant.

"My mother is a blacksmith. I might know the style of the dagger if I examine it."

Michael still hesitates but says, "Well, I do not feel any energy in this, just an echo. I'm sure you won't be cursed if you touch it, and I do not detect a curse on you, although you grabbed it." Michael hands me the dagger. I grasp it firmly by the hilt and take a closer look. My feet freeze in place, and as I blink, everything around me turns an obsidian color. I am frozen in place. I move my eyes to look at Michael, but he has turned into an obsidian statue. The sky is still my only source of light, although dim.

"Feels good to move again, doesn't it?" Valke says as he appears next to me.

I try to move but to no avail.

He stretches and says, "It is good to see you again, Ruffus of Bern." He says this as if he's greeting an old friend.

I force myself to move, but still to no avail. Valke notices and points down. I look at my shadow and see Valke's shadow holding mine in place as if the shadow and Valke are two separate entities.

"Tsk, tsk. You're in my realm right now, dear human. You see, that dagger you touched gave me enough power to leave my prison," he says, smirking. I gulp and find my voice in my head. "I slew you. I saw your spirit leave your body. You were exorcised."

"By you, a non-priest, a normal, non-magical human, but you are correct. You were able to exorcise only half of me back into the underworld, but my other half you trapped in this item." His shadow moves my sword arm, forcing me to unsheathe Coal. The origin of his shadow is my sword.

"You see," he continues, "I need a soul to remain in your realm. I had one." He bursts out laughing. "Actually, I had multiple. I killed a lot of creatures and harvested them like cattle."

I glare at him. "This sword has been through multiple enchantments and blessings. How were you able to exist in my sword?"

"The stronger the light, the bigger the shadow that is cast. You humans might know that we are weak to holy magic, but you forget holy magic is weak to us," Valke says as he squats in front of me, caressing my face, looking deep into my eyes, as if searching for something.

I glare at him. "What do you want, daemon?"

His expression softens, and he says, "To be whole again, to rule this world, add to my power. You know what a hungry creature like me wants."

"I will not help you. I hope you know that."

He laughs and playfully slaps my face. "You have no choice in the matter, Ruffus. I know everything about you, as you know about me."

I feel a tug on my arm and see his shadow let me go. I seize the opportunity and quickly step forward, unsheathing Coal and thrusting it at Valke.

In turn, he grabs the hilt of my sword with his hand and

grins. "My time is up, Ruffus, but I'm sure we will have a chance to speak again. I mean, you do know a friend of mine." He begins to meld into the darkness, creeping back into Coal's shadow.

His voice echoes in my head. "We will keep in touch."

I blink, and the world returns around me. I never pulled my sword—it was all in my head. I drop the jagged dagger from my hand, and Michael quickly catches it.

"By the Three! Ruffus, be careful."

I shake my whole body in disgust.

Michael carefully wraps the dagger, putting it in his bag. "Ruffus, what's wrong?"

I lie. "Just thinking that this was used to kill people gave me a shiver."

Michael nods. "I agree, it is quite the horrific artifact, but do not fret. With this in our possession, some of the conjuring will stop. We did kill the daemon who I suspect was the necromancer, although, for a second, I swear I could feel a daemonic presence around us."

"I think I need a holy water bath after this!" I say as I touch my cheek.

Michael giggles. "I think you would burn up."

"Oh, ha ha, Mr. I-Used-to-Be-a-Necromancer," I reply.

Michael rolls his eyes at me, shaking his head. "Next time, I might take a second to heal your wounds. Now, let's press on forward. I grow tired of this place."

"Agreed, let's find the other two," I say, but I think of the horrors that just happened. I cannot tell Michael that there is a daemon spirit in my sword. He will probably want to forfeit the mission and put me under watch until they can detect Valke in the damn thing. It's a luxury that can wait.

"Ruffus, I am as exhausted as you are, but let's pick up the pace and hurry to our location. I have an off feeling, and it's making me nervous," Michael says as he examines the map on the ward, quickly looking up. "By the Three!" he says happily. "There, that's our destination!"

Michael points at a magnificent marble building standing high above all others with columns as high as oak trees and a staircase that would make a runner groan. The triangular roof has odd carvings and drawings of humans and what look like taller humans giving water to them. On the top of the carvings, it says, Banca Regelui. At the top of the building's staircase, blood is dripping down and a multitude of dead bodies are lying around.

As we both make it to the staircase, I ask Michael, "What does that say?"

He looks at me, too, then looks up and reads aloud, "Banca Regelui." He stops to think. "It is an old human dialect from the nomadic tribe that came from the continent next to us. I think it means 'Bank of the King.'"

"How did nomads build this?" I ask.

"I do not have that information, for this is the first time I have seen it outside a book," he says, pondering.

Our curiosity is put on hold as we hear a roar coming from inside the building. We look at each other and make a run toward the noise. My legs are on fire as we sprint up the staircase, and I curse under my breath at whoever invented staircases. As beautiful as they might have been, the enormous doors are now smashed clean as if a bull went through them.

As we get closer, we can hear the sound of battle coming from inside the building, metal clanging, and the all-but-comforting sound of Erol's victorious roar. As we make our way, we see Erol on top of what looks like a giant undead lying on the floor with Erol's polearm stabbed through its chest.

Erol flexes his arm and says to the undead, "Pathetic spawn of magic."

Trist is behind him, shaking her head in disagreement and annoyance. "Warrior, have you had your fun?"

Erol huffs.

She walks toward a pillar, placing her ward on it. With a snap of her finger, the parchment begins to glow brightly in white light. It pulses, and instantly, as if a weight lifts off my shoulders, I feel relaxed. The whole room bursts in white light, blinding me and escaping to the outside. The entire area is now underneath a dome of light, brightening everything. The smell of pestilence begins to fade, and the feeling of dread melts into newfound hope.

I open my eyes to see Erol rubbing his, and with a heart now filled with joy, I say, "Erol, I'm glad to see you alive!"

His ears perk, looking towards my direction. His bloodied face shows a stunned look that rapidly changes to joy. He runs to me and picks me up, sniffing me all around, saying, "You are safe!"

Michael walks up to Trist, hugging her. "Thank the Three both of you are safe."

She hugs him back. "They are with us on this perilous journey, my friend!"

I push off Erol, who looks at me and inspects me from top to bottom. His face changes to one of knowledge, and he says, "You battled hard, my cub. Come, tell me of your victory so I can tell you mine!"

I quickly inspect Erol, noticing his armor is dented and broken, with new cuts and bruises and missing a new chunk of fur on his calf. He sits down and sighs, happy as I pat his chest and say, "You took a hell of a beating."

"Does it impress you, cub?"

I smirk and check my belt pouch, pulling out a small container with medical balm. "I will be impressed if you don't flinch after this."

"I am strong. I can handle—"

He bites his lip when I put a small amount of ointment on his calf wound. Trist and Michael walk toward us, talking about their journey after sitting next to Erol, who is twitching in pain and smiling.

"This beastman," she pauses and says, "bestlia saved my life multiple times. His bravery and strength kept me alive and filled me with the hope of victory through all our battles." She taps Erol's shoulder.

Erol tries to nod but slumps to the floor, still biting his lip, moving his tail uncontrollably.

Michael sees me inspecting Erol's wounds and asks, "Do you require my help, Ruffus?"

"I got this. Rest up so you can heal us if we wind up in another battle."

Michael nods and sits down, examining himself for wounds. Erol gasps as I begin to stitch him up and says, "You are a strong fighter. A human woman of your caliber would make a great breeder of soldiers."

Trist scoffs and takes off a piece of broken shoulder armor. "Was that a compliment?"

"Coming out of Erol, yes, pretty much. He is not very tactful," I say, holding my laughter.

She smiles and says, "Well, thank you, my training keeps me alive."

Erol gives her a thumbs-up as I apply ointment to his stitching.

"Where were you both, and how did you get here?" I ask as I start to inspect myself for injuries.

"When the ground started to shake, the warrior and I fell inside a ravine, only to appear in the auction house, a few houses down the road from here. In there, an odd mage, which I believe to be our target, attacked us and summoned hordes of unspeakable evil ones. He then laughed, and as quickly as he came, he left." She points at the dead giant.

"It was a glorious fight," Erol adds.

"What exactly is that?" I ask, looking at the beast.

Michael stands up and moves toward the monster nonchalantly. "How grotesque. It's an abomination is what it is—multiple bodies stitched up to create this giant."

"Michael, don't you have to free the spirits as you did with the other monsters?" I ask as I put ointment on my neck.

"The ward's magic did that for me." He points at the pillar where the ward is still shining brightly. "It's holy magic sends them off, allowing us to move quickly and not perform a ritual for each undead we see."

"Pity the death of the necromancer does not complete this mission," Trist says as she finishes up wrapping bandages on herself.

Erol licks his thumb and wipes it on my face. "I will heal you."

"Truly, I feel as healthy as I can. We can thank Laura for the medical supplies she gave all of us. Really does the trick," I say as I dry my face off.

"Yes, I feel as if I were born today," Erol says, stretching and flexing in satisfaction.

"Stop flexing, Erol. You will rip the stitches," I say in annoyance.

Erol grabs me, gently pulls me closer to him, and whispers, "My cub, you are fine, right?" His demeanor changes, and he looks behind me.

I whisper back, "Why are we whispering, and why would I not be?"

He puts his head on my chest and sighs in relief, letting his guard down. "Thank the spirits," he says quietly. After a quick pause, he lets go of me and stands tall. He looks at his armor and removes the pieces of metal that would not offer him protection as I remain on the floor, sitting dumbfounded.

Does he know about Valke?

"No, the beast does not know," Valke says in my head as he appears next to me.

I jump and abruptly move away from him as everyone else looks at me.

I give a weak laugh and say, "Spider."

Trist and Michael shake their heads and finish talking as Erol shrugs and walks toward the giant to retrieve his weapon. Valke moves closer. "Now, now, do not fret. Only you and whoever has an acute insight can see me. Others might feel my presence, like your sibling, the priest over there, and whoever else has been possessed before."

Can you get lost, daemon?

He smirks. "I have constantly been trying to possess you again and keep failing. Your damn sword and its blessings keep preventing me. Now this ward has added another layer of annoyance to me." He flicks the hilt of my sword.

"Cub?" Erol walks up to me with a concerned look on his face.

I quickly look toward him, then the floor. "Damn spider keeps following me."

Michael taps me on the shoulder. "You killed a possessed elf, nihldrens, revenants, hunters, and a banshee. How is a spider scary?"

I laugh nervously and watch Valke walk toward Erol, sizing

him up. He walks behind him and licks the wound on Erol's cheek.

"I will enjoy drinking his blood when I take control of you."

Erol scratches his cheek and shivers just a bit. He looks in the direction of Valke, but his expression doesn't change.

Trist stands next to Erol, making Valke vanish in a puff of shadow. She takes a deep breath and says, "We have rested enough. Let us continue our journey through this hell. Hopefully, we can communicate now with Mrs. Hearth and inform her of our status and what has happened."

We all nod and pack up our medical supplies. I glance toward the ward to see it meld to the wall, disappearing. With that, I walk out last through the broken doors of the building and stare out into the sky. The area outside is brighter. Thanks to the dome we created, a ray of light shoots to the sky and connects with the cathedral on the horizon. As I look down, I see Erol waiting for me at the bottom of the stairs.

Every step I take to get down feels as if it's my last since I have a daemon attempting to possess me at every waking moment, and the dream I had in the cathedral keeps haunting me. Erol greets me and wraps his arm around my neck, pulling me closer. He unknowingly comforts me until I feel another hand grab my arm. I look and see Valke walking next to me, looking forward, holding me. His eyes meet mine, giving me a gleeful smirk. I quickly look away, placing my hand on Erol's arm. He shivers and looks at me happily.

"I am here. Don't forget that, my cub, and so are they," Erol says in a comforting tone, pointing at Trist and Michael, who are waiting for us.

"Yes, they are," I say, trying to ignore Valke until he says, "So am I."

Separation Anxiety

We reach the dome's end and hesitantly walk through it to the gloomy, pestilential smell that this town has to offer. Trist was able to communicate with Clover, and she informed us that we have to head southwest. Looking at my compass and map, I point us in the right direction. The sky is a bit brighter, allowing us to see farther, but still, it is a hindrance. The easternmost point of the town is now secure. Hopefully, if there is anyone alive in there, they are safe and sound. Our next stop is the hospital in the southern part of the town. Clover tells Trist that there are people barricaded there, which will be ideal for the second ward. From there, we will head east and finally north. "Only three wards to go," I say quietly as Trist leads us down the road.

"Why do we not go to the north now?" Erol asks.

"Seems there is a large horde of monsters blocking our way, denying us safe access to the castle," Trist says as she scans the area.

"We could have fought them all and brought ourselves glory. Might even learn a thing or two from me," he says as he walks up to her, playfully shoving her.

Trist tries to hide a smile and says, "We will fight, big tiger, and I will show you who needs to pay extra attention to training and discipline."

Michael glances at me with a disturbed face.

Erol smirks, puts his hands on the back of his head, and says, "It would be an easy fight. You trust much on training and not on instinct or experience."

"I am Arcadia trained. My master in combat will referee our fight, then. And after I win, you will owe us a good night, as you lot from the Warriors Guild always say." Trist says authoritatively.

Michael glances at me again and mouths the words, "Do they?"

I flail and shrug.

Trist catches Michael and me. She quickly says, "I mean for him to buy us food and beverages."

"Seems fair to me," Erol chimes in innocently.

Changing the topic quickly, I say, "I would have liked it if Arcadia had given us horses. It would have been quicker for travel."

"Well, Ruffus, your cart was supposed to aid us on that. That is why they gave you extra horses," Michael says in a pondering way.

"That is correct, Michael," Trist adds in a slightly annoyed tone.

"Their weakness got them killed. If they were beast tamed, they might have survived the trip."

"I have never ridden on a beast-tamed animal before," Michael says. "How do they differ from elven or human trained?"

"Well, they eat the meat of their enemy, and we feed them the blessed milk of the Great Bull," Erol says as he scratches his jaw.

Michael stops for a second and then quickly continues to walk, saying, "You mean one of the deities from the Wilds?"

"Yes," Erol says as he checks his bandaged hand.

"Oh, well then, I had no idea cow's milk was valuable enough to get blessed," he says, astonished.

"What cow?" Erol asks. "No milk from cows, just by a bull that the shaman blessed."

"But bulls do not give milk."

Erol stays silent as Trist says softly, "Ew."

Michael refrains from asking more questions as he puts his hand on his mouth.

I look up and see the shine from one of the moons in the cloudy sky. Trist notices and says, "The autumn moon shines so brightly, even though it's not nighttime yet. The desert must be celebrating its festival soon."

"A festival sounds fun. Is it a harvest celebration?" I ask.

She nods and stops, abruptly putting her hand back to stop us as the fog starts rolling up in front of us. We all pull out our weapons as Michael walks next to Trist. He points his index finger at it, releasing a spark of light.

"Is it natural?" Trist asks.

The fog rapidly descends on us, making it harder to see. Michael summons a bright light next to him and says, "We are in a forest, so fog is normal. I do not detect evil in it or any anomaly, but I will keep my senses alert."

As we traverse the fog, it begins to get thicker, and it's harder for us to see well.

Michael keeps firing tiny sparks of light toward the fog, giving some illumination on our way, until he says, "I am detecting a disturbance. We must be getting close to our destination."

"How do you know that?" I ask.

Trist answers me. "Because fog does not roll until morning, and that time has passed."

"Be careful, cub. The fog is getting thicker, and I have lost my sense of smell. Get closer to me."

The fog gets so thick that I can't see my hand in front of me. I keep following the light that Michael created, and I stop as I rub my eyes. "Erol, do you have a handkerchief? I feel something in my eye, and I do not want to rub dirt in there."

No one answers. "Erol?" I ask again.

I look at the small light that has been guiding me and walk up to it, still rubbing my eye. I see the small floating orb of light clearly, but it isn't floating near Michael. It is lazily just floating in front of me.

"Michael?" I say louder. Silence looms.

"Trist? Erol? Where are you?"

The small light begins to fade, flickering on and off as I start to panic. I turn to look, but the fog is so thick that now I can't even see the ground.

"Shit." I take a deep breath and count to ten, calming myself down enough to think clearly. "I am in a fog and lost my companions. I have been in worse situations. Any second now, someone will notice I am missing, and in the meantime, I will talk loudly so they know I'm still here. If there are monsters here, they can't see me since I can't see them, but they can hear me, so I will be quiet now."

Then I hear Erol's voice behind me. "Are we lost, my cub?"

I quickly turn, only to see Valke grinning at me. I fall on my butt with a small yell as Valke laughs.

"Go away, daemon! Can't you see I'm in trouble?"

"Actually, I can't see it at all. But all this desperation and fear are just too good to pass up." He quickly perks up and says, "Move to the left."

"What?" I ask.

Valke grabs my hand for a second, and I lose control of my feet. They jump by themselves to the left, moving me. A few seconds later, I hear a loud crash where I was just standing.

Valke now raises my hand, making my feet jump up, dodging a chain that would have swiped me off my feet. He lets go and looks toward my left.

I curse loudly, "Let go of me, daemon!" only to see Valke make a chair out of the fog.

"The more you panic, the more you lose control, giving me the chance to finally possess you. So I will remain here to see you slowly seep into more madness," he says as he keeps looking to the left.

"What's attacking?" I say in a panic as I run aimlessly. "Remain calm, Ruffus. The more you move, the harder you are to hit."

Valke seems impressed and says, "It's a ghoul. A big one, at that." He yawns but quickly grabs my arm, making me somersault forward and out of the way of another loud crash.

"Stop controlling me!"

"Believe it or not, I'm saving your life, meat bag. If you die, I die. Now, jump up," he says, growling at me.

I jump as high as I can, only to see an enormous metal ball with spikes and a chain appear from the fog and land a foot away from me, dispersing the fog.

"By the Three!" I exclaim as I land on top of the ball and chain.

I grab a knife from my coat and throw it after the chain, only to hear the loud clang of metal hitting metal. The fog begins to let up, and I can see around ten feet away from me, showing me a heavily armored monster. The ghoul is taller than Erol, wearing as much armor as Trist and as ugly as they come. My knife hit its helmet, tipping it and showing me a rotten, yellow-looking undead that makes my stomach churn. It growls as it fixes its helmet with both its hands.

"For both our sakes, you should run. The beastman is not here to save you, and we both know you don't stand a chance."

With no other choice, I do as he says and sprint away into the fog. I concentrate to see if I can hear anything resembling Erol's roar, Michael's spell, or even Trist's commanding voice. The only sound that reverberates in my ears is the noise of tiny feet pitter-pattering and a loud metal rattling noise coming from behind me. As I run deeper into the fog, I can see two lights in the distance. With the hope that one is Michael, I run toward them. The mist starts dissipating, allowing me to see farther and farther until, in front of me, I see two lanterns and what looks like a somewhat damaged building surrounded by a metal gate.

I climb through the gate and run toward the broken-down building. There are no bodies around, making it easy for me to keep running straight. I look toward the top of the structure to give me an indication as to what this building might have been. The top consists of a bell statue, and beside it is a rod with a single snake coiled around it—the symbol of medicine.

"The hospital," I say aloud as I run toward the shut doors. I make my way through the staircase, running past the two lights that guided me, and slam through the doors. They open quickly, as if they were waiting for me. The doors hit the wall behind them, creating a loud echo. Hastily, I reach for both heavy doors and shut them slowly, backing away. My foot hits a wooden beam on the floor, and with all the strength I can muster, I pick it up, using it to bar the door. I turn my back, slowly sliding down and sitting on the cold stone floor, panting and trying to catch my breath. Wiping the sweat off my forehead, I let a quick whimper and a tear out of my eye. I put both my hands on my face while I grind my teeth, trying to recover.

Loud footsteps from outside snap me back as I roll away from the double door. A loud grunt and a gurgling roar shake the door violently but cease after a few loud bangs, cracking the wooden beam slightly. The sounds of loud footsteps grow farther away until all I can hear is silence.

I shake and hug my feet. "I want to go home, please. I just want to go home! Gods help me!"

A memory of my father comes unannounced to my mind. It was a time when I was younger and had an argument about how I needed to pay attention to my safety. He took me to some ruins near our village for the purpose of learning about his job as an archeologist. He would constantly remind me to observe my surroundings and tried to teach me that noticing the minute details might help me understand a problem. He would then go on about how paying attention had saved some of his colleagues' lives. I told him that I did not care for him or other people and to stop preaching to me like I was a little kid. I ran from him and, to my luck, found a new room unexplored by anyone else and accidentally activated a trap, sending a stone golem after me.

I ran far, but I remember what he told me. "Stay vigilant. Stay focused. In our moments of panic and fear, we must remain in control of our senses. We as humans survive because we thrive on emotions, but that does not mean we let them control us. There is always time to think and reflect. Clarity always comes to those who look for it, even when the metaphorical ship is sinking. If you are ever in a situation when all hope seems lost, think of the ones you love. It might be me, or your mother, Yubia, or even Juratan. Always remember someone out there is looking for you. Just make sure you are looking for them too."

As I ran, all I could do was think of my father. I thought of how I was a fool to ignore his warnings and disobey him when he was only trying to protect me. I ran to find him, not for me to be saved, but to warn him and maybe save him. He found me first, and he used his magic to fight off the golem, protecting me. After the ordeal, we both sat down, and he hugged me as tightly as he could.

I looked at him and asked as I wiped my tears on my arm, "How did you find me?"

He looked at me and kissed my forehead. "I thought of you. Even though I might be angry, never think for one second that I don't love you. You and your siblings are my light, my hope, and my greatest achievement." He punched my shoulder and said, "And thanks to you, I now know of the new hidden dangers of this place. I am lucky and blessed to have brought you here."

I cried, and for the first time in my life, I felt that I had saved someone I loved. The ruins proved to have more hidden treasures and traps, and thanks to my father and me, the expedition ran smoothly and no one died on our watch. The success brought us a royal envoy from River Front, and my dad received commendations and more funding for his excavations. That's when he gave me his old handkerchief and said, "Keep this near you always. It was my first find when I was a child. My teacher told me it was a piece of cloth woven by the gods themselves. May it always remind you of your achievements and be a reminder that I will always be there when you need me, through better or worse."

The memory fades, and I wipe my tears away from my face, standing up slowly, feeling less sorry for myself. I look around the room and see it dimly lit by candles, almost making it cozy enough, even if the furniture around me is destroyed.

I reach for my belt and unbuckle it. There is a small, hidden compartment where only a single piece of cloth fits underneath the leather. I open it and grab the small piece of fabric with only two letters embroidered on it: *M* and *B*.

"Marcus Bern. Dad, thank you," I say softly as I kiss the

cloth, quickly putting it away, fixing my belt, and running my hand through my hair.

I walk toward a window and look outside. The lanterns that were lit are now turned off, and the fog rolls toward the hospital. I sigh and turn around, only to see dimly lit corridors and staircases going into the unknown.

I scratch my head, shake off my fears and insecurities, and say, "Here we go. Let's find a spot to ward this place." I pull out the parchment and check the map. "Guess I have to go to the top of the hospital." I put it back into my pocket and make my way to the staircase.

I stop and look at my right hand and say, "Erol, where are you? I pray that you are safe." Making a fist with my hand, I look up. "Even if you are at the ends of this continent, I will always be here to find you, and I know you will do the same. And if you are in trouble, it is my turn to save you."

Rule of the Rose

The darkness in the corridors seems endless, as if I'm staring at the void itself. I decide to use a present given to me by my father, a small scroll the size of an oak leaf tied by a thin green blade of grass. The scroll contains a low-grade illumination spell that will last me a day if I use it constantly. I carefully untie the scroll and open it. Inside, I can make out a few magical symbols on the parchment. I clear my thoughts and say, "Illum," as I tap the open parchment with the blade of grass. A tiny wisp escapes and sets itself on top of the blade of grass, brightening the room a little. It feels as if a tiny candle is floating and following me. Impressed, I put the parchment away in my pocket again and trek on.

I make it to an enormous room that is filled with dead bodies. Oddly enough, each of them is covered by a linen sheet and organized on one side of the room. The walls are stained with blood, while all the furniture is gone or wholly dismantled. I walk to one of the corpses. Kneeling, I remove the top part of the linen to see that these bodies look as if they were killed a few days ago. I sigh and give a quick prayer as curiosity strikes me, and I take the whole cover off to see the naked body. It has minor puncture wounds on the neck and thigh and near the armpit. The rest of the body has tiny shards of stone embedded in it. "Malek was here," I snarl as I carefully cover the body again.

The sound of footsteps above me startles me enough to grab my small illumination source and hide it in my hand. I crouch down and walk toward a new set of stairs that take me to the third floor. I turn off my light by pulling out the parchment and saying, "Off." I peek through the doorway on the third floor only to see another dimly lit hallway.

There is furniture on the sides. It looks as if everything was put there to make a barricade, but it failed, and the cushions were ripped apart. I make my way through quietly. I can faintly hear crying and whispers.

The lit candles on the wall look as if they are freshly replaced, hinting that there are other living things here besides me. As I reach the end of the corridor, I peek inside the room to see that I am entering a sunroom. The glass ceiling lights the area enough for me to be able to see all around.

Valke walks right past me as if he owns the place. I stand up and quietly follow behind, surveying the area for dangers.

"You know, if you allow me to possess you, I can destroy the real threat and even save this town from a holy purge," Valke says passively.

Ignoring him, I walk through him, making him dematerialize and rematerialize next to me.

"A perk of this pact is that you would have all my powers, making it easier for you to find your friend," he adds.

There is a counter with an odd glowing rose floating a few inches above it at the far side of the room. As I reach the counter, I see a shadow move, running away from the room I am in, startling me.

"Who goes there?" I say bravely.

"It is just an eldar child," Valke says blankly. "Just a small snack for the monsters."

The sound of her running and whimpering distracts me,

and I wonder if I should follow, but my better instincts tell me to let her go. I move to examine the rose on the counter. As I am about to grab it, a loud clang comes from the corridor nearest to me. More shadows move away from this room, and I catch a glimpse of a child running in the direction from which I came.

I slowly walk toward the hallway where all the noise is coming from. I realize that I hear the sound of combat. Now running toward the noise, I quickly reach a smaller room with a few deceased bodies on the side covered in linen. Above them, I see a map of this hospital. I try to memorize it, but the sound of battle seems to be moving farther away. I quickly follow it, only to be met by another staircase.

The sound is getting louder by the second as I get near a new room, and as I peek inside, I see Trist locked in battle with two other creatures that look like living shadows. I run into the room, and to my surprise, the doors slam behind me, silencing the whispers and moaning. The only noise now is Trist's grunts. She bashes one of the shadow-looking humans in the face, and with her mace, she relentlessly smashes it on the second enemy, knocking both on the floor.

"Trist!"

She quickly turns toward me, crouching with her shield in front of her with her mace high in the air, ready to strike. "Who are you?"

I stop dead in my tracks and respond, "It's me, Ruffus!"

"Prove to me you are Ruffus, as those two were also Ruffus and now lie dead on the floor."

I glance at the shadows and see no resemblance. I pull out the ward she gave me and show it to her. In turn, she lowers her mace, relaxing her stance. Valke casually strolls over to her, glancing over her shoulder at me, smiling. Trist's eyes quickly dart at him, examining him up and down, giving him a dry look.

Seeing that Valke is visible to her, I unsheathe my sword and get into my battle stance.

Trist, seeing this, asks, "What are you doing, Ruffus?"

I remain silent and slowly begin stepping backward, not taking my eyes off of her.

"Ruffus, where are you going?" she asks angrily. "We need to stick together."

"He knows you see me, human," Valke says as he turns to face me. "Oh, Ruffus, dodge left now."

Moving without thinking, I jump left to see another Trist next to me, swinging her mace. It narrowly misses me, slamming on the floor, leaving a sizable dent. Quickly, I glance back and see Valke and the other Trist staring at each other.

"Pity," the second Trist says as she lifts her mace from the floor. "Here I thought this would be an easy fight. No matter though." She begins to shimmer in a faint blue hue, changing into her proper form.

She turns into an exquisite middle-aged woman, dressed in a long black dress that complements her body very well, exposing just enough of her chest, with her pale leg sticking out of the thigh-high slit on one side. She stands taller than me. Her face could rival the beauty of an eldar or even a nymph. Her lips are red as a rose, but her eyes are exhausted and have seen better days. She holds a magnificently crafted and decorated rapier that shines beautifully with even the slightest hint of illumination. The decorations remind me of the glowing rose I saw in the other room, making me wonder if it belongs to her.

"Darkness will consume you soon. I have already trapped two of your three companions, and you are not far behind." Her voice changes from Trist's to one of sweet noise. It's melodic and smooth. The accent is thick and slightly hard to understand. Unlike Trist's, hers is thicker, and if we were in other circumstances, I would just want to hear her speak.

She begins to glow once again in a cerulean light. The little luck I thought I had left feels like it vanishes entirely as she does, only for her to appear in greater numbers, filling the inside of the room. The same smirk paints all their faces as they all say, "Give up, monsieur. It does not matter."

Valke appears next to me and whispers, "This is one of those times you should run."

"Yeah, I think I agree with you."

The Illusionist

I have seen this magic before! I think as I kick the door open and run out of the room.

Valke whispers, "How fascinating, an illusionist! This is rare magic. How have you witnessed this before?"

I run past the hallway, jumping over a few obstacles while thinking, *Figure it out for yourself, daemon!*

"Then I shall!"

My head begins to hurt as Valke probes into my memory. He finds that my parents took me to the circus in town. One of the acts was a man who could create illusions of himself, and as a child, I was mesmerized by his magic. All of his clones were a part of him. They all moved in sync, creating a spectacular show. I even begged my parents to let me join the circus so I could become him.

Never do that again, I think in the angriest tone of voice I can imagine.

Valke, in turn, whispers, "How adorable."

I make it to the sunroom, and quickly, I take a new exit, noticing the rose isn't there anymore. I look to the walls to see a map, and on top of the map, the words "Hall of the Minds" are written in bold letters.

How appropriate. I do feel like I'm losing mine.

"Rightly so," Valke adds.

Can you make yourself scarce, daemon? I think as I try to find a good hiding place.

"Think this through, meat bag. Where would I go? "

I can tell you a few places you can crawl back inside of.

Valke remains quiet as I run forward, deeper into the ward. I find a room to the side with a still-functioning door. Slowly and quietly, I close it, and to my surprise, I find a locking mechanism. After latching the door, I crouch again and inspect the room to see if I can find anything useful. I realize that the room I am in has three more doors, each facing a different wall.

From all directions, I hear moaning and a few screams, making me feel entirely unwelcome. As I quietly move around, I lose my footing and slip on the floor, grunting loudly and cursing. I face the floor and see that I've fallen on fresh blood. Curiosity falls on me as I follow the trail while sheathing Coal. I make it to a tall metal door with a few dents on it, giving the impression that someone or something has been trying to get out. Then, halfway to the top, there is a small window, and I stand on my tiptoes and look inside, bracing for something to jump at me.

I can see Trist tied up on the floor in the small room, a small puddle of blood spreading out from underneath her, while Michael is bound and gagged with a few cuts on his face. He is groaning in pain, trying to release himself from his bonds.

I whisper to them, "Michael, Trist, I'm here!"

Michael looks at me, glaring, and says something into the gag. Trist, on the other hand, doesn't move much but reacts to her name. I quickly pull out my knife and whisper to them, "Here, take this knife and untie yourselves. I will open the door." Michael nods as I drop the knife in. He swiftly moves toward it and begins to cut his bonds. I step down and look at the locking mechanism on the door. It glows blue. "This is new." I tap the lock, but it ends up giving me a slight jolt.

"Well, this is bad if I can't pick the lock." I unsheathe Coal and raise it high. "Might as well break it!"

I slam down on the lock, only to make my whole body vibrate as my sword hits it, creating a loud echo that reverberates around the hospital. I stop shaking and say out loud, "Not the smartest idea I have ever had," only to hear an "mhmm" from Michael.

I stand on my tiptoes again and whisper angrily toward him, "I do not need any of your sass at this moment."

Michael groans loudly, and I can feel him rolling his eyes at me.

Before I can answer back to him, an odd scent catches my attention. It smells amazing. It's jasmine with lavender and, somehow, soup. It entices me, and I cannot resist the aroma. My body and mind are on a mission to find the origins of this fragrance. Michael starts banging the door with his feet, and all I can think is, *Good, he is free. Where is this smell coming from?*

Michael keeps banging hard, and it begins to annoy me. I leave the room and find that the aroma is coming from the chamber I had locked before finding my allies. The rose has appeared here, as if by magic, glowing a violet light. I slowly walk to it, forgetting all my problems, thinking about how nice it will be to smell the flower or eat it.

Valke appears next to me, warning me to pay attention, to stop, but I don't listen. I can't care any less about what he has to say to me. Valke begins acting erratically, as even he tries to stop me from moving, but something in me shuts him down.

"The nerve that daemon has, trying to stop me from achieving happiness," I say as I kneel to grab the rose.

It begins to drift away, making me sad, but it lands in the hands of a dark-haired maiden.

"What is a woman like you doing in a place like this?" I say aloud.

She sighs in relief. "Thank our ancestors, you are real and not an illusion!"

I fix my hair quickly and stand tall, "I am Ruffus. I am here to save you." I look at her flower. "Is that yours?"

"Yes. I work here in the ward as an aromancer. I help people relax with perfumes and smells to help them heal their minds and bodies. Sadly, it's a lost art in many places, but here in White Wood, it's highly accepted."

Valke appears next to her but doesn't say a word. He rapidly walks next to me, and I don't see her notice him.

"There are people here who have been trapped for days. I have been able to keep them calm with my scents, but there is not much I can do. Then the illusionist came, and"—she looks away and tears up—"she fed some of them to some unholy creatures."

I walk up to her and hug her, which in any other situation I would not have done, but I felt compelled to. "Do not worry. I am here. I will save all of you."

She looks at me with tear-filled eyes and says, "How?"

"All of us have wards with holy magic imbued in them. Once I activate mine, this area will be safe, and help will come." I try to calm her.

"Thank the ancestors for you!" she says, overjoyed.

I think to myself, *Wow, what a catch. She is beautiful, and I'm her hero.*

I hug her, only to hear a racket behind me. I separate from her and look away to see Valke threw some cups to the floor to grab my attention. I scoff and turn to face her again, only to feel a sharp sting in my stomach. I look down to see the stem of the rose stabbing me as she holds the flower. She begins to glow and transform into the woman that I've been trying to run away from, and the rose morphs into her rapier.

Every time I try to breathe, I choke, gasping. My knees start to buckle as I grab the rapier's blade with my hands, trying to push it away from my body. Her weapon is so sharp that it cut through the hide of my gloves and the under armor I have on. All my senses rush back to me, and the feeling of pain wracks my body. I'm able to move back from the blade only to fall on the floor, gasping for air.

She walks next to me and steps on my chest with her stiletto heels, stabbing me through the ribcage. I attempt to yell, but I'm now choking on my blood, coughing violently. She speaks down to me, "Unworthy." The woman's voice returns to normal. "To fall for such an obvious trap. Men are easy."

She elegantly moves her sword, removing most of my blood from its blade. She then pulls a small napkin out of thin air and wipes the blade clean with one stroke.

Valke appears next to me, raging down. His face seems to change into panic, and he says, "Idiot! How will I escape now? I'm tethered to your sword, and the magic on it makes me tethered to you! If you die, I die!"

"Silence, daemon. You are but a pawn to his will. You have no real power on this plane of existence," she demeans him.

Valke's eyes fill with rage and begin to glow menacingly. "Silence, mortal! I will eat your very spirit when I free myself from these binds!" He charges at her but stops when she points her weapon at him.

"Learn your place, filthy dog!" she says in a commanding tone. "This is Black Rose, the legacy, my legacy of the Pryde lineage. It is designed to kill lowly creatures like you. Even if you are captured in his blade, all I have to do is shatter it with mine, and you will be sent back to the depths of the underworld. You would not be the first one I do it to."

As they stand off against one another, I slowly move to grab a syringe out of my belt pouch, but my hands are too numb and cannot move well. I try to speak, but the immense amount of pain I am in only lets me get one word out: "Help."

Two shades that look like her appear, grabbing me by the arm and begin to drag me away toward Michael and Trist. I can see Pryde walking behind me, looking at her nails as if nothing has happened. As we near the metal door, it's thrown wide open, letting out a blast of light, killing both shades instantly and making Pryde flinch, jumping a few good feet back into the room we were just in. As the dust settles, Michael aims his hand toward her and says, "Repent." A strong blast of light pushes her farther back, cornering her against the wall.

Michael heaves heavily and places his hand on the wall next to him, causing it to glow. The magic rushes toward the door, creating a wall of light and trapping us in the hallway.

Pryde gasps in shock and says underneath her breath, "Insolent fool."

Enraged, Michael yells at her, "Heretic! You shame the Pryde family lineage!"

"Who are you to accuse me of this, priest?"

Michael puffs his chest and says, "I am Michael Ravenholme! Our families are allies. My great grandfather helped build the Black Rose rapier for your mother!"

"Ravenholme? You mean the disgraced family with a necromancer for a child?" She spits on the floor. "I would have ended you if I had known you were the necromancer. I would bring honor to your namesake!"

Michael glares at her and says, "You disgrace your departed mother."

Pryde sprints to the wall of light and stabs it at lightning speed, trying to break it, but with each hit, she recoils, sending her into a frenzy.

Michael smiles as he looks at the glowing wall, lightly mocking Pryde's assault. He turns his head toward me and says, "Good to know the bloody mess on the floor is you. I was fooled by her, thinking she was Trist."

Trist wobbles out from the cell, looking as if a cart full of bricks hit her. She says in a pained voice, "She attacked me from all sides with her illusions. I can't move correctly. Her rapier seems to exude poison."

Michael puts both his hands on the wall, saying, "Correct." Trist shakes her head lazily. "He administered some of the alchemist's antidotes she gave him. I can do the same to you, but I will need your help, Ruffus."

"How dare you imps talk about me as if I'm not present!" she says in a fury, still attacking the shield.

Michael grunts as he keeps his concentration on the wall of light.

With conviction, she thrusts her rapier to the center of the barrier, making it crack. Michael gasps and grinds his teeth as he keeps the wall up while she continues her onslaught.

Trist kneels behind me, slowly raising my head and putting it on her lap. Her hands tremble violently, and I can see a frightened look on her face. Using what strength I have left, I grab her hand, looking at her calmly. She takes a deep breath and pulls a thick needle out of her bag. She looks at me, pained, and tries to speak. Still grabbing her hand, I slowly pull it toward my chest. She nods understandingly, and with a quick motion, she stabs me in the chest with the needle, administering the antidote. I cough up blood and accidentally hit her face with it. Unfazed, she wipes herself clean. "Okay, Ruffus, it will take a few minutes for it to work. Please stay with me." She removes the needle and helps me sit up against the wall.

With loud cackling laughter, Pryde unleashes a tremendous

flurry of hits at the wall. Michael falls to a knee, gasping for air and trying not to lose consciousness. Her laughter suddenly turns to silence as a growling beastman enters the room, grabbing her blade-wielding arm.

"Did you kill him?" he says softly.

"Unhand me, beast!" Pryde yells as she jumps, kicking Erol in the face.

His head does not move from the impact.

I look at Erol and fear for Pryde, for I have never seen him so angry. His eyes are glowing red, his fangs are showing, and I can see his veins through his fur as they pump blood to his muscles. She tries to move quickly, but a loud snap echoes in the room. Her face turns from pure anger to unbearable agony in a matter of seconds as Erol breaks her arm.

He slowly brings her to his face and asks again in a low tone, "Did you kill my cub, my Ruffus?"

She gasps in terror.

He flings her across the room as if she weighs nothing, slamming her into the wall with force. Erol growls softly as he walks to her, holding his polearm, ready to impale her. With tears in her eyes, she starts to glow blue and creates multiple illusions, all of them injured in the same exact location.

"You will pay for that, beastman!" all of the illusions yell as they shift their weapons to the other hand, attacking in unison.

Erol sweeps his weapon, successfully shattering some of the illusions that charge at him. Other illusions hit their mark and stab Erol in different parts of his body. He is still unfazed, and with a roar, he shakes the room. Pryde, in turn, continues creating more illusions, but he keeps shattering them like glass, sauntering toward her.

"I can smell his blood on you. I know who you are—your mirages cannot fool me," Erol continues to growl at Pryde.

Her face changes from anger to panic, and a wave of her illusions rush to her side, covering her. Erol just swings his polearm, destroying half of them in a clean sweep, knocking the rest down.

Erol yells loudly at her, "You fight me like a weakling! Hiding behind your puppets will not save you from me! You took my most precious possession from me. Now, I will take everything from you!"

Pryde stands up tall and mutters, "You welp, you dare think you are above me?" She raises Black Rose, and, putting her injured arm behind herself, she yells, "En garde!"

With her broken hand, she drops a rose on the floor. She materializes and stabs her rapier on the stem. The room erupts in rose petals, releasing a powerful aroma that engulfs us.

"Erol! Don't breathe! It's poison!" Michael yells, quickly looking back at us. "Do not fret, Trist and Ruffus, my shield will filter the poison."

A fight finally breaks out between Erol and Pryde. Erol blocks her incoming attacks, easily parries her flurries, dodges her lunges, and counters back with such fluidity, I am awestruck.

"My gods, what a fighter," Trist says, admiring him also. "Such brute strength, tactic, endurance, and will."

I yell in pain as she stitches me incorrectly. In a low, raspy voice, I say, "Pay attention!"

Michael is in awe as he says, "It's like they are dancing." The rose petals remain in the air thanks to the combatant's movement and the force of Erol's swings. Pryde is able to stab Erol multiple times in his back and legs, but to no avail since Erol is in an all-out frenzy. He raises his weapon, spinning it with grace while she jumps to strike him down. With a block, Erol grabs her weapon's blade with one last fluid motion of his hand, lets go of his, and falls on top of her with a slam.

Erol speaks calmly. "Who were you?"

She gasps in pain, with tears in her eyes, but she says clearly, "Vanessa Rose Pryde, heir to her house, master of Black Rose, the daemon slayer."

"I did not ask who you are. I asked who you were." Erol raises his head and opens his mouth, and with a roar of anguish, he bites her neck, tearing her skin apart. The rose petals begin to fall as Erol sits back up, spitting her blood out. Her body starts to crack and shatter into a thousand pieces, turning into a bed of rose petals, leaving a single white rose on top.

"She got away," Erol says dryly as he picks up the white rose.

Michael drops the barrier and runs toward Erol with a gasp, who is still kneeling over the rose petals left behind.

"Erol, please breathe into my hands," Michael says as he extends his arms to him.

He gently pushes Michael's hands away and looks up. "I grieve, Priest, for I have lost him. I lost another, my cub, my friend, my lo—"

My loud cough interrupts him. He turns his head and sees me. He tries to get up but falls, wheezing.

Michael puts his hands on Erol's nose and says, "Fool, just breathe normally. I will get that toxin out of you, but I need you to stop squirming and breathe for me."

Erol exhales black smoke out of his nose. Michael grabs a vial and fills it up with the black fumes, carefully encases it, and puts it in his bag next to a small vial of blood. He stands up, pulling out his ward, and says, "This is as good a place as any."

Michael stumbles to the wall. Placing the ward, he turns his back against it and slowly descends to sit. He raises his arm and snaps his finger, successfully activating it.

Light engulfs the room, and we can all feel a weight lifted

off our shoulders—again, the same as before. The hospital brightens up with holy light, allowing the spirits and souls to transcend.

Erol gets up, sluggishly walking toward me, and, with a thud, he falls next to me. His eyes water and he lets a small tear out. I push off the wall and fall on top of him. I can hear a slight purr coming out of him.

In a raspy voice, I say to him, "Found you."

He smiles and closes his eyes, groaning in pain.

Michael limps up to all of us and says, "Lucky us, we are in a hospital. We will feel better in no time."

We all stare at him with a weak glare.

He sighs. "I bet five gold if Ruffus had said that, you all would have chuckled."

I muster my strength and give Michael a thumbs-up.

It takes around an hour to patch ourselves up after our encounter with Pryde, but as we heal ourselves, people start to come out of rooms. Some of them are doctors and help us recover faster with healing magic, allowing Michael to rest and take a nap. They thank us for saving them and tell us that Lady Pryde saved the hospital. She brokered a deal with the geomancer to keep the children and to leave our deceased alone. She even provided first aid to most doctors and warned them not to go outside until she got a rescue party.

"Hard to believe she actually helped people," Michael says as we all make it to the entrance of the hospital.

"Agreed. She hunted us like cattle, one by one," Trist chimed in.

"I am no cattle. I'm a bestlia," Erol says proudly.

"Yeah, yeah, Erol, I'm sure even the undead know you are a bestlia," I say, slightly pained and equally annoyed.

As we walk out, Trist turns around and says to one refugee,

"Please take this, Doctor. Barricade yourselves in here. Aid will come to you."

The doctor nods and asks, "How will we know our allies?"

Trist pulls out a small emblem. "This is the Prime Emblem. All Arcadian soldiers have this on their person. It is made from silver and copper so that no undead can touch this. Trust in Arcadia. They will come and rescue you."

After we resupply with medicine and get a few bites of jerky to eat, we all step outside and look toward the sky. The smoke and clouds have dispersed, showing us the moon shining down at us. The full moon lights up the sky, creating much-needed light, allowing us to see better in the dark. The only problem is that it has a red corner, and it is spreading.

"By the gods," Trist gasps as Michael chants a small prayer for all of us.

Erol is stunned by the moon.

"Well, we are royally screwed, aren't we?" I say, disheartened as the cries of wild creatures fill the air. The wailing of monsters reminds me that we are still in danger.

The Truth of the Matter

"**T**wo of the four districts have been warded. If any undead walk through it, they will die again. Right?" I ask.

"In theory," Michael answers.

"Okay, so if anyone happens to die inside the warded area, their spirit will be immediately sent back to wherever they go."

"In theory."

"If necromancy or any chaotic magic is used, it will be nullified. Meaning undead should be weakened, right?"

"In theory."

I stop and look at Michael. "'In theory' still has many variables!"

Michael nods.

"So, since it's all 'in theory,' you mean to tell me this might not actually work?"

"Ruffus, it will work. You have already witnessed the power of the wards. Now, have you seen any undead lately?"

"No, I haven't, but honestly, I feel like we are rats in a maze! Walking into a trap. Reacting instead of being proactive."

"My cub, you know I am bestlia."

"Yes, I know," I say, feeling exhausted with the conversation. "That is not what I mean, Erol!" I put my hands on my face and try to calm down.

"I know it is hard for one to see, but have hope and faith in this plan. It will work," Michael says as he grabs his book from his belt and taps it.

Trist chimes in, "If I may say, Priest, I can see why Ruffus is worried."

"Go ahead, Trist," Michael says in defeat.

"This holy magic field nullifies all other types of magic that do not complement it. As you say, holy magic is powered by faith and hope. I know you know this." She looks at me, waiting for a reaction, but I kept quiet. "Arcadian magic is devotion and willpower, a perfect combination of emotion and clarity. It works in this zone, although dampened. Elemental magic, wild magicka, and other types of destruction magic are, in theory, suppressed. The wards work to calm emotion, which powers magic."

"So, it's a form of control to make people feel nothing?" I ask.

"No," Michael quickly answers.

Trist continues, "Yes and no. Yes, in the way that it helps law enforcement control chaotic minds and strengthen our resolve, and, no, because people have the willpower to choose what they want to do, whether they resist or comply. It is the reason why Arcadia recruits mages and priests, so there is a balance. As you know, too much of a good thing is always bad. This town in particular—"

"Captain," Michael interrupts, but Trist stops him.

"This town, as you know, only has a singular cathedral and a few churches. The royal family closely monitors the sanctifying and holy acts for reasons unbeknownst to Michael and me. Magicka users rule this town because the forest we are in contains an untapped and enormous amount of energy, perfect for magicka users to hone focus and learn. I also could use the power in the forest to train my skills, but I choose not to."

"So it's all a choice?" I ask.

"Yes, it is all a preference. I can safely say Lady Helena has come here to train and knows the royal family personally, but the master librarian, her brother, chooses not to hone his skills here. He uses other more archaic ways," she says confidently.

"So holy magic is strong against magicka, but magicka counters holy magic?"

Michael nods. "Yes, this is true."

"So can the wards be used against us?"

"No, Ruffus. Understand that no magicka user can dispel the wards. Also remember Mrs. Hearth is a magicka user, but she is just channeling its magic, not using it. Everyone has this ability, even Erol," Michael states.

We all look at Erol, but he is picking his ears.

"But again, she can activate the wards remotely, or did you forget?"

Trist chimes in, "There are several archmages and priests at her disposal. She can only activate them with the priests' help. Again, remember she is a conduit and has been training to use holy magic. In a normal situation, no one can remove those wards."

"Michael, does Trist know about your past?" I ask. They both look at each other and nod in unison.

I start, "Other than keeping information from me and Er—"

"I knew, my cub. It was in the mission information back at the cathedral," Erol adds. "That's why I asked you if we could trust them."

Michael smiles and says, "Information is key to victory."

I huff in anger as Trist asks, "What is your worry?"

"Let me use healing magic for an example. I learned a few

hours ago that holy magic, if applied wrong, can turn into necromancy. In turn, necromancy is an extension of holy magic since both schools know how to return the spirit back or send it off. What would stop a necromancer from turning our wards into a weapon they can use? Michael, you of all people know how easy it is to revive someone wrong accidentally."

Trist remains quiet.

"Ruffus, do not forget, Mrs. Hearth and her crew can detect if something or someone is tampering with magic, and they would know how to counter it," Michael assures me.

"Then explain that to me!" I point at the moon that is now red along one-eighth of its circumference.

Trist bites her lip as Michael answers, "A complete anomaly."

"Is that the truth?" I ask.

Trist looks at me and says, "I truly don't know. All I do know is that it is a bad omen. Where I'm from, it is said that daemons are out and about."

"Back home, it is said that djinns are about to cause mischief," Erol says uncomfortably.

"I believe it is just a natural anomaly. We have all seen a blood moon before. I have witnessed several," Michael reassures everyone, but I can see he is withholding a tad bit of information.

"Michael," I say, putting my hand on his book.

The party comes to a complete stop as Trist quietly observes us. "I sense a 'but' in your mind."

He looks away.

"Swear on the Holy Book of the Divine and the Scriptures of the Three," I say commandingly. "Swear on the books of the hierophants that you do not have more information."

Michael shakes his head and bites his lower lip. "In the ancient scriptures of the first book, it says that evil stirs uncontrollably in the month leading to the blood moon. As you know, a blue moon is considered holy by all theology. Scholars and holy men ignore a blood moon because they fear that by acknowledging the moon's potential, it gives power to everything unholy. What I can surmise is that Cardinal Ludwig wants to show the world that this kingdom is evil. There are rumors of unholy beasts and the practice of immortality. When I went to research this place, the books were missing from all the libraries. Only horror stories of monsters were left. The only place I found some information was a book the cardinal gave me stating the atrocities that this royal family has committed. It even went as far as stating daemons have possessed them all."

"The church ignores a phenomenon that brings power to its opposite? That seems very—"

"Foolish. Your story checks out. When I went to the library, I could not find anything other than horror books and folklore about this town," Trist chimes in.

"I understand that, and hence the reason why Cardinal Ludwig wants to purge this town. He believes that the royal family practices ancient or chaotic magic, and the events leading to this are their fault—another reason I was sent here. I have to report what I see to Cardinal Ludwig. I provide the information that might give him enough leeway to use such drastic actions," Michael says, seeming ashamed and somewhat repulsed. "Look, I do not condone the death of a royal family, but if they are evil, we must stop them."

"But blood moons have happened before. Why now? Why is this the blood moon that the cardinal believes the royal family will use to empower themselves when they had many other chances?"

Michael shrugs. "Checks and balances of power? The struggle between kingdoms? A new change in leadership that does not trust foreign powers?"

Trist says, "We both know too much holy energy can kill if not weaved correctly. Would the cardinal sacrifice the lives of innocents and ours to get his way? Do the others at the council know?"

"Yes, and the reason Mrs. Hearth is here is as a median for Lady Helena to have a second opinion on the matter," he tells Trist, who begins to rub her eyebrows with her hand.

"What is in it for you?" I ask.

He looks directly at her, then shifts his gaze toward me. "He would restore the Ravenholme lineage. It is my fault for accidentally practicing low-grade necromancy. It is my fault my ancestor's mansion was revoked, and my family had to move away from High Town in River Front. He offered me a second chance."

"As I understand it, you are here to report to Ludwig and plea for his support to aid you. If the cardinal gets his way, innocents die," I say as Michael looks down.

"Human priest," Erol says, surprising all of us, "you have to live with the burden of the errors of your ways. It creates strength and resolve, but I ask you, is your family in peril?"

"What?" Michael says as he looks at us for answers.

I get ready to talk, but Trist puts her hand up toward me. I take the cue and remain silent.

"I will ask again: is your family scrounging for food or in peril every night, or do they remain together and support each other?" Erol asks dryly.

Michael stammers, looking at us to jump in, but Trist and I remain quiet. He quickly shifts his gaze toward Erol, who crosses his arms, waiting for an answer. Michael slowly looks down and moves his head side to side. "They still consider me a son, and we have money for food and a home. They have taken up the craft of trading."

"Then you are blessed, Ravenholme," Erol says as he uncrosses his arms, walking past him and us, now leading the party. He looks back at us and says, "We all have things that we cannot control or change. Doubt brings weakness, Priest, and I have seen you protect everyone. You are not weak, and if you ever needed help, which I doubt you will, you can always rely on us." Erol's expression softens. "I can understand your quest to reclaim your place in this world. Know there are hardships ahead, and you are the only one who can fix them. Do not let someone with power control you like a puppet. In the end, they can cut the strings and let you fall in the abyss."

Michael looks at me in surprise while I look at Trist, impressed, as she looks at Erol and says, "I think that is the most I have heard you say since we have met."

Erol shrugs. "I have had enough of the conversation and want to keep going forward—no need to stay stuck and reminisce on old times. To me, it seems that Ravenholme is used as a martyr for a fool's fear. It is quite cowardly to sacrifice anyone for the comfort of this cardinal's mind. A real warrior fights in the front lines instead of hiding behind the safety and comfort of a title."

"Thank you, Erol. I needed perspective," Michael says as he follows his lead.

"As for the blood moon, I knew one was coming soon, and if the foe empowers itself, it will be for its benefit, as we are stronger than it," Erol says as he looks toward the sky. "It feels as if the cardinal uses this moon to ignite fear in our hearts, to see his point and make it unpleasant." He scratches his neck. "What is better word?"

"Irrefutable?" Trist chimes in. "He is trying to make his argument irrefutable by using scare tactics so there is a reason to attack White Wood, using a natural phenomenon as a sign of the gods that this place cursed and evil." He smiles and nods. "Make his point to attack irrefutable." "Your friend is full of surprises, Ruffus. I think Michael realized that the cardinal was using him, and when we get out, I will make sure to report to Commander Leto." Trist smiles as she walks away, following them. "I had an inkling but no solid proof."

I remain still and look up to the moon, thinking, *Purge by holy flame, and Clover says holy magic backlash will create rifts that would allow holy to enter. I wonder who the real enemy is here. It can't be us—we are saving people from the undead. Then again, Michael would have allowed a purge in this town because Ludwig influenced him. The only person in real danger here is Clover. She holds the key to controlling the magic in this town. If she goes, we all go. But if the blood moon empowers chaotic magic, she and the archmages should be fine.* The thought makes me shiver.

I glance toward the cathedral, seeing tiny flickers of light floating in the air lazily, and can't help but think of all the bad that has happened to us in the past hours. What other horrors are waiting for us on this mission with only two more wards to place? The undead have relentlessly tried to stop us as if they knew what we are up to. Malek was a daemon, but he died, and I thought he had the power to control the dead. Michael made sure he sent him off. Whose hand is at play? Could it be the royal family? Malek possessed the king's jester, and Laura did mention trouble with the royal family. Erol yells for me to keep up, snapping my mind back. I begin to run toward them, thinking, We will cross that bridge when we get to it.

An Old Friend

As I catch up to the group, I get a feeling of dread deep within me, as if I've eaten too many salty pork rinds. Nauseated, I fall to my knees. I cough violently, ready to throw up, but nothing comes out. I fall back, sitting down, closing my eyes, taking deeps breaths to calm myself down. My eyes water as I cough violently again, expecting to throw up. Michael rushes to me and quickly places his hand on my forehead.

"What is going on, Ruffus?" he asks as he moves his hand to my neck.

I groan and fall on top of him, dizzy and confused.

Erol kneels next to me, inspecting my body, looking for anything out of the ordinary.

As quickly as my episode comes on, it ends, and I open my eyes, feeling as good as new. Both Erol and Michael look at me, puzzled, and help me get back up.

"Are you okay?" Michael asks as he cleans the dirt off my back.

I shake as my hand, without my consent, moves to my nose, wiping the blood out of my nostrils. They all stare at me, confused.

"I think I'm okay," I say, hesitating, wiping the blood on my sleeve. "I felt a deep dread and fell ill."

Michael abruptly stops and stares behind me as Trist runs next to us in shock, looking at the same.

I turn and glance at the towering beams of light from the wards we placed around the cathedral. They are shining brightly, connected. The lights are hovering frantically as they head toward the cathedral, but something catches my eye—a small ray of light hitting the sky as if it's trying to reach the beam. A small, bright creature is jumping around the rooftops of the burning buildings, shooting the beams. The hair on the back of my neck stands up as I remember seeing this creature twice before.

"I take it you felt it, too, Trist," Michael says quietly.

She nods and says, "What in Arcadia is that?"

The figure starts jumping close to us, still shooting small rays of light to the sky.

"Oh gods," I say, clutching my stomach.

"I feel it too, Ruffus," Trist says as she pulls out her weapons. "That nauseous feeling is one of sensing."

I lurch forward as I put my hand on my mouth and burp loudly.

"I feel a summons, but it is very far away," Michael says as he grabs his book.

Erol pats my back, saying out loud, "I smell topsoil."

I regain my composure, thanks to Erol, and look at the creature coming right at us.

Erol takes a few steps back and says, "Listen." He sniffs the air and adds, "Smells."

There is an odor of rotten flesh overpowering the scent of the burning building now. A gust of wind blows in hard from the direction of the jumping creature. It reaches the top of the building nearest us, and my eyes meet the enemy. Those eyes glow emerald green.

"Oh no. It's him," I murmur.

Erol growls and says, "Cub, is that—?"

The creature screeches loudly and points its thin, hand-like appendage toward us, releasing a narrow beam of light straight for us. Immediately, I react by pushing Erol away and tackling Michael and Trist. The beam misses all of us, but the impact makes a hole in the ground as the force of the explosion pushes us away. Small chunks of rocks fall on top of us, hitting my head, but as we recover from the blast, the creature jumps high into the sky, landing on another roof, staring at us as it makes clicking noises and twitches.

"My gods, is that an actual rakefire?" Trist gasps.

"A wraith that can physically manifest magic? Unheard of!" Michael says, looking fascinated. "Only in legends—"

Erol rolls to our side. His face shows fear and worry combined.

"Whatever it is, it almost got me killed, even before we got into this damn town, and if it's here, the rider will be right behind!" I say as I stand up, facing it.

The thin, scarecrow-looking creature violently begins to twitch, and with a blood-curdling wail, it jumps and shoots a row of houses blocking our path west. The row of houses around us begins to shake as doors slam open, revealing a horde of revenants making quick headway toward us.

"Our path is blocked!" I yell, and look around.

"Head north! Quickly, through the living quarters!" Trist commands as she puts up her shield and runs.

We all follow her, and like a boulder going down a hill, she knocks every single revenant out of our way, creating a path for us. As we run through the street, our approach is obstructed by two abominations eating the carcass of what looks like a horse.

I yell at Trist, "Alleyways!"

The abominations hear us and quickly throw a horse and carriage toward us. Michael and Trist dodge to the left as Erol grabs me, pulling me to the right with him.

"Divide and meet us at the castle!" Michael yells.

We separate through the different alleyways, headed toward the horizon where the castle is. Our run is quite far since we are south and the castle happens to be north of us.

Erol runs right behind me, dodging small cutlery that has been thrown at us by whatever monster is above us. We reach a dead end when Erol suggests, "Climb!"

With the momentum I have, I jump toward the wall, reaching a wooden beam. I carefully make my way to the top until I see an open window. Skillfully, I somersault into the window, rolling inside the room and knocking a few revenants down. They are busy feasting on a body, and I quickly unsheathe Coal, slashing the remaining revenants in the room only to get hit by Erol's body as he jumps, smashing through the wooden window. We get back on our feet as I glare at him. He, in return, gives me a quick wink and abruptly grabs me by the collar, throwing me on his shoulder.

"Sorry, cub, but you are quite slow!" he says as he jumps through a hole in the room.

We make it outside and run along the tile roof. "Hold on, cub!" he huffs between sprints.

I look at his polearm on his back and wonder, How does he do it? How does he run with a polearm, a small satchel, armor, and me on his shoulder? As I lose myself in that thought, a rock smacks me on the face.

Erol yells, "Ready?"

"For what?" I respond as I grab his fur.

With a mighty roar, he jumps to reach a new rooftop, which is higher. The landing isn't graceful. He tumbles down as I dodge his weapon and accidentally rip some of his fur off him. We both roll, hitting the hard roof, knocking down a revenant that was minding its own business. Luckily, we aren't injured.

Erol groans between bursts of laughter, saying, "This is the farthest and highest I have ever jumped!"

I slowly stand up and kick him. "You could have stuck the landing better."

Erol pulls out his tongue at me with a coy smile on his face. I grab his arm and try to pull him up, but a sudden chill catches me by surprise. I exhale and see my breath.

I look to our side only to see the thin, scarecrow-looking creature on the neighboring rooftop. The rakefire clicks loudly, looking me up and down. It raises its thin arm to the air, releasing a bolt of light into the sky.

I hiss, "Shoo, go away."

The creature jumps backward and out of sight instantly. Dumbstruck, I look toward the direction, only to hear Erol say, "Did you just shoo it?"

I turn to face Erol, who is as shocked as me, and shrug. "Guess I scared it?"

Seconds later, a creature tackles me, and I fall on top of Erol. We both roll to fling the creature off, standing and facing the direction of the attacker. A bat, the size of a fat piglet, flutters around us erratically. Without warning, a swarm of them appears like a rolling cloud. The creatures bite and scratch us, trying to knock us down. They let out a quick screech every time they attack, which is remarkably unbearable to withstand.

Swinging my arms wildly, trying to knock them out of the sky, I yell, "Damn it! Where did all these screechers come from?"

"Too many of them to hit!" Erol says as one of them flies into his mouth by accident.

A strong gust of wind knocks the beasts out of our way. As we look toward the gust's direction, we see an old friend again on the neighboring rooftop: the gigantic horse that carries the rider. The creature jumps in place. As it lands, it demolishes the house beneath its hooves. The horse kicks the next two houses connected to the destroyed one, creating a slight tremor around us. Dust and debris cover the whole horse when it finally gets on its hind legs, releasing a loud war cry.

Multiple whispers and voices speak inside my head until a definitive one says, "Kneel before your king!" as a body starts to form on top of the horse.

I look at Erol, who is already holding his polearm, ready to fight. "We must find the others. We cannot defeat him!"

Erol glares at the monster below and looks at me. His angry face reminds me of how he almost died, and I know he wants revenge.

"Erol, please!" I beg.

He snarls at the rider but quickly puts his weapon away, pointing behind me and running. I quickly turn to see the castle is far on the horizon. We jump from rooftop to rooftop, cutting a straight line. I grab a throwing knife and cut clothing lines so we can cross long distances.

The whispers in my head are relentless, almost driving me mad. They all say the same thing: "Run faster, prey. He will die by my hands. All hail the king!"

A deep voice pierces my head, saying, "My subjects will catch you. You will not escape my wrath!"

The castle is still a ways away. We would both get tired before we even reached the halfway point. I see golden flashes of light and a path of undead bodies on the floor not far from us.

Trist and Michael must be alive!

"What are all these voices doing in your head?" Valke's voice pops in. "I am attempting to possess you. Almost did it, too! Now all these random voices are costing me my concentration!"

I need information, you freeloader! I think.

"What about?" Valke appears next to me, floating at my speed. He turns his whole body to look behind us and sighs. "Is there a reason why you are running away from this fight? It seems every time I sneak a peek out of your mind, I always catch you running, lost, or close to death. Also, is that the king of vampires, the Ancient Slayer?"

We make it to a stopping point, for the next jump is too far away, and we have to cross a river. Erol finds an extended cut of rope and quickly ties it to his polearm. He jumps back to sprint forward, releasing the polearm, which clears the gap efficiently. On the other side, the polearm smashes through a window in a bell tower.

He tugs on the rope and secures it on our side. Without thinking, he grabs me and, with all his might, throws me across the gap. I yell in a panic and unexpectedly grab the tight rope and shimmy myself to the other side as Erol turns, throwing a basket of laundry on the rider below. The laundry goes through the rider but blinds the horse, making it come to a complete stop. I make it three-fourths of the way as Erol begins to shimmy on the rope.

As I make landfall, I find a longbow on a balcony with a quiver of arrows next to a guard's body, the guard missing half his face. The guard twitches, and without remorse, I step on his head, bending his helmet, successfully stopping him. I grab the bow, attach the quiver to my belt, and jump back out to the highest point of the roof. Erol is already halfway through the gap. The horse jumps high in the air to land on the building. My senses sharpen in a way that feels like time is slowing down. I see my opportunity. I nock an arrow, pull back on the string, aim carefully, and with a loud tsha, release and say, "Eat shit, you undead beast."

The arrow whistles through the air like a comet in the sky,

hitting between the armor under the horse's chest, right into its flesh. The horse flinches in the air, turning sideways, landing on the corner of the building. The rope vibrates furiously as Erol holds on, not looking back. I nock another arrow, aiming carefully. Once more, I can clearly see the horse attempting to climb as the rider grabs the ledge. I take a deep breath and release the arrow. It flies directly to the horse's face, hitting the red socket it has for an eye. With a loud whine, it falls behind the building, creating a slight tremor.

Erol makes landfall, quickly retrieving his polearm. He rushes at me, picking me up. "You would shame the game hunters in my village, my cub!" he says ecstatically.

I drop the bow and secure the few arrows I have. "Asshole had it coming."

The small victory we'd acquired comes short when a green bolt of light comes from the direction of the fallen horse. Erol glances at me and, again without warning, jumps off the roof. The green bolt changes direction, hitting the pillar of light on the cathedral, creating a loud, crackling boom.

Valke! I concentrate on yelling in my head. *Only top-tier daemons can remove wards, right?*

"If they are strong enough, yes," he replies.

Did the rider summon a daemon or undead? I ask.

"He already has," he replies nonchalantly.

I hesitate. *What did it summon?*

"A trickster daemon. The rakefire, or, as you know him, the thin scarecrow," he replies. "He is created to deceive, misguide. The king, or rider, as you call him, is not targeting us directly, and if he wanted the wards gone, he would have already done so. I can sense him attempting another summons. The trickster is with him."

How did the rider appear without our notice? I respond.

"The trickster is the one who created the portals, allowing all of the undead to roam so freely in this town." Valke seems preoccupied with something else.

Then who summoned the rider?

My head begins to hurt. I feel an immense tug on my chest, shortening my breathing. I squirm violently, falling off of Erol's shoulder. We both tumble while I'm screaming in agony as if my head is being split in two. "Ruffus?" Erol shakes me as I place both my hands on my face and close my eyes. "Cub, what is the matter!" His hands begin to shake. "Answer me!"

The pain finally stops. I open my eyes to see Erol's face, looking into my eyes. I shake my head as I sit back up, groaning, quickly saying, "I'm okay, I promise. I must have injured my head when the rock hit me."

Erol moves my hair and searches for a wound. "Which rock?"

"All of them," I say, unamused.

Erol flicks my nose and giggles. "If you ate more of my food, you would be strong as the bull."

I stand. "I'll take everything but the milk."

All around us calms down, but we keep moving quickly, hoping the rider is still incapacitated. We look down on the street and see a multitude of undead roaming aimlessly. We then decide to stay on the rooftops, traveling through them. We make it to a beautiful plaza, and to our disbelief, we see Michael and Trist finishing off an abomination.

We both jump down and roll to the floor, surprising Michael. "By the Three, where did you both come from?"

"The rooftops," Erol says as he walks up to the abomination, examining the kill. He looks at Trist, who is clearly exhausted, giving her a congratulatory pat on the back. "You must tell me how you defeated him."

Trist exhales. "After we finish our mission."

Michael interrupts them by casting a shield spell, blocking a volley of javelins hurling toward us. "We are not safe here!"

I look toward the sky and see gargoyles coming our way, throwing more projectiles at us. Trist grabs me by the hand, leading me underneath a gatehouse. Right behind us, Erol picks up Michael, throwing him on his shoulder. The gargoyles seem to disappear abruptly as they fly over the gates toward the castle.

"By the gods, I do not know how we all made it," Trist says, exhausted, as she limps toward the mechanism that opens the gatehouse from the outside. With a loud grunt, she attempts to move the wooden lever but fails.

Erol puts Michael down, attempting to move the lever, but to his surprise, he can't move it.

"We have incoming!" I yell as I pull a throwing knife out of my pockets. The horde of revenants now come running toward us.

"I didn't know they could run," Erol says as he attempts to move the lever again.

"They are not supposed to!" Michael adds, surprised.

Trist runs alongside the wall and beckons us to come. None of us hesitate, sprinting to her, hoping she has a plan. When we reach her, she kicks in a wooden door reinforced with iron but falls down, grabbing her leg in pain. Erol quickly runs to her, taking her shield as Michael and I move her out of the way.

Erol takes a few steps back and runs with all his might with the shield up, smashing through the door. He falls inside, making an almost comical racket. From the inside, I can hear a low "ow" coming from him.

We pull Trist inside the door, laying her against the wall, as Michael runs back and slams the door shut while I push a heavy wooden table to block the entrance. We high-five only to be interrupted by the sound of scratching and pounding against the door, slowly breaking through the wood. Erol picks up another table and sets it on top of the other, successfully creating a stronger barricade.

After a few minutes, the noise dies down, allowing us to all sigh in relief.

Michael walks up to Trist, wiping the sweat off his forehead. "Let us see what went wrong." He kneels in front of her leg to inspect it. His hand begins to glow a faint blue, slowly hovering above her wound. After a few seconds, he asks, "Better?"

She swallows. "Much better."

A few candles light the room, allowing us to see that we are in a small barrack inside the gatehouse's wall. The only things inside the room with us are two bodies on the floor, neatly placed next to each other. Michael carefully walks toward them to inspect them. He removes their helmets to see that they are young soldiers. Curious, he moves the head of one and looks at his neck.

"Vampires."

"Are you sure?" Trist asks nervously.

He nods, showing us their necks. They both have puncture wounds on the jugular.

Erol wanders off but returns quickly. "We are safe here for the moment."

"Let us continue," Trist states as she pulls a small piece of jerky out of one of her pockets.

I walk around. "Where are we?"

Michael takes a waterskin out of his side bag and takes a big gulp. "We will soon find out," he says as he wipes his mouth with his arm.

Erol pushes on another door on the opposite side of the

room but cannot open it. "There is a barricade on the other side."

Trist stands up and pushes on the door. "You are right. This means there might be survivors on the other side!"

Erol and Trist manage to force the door open with a strong push, causing the barricade to tumble down on the other side. A cool mist creeps into the room, dropping the temperature enough for me to see my breath slightly.

Erol takes a big whiff of the air. "There are humans here, and elven and odd beasts!"

We all walk out of the room into the castle town. We see our objective, White Wood Castle, close to us.

We all stare at the magnificent-looking structure, "It rivals the castle in River Front."

Everyone nods as Michael walks forward. "We are indeed blessed that we made it to the castle town. I do not think I have ever run so far or fast in my life."

We follow Michael's lead, looking around at the rows of houses and the shops around us. They are all astonishing. To our surprise, there are no dead bodies or bloodstains at all in any of the buildings and adjacent marble roads.

After walking a good while, we make it to a central plaza, which has a beautiful, still-working fountain with a lifelike sculpture of a woman holding an orb in her hand. That is where the water is shooting out.

I move closer and find a plaque embedded in the rim of the marble fountain. I read aloud, "Princess Orchidia Veil, daughter of Malcolm Veil, the Immortal King of White Wood."

"Ze gem of this forest, if you ask me, no?" says a stranger's voice with an accent that reminds me of Pryde's.

We all turn, drawing our weapons, only to see a handsome, middle-aged man with expensive-looking clothes walking toward us. He looks exactly like Vanessa Pryde but in male form.

"Hold!" Trist yells at the man.

He stops, raising both hands. "I come, oh, how do you say, oh yes, peace. Please stay your arm, soldier of Arcadia," he says calmly. "Although, you are the ones surrounded. Unless you mean to cause me harm, I suggest you all sheath your weapons." I glance to the sides to see the windows open with arrows pointed at us. Hesitantly, we all put our weapons away, and to our fortune, the arrows slowly point down.

"*Très bon,*" the man says in a low voice. "Now, on to business. My name is Locem. I am the queen's bodyguard," he says in a proud tone. "Welcome to White Wood Castle Town. This area is known as the Pale District. I was sent here by the queen to greet you, as she would very much like to meet you all."

We stand still and look around us as people start to come out of the houses and shops: beastmen, humans, eldar. Most of them wear expensive-looking clothes, while others look like vagabonds.

"Are you all refugees?" Michael asks. "If so, the cathedral in the middle of town offers sanctuary and fresh supplies."

"*Oui,* we know. We all saw the holy magic pillar, and our scouts know what you carry," Locem answers back politely. "But the Cathedral of the Soul Tree does not offer sanctuary for all of us."

"What do you mean?" Michael replies.

"Well, you see, not all of us are technically, how do you say, human." Locem smirks as he shows us his fangs.

Queen of White Wood

We are escorted forcefully, thanks to Michael. He decided to make trouble when he met his first-ever vampire by grabbing a small stick and threatening to impale it in its heart.

After a long conversation, Locem decided to take us to see the queen, but this time, with an escort.

The castle is as magnificent as it is old. The stones on the castle walls look as if they are brand new, even though some are stained with blood and missing a few bricks. If the castle weren't under siege on the other side of the walls, I would have loved to walk around the courtyard. The garden is magnificent, although somewhat destroyed, thanks to a few dead gargoyle bodies bleeding all over the bushes.

The archers on the walls are scarce and attempting to shoot down incoming attacks from the screechers as gargoyles circle around the outside. One does manage to break through and smash through a tower window, but it falls quickly, with multiple needles embedded in its body. War hounds heavily guard the gatehouse for the castle, a few by a human and a sinister man whose aura envelopes me in fear and whose face is covered by a cowl.

Michael stops to stare at this man, only to be picked up by Erol.

He whispers at us, "That was a warlock! They are practicing illegal magic!"

"Quiet, Michael!" Trist hisses.

The inside of the castle is dark, with only a few candles lighting the high walls and our way. The hallways echo with the cries from the outside, making the atmosphere quite unpleasant. The walls are decorated with old oil paintings of all the royal family members, and to my surprise, they all look the same, as if they feature the same person posing for them.

"You are approaching the throne room," Locem announces. "If I even suspect treachery against Her Majesty, I will feed you to the dogs myself after my warlocks torture you." He looks directly at Michael.

Locem pushes two enormous oak doors open, revealing the throne room. It is well lit with a magnificent chandelier on the walls and has canvases of the town and the forest. The throne is enormous, and it looks as if it were carved directly out of a yew tree, with its leaves still hanging to the side. On its right side, four smaller seats are present, elegant but not as magnificent as the throne, and four others are a step below to its right.

I see a magnificent-looking crown made of pearls and gold resting on top of a white pillow on the throne. Standing next to the throne, a pale, beautiful woman gazes toward us, dressed in a blood-red gown with a pearl tiara.

With a graceful but worried voice, she says, "Welcome to White Wood. My name is Orchidia Veil the Seventh."

Trist takes off her dented helmet, walking a few feet in front of us, and kneels. "My name is Trist, captain of the Arcadia Forces. And these are my companions, Ruffus of Bern, scout for River Front."

I walk next to Trist, bowing as gracefully I can. "Michael Ravenholme, priest of the Three."

Michael's eyes shift toward Trist and then to Locem. He walks up next to me, bowing as he says, "May the light embrace you and cast all shadows away."

The queen nods and says, "Same as to you, Michael Ravenholme."

Trist pauses. "And last, this is Erol of the Wilds. A renowned warrior of River Front."

Erol walks in front of all of us. He nods and quickly moves one of his arms on top of the other and bows.

The queen seems fascinated by Erol, giving an approving nod to him. She sighs and smiles, delighted to see all of us. She walks closer to us and says, "Please rise. You are all welcome in this court. I thank the Pale Tree you have made it here."

We all stand, thanking her.

"As you can see, my kingdom is in peril. I have sent aid to my people, but so few of them remain," she says, looking pained. "I am glad help came when White Wood needs it most."

"Your Highness, I fear we are losing the kingdom. What has occurred?" Trist politely asks.

The queen looks away as her hands close, creating a fist.

Locem walks toward her gently and places his hand on her shoulder. She grabs his hand in comfort and sighs. I glance at Michael, who I can tell is analyzing what he has just seen.

That's too friendly of a gesture for a guard to touch a queen like that and for her reaction to being so carefree.

"How much history of White Wood do you all know?" Locem asks as the queen shifts her gaze toward the throne.

"Just what some books in the library state," Trist replies.

I pull out my notes of what I found in the library and what Clover told me at the cathedral. I volunteer to share my information, keeping it short but hopefully insightful. The group agrees as the queen and Locem listen carefully to what I say, waiting for me to finish before adding, "The history has been told correctly to some degree. I commend you on your information gathering, Ruffus." Locem sighs. "We do not have much time, but I can fill in some of the gaps in the story from the past. It will hopefully hold some clues to the present danger so we can prevent a gruesome future that we see ourselves in.

"As you know, the boy saved by the goddess who eradicated the corrupted druid became the guardian of the forest. His name was Erkes Veil. His power rivaled that of a demigod, but he was kind and just. As the forest regained its former glory, people began to explore to claim its untapped power. He established a small hamlet, which he called White Wood.

"The old hamlet is, in fact, Castle Town, and he built it with the help of the forest elven and druids who pledged allegiance to him. He was loved and renowned by all. Thus, he was crowned the king. Days became weeks, weeks became months, and many years that time forgot to tell passed on, creating a population surge that the forest could contain. The hamlet grew into a town and into the city we now know today."

A platoon of archers ran through the throne room toward another entrance.

"White Wood prospered in the magic trade, creating tension between the other young kingdoms, and soon after, the war came. King Erkes single-handedly defeated battalions of men, beasts, elves, and dwarves who threatened White Wood. This bloody campaign gave him the Immortal title, and people remembered what he was, a monster, and some in White Wood sought his power to become him."

The queen adds, "In the king's bloodlust, corruption reawakened during the decades of war, weakening his willpower. His people saw him draining men of blood amidst the battlefield, but back then, no one knew what a vampire was on this continent, but some knew of the horrific creatures of old, and daemons drank the blood of their victims in other locations of this world."

"Seeing how slowly he lost control at the sight of blood," the queen continues, "he locked himself in his castle, scared of his old, tainted blood and the curse he had gained as a child. His wife of twenty years, Orchidia, was the only human who could calm his appetite by giving him her blood, and out of fear of killing her, he never took more than he needed. My ancestor. Their love saved the king from corruption, but love could not save him from those who seek his power.

"The king offered his power to her, but she always declined it, for the simple fact that she wanted to live a mortal life with her children, and the pain of outliving a child was one she could not bear. For the first time in eons, Erkes felt human again, and the people quickly decided to live in ignorance of what he was because nothing terrible came out of it."

A slight tremor makes us all slightly lose our footing, and a painting falls off the wall. Locem holds on to the queen. "My queen—"

She shakes her head and continues, "During the Blood Moon Festival, where we as a kingdom mourned the dead and communed with the spirits still in the forest, the king was attacked. Holy men from an unknown part of the continent came and successfully dealt a blow to the king that not even his immortality could protect him from. To this day, we do not know what magic they used to put him in a coma or if it was even magic, but this drove the queen into madness.

"As the king was buried, she stole a vial of his blood and consumed it, becoming a vampire. In her rage, she killed half the population of White Wood and their guests from other kingdoms, trying to find the assassins who were sent for her beloved. Using her blood on others, she created an army of brand-new vampires to help her find the assailants, which caused havoc in the forest. The city burned as mages, druids, and soldiers held back the assaults during the festival. This is where the omen of the blood moon came from and the reason why people fear it.

"Her son, Malcom Veil, the eldest of seven and firstborn of the king, rallied his men, and with the help of the blood moon's empowerment, he used old forbidden magic and was able to save White Wood from his mother. Before landing the final blow on the queen, she realized what she had become and yielded. Ashamed, she requested to be buried with her loved one and put under a spell that would let her sleep until her husband woke again. The royal necromancers and warlocks who were still loyal to her obeyed, and now—to this day—she remains buried deep beneath the castle in the royal catacombs, holding hands with the first king. From then on out, the story of the royal family's affliction was turned into a legend, and now the blood moon reminds us of our history, but to the common folk, it brings a dark memory of evil."

Locem sighs, looking at the queen once she finishes the story.

"The king was a good vampire?" Michael scoffs. "Unheard of. It feels like I just listened to a fairy tale."

A few guards step forward, but the queen raises her hand, stopping all of them.

Locem glares his black eyes at Michael, annoyed, and calmly says, "Michael, you do know fairies are quite evil creatures? Well, around in this forest, they are." He walks closer. "The fay are known to kidnap travelers and bleed them dry so they can make sweets and cakes out of their blood. Did you know that? Or did you assume they had no chaotic nature because they use holy magic? Sometimes real monsters hide in the light, with no shadow cast."

Michael scoffs at Locem but remains quiet.

Trist interrupts, "Locem, trust us to protect all citizens of White Wood, alive or undead. It is our mission."

"Although my duties to the church might be my core value, I am entrusted to make sure the safety of White Wood's citizens is my main priority," Michael says, pained but not forced.

Locem puts his hand on Michael's shoulder and says, "Believe me, Priest, I can understand your values more than anyone here."

I step forward and ask Locem, "What did I have to learn from the tale you told of White Wood? What I understand is that the royal family are a coven of vampires, and that mages here practice ancient magic and chaotic magic more than wild magic."

"To a point, yes." The queen nods and says, "Then, a few months ago, there was an amazing discovery of immense proportions. One of our best druids found the Pale Tree and the bark, the same one my ancestor used to receive her gift. We know the tree empowers this forest, and we wanted to examine it. As our legends say, its sap can cure any illness. Its fruits can be used to sustain our special citizens without having to injure any others." She pauses for a second. "As you know, when the queen went mad, she turned a lot of the nobility into vampires. Malcom only killed those who were truly feral, saving most nobility. I am a descendant from one of those families and the royal bloodline of the first vampires. Although I, myself, am not a creature of the night."

Michael looks up surprised, but Trist is the one who speaks to her. "You are not one of them?"

"No," she politely answers. "Nor was my sister, or my mother or her sister, or her mother before that. The only female vampire to exist in our history is the first queen, and that is because she took her husband's blood. You see, females born from the vampire bloodline can choose to become vampires at a young age. We were given the will to resist by our god. Males have no choice on the matter. They either fall into corruption or grow from it. There is a reason the royal families and the noble's lineage are mostly filled with women. Most men do not make it and get killed by their fathers."

"But do you carry the affliction?" Michael asks.

"Yes," she answers. "If I were to have a son, he would become a vampire. If I had a daughter, she would have the choice."

I ask, "Why don't women choose to become vampires?"

"In this lineage, we are reminded of the value of life and the cost of immortality, and it makes sense for us not to want to outlive our children," she says as she looks toward the doors leading outside. "We will speak more of this at a later time though."

"My queen?" Locem asks, worried. "What do you see?"

The ground shakes again, but enough for all of us to feel the tremor's potency.

"They are getting stronger and more constant, my queen," Locem says, looking to the ceiling.

"Locem, make sure all living refugees and soldiers make it to the cathedral safely and continue taking the nobility to the catacombs, where the warlocks and necromancers protect the last living members of the royal family."

Locem stands tall and salutes her. He leaves.

She turns to us with a sad expression. "We believe my brother corrupted the Pale Tree. He wanted to become king early. It was entirely out of his character. Noticing this, my father did not allow his time to end, for he thought my brother was not ready to carry this burden. With the help of the jester, my brother assassinated my father and mother, the king and queen, and members of the royal family that were here.

"He tried to open the Tomb of the Immortal One, but I was able to stop him with the help of my warlock and necromancers. He somehow became feral and used his magic to turn the spirits in the forest against us. We are sure he was the one who raised the revenants and the forbidden creatures that have attacked you. After that, my brother taught that disgusting jester horrific spells and became stronger, and my mages told me he even summoned a daemon to help him take over. Even his betrothed wanted to stop this. She felt the daemon and pleaded with my brother to stop."

"And the rider?" I interrupt. "The one who calls himself the king?"

She looks down. "That—" she hesitates "—was my doing."

I stop writing in my notebook and stare at her as Erol's fist clenches.

She wipes her face. "My necromancers told me that the king, my father, was dead. Out of grief, I tried using holy magic without thinking to revive him. My necromancers warned me and tried to stop me from misusing magic. I accidentally summoned the wrong spirit, creating this abomination."

We all remain silent until I close my notebook, making a small echo in the room. "You beckoned a daemon by mistake, and he summoned others—the rakefire, the hellhound, and multiple minions that ascended. Then your brother summoned more."

"I sent Lady Pryde to hunt the daemons down and plea with my brother to stop. If anyone on the outside knew what has transpired here—"

I interrupt, "She was our enemy in the hospital. Almost killed us, too."

"Her mission was to subdue the threat to our kingdom and destroy any daemon she encountered."

She attacked us because she felt Valke on my sword, I realize. Me being near everyone gave the impression that one of us was possessed. It could have been the reason she hunted us one by one.

She continues, "If my brother succeeds in destroying the Pale Tree, the backlash of unstable magic will destroy the forest. He needs my ancestor's power to do this. But we have created a fortress here and he has not been able to penetrate it."

"By the Three, the destruction would create daemons and holy portals!" Michael says as if he only realizes it now.

Erol whispers to me, "Why is that so bad, cub? The holies are good."

"Not necessarily, Erol. Holies are against new things, new ways of thought, or new techniques. Call them old-fashioned. Whereas daemons' chaotic ways of thoughts create new ways of thinking."

"So, what are we, then?"

"Mortals, I guess. We abide by all laws and none. I can steal a cookie and then give it to a hungry man in need. I don't think we are bad, just opinionated. We have a choice, while they don't, or that is how I understand it."

The two giant doors burst open, and Locem walks in with haste. "My queen!" He kneels. "The gates to Castle Town are about to be destroyed. We have taken heavy casualties."

"Bring all to the castle and fortify the doors. We will not let White Wood Castle fall!" She orders, "Guards, bring my armor and sword." She points at a pair of guards who nod and run. "Locem, is it my brother?"

He looks grim and answers quietly, "It is the late king."

"By the Pale Tree, he must be here for them too. I will protect my people! I will protect the tomb!" the queen shouts. "Take my wrath with you, soldiers and mages! Make our enemies pay with blood and bring me victory! For night! For White Wood!" All the soldiers and mages in the castle rally and chant, "Long live the royal family, long live the night! Long live White Wood!"

The aura of the room changes as Erol walks to the queen and says, "Let me and my cub fight. We have a score to settle with the creature."

He looks at me with conviction, and I nod at him.

"I will provide support from the ramparts, so no monster flies in," Michael states. "All I need is an unstrung bow."

"I will remain here with Locem and Her Royal Majesty if I'm allowed to make sure no civilian is left behind." Trist looks at Locem.

"What do we do with the ward?" I ask.

Michael walks to Erol. "Erol, please give me your ward. I can make it so we won't harm any"—he hesitates—"special party involved."

The queen's smile brightens up the room. "I will take you to the best location for the ward," she says gratefully. "Locem, make sure the warlocks and necromancers shield the nobility and civilians from this ward."

Locem nods and springs into action, with Trist taking a handful of guards outside.

"Ruffus and Erol, please come here," the queen beckon both of us.

We both stand and salute. With a warm smile, she closes her eyes and raises her hand. It begins to glow brightly. "Both of you pull out your weapons."

We do as she asks, and with her index fingers, she touches both our weapons, and they begin to glow faintly. She wavers, only to be quickly caught by a guard. She thanks him and stands up, saying, "Your weapons can now injure ethereal bodies. This is my blessing of the royal bloodline to our most renowned soldiers. Use it wisely." She catches her breath, "Ruffus, your weapon—"

"We will not waste this blessing, Your Royal Majesty." I interrupt, bowing gracefully as Erol lowers his head.

She tilts her head slightly and nods in understanding. "Be careful."

Locem returns with a multitude of people, pointing them to the back of the throne room. He has his weapon pulled out, which is a rapier a lot like Pryde's. He walks to us and says, "Do not fret, you will not fight alone. Once we are done, we will provide assistance."

"How do we kill him?" I ask.

"With the blessing you received, you can damage the body," Michael says. "All you need to do is destroy the heart. It contains the spirit or the controlled soul."

"What about an exorcism?"

"We do not have the resources or time, Ruffus. The ward is not strong enough to tackle him," he replies.

The ground shakes harder.

I look at Erol. "Time for a good old-fashioned scrap."

"It is, my cub. I have been waiting for this fight!" He smiles at me.

Michael interrupts, "Please, both of you, be safe, especially you, Ruffus. I know how reckless you can be." He grabs an unstrung bow that was handed to him by a guard.

He enchants it with a quick prayer, making the bow sizzle as if it were on fire.

"What are you doing?" I ask.

"It is called a Holy Stinger's Bow, my weapon of choice. I can aid people from a distance and more accurately attack my enemy," he says as he examines it. "All I need is a bow."

"You are not a boring old priest, are you?" I smile.

"No, Ruffus. I am an enforcer, or in your terms, a battle priest," he boasts.

"Oh, a title, how important!" I tease as he rolls his eyes. We all change the direction of our gaze toward the doors.

In unison, we say, "He's here."

Battle in the Castle

White Wood Castle is now warded. The refugees hide in a hall guarded by the queen's best guards as the special refugees are safe underneath the castle in the Royal Family Mausoleum and catacombs. To everyone's surprise, the siege on Castle Town is spreading quickly toward the castle itself. The revenants, abominations, nihldrens, gargoyles, and elementals are moving erratically closer to our last bastion, and there are not enough guards to stop them.

As Erol and I make our way down to the courtyard, we both see the battle up in the ramparts. Screechers and gargoyles are unrelenting, savagely attacking the guards. The only saving grace is that Michael is rallying them and leading an assault next to some warlocks and archers. A few abominations try to sweep the archers, but the pikemen and lancers keep them at bay.

The ground shakes violently, and Erol catches me before I fall down the stairs with a quick swipe from his arm. I look at him to thank him, but the words disappear when I see his stern look as if he were preparing himself for a battle that all others would envy. We make it to the castle gates, where a few soldiers and mages are holding back the horde of undead, making sure the gates remain closed. A warlock yells a terrifying spell and disintegrates all the monsters in front of him, giving us the ability to cross the gates safely.

The warlock falls on his butt and says, heaving, "Your trial is here. For the blood moon, win!" He falls quietly back, lying on the floor as a few soldiers drag him to the castle. The soldiers close the gate behind us, wishing us a victory as they look up toward the ramparts.

The rider is in front of us a good few meters away, his horse standing still as he hits the cobblestone floor with his hoof, creating sparks. The rider faces us with a slow turn and stares us down as we both draw our weapons and stand ready for the fight.

I say to Erol, "Here we are, trapped with a powerful foe with no backup."

I am nervous. We have already been fighting to survive all night, with few moments of respite. The only thing keeping me going is the rush of adrenaline and a few potions that give me a quick boost of energy. At least I have Erol with me. Even in the darkest of times, he seems to shine and rally me with his positivity.

The clouds churn above us as more thunder elementals attack the ramparts. Lightning flashes as the sound of thunder rattles my insides while the noise of battle gets me ready for the skirmish. Tiny drops of rain fall on me, and the intensity increases with each passing second.

I quickly glance at Erol, who is murmuring something under his breath. His eyes glow red with anger as his tail twitches rapidly behind him. After letting out a big sigh, he glances at me with his red eyes and smiles. With a smirk of my own, I nod at him, and as quick as lightning, he runs off to join the fight for the castle.

The rider cackles maliciously as he sees Erol charge him, and with a grand sweep of his sword to the floor, he sends gravel flying in Erol's direction. He can withstand the impact but is pushed back a few feet, denting the little bit of his remaining armor. While the enemy is distracted with Erol, I dash behind the horse, and with Coal, I slash at the horse's back leg and succeed in injuring the beast. Whining loudly, the horse loses its balance, and now all the attention is on me.

I somersault back, dodging the horse's tail whip, but I am not quick enough to avoid a punishing kick from the horse's other leg. The backflip absorbs some momentum, but the powerful kick lands on my chest, sending me flying back. With a loud grunt, I twist my body in the air, sticking my landing and preventing any more injury.

Following up on his attack, the rider hurls his sword at me, but I throw myself on the floor, dodging it in the nick of time. The great sword hits a row of houses and shops behind me, causing the entire block to crumble and fall. Erol roars at me to move out of the way, but I am prone and unable to react in time. The debris crashes on top of me, squishing me and pinning me to the ground as a beam of wood and stone hits me all over my body.

Oddly enough, I feel no pain, just weight on top of me. I start to wiggle out and try to find a way out of there. I can hear Erol yelling loudly, and the sound of steel bashing against steel follows quickly. I keep twisting through the wood and gravel until I see a small flash of light, giving me a direction to follow. I move closer and feel a rush of cold on the lower half of my body after a poorly placed wood beam crumbles down. I move my toes and legs and conclude that I am still whole. The cold races up my body and is up to my stomach now. Then a thought hits me: water!

The storm is causing a small flood, and I am trapped. This gives me enough reason to try to move to another area. Another violent flash of light appears through a much bigger hole. I smile and crawl away, but an explosion comes quickly after, knocking more debris ahead and behind me. I make it to the spot and see it's big enough for only my arm to pop out. The freezing sensation is now up to my chest and rapidly climbing up to my neck. I pop my hand out of the small hole and try to feel if there is anything I can push away.

I gasp as I feel a firm grip grab my arm and pull me out of the wreckage. The building behind me rumbles as my eyes focus to see my savior. It is Trist, but her armor is bloody and even more dented.

"Shake it off, soldier! Erol needs our aid!" she commands as she lets me go and runs to the fight.

I run behind her and yell, "How long was I trapped down there?"

"We just arrived at the scene now. It took around twenty minutes to get everyone to safety and ward off the catacombs. Only the queen and Michael can enter," she answers quickly.

I see Erol with multiple bright arrows sticking out of his back as he valiantly and savagely blocks attacks. Another arrow lands on Erol from Michael's direction, and with a mighty roar, Erol moves at lightning speed, retaliating and landing blow after blow on the horse and rider. To his side, Locem is killing revenants as quickly as Pryde did, leaving a small mirage behind him. He jumps, and with a single thrust, multiple flurries appear, stopping a horde of abominations and an elemental.

"Ruffus! Abominations have breached the gates!" Trist yells as she quickly changes direction toward them.

I race off to intercept them when a flurry of bright arrows strikes all of them. I glance in that direction. The onslaught keeps coming from Michael, and he aims at me. A swift bolt hits me square in the chest, and I feel a burst of energy surging through me. Although it is dark and he is far away, I can see him smile and mouth the words, "Fight on!"

The abominations bellow loudly and begin to recover from

the attack, just as I arrive and pick a fight with the horde. Trist joins me after a few seconds, shouting at them, successfully gaining their attention. I take my opportunity and slice their legs, making them fall to the ground, and with a powerful smash from her mace, Trist finishes them off.

"Behind us!" Trist yells as she raises her shield, bracing herself.

As I blindly dodge, I hear a loud bang and see Trist knocked back to the castle wall next to the doors. I roll and face the rider, only to take a good look at him. His horse is cut up and bleeding out black ooze. With a loud whinny, the horse gets on its hind legs, attempting to stomp me flat. An arrow hits the creature, buying me the second I need to react and backflip, doing a set of somersaults. The rider charges at me only to miss me, taking an opportunity to enter the castle behind me. I curse under my breath and stand still, analyzing what happened.

In an instant, Locem yells, "Fall back to the castle and protect your queen!"

Everyone retreats to the castle as the archers cover them.

"Ruffus! After him!" Locem yells at me as he sprints past me into the castle.

I yell at Erol, who is limping toward me, "Get Trist! I will finish this!"

I sprint behind Locem, ready for battle, as a trail of black ooze guides me to the throne room. I see brave soldiers groaning around the corner and a few corpses of mages and warlocks on the floor. In their hands, I see items that look like they could have potentially stopped their enemy, if only I knew how to use their magic. The throne room's giant doors are collapsed in as if they were made of weak wood. Near the throne, I can hear the queen yelling and the monster's loud laughter. I run as fast as I can, hoping for the best.

The rider is smashing something in front of him but abruptly stops, moving back and blocking a flurry of light bursts. I can see Michael with his hands up, inside a dome of light that has visible cracks.

"Michael!" I yell as Locem stops me from getting near.

"Ruffus! The spear on its body! Its beating heart is on the tip!" Michael yells, obviously in pain.

I see what Michael is talking about and quickly run toward the heart as Locem runs to aid Michael and the queen. I jump and throw two knives directly at the monster's heart, but the world stops. I am trapped midair as Locem is frozen in place, grunting. The rider slowly moves, trying to break free as Michael and the queen look surprised.

"By the gods!" Michael yells. "Show yourself, daemon!"

A voice echoes in the room. "I found my way out, meat bag.

Oh, what an inopportune moment you chose to show up, Valke! I think.

"The one and only," his voice speaks in my head.

Both my knives reverse, impaling me as I fly across the room, smashing into the dome Michael created. I gasp in pain as Locem is thrown like a ragdoll, breaking the throne on his way down. The rider is knocked back a few feet toward the throne room entrance and violently yells toward the ceiling.

All of our shadows connect, and Valke erupts from them yelling as he lands on the floor in front of the rider. "I will not have you interrupt me. That heart is mine!"

"Daemon spawn, you were summoned to aid me in killing your opponent and take his spirit! How dare you turn on me?"

"Lesser daemon, you stole the king of White Wood's heart and possessed him. Such power will raise me to greater heights once I kill you!"

"Fool, you have broken your contract, as the hellhound has

with his master! Now suffer as I devour you and send you back to the pits of hell where you belong!" The rider's horse charges as the booming voice erupts in my mind.

With a loud bellowing roar, the two creatures exchange blows with immense power. The throne room becomes a battleground for titanic figures thrashing and destroying the environment.

Meanwhile, Michael drags me into a corner with the queen as Locem limps toward us. "By the Three, you are lucky to be alive! The knife hit you inches away from the heart!" Michael states as the queen stabilizes me. "I knew there was another daemon here. I've felt him since we met! How on earth are you not possessed?" He stares at the battle.

I groan in pain as the queen removes the second knife from my stomach. "Luck, I guess."

"You should have told me! We could have prevented this!" Michael scolds me.

"I had no idea!" I say, hurt.

"Gentlemen, leave your squabbling for another time. We have pressing matters at hand!" Locem says, interrupting both of us as he takes a quick lick of my bloody throwing knives.

I yell at Locem, "Could you not do that?"

He looks a tad ashamed and says, "My apologies, I am new to this gift."

The queen pushes a stone on the wall, opening a trap door on the floor. She looks at us and says, "Through here!"

Locem and Michael carefully move me down the trap door. "Has this always been here?" I ask, mildly annoyed.

"They are all over the castle, my friend!" Locem says as he carries me, eyeing the blood drops on my duster. "How do you think spies keep a tab on everyone in the castle?"

Michael interrupts. "Where does this lead to, Your Majesty?"

She snaps her fingers, and the room lights up with fire braziers, illuminating up a path. "This is the old passage to the cathedral. We need to take a left here," she says as she leads the way.

"What about Erol and the others?" I ask as Michael and Locem help me walk.

"Captain Trist knows of this passage. She will bring the rest of the guards through."

I stare at him, and he reassures me, "Do not worry, there are multiple entrances that lead here, as I said. They do not have to go through the same one we took."

"There they are!" the queen says as she runs toward a dark room.

In front of us, there are ten trollies connected on a rail system. I have read that this human invention was built using steam and metal wheels, but I have never seen them in person. The closest contraption that comes to mind is a mine cart. They look big enough to take around thirty people per ride.

"This station holds twenty carts," Locem states. "As you see, ten are gone. These will be enough for the guards and us."

"Ruffus, do not worry," Michael says as he pulls out a handkerchief. "Once we get to the cathedral, we can try to give you proper medical attention. Do not worry about that daemon—what's in the past is past. We have been through too much this night."

I nod at Michael, who wipes the blood off my forehead and lights some incense.

"What's that for?" I ask.

"Other than calming us down, it's so Erol can find his way to us," he says as he ties the small silver ball to one of the braziers.

We all hear footsteps echoing through the furthest corridor, and Locem looks out. "It seems our companions are coming now!"

Soldiers break through the darkness, limping toward us, but they seem to be groaning and not speaking.

"Balance be achieved! Arm yourselves!" he says, aghast. "Revenants."

"That is impossible! The ward is strongest at the castle. They should not be even able to—"

"Unless what, Michael?" I say frantically.

"The wards have been compromised. That would explain why there are two daemons in the throne room!" he says, panicked.

The fact that I was right usually makes me feel worlds better, but I don't particularly appreciate that I was right on this occasion.

On the other side of the room, fast footsteps echo, and out of the darkness, a multitude of wounded soldiers pour toward us. Erol is leading them as he carries Trist by his shoulder.

We all yell at them about the danger, but a few shielded guards sprint and make a small wall, stopping the revenants and allowing the guards to begin boarding the trollies.

One of them yells, "My queen, get to safety. We will hold them!"

Erol quickly limps to our cart and puts Trist against the cart wall. She seems exhausted and clutches her left arm as if it is broken. All the soldiers mount the remaining nine carts. After they finish, a mage steps out and pulls a lever, making the trollies move.

The queen rushes to the back of the trolley and yells, "Soldiers, haste! Jump!"

Sadly, the warlock and the shielded soldiers remain behind, holding the revenants. As the cart drives away, the warlock yells loudly, "For the night! For White Wood!"

Soon after, a loud explosion echoes through the tunnels leading to the cathedral.

Dagger Fall

"So, it only took a night of terror to discover we could have traveled quickly around town on this," I say in annoyance to anyone who might be listening.

The underground trolley system was built to escape to multiple destinations in case of an emergency. Looking at the rails, it seems to operate by a force unknown to me.

"What is pushing us? Air, steam, or magic?" I ask Michael.

He looks toward the rails and ponders, but he ends up looking at me as confused as I am.

Around five minutes pass, and we feel a tug on the trollies. Slowing down, we come out of a cave and into a room just like the one we fled from, except much dustier.

"Thank the Pale Tree, we made it." The queen sighs in relief. "It looks like my soldiers made it too." She gazes behind her as other trollies begin to appear.

In the distance, on the platform, I can see Laura waiting with a grim look on her face. As we dock, she sends the wounded soldiers to the catacombs of the cathedral, which has been turned into a makeshift medical ward. Refugees are walking around, helping move boxes and learning how to use the little medicine left from Arcadian soldiers.

After all the guards from the castle disembark, an Arcadian

soldier approaches us. "Your Majesty, the cathedral is overrun," he says, kneeling in front of us.

"How is that possible? The shield is being protected by—" Michael states but is interrupted by Laura, who's coming over.

"I can answer the how." Laura fixes her glasses. "A refugee who was claiming to be royalty visited us. The door guards granted him sanctuary after he showed them a royal seal. As he walked to the mages, the soldiers of White Wood recognized him but seemed to be too stunned even to move. In a blink of an eye, he attacked the archmages and the priests. It was our prince.

"Clover was able to push him away and create a shield for the rest of us to take shelter here under the cathedral. The barrier is so potent that I cannot even penetrate it. I don't even know if Clover is still alive." Laura's gaze turns to me and sees me propped against the trolley wall, Erol fixing my hair, Trist next to me, barely conscious. Laura passes the queen and Michael, running to us. "These two are in dire need of medical attention." She looks at Erol, who is looking exhausted. "Erol, do you have the strength to carry them?"

He slowly and painfully nods.

"Good, now let's move them carefully onto a cot," she says as she passes her hand across Trist's forehead.

Erol picks me up as gently as he can, but I can feel his muscles trembling and his limping gait, making him groan every time he steps. A few soldiers see what he is doing and assist with carrying Trist. A hanging cloth gives me some privacy to remove all my clothes so Laura can accurately examine me.

Laying me on a makeshift cot, Laura places her hands on my stomach and begins to check my stab wound. "A rapier made this, and around your bandages is a small stain." She picks them up and looks at the old bandages while she squints, making a funny face. "Looks like traces of nightshade." She puts the old application down on a silver plate as she checks the stitching on my stomach. "Whoever did this was in a hurry or distracted—sloppy." She carefully removes the seams and quickly but skillfully re-does them.

"Ow," I complain quietly.

"Oh, hush," she says as a weak smile escapes.

"How is everyone else?" I ask, trying to make conversation. "The Arcadian medics and priests are looking after the injured," she answers as she injects me with a syringe filled with odd, green-looking liquid. "I just administered an antivenom that will flush any remaining toxin from your body." She stands from her chair next to me and fetches a cup with clear-colored liquid inside. "Here, drink this."

I take it from her hand and chug it, instantly feeling refreshed. "What was in there, some potion to give me a boost of energy or make me stronger?"

She raises her eyebrow and says, "It is just water. I am sure you all are dehydrated." She sits next to me on the cot. "We are almost out of medical supplies and food. We also have no means of communication with the outside world. We need to leave town now. We were lucky one of the cardinals here told us about the underground and we found you. Sadly, there were no trolley carts and we did not know what they did."

I look at her, surprised, and lay my head down, then I ask her, "How did we lose so much?"

"When we were attacked, I had only managed to move a few supply boxes down with the help of"—her voice starts to break—"Lynn."

I remain silent and brace myself for what she has to say. "He took her." She wipes her eyes. "The man used some kind of magic and pulled her away from my arms."

I sit up and hug her. She hugs me back gently, quietly sobbing on my chest. After a few seconds, she pulls away and says, "Go rescue her, please. I will do anything—"

I shush her quietly as I get off the cot and put my stained, damaged clothes and armor on. I look at her and say, "I'll do it free of charge."

She smiles and scoffs. "Yes, okay."

Trist walks into the makeshift room by moving the hanging cloth out of her way. For the first time, I see her without any armor on. She is wearing a stained green tunic and tight black leggings that have a few rips in them. Both her hands are wrapped up in bandages, and her face has cut marks.

She walks next to Laura and sits on the cot. "The sun is supposed to be rising soon. There is a small clock down here, and it says it's three in the morning. How did we lose so much time? Scouts from the outside say it's still pitch black out." She scoffs. "Scouts." She puts her hand up and massages her eyebrows. "It's not even an accurate report. Soldiers can see through the grates above ground."

"The Three wills them to try, at least," Michael says as he walks in. "Do not lose heart, Captain, they are trying to assess the situation as we are, but I do have news."

We all shift our gaze to him.

"I know where the prince is," he states.

"How?" we all say simultaneously.

"I grabbed the last ward after we put our weapons and bags outside. Remember, the parchments are bound with each other. They all need to be activated before they are destroyed, and Clover will have the insight to control the backlash with the help of the archmages and priests. As we saw, daemons entered a warded area, meaning after the castle was warded, someone reversed its spell."

"That means Clover has to be suffering a backlash," Trist adds.

"Correct. The most novice seer can feel such a strong point of magic," Michael says as he looks toward the ceiling. "This last parchment is the final catalyst and the only thing remaining that is keeping Clover alive. If all the parchments are released, the holy magic would be too powerful for even Clover to contain, making her a human bomb. The explosion would release wild magic in the area, allowing rifts to be opened by holy creatures or daemons, creating an Armageddon."

"Well, where are they?" I ask.

Michael and Laura point toward the west.

"You feel it, too, Laura?" I ask, surprised.

"I feel something like Michael, but I have been too busy to even think about it," she responds.

Trist stands up.

Erol walks into the room, almost fully naked. "My cub! I have brought you bread and grape," he says as if nothing happened tonight. His limp is gone, and he looks as if he never got injured. "Have I interrupted something? Good, leave my cub so that he can eat his grape."

"Just one grape? Not grapes?" I say, dumbfounded.

"Yes, it is a special grape. I carry it in a hardened metal container, so I don't squish it by mistake. It is what makes me as strong as me." He smiles as he holds out a small red-looking grape in one hand and a small piece of bread in the other.

Laura stands, getting a closer look at the grape. She gasps and quickly takes it from Erol's hand, examining it. Erol is about to speak when she shushes him. "By the gods, this is a provelian seed! A grape would not be this hard, first of all, Erol. Second, this is a rare and sought-out alchemical—"

Erol interrupts, trying to take the seed back but failing.

"Human, that is a grape! My kin grows it easily by the barrel, and he calls them grapes."

"Erol, these are worth two hundred and fifty gold a seed! Now I understand how you recover inhumanly fast! One-sixteenth of this can restore a full-grown adult in mere minutes, and if carefully brewed, it can—" she says in excitement but is interrupted.

"I have eaten two already," Erol says nonchalantly.

She glares at him. "I, at times, wonder how you are even alive."

"Take it, Laura. We will be fine. If you can quickly brew anything to help the guards, do it."

She smiles, thanking us.

"I will rally the soldiers and get an assault squad ready to retake the cathedral. After that victory, they will escort the royal family and the refugees out." Trist bows and walks confidently outside.

Michael follows her and says, "I will meditate to pinpoint the exact location of Clover. Please come and get me when we are ready to go."

Laura continues to examine the grape, leaving the room in a hurry.

I walk to sit down on my cot, feeling funny, jittery, and unfocused. Erol sits next to me and says, "You are kind of heart, my cub. I would have never shared the grape with them. I only care for you!"

He hands me the bread, and I break it in half. "Here, you need food too. I know you must be hungry."

Erol grabs his half and shoves it in his mouth whole. He chews it and says, "The elf woman will be fine." He swallows the bread. "I talk to her husband. He says she is strong. I am not worried," he says reassuringly.

I nod and take a bite of my bread.

Erol gets closer to me and puts his arm around me, whispering, "I know you want to save her. She reminds you of your dead kin. Have faith. No harm will come to her. I will be there, and I am stronger than a prince!"

I lean against Erol. "This has been a horrifying night, and it is not over yet, not by a long shot. Now Clover is in danger, and this talk of necromancers does remind me of Yubia and her death."

He chuckles, "All will be well. That is what we do. We work to help others. Do not worry. Also, you have something on your side to help."

"You?" I say, and roll my eyes.

"Yes, but you have the experience, and now we know how to save her, and once we save her, we will be rewarded by the husband with food and drinks."

"Well, when we do save her, I'll tell her you did it for the food," I say, smiling.

He bumps his head on mine. "Go now, grab your knives and strong rope so we can drag that prince back here."

We both stand up, and I receive an unexpected hug from Erol. He then proceeds to walk out of the makeshift room, stretching. I finish getting dressed and follow, quickly thinking of what items I might be missing.

As I look at my equipment, I see all the burn marks, cuts, and chunks of fur missing on my leather duster. The chainmail has dents, broken links, and melted pieces. As for my pants, they are all torn up with burn marks on them. I quickly assess my inventory. I have around eight throwing knives left; a small grappling hook with Knitting Guild-grade rope, which would hold my weight fine; only two syringes with medicine in them; and a small syringe with antivenom. My blinding powder is still good, and my boot knife is still in place.

Next to my stuff, I notice the dagger Malek used to summon the banshee. I grab it and hook it to my belt, just in case I run out of knives or am disarmed. Finally, I inspect Coal. No visible damage or dents can be seen. I smile as I think of how much effort my mother put into making this sword.

Trist walks up to me with minimal armor on. Her breastplate is full of dent marks, and her cape is almost entirely torn off. Her shoulder guards are dented, and half of one is too broken even to equip. Her plate legs squeak as she bends the knees, and her helmet is now too damaged to even wear. The shield has holes through it, and the emblem on the middle is all but gone, but her mace is still in good shape, although bloody.

Michael walks up with a scrunchie as he works on his hair. "Laura is going to provide all the soldiers the last of the medical supplies." He hands us four small pouches. "These are ours."

Michael has the look of a man who has not slept for days. His hair, now greasy and dirty, is too wild to brush. His robes are all tattered and torn, covered with blood spatter. His hands are freshly bandaged, and his face has a few cuts. He lets out a long sigh and says, "I do not know about you, but I am exhausted."

"You just need to work in the fields more and do less reading," Erol says as he walks up to us, bumping Michael playfully.

Erol has no armor on. It seems it is too damaged even to wear. He has his leather harness that protects the left side of his chest but exposes his upper torso and back. His pants are full of mud and stains. I see him trying to hide a limp, and I am reminded that he is the most injured one of us all. His chest is full of cuts. His face has a small chunk of fur missing. Although he knows how to hide exhaustion, I can see in his eyes that he could sleep for days. His arms are bandaged up, and so is his stomach. His tail moves weakly side to side as the tip of it is bandaged up.

Trist looks at all of us. "Good, we are all here and ready." She pauses for a second and says, "Men, our mission has changed. We are now going directly to the source of the problem: the prince of White Wood. As of now, he has taken two hostages, Lynnet and Clover. Both of them are powerful hosts of magic. We do not know what he plans for the child, but we know why he has Clover. All remaining soldiers and refugees willing to fight will guard the queen and the injured refugees, escorting them out of this nightmare. But we are the front of this, so we must cut a path through to the cathedral. If one of us falls, we must keep going forward. Any questions?"

Erol laughs and yells, "For our glory!"

The area gets quiet, and the people around us glance toward us.

Trist speaks loudly and says, "The soldiers of Arcadia do not know death!"

All of the soldiers of Arcadia yell in unison, "Arcadia!"

I look around, and everyone seems to gain spirit and hope. Who knew such chants increased morale? As my friends and I walk up the stairs to our impending doom, I whisper to myself, "We will find you, Clover, Lyn. For White Wood and its people."

Bread Crumbs

As Trist opens the barricaded doors to the cathedral, we meet a wave of revenants. With speed and precision, we put them all down without breaking a sweat, clearing a way for the soldiers behind us. As we make our way to the center of the cathedral, we see three screamers. Without a doubt, these monsters are the bane of any adventurers. These undead creatures stand around seven feet tall and are lanky, with long, thin appendages that look like needles, and a mouth that can unhinge itself, dropping down a foot.

With a human-like structure and brown in color, these creatures are apparently created by torturing men and dislocating their appendages, so they grow tall. Warped by magic, they are known to reside in caverns where they can attach themselves to the ceiling, awaiting their favorite prey—us. Their small but powerful claws can rend flesh easily, and what gives them their name is the piercing scream that is almost as powerful as a banshee's. It can disorient, paralyze, or rupture an eardrum if an unlucky soul gets too close to them. The only saving grace we have to defend ourselves against them is that they're slow and need all four appendages to move around.

They are all focused on a glowing green shield that an archmage projects around himself. Relentlessly, they stab the shield, making no dent but projecting a horrible gurgling noise out of them.

Erol whispers to me, "My cub, get the one on the right. I'll sweep the other two."

Quickly and quietly, I make my way behind my target, waiting on Erol's signal. Trist and Michael quietly hide behind rubble, ready to back us up. Erol nods at me, and with a substantial jump, I drive my sword into the back of the monster's neck.

Unable to react, the screamer drops to the floor, making a horrifying muffled sound, grabbing the attention of the other two. Startled, the other two monsters take a deep breath, readying themselves to blow up my ears, but I just wave at them as Erol swings his polearm, removing their heads in a clean sweep, releasing a long puff of air out of their necks. My screamer gets up to its knees.

Erol walks up to it, smiling. "Lucky, we have fought this before, cub!"

"I know. I remember you were in the hospital for a week straight after one screamed in your ear." I move away as it stands on its thin legs and I yell, "Finish it!"

Erol jumps toward the creature, grabbing the hilt of my sword. He forces Coal down, slicing the screamer in half.

"I do love your sword, cub! Sharp enough to cut bone. We should gamble later!" he exclaims as he slashes the air around him. "It tingles when I grab." He chuckles.

I shake my head. "Fine, if I save your life tonight, you have to come with me to Bern and ask my mother to make you a new weapon," I say, walking up to him.

Erol flinches, "I am not worthy to meet the matriarch of your family! She will eat me alive!"

"She won't eat you! Might stab you, but definitely not eat you on the first night," I jest.

Michael clears his throat at both of us, walking toward the barrier, tapping it with his finger, saying, "Archmage, you are safe. It's me, Michael."

The archmage wakes up from his meditation, and in a frightened tone, he says, "How do I know you're not an enemy?" Michael pulls the last ward out of his pocket, showing it to him. The archmage sighs in relief, slowly bringing down his barrier.

"My priest, they took Lady Hearth and a child away," he says as he stands quickly, looking around.

"We know. We will get them back. For now, I need you to gather yourself and help escort these people out of White Wood."

The archmage nods. "It will be done, but please allow me to show my respect to my fallen friends. When I am far enough from White Wood, I will set communications with Meister Helena and report everything. I pray they make haste."

Trist walks up to him and says, "With communication abruptly severed, I have a hunch River Front will rush the battalion here. Now, Archmage, take my knowledge and file a report for the meister and Commander Leto."

"Yes, ma'am," he says as he raises his hand, placing it gently on Trist's forehead. With a quick chant, he pulls a tiny, bright wisp out of her. "I will keep this safe. My knowledge guides your path." He bows and places the wisp in a small crystal bottle as she nods and rubs her forehead slightly.

Locem appears as if from thin air and says, "The area has been cleared. I will start the evacuation."

We all jump, startled, looking at him as he cleans his rapier with a handkerchief.

I look at him in detail and think, He really reminds me of Pryde.

Trist shakes her head and asks Michael, "Where to now?"

He closes his eyes and says, "The last place I can sense a powerful magic entity, on the western end of the town."

Locem gasps and says, "But of course! The west area of White Wood is where the old queen spread the plague of vampirism. You must be careful. There is a tower there that holds the corpses of many of the feral vampires underground." He beckons a White Wood guard toward him. "Begin the evacuation. I am leading toward the eastern gate. It is the most direct path to River Front. Send the scouts out now."

The guard bows and spreads the news, creating movement around us.

"Locem," I say, catching his attention. "I never asked, did your scouts find the refugees in the medical ward?"

"Our last report said that they wouldn't leave until Arcadian soldiers come to their aid," he replies. "But they were rescued. Thanks to Lady Pryde."

"Locem, might you have any information about our enemy?" Michael asks.

"As you know now, or could have guessed, the prince of White Wood is to blame for all this chaos. His name is Alexander Veil. He has studied ancient magic since he was a mere boy and is a prodigy in pyromancy. His fiancée is my sister, Lady Pryde, and to my sadness, I do not know if she aided him in this madness."

"We have had an encounter with her," I say.

He glances at me, bites his lower lip, and asks, "Is she still—"

"Alive? Luckily, she is, but she was heavily injured when she took on Erol by herself."

Locem glances at Erol with an uncomfortable look as Erol licks his lips, smiling evilly at him.

"Good, she still lives, then," Locem says grimly. "I might be able to make her see reason when I find her later." He slowly raises his hand, rubbing his eyebrows. "Ruffus, your weapon and the beastman's are the only things that can deliver the final blow to Alexander."

"Queen's blessing?" I ask.

Locem nods. "Also, she requested that you bring back at least his body. He might have gone mad, but he is still her sibling," he says, ashamed. "I feel responsible for this. If I had noticed his change in behavior . . ." He places his thumb in his chin. "He was who turned me into a vampire. My sister was not happy."

"We will do what we can," Trist says, comforting him. After a brief pause, she turns to us and says, "Let us finish this nightmare. Our candle has burned, and now we must make haste, for we have run out of time."

As we all rush to the front doors, I ask Trist, "Will they be fine? I mean, we do not know how the outside looks! All manner of creatures might overrun it."

"These are Arcadian soldiers, White Wood royal guards, and a powerful archmage from the Mage Quarter. I have faith that they will be fine," she assures me.

As we make it to the broken double door, Trist stops and looks at us, but Erol speaks first. "We are ready. No more words."

She nods, and with my help, we push the broken doors open, revealing a horrible sight in front of us. The clouds are blocking the light every few seconds, and the sky is dark velvet red. The wisps floating above the cathedral are now glowing orange and red, moving aimlessly in the sky. Some dissipate as others whisper to us a language long forgotten that none of us understands. Where the bright pillars of light once stood now, there is an opaque red light in its place.

"By the Three gods of this realm," Michael says in a low

gasp. "All the lost, corrupted spirits. Never in my whole life have I witnessed this much corruption of the dead." He snaps his finger, creating a weak spark of light. "My magic is weak here. I can still perform the miracle of healing, but stronger spells will take me time to conjure."

Erol stands behind Michael, sniffing the air. "There are creatures here I cannot identify," he says as his gaze turns down and he notices a sword. "Priest, take this sword I found. Your book is not hard enough to break a bone, and its cuts are laughable."

Michael genuinely looks hurt by the comment and says, "I will have you know this book of holy miracles has saved entire villages! It has been passed down by generations of enforcers and even saved your life numerous times!"

Erol stares blankly at him as he hands him the sword. "You say your magic is weak, Priest. No monster will wait for you to cast a spell."

"He has a point," I add.

Michael glares at me, and in a huff, he puts the book away in his bag and grabs the sword. "I will show you how proficient I am in arms combat," he growls.

"Don't grab the handle like that. The grooves will make it fall out of your hand if not properly gripped," Trist adds with a smile. "Whatever happened to your unstrung bow?"

"After too much magic, it snapped," he says.

"Pity," we all say in unison.

"Have you ever wielded a sword before?" I ask.

"Of course!" he answers quickly. "I am just not as adept with a blade as other people."

"Then good thing I am coming with you!" Laura says as she walks to us.

I turn to see she has a vest on with vials hanging on each

pocket. Her satchel seems to be cluttered, full of small items, scrolls, and a dagger holster.

We all stare at her and nod at her decision to join us.

"None of you ask why I want to join your band?"

"As long as you can kill and defend, I will be honored that you are with us," Erol says as he inspects her.

"He pretty much sums it up, Doc," I agree.

"Well, good, then," she says, mildly disappointed as if she had a whole speech ready for us. "Now that this is settled, all of you gather and drink this." She pulls out four vials of bright yellow, glowing liquid from her bag.

"What is it?" Trist asks as she takes one.

"Well," Laura says, "it is a compound I made with purified water, flash bug oil, and king scarab—"

"What does it do, Laura?" Trist interrupts.

"Oh, well, yes, it's a tincture that will increase mental stability and deny psychic attack from an unknown source and can help us identify a possession. A simple touch can warn us if someone is under the influence of another being. The flash bug oil will react to warming the point of contact. This is just in case we get separated." She smiles as she hands one to Erol. "Drink up!"

Erol takes a gulp and coughs uncontrollably. "It tastes like when my cub made me drink ocean water!"

"That would be because this tincture also contains rock salts!" she replies, waiting for the rest of us to drink it.

Trist takes a drink and seems utterly unfazed by it as Erol falls to the ground, heaving. Michael raises an eyebrow at Erol and takes a drink after he cleans the opening of the vial. Just like Erol, Michael starts coughing uncontrollably, gasping for air. I hesitate to drink mine, but all eyes are on me as if silently taking a bet on how I will react. With no further thought, I drink the content of the vial as if it was a strong shot of alcohol, only to burp and give a weak cough. The taste is as if I took a block of salt and ate it with salted pork and overdone fish, but it doesn't affect me as much as I thought it would.

"Just as I suspected!" Laura says as if she was enlightened. "Erol, you were a prime candidate for possession!"

"Water!" he exclaims.

Laura pulls a small vial of pink liquid out of her pockets. "Drink this, Erol."

Erol snatches the bottle and drinks it until the last drop, and after the last gulp, he sighs in pure relief.

"It seems your mental state was prime to be possessed or attacked by any being with the ability to probe minds. It boggles my mind that you have not been targeted though. The gods must be on your side." She quickly pulls out a notepad, jotting down a few sentences.

"Why did I not cough?" Trist asks.

"I hypothesize that your Arcadian training saved you."

Michael wipes drool off his mouth and says, "Gods, that was horrid."

Laura looks at Michael and says, "Because you practice magic, you are more susceptible to possessions. The saltier the tincture tastes, the more protection you will receive. I'll explain more later. We have to get moving!"

Erol grabs my satchel and drinks my waterskin whole.

Michael pulls out the ward. "This will give us a general direction on where we have to go. With luck, we will find—"

"I have a better solution," Laura interrupts. "Breadcrumbs!"

We all stare at her, confused.

"It's silver-infused quartz heated with—"

"Gods," I interrupt, "we don't have time for this. What does it do?"

Laura fixes her glasses and says, "Look down on the ground. Lynn dropped a trail for us. I gave her a locator just in case she got separated from me."

I focus my eyes and see a small glittering trail leading away. We all follow the path leading us to the unknown and, hopefully, our last confrontation.

Requiem: The Division

The screeching and bloodcurdling howling of the nightmarish creatures running rampant through the city echoes throughout the night sky. The smell of death and decay intensifies with each passing second as the city's last breaths of life are slowly being extinguished by the undead creatures that now inhabit its walls.

The trail leads us to a guard post with a hidden trap door, concealing a small station with one cart. We all take a vote and decide to hop in and hope that the cart takes us in the right direction. The mechanisms unlatch and boost the cart's speed, making us all hold on to a small piece of metal so we will not lose our balance and fall on the cart's floor. Screechers living in the underground tunnels try to attack us, but the cart is too fast for them to keep up.

"It's almost over. Hold on! We are coming in too fast to the station!" Laura yells as she braces herself.

The cart comes to an abrupt stop after losing some speed, throwing us all off. I land on a few wooden crates, but I am uninjured. I quickly get up, brushing woodchips off me and making sure I have nothing impaling me or any broken bones. "Is everyone all right?" Trist asks as she groans, sliding off a bag of flour.

Laura brushes sugar off her hair as she moves away from

a bag of sugar next to Erol, who is upside down, lying against the wall with what looks like honey dripping on him.

"Nothing broken or too injured," Michael adds as he pulls an onion out of his shirt.

"Where are we?" I ask, walking toward Erol, who has a slight grin as he eats honey off a pot.

Laura inspects the room quickly. "An underground pantry, perhaps, or storage for food. It is connected to a guard post. Maybe we are underneath a kitchen?"

My stomach is growling loudly as I look at a table filled with bagged dough and somewhat fresh-looking apples.

"No time to dawdle. This cart must have taken us in the wrong direction. I cannot see our trail!" Laura says as she looks toward the floor.

"Let's move," Trist says as we all go toward the door on the opposite side of the room.

We all leave the pantry, making our way toward a kitchen that appears empty, with no sign of anyone having been there for a few days. Leading the way, I quietly walk out of the kitchen to a dusty, empty dining room. On the table, there are plates with some food still on them. A few bugs are having a feast.

"This is a mess hall," Trist says quietly as she leaves the kitchen, joining my side.

"It seems it has been abandoned for a few days," I say, carefully walking toward a set of double doors at the far side. I slowly open one of the doors just enough to peek outside. All I can see are a few bodies on the floor immediately in front and the darkness of the sky. I pop my head out and see the immediate area is clear of any monsters.

I hear stumbling behind me, and Michael gasps for air. I carefully put my head back inside and close the door as Laura says, "Michael! What's wrong?"

I turn to see him shivering and holding his head with both his hands. Laura caresses his face and calmly says, "Breathe."

Instantly, I feel a massive headache. I fall to my knees. The pounding sensation inside my forehead feels as if someone has driven an ax through me. I feel a shift in the air as if something is incredibly wrong.

Erol stumbles to me and says, "I felt it too. Something is now here."

"Erol is right," Michael says, pained. "Something just arrived, and we all felt it. We are extremely close—stay sharp."

Trist stands up, shaking her head as Laura catches her breath next to Michael. Erol helps me up, tapping my face with his hand as if he is trying to wake me up.

"I'm fine, Erol," I say to him.

Trist walks up to the door, pushing it open as she grunts in pain. "Get up, all of you! We have company!"

We all spring up to our feet to see three revenants shambling their way near us out of the darkness. Laura gasps excitedly, "There, on the floor! Our trail!"

A surge of bravery enters my body. I quickly unsheathe my sword and run past Trist. With my momentum, I cut down two revenants, slicing the head off the last one. The skull lands on the floor with a splat, and I scoff. "No time to waste, then!" I turn my gaze toward Erol and smile. "I just got three. How many do you have?"

Erol smiles as he walks out of the building. "My cub, you are in for a competition you will not win."

Following the trail, we encounter a medley of undead monsters waiting for us at every corner. We fight a few banshees, revenants, nihldrens, and screamers and two feral ghouls. As Erol and I take down monsters, we call out the numbers of our slain victims.

To all of our surprise, we see Laura is quite adept in combat. Instead of a typical hack and slash, she can whittle down enemies with alchemical explosives and precise white magic. With Michael's help, she can heal us faster and provide us with enough adrenaline while we fight.

"Are they never-ending?" Laura yells as she swallows a vial of green liquid and spits fire out of her mouth.

"Feels that way, doesn't it!" Michael yells, and stabs a revenant while he smites another.

Trist kicks a screamer in the jaw and bashes its head with her shield, spraying a mess of blood on herself. "By the gods!"

"My cub, duck!" Erol says as he swings his polearm, decapitating a few revenants and killing off the last nihldrens. He laughs and yells, "Forty-seven!"

"Look, the trail leads to that old chapel! Erol, throw me to the roof next to us!" I yell.

Erol quickly runs to my side. Picking me up, he says, "Fly." I tap him on the hand, bracing myself. He nods, and I feel him spin, throwing me with immense force toward the roof of a small shop next to us. I twist my body in the air, grabbing the ledge, pulling myself up with surprising ease. Once there, I start to jump rooftop to rooftop toward the chapel, making sure I am following the trail down on the ground. There is a multitude of monsters protecting the very well-kept-looking chapel and blocking our path.

From behind me, I hear Trist calling my name. As I turn, I see a flask coming straight toward my face, with a yelp I barely catch it, almost losing my footing and slipping down off the roof. The flask has a red churning liquid and is very warm to the touch. From afar, I hear Laura's voice telling me, "Shake it hard and throw it toward the enemy, far from us!"

I do as I am asked, shaking the flask violently.

The liquid churns and begins to emit a bright light, heating my hand rapidly. I throw it toward a cluster of monsters far away from everyone. I see Michael creating a shield with Laura's help.

Before the flask hits the floor, it erupts, creating a violent explosion that shakes the foundation of the buildings around it. The eruption sends a cloud of fire rushing through the streets, almost reaching the rooftops. Rapidly, I cover my face with my coat and feel an immense heat upon me. A few seconds pass as the temperature falls, and I feel safe enough to pop my face out again. The roof I am on has patches of orange-looking fire burning brightly, and as I crawl toward the edge of the roof to see the street, I let a small "wow" out of my lips. All of the undead have turned into ash, creating a safe pathway toward the chapel.

I yell toward Laura, "What was that?"

The group runs toward my building as I jump down.

"It is called the essence of hellfire! I was able to extract some from Lynn's puppy and made a powerful concoction!" She looks at Erol and says, "If my math is correct, I have downed around two hundred monsters plus the six I had already under my belt."

Erol scoffs and looks away from her and says, "After here, you are getting me food. The smell is making me hungry."

Michael stares in a worried way at Erol as Trist says, "Good to know burnt flesh makes you hungry."

Around us, a gale of wind knocks us all down to the ground, turning off the fires as a booming voice echoes, "This is as far as I willingly let you go. You have all been useful in placing holykantira wards around town. Your aid has been noted and furthers my purpose."

"Holykantira? Wait, Father has mentioned that holykantira is what ancient civilizations called holy magic," I mumble under my breath.

"Who is speaking?" Trist demands.

"We have many names. The Reckoning, Horsemen, Angel of Swift End, the Vampire King Slayer, but for now you know my vessel as Alexander of White Wood."

"By the will of The Three, surrender, Alexander! Your minions are defeated, and your fiancée has fled. You have no chance of winning!" Michael pleads.

The voice reverberates in my mind. "Priest who serves the teaching of holykantira, you dare order me? Your filth has no place in this world for a user to turn to necromancy! You will be the first to feel the embrace of death!"

"Give us back Clover and Lynn!" I demand as we run for the chapel.

"Ahh, you must be Ruffus of Bern. Your name has been whispered in the veil, and the she-elf mutters your name. She speaks of you in her trance. Come to us and awaken her."

"Where is Lynn?" Laura yells as she runs behind me. "I swear upon my life, not even the Three will stop me from killing you if you hurt her!"

"The alchemist Lauralee Rye, come to us, for I need your assistance. You see, the one called Lynnet, the prodigy child, is defending the she-elf with my hellhound. Her insolence is causing a delay in the reckoning of White Wood. I require your body to trick her."

As we near the gates of the chapel, the ground shakes violently, knocking all of us down as a fissure opens, letting out a blood-curdling scream.

"Alexander's eldest sister will recover both of your bodies." The echo laughs as a multitude of red wisps dive into the gap.

A bright pillar of light erupts out as a sobbing woman begins to float slowly from it. Once the light subsides, I can get up and see a finely dressed woman levitating around four feet over the top of the fissure. She looks similar to the queen of White Wood but older. Her flesh is still pink as if it was alive but a few seconds ago. She removes both hands from her face, revealing deep black eyes with white irises. Melancholically, she asks, "Hero, tell me, is my sister alive?"

Laura lets a tear fall down her cheek. "Laura, please answer me," she says.

"Yes, Princess Antonia, she is now the queen of White Wood." Laura's voice breaks.

She lets a small smile escape her tired-looking eyes and says, "Thank the Pale Tree." She pauses for a moment. "Sadly, I am now bound by the ancient magic. In mere moments, corruption will take its place, and I will not be able to control myself. Prepare yourselves."

The booming voice echoes around us, saying, "Pure to the end, now go."

More red wisps meld with the late Princess Antonia of White Wood. With a small gasp, her floating body goes limp and starts glowing red.

Michael walks in front of all of us and says, "She is powerful in the holy magic arts! Her spirits attempt to fight corruption even now!"

"Yes, she was the bishop's apprentice here in White Wood," Laura adds. "Her grace and kindness, her heart and life were always devoted to helping the undead and afflicted. She meant to save all."

Antonia's body snaps back and lets out a screech. "Ironic, is it not? For me to purify so many feral vampires and cure so many, and now become undead—and not by choice? For one who has fought chaotic magic to now be turned into a puppet of it?"

"You are strong enough, Princess! Your holy magic has saved your mind! Use it to cleanse your spirit and remove the corruption!" Michael pleads.

"The creature who controls me has a stronger attachment to the sacred arts. He is stronger than me, and until he is vanquished, I am under his control,"

"Where are they, Your Majesty?" Trist asks.

She points at the chapel. "In the catacombs with three others: the child, the elf, and my brother. I cannot let you pass. I cannot control it."

Michael points his sword at the princess and says, "When I say go, you will all run toward the chapel. Do not look back, and do not wait for me. Do as I ask."

"She will kill you, Michael! We do not know what manner of undead she is!" I reply.

He smiles and says, "You also forget she knows the same school of magic as I do."

Antonia interrupts, "I am deeply sorry, but this is the end of all of you. I will use only white magic, so your spirits are released to the Pale Tree, and you do not fall under its control. Please forgive me." Her hands begin to glow brightly, summoning an immaculately beautiful golden sword. We all see she can't touch it as it floats around her hand. She raises it, and I feel a deep burning sensation under my skin.

"I will boil all of the sin and corruption out of you all, and once you are weak, I will save your spirits!" she says as the sword glows brightly.

"By the Three! She is about to unleash holy fire on us! Flee to the chapel and leave this fight to me!" Michael's sword erupts with white light. He looks at us and says, "Go!"

I grab Erol and Laura's hands and run toward the entrance of the chapel. Before Trist runs behind us, she looks at Michael and says, "Light guide a path for us."

With that, she runs toward us, leaving Michael behind as the moon in the sky turns almost entirely red.

Requiem: Heretic Priest

May the Three protect me because I am in so much trouble! I keep thinking to myself as I hold Antonia away from the rest of the group as they run to the chapel. Think quickly about your training, what do I do now?

"Your efforts are valiant, Priest, and your skills have bought your friends time from my wrath," she says as her feet touch the ground.

"Princess Antonia, fight the corruption in your spirit! You can beat the hold and free yourself from the magic's grasp!"

She, in turn, smiles and breaks from my magical snare, rushing me quickly. I jump out of the way, only dodging in the nick of time with a minor cut to the shoulder. I turn on the ground to see her look at her sword with a drip of my blood on it. As I get up, I slap my sword hand on my wound, healing it, biding my time and praying that I can develop an idea.

As she observes her sword, she speaks softly. "I am bound to kill you, Priest. Even though it is not what I wish, please help me end my suffering."

I grab my book to see what miracle I can use, but a gale of wind knocks it out of my hand, throwing it a few feet away from me. I look up to see Antonia slowly walking to me with a look on her face that tells me how she will peacefully end me. I grip my sword harder and concentrate to infuse it with a vast amount of holy magic. It is pretty tricky for me to muster the ability to cast any miracles since this area weighs me down with its chaotic aura. Still, in turn, this is advantageous since my enemy also needs time to cast a miracle.

As she raises her sword to charge her next attack, I run as fast as I can to attack her and hopefully win this battle, but as I am upon her, she quickly spins away, raising her hand, releasing multiple bolts of light directly toward me. I deflect most of the bolts by grounding myself, allowing me to absorb some of the attacks and inviting the magic to flow through me. I don't take in an immense amount of energy, which would've been fatal, as I am not trained to conduct a large amount of holy magic.

I attempt to stab the monster again with my now-empowered sword, but again I fail, and the frustration of being toyed with sets in.

"I knew magic would not work on you negatively. Hopefully, you were able to direct my miracles to aid you." Her face twists, and she looks more menacing than before. "If my holy magic will not end you, I will have to adapt to physical combat."

Quick as lightning, she is upon me, close enough to notice how much taller than me she is and how she has massive fangs in her mouth. Her mouth unhinges as she tries to bite my neck. I instantly use a spell and push myself away from her attack, landing next to my book. Impressed with my survival skills, I grab the book and push myself up before she recovers from the spell.

An exorcism, this has to work! But she is not possessed— she is controlled. Okay, I got it. I will turn her into a martyr! She has to ascend—oh gods, only if she sacrifices herself will this miracle work! I think to myself.

As I snap back to reality, I see a volley of bolts of energy heading my way. I am too stunned to move. With no way of defending myself, I become a pin cushion, getting hit by all of the needle-like projectiles. My blood feels as if it's boiling and ripped apart from the inside out. Instinctively, I focus on my hand, creating a glow that rivals the light of the sun. A second later, a massive bolt of energy is released from my hand directly at Antonia and also creates a thick barrier of pure, holy magic around me that lights up the area as if it were midday. The bolt smashes into Antonia, encasing her in a wall as she falls to the ground.

She stands, smiling, as she taps the barrier around her. "You are a smart man, just what I would expect from an Arcadian-trained priest: use my magic to create a spell powerful enough that an undead like me can't manipulate it easily. Bravo."

My legs shake as I cough up blood and pray to be healed enough by my miracle. I shake my head. "How can you even use holy magic if you are undead? You are a living contradiction!"

"It is odd for an undead such as myself to use holy magic, but as the warlocks and necromancers bless their undead, I can bless myself to withstand the impact of holy energy." She taps the shield with her finger, making it violently crack.

"Necromancy."

"This skirmish has gone long enough, Priest. I have to end this now so I can complete my contract," she says, tapping the barrier again.

"Princess, tell me, how do you know he will release you?" I ask.

"Hope," she mutters. The sword she controls shrinks and turns into a dagger, and with a quick thrust, she shatters the barrier, charging at me at lightning speed. I concentrate on thinking of the word *hope*. As I close my eyes, everything around me mutes, and the only sound I can focus on is my heartbeat, which slows down to a calm state.

I open my eyes and see everything as if it is in slow motion as Antonia stabs through my barrier. I see the cracks slowly getting longer and longer as the light dissipates around me. Her eyes are full of grief, sadness, and hate for what she is doing.

"By the Three, I will save you," I whisper as she inches closer to me.

Her hand grasps the dagger, and my hand slowly reaches for my chest.

My heart beats loudly.

As the dagger pierces my skin, I move my other hand to reach for her face, touching her icy skin.

My heart beats even louder.

I feel the dagger now reaching my chest, just inches away from my heart, and before it pumps one last time, I unleash a blast of energy to the blade and her face. I can feel the dagger pumping energy into me, and I am releasing it right back out to her. I close my eyes as I feel the weapon pierce through my chest deeper.

As I reopen my eyes, I can see that I'm in a field of grass, but everything is white and hazy. Right in front of me, a glowing red orb floats lazily a few feet off the ground. The shadow it casts is of multiple creatures writhing and flailing on the floor as if in constant agony. This is a corrupted soul, the energy used to bring the dead back to life again.

"Tell me, Michael, what does death feel like? Is it an embrace of a friend or a terror to you? Is it a relief or a burden?" I hear the princess's voice asking me.

"I would not know, Your Majesty, for I cannot feel death's embrace," I say as I turn around to see her.

"Impossible. I stabbed you through the heart," she whispers. "I felt a soul be released."

I can't help but smile. "There is a reason why I was sent to this town, Princess. I used to practice necromancy. And I know all its weaknesses and strengths."

The princess falls to her knees, and bright red orbs erupt out of her body.

"You see, I knew I could not win this fight, especially not against you. You are stronger, faster, and better at miracle work than I am," I say as she coughs, violently releasing more red orbs.

"I learned something during my time in White Wood. Like what Captain Trist taught me—even a mountain can fall if you push hard enough."

The princess gasps and begins to yell in pain while glowing a bright golden light.

"Or what Erol taught me." I laugh a bit. "Actually, he taught me to literally go all-in on a bet and in a fight. I guess he will be proud of me when I tell him I got stabbed in the heart. I wonder if he will call me cub or some other type of pet name after I tell him how I defeated you."

The last of the red orbs escape her body, melding with the lazy floating one behind me.

"And as for Ruffus? Well, he taught me patience and not to be so closed-minded. Although he tested my patience." I walk up to the princess. "If you are curious as to where we are, Your Majesty"—I look around—"we are in my spirit. I decided to let myself be possessed by you when I touched you, absorbing all the souls inside you and compressing it to this." I point at the floating red orb.

"Also, Laura's potion allowed me to keep control of my mind as you came in. You see, in necromancy, a person can evade death if they can absorb enough souls. When I touched you, I tried to revive you, pushing the souls away from you to me. All that is left is a husk of pure, holy energy now stabbing me, but as I saw how I was able to transfer your energy to my own, I decided to cast a regeneration spell on myself."

The princess smiles as she lies on the floor.

"Lady Helena taught me how to use holy magic and ancient magic correctly enough for me to be able to use this. Now please close your eyes, and let me release both of us, returning you to the Three's embrace," I say calmly.

"Will you live?" she asks.

"Well, this was an uncalculated risk, so I hope I will be in critical condition as I use the holy magic left in you to heal myself from the stab wound you inflicted on me and use this corrupted soul's energy to push you and the blade off me. Then I hope Ruffus and the others find me and heal me," I say calmly.

I close my eyes, loudly chanting my spell, releasing the princess. She explodes in a multitude of colors that float around in the light.

I let out a long sigh and sit down on the floor. I look next to me to see the corruption slowly dripping onto the floor. I wave my hand, and a bright light consumes the orb, replacing the red with golden light.

"Now that is cleansed," I say as I lie down on the floor, pondering whether my idea will work and realizing I have no clue about how to get out of this current state if my first plan fails. I close my eyes and hum a hymn to see if I can come up with an idea to start the process of waking up.

As I lie there, memories of my life come back to me as if they're happening right in front of me. My father sent me to be a priest as a small child of six to secure a position, hopefully, in the king's cabinet—all noble families with multiple sons and daughters sent at least one of their children to the church.

My older brothers became knights, and my sisters became

politicians. I never wanted to be a priest. Since I was a child, I always wanted to work with wood in a vineyard, build houses, be a carpenter, or even step on grapes to make wine. Once I told my father the desire, he almost disowned me, for at that time, having a foot in political power meant the noble houses had more control and wealth in the kingdom.

I resented him for that, but as a good son of Ravenholme, I became the best priest at the mere age of fifteen. I grew close to a boy who shared a room with me. He and I were inseparable—we ate, laughed, cried, and prayed together. One day he fell ill, really ill, so it only took five hours for the disease to claim his life, creating a void in mine.

Broken and defeated, I stole his body from the hospital, took him to a graveyard, and attempted the miracle of a resurrection on him, but I was not powerful enough. As the light rain hit my face, I denounced my faith, for I did not believe that the gods would be so cruel to take something as innocent and precious as him from me. My world felt empty as the rain hit my face. I lay kneeling in the mud, crying quietly, gathering hate for the unfair fate that had befallen me.

Until a creature dressed in brown robes accompanied by a small girl approached me. With crooked teeth, it smiled and asked in a calming tone, "What has you vexed, my child?" as it looked at the body that was in front of me.

I did not move but shifted my eyes to the small girl. I knew her. She was a recruit that the pastors and the archbishop at the time talked about with great praise. They called her a *medium*, someone who could speak to the spirits of the dead. She was from the coal mining town of Bern. Acknowledging this, I asked the child if she could hear him, if she could see him, if she knew where his spirit was, but the odd creature was the one to answer me.

"My dear boy, he is still with us! If you can cast the miracle of rebirth, he will come back to you!"

"I am not strong enough," I replied as I shifted my gaze to the body.

The stranger let a small chuckle escape and said, "My young lad, you are in a cemetery. The trained eye can see souls floating around the graves. Use them to empower yourself. Use them to gain your beloved friend back."

It made sense I could use that power. I asked the question that doomed my family name for the next twelve years: "How?"

Suddenly, I feel something light pounce on my stomach, and something else touches my forehead, snapping me back from my memory. I open my eyes and sit up. Looking down at me is a tiny tabby kitten, staring at me blankly. I close my eyes and rub them, thinking I'm going mad, but when I reopen my eyes, I see a ferret where the kitten was. Confused, I stand up, and a tiny mouse falls from my shoulder to the ground, but before it hits, it morphs into a falcon, flapping its wings and landing next to the ferret.

"What in the world?" I murmur as a seal appears next to me, awkwardly staring but looking at me in the eyes. The sound of whispering children and adults begins to engulf the area, and an all-too-familiar voice greets me from behind.

"You have done me a great service, Michael."

I turn and see Antonia in a beautiful turquoise gown, glowing brilliantly. Her eyes are now a pale violet color with a smile that could stop my heart completely. Her hand extends as a frog appears in her palm. A second later, the frog turns into a puff of smoke, revealing a wisp.

"This wisp will send a message. This is my gift to you." She caresses the wisp.

I gently grab the floating wisp and whisper to it, "Find Lady Helena and tell her all that has happened."

As I tell the wisp the story, I cannot help but think my part of this mission is now over. I have to pray that the rest of my unusual new friends can see this mission through till the end and save us all.

Descending

We make it to the chapel, not looking back but hoping for the best. It is smaller than how it presented itself, and no sign of damage is notable on the outside. The rose garden is still intact, the pillars have no bloodstains, and there is no sign of any undead at all. Trist closes the metal gates behind her as Erol opens the double doors to the building. The inside is bright, as all the wall candles and chandeliers are on, lit with a bright white fire. We slowly walk toward the altar, making sure we do not get ambushed.

Erol sniffs the air and looks at me. "The elf and the child were here. Their scent lingers," he says quietly.

As Trist closes the doors behind her, she says, "I pray to the Three we made the right decision for Michael. I have never left anyone behind." She turns and seems surprised by the condition of the chapel. "This place seems to be in pristine condition, even though there is a war outside. How is this possible?" She walks to us as she looks toward the ceiling.

Laura moves away from us toward a stained-glass window. "Yes, you are correct. There is no trace of undead here. The windows are dusted, everything is clean, and the smell of incense is present. Do you think this is a sanctuary?"

I place my hand on the white linen of the gold-and silver-gilded altar, looking at the symbol embedded in the middle—a four-pointed star with a sun in the background. "This is the mark of a holy. I wonder if there are any other chapels like this in the town."

A soft-spoken voice startles all of us. "Sadly, no, all of the other chapels have been destroyed."

We all face the voice's direction to see it came from a chapel nun wearing white-and-black robes with the emblem of the holy on her chest. She is an average-looking female human with dark hair and tired eyes. Her face is bruised with blemishes and marks, and her hands have cut marks as if she has been whipped. Her robes are well taken care of but dirty as if she has not changed in days. She bows as she fixes her hair, saying, "Welcome to the Church of the Holy."

We all draw our weapons and steel ourselves for a fight, but as she rises from her bow, she calmly and almost tearfully says, "Please, no weapons, no more fighting."

"Identify yourself!" Trist demands.

"My name is May. I swear on my church and life, I mean you no harm!" she says quivering. "I am the last servant who is alive in this church. The rest sacrificed themselves to save him. They are all in the undercroft, dead." She covers her face with both her hands.

I calm my stance and sheath Coal as I walk up to her. I pull out my dirty handkerchief and dab it in a chalice on the altar filled with what I think is holy water. As I get near her, she lowers her head and shakes as if she is waiting for me to beat her. I remove my glove gently, place my fingers underneath her chin, and raise her glance up to me as I wipe her tears off with my handkerchief. Behind me, I can feel Erol about to jump on her if she even thinks about moving a muscle.

I whisper to her as I clean her face, "There, there, you are safe with us. Please stop crying."

Her eyes look at me as if I have shown her a type of kindness she has not ever witnessed before, and she begins to sob quietly, hugging me.

I can feel Erol having an emotional crisis behind me, but I ignore him and say, "For us to be able to help you, we need to know what you know. Can you do that for me?" I hug her back.

A few seconds pass, and she lets go of me and takes a step back, regaining her composure. She fixes her hair again and says, "The prince is not who he says he is. He has been taken over."

Trist walks closer to us, still with her weapon and shield at hand. "What do you mean, he is possessed?"

The nun looks toward Trist and says, "Before His Majesty went into the forest, he came to us to learn more about holykantira, ancient holy magic. He got a letter from a cardinal outside this kingdom informing him of what our church and miracles could do for him and his ailment of vampirism." She pulls out a bloody handkerchief from her pocket, cleaning her nose.

Laura puts her vials away and asks, "Why did he come here and not the main cathedral? The bishop lives there. If he got a letter from a cardinal, he should have gone there first, and like royalty, he could have summoned the bishop with ease."

"Truthfully, I do not know. We here pray to the holy more than the Three. We think of them to be messengers of truth and purity since, in ancient texts, they were the ones who taught eldar and common folk how to use holy miracles. But he also visited the various cults of daemonology and the pagan churches. We thought he was doing research, but—"

The chapel begins to rumble, unexpectedly making the nun duck in fear.

"We must go now," Erol says, looking at the ceiling as he squints his eyes to be sure nothing will fall on top of us.

I look at him and ask, "My friend is right. Is there anything useful you can say before we investigate the undercroft?"

"Yes," she says quietly. "My former colleagues are now in control of the creature. I choose to denounce my faith here and now. Nothing good should have the ability to do this."

It clicked in my head that a daemon was not the cause of all these problems. When Valke talked about the creatures in White Wood, he mentioned a hellhound, the rider, who is a rakefire, and a trickster daemon possessing the jester. They all have the same thing in common: they all are looking for their freedom—it may be Valke's freedom from me, the hellhound from Lynn, and the rider with the release from the one who summoned it. They are all under a type of control, and the prince is systematically using them as pawns to create chaos instead of joining them. Antonia was summoned by a creature that can control holy magic and kept her in control. Unlike the daemon that we fought, he lost control of his summons. The only building that is not destroyed and ignored the chaos outside is this church.

"Leave town. There should be a caravan headed to River Front on the other side of the city. Find it and escape with them. Tell them all you know," I order May.

"I cannot leave them. What if—"

"Go. Now. I won't ask again."

I can see the fear in her face, but I'm sure she understands the gravity of her situation. With a quick nod, she runs past Trist out of the chapel doors.

"Either you are brave or a complete buffoon, Ruffus of Bern!" Trist yells at me in anger. "That could have been an enemy for all we know, and you just provided the location to the caravan! How in the Three's name can you trust her!"

I look at her and smirk. "Call it a gut feeling. If she were undead or a magic-based creature, other than this holy magic, the handkerchief with holy water would have made her react. I paid some attention when Michael spoke. Also, I removed my glove and touched her skin and did not get the warm and fuzzy feeling that she was controlled, which I would have felt with the drink Laura gave us."

Trist's eyes widen in surprise as she shakes her head. "The gods gave you luck, or you are just smarter than you look. Do not waste it. At least your gamble paid off."

"You paid attention to me when I talked about the tincture," Laura murmurs loud enough for me to hear.

I hear Erol holding in laughter, and I look at him, annoyed, and ask, "Something funny, furball?"

He shakes his head. "You are pretty."

Laura walks to where the nun appeared from and says, "There is a staircase here and a weak barrier. She must have tried to seal this place off." She puts her hand through. "It seems it's to keep whatever is on the other side in. We can safely pass through, but I do not know if we can come back out." A few sparks fly from her palm as she tries to pull her arm back through the barrier, knocking herself down.

Trist runs up to her, helping her up. "Are you okay?"

Laura fixes her glasses and stands up, saying, "My hypothesis is correct. This enchantment is to trap people within. Funny enough, it seems to keep white magic users in. The only reason I was able to pull my hand out is that I know how barriers work, and I thought if—"

I interrupt, "You are doing it again, Doc." She smiles and looks down.

Trist gazes at the door and says, "This is the point where we might not return. We don't know what is under here, and a fierce enemy is waiting for us." She turns to all of us and says,

"Whatever happens, I am glad I was able to fight alongside you all."

"Sounds like we might not survive this encounter at all!" I say mockingly.

Erol walks up to me and places his hand on my shoulder as Laura nervously smiles. Trist looks down as if she is trying to come up with something to say.

I sigh loudly, "Well, what are we waiting for? I want to die while I am young, and you all are keeping me from that!" I look at all of them as I walk past Trist and through the barrier, going down the stairs.

"Knowing him, he will need medical attention after we are done here," Laura says as she passes through the barrier after me.

"That idiot," Trist says as she smiles. "I will have to help him out of this, and I do not know how you have the patience for him, Erol." She passes through the barrier, shaking her head.

Erol stops and sniffs the air around him. "Michael, you survived." He inspects his polearm, running his finger over the blade's edge, drawing a tiny drop of blood. He quickly pulls out the charm I gave him when we started this journey and smears the blood on it. With a small prayer, he kisses it and ties it onto his harness, sighing in exhaustion. "Once we are done here, I will take Michael to dinner. I hope he likes dragon marrow. Mhmm, that is delicious. He'll eat it. I know it." Erol walks through the barrier, continuously murmuring things that we will do in the future.

The descent is nerve-wracking, as the staircase echoes with cries, making me wonder why I was the first one to pass through the barrier.

As we all reach the bottom, an enormous room opens up before me, showing me the source of the eerie noise. I wave everyone behind me to crouch and follow me behind a few boxes, hiding us from the people in the room. In the corner of the room on the far side, we can see three human-like creatures containing Lynn's stuffed animal inside a small barrier.

These creatures around the room look exactly like nuns and priests, but they are pale white, like parchment, and glow with an eerie aura around them. On the other side, seven more creatures prepare scrolls and chisel down symbols on a stone slab where Lynn is bound with rope.

Lynn tries to use magic, but it backfires on her, causing her to wail in pain. Laura has to cover her mouth for a second. I look toward Trist and whisper, "What are they doing to her?"

She whispers back, "It seems they are trying to siphon her magic away from her, but the child is resisting."

Erol sniffs the air and points to the tunnel that is not guarded. "The she-elf is that way. We can sneak and reach her."

"We are not leaving Lynn!" Laura whispers angrily.

Trist calms her down and says, "They are, but we are not. Ruffus, Erol, go on ahead and find Clover and stall for time for us to get there."

"Will you be all right?" I ask.

Trist smirks at me and says, "I've taken down more ghouls and monsters than I wanted to count while surviving this town. You are not the only skilled person in this group."

Erol smiles at her and says, "Good fight."

With that, Erol and I sneak our way to the tunnel successfully. I look behind and see both of them discussing a plan, and all I can think of is, *Finish them off quickly and come back to us safely.*

Erol beckons me quietly as we both run into the shadows, ready for our encounter.

Requiem: Knight of the Desert

As the only female in my family, I was always treated differently. I was never allowed to do anything my brothers did, like leave the castle by themselves or go to school or social gatherings. I was told and taught to take care of my ten older brothers and four younger ones since the age of five. As a female, I know how to sew and cook, and I trained to become a great bride. As a child, I never understood why I was so hidden from the world, only to find out that it is rare to give birth to a female in my clan, and we are considered treasures and valuable political tools, like an oasis in the desert.

When I was six, my mother first took me to the desert, hidden away in a basket that her camel held. She disguised herself as a traveling merchant, hiding her face and deepening her voice. Once we were far enough from society, she would take me out of the basket and train me to become strong. My grandfather taught my mother how to be a warrior, so my mother passed down his teachings. I became strong, agile, and resilient.

When we were home, she would hide trinkets in the castle and make me sneak around guards to find them. At the age of seven, I was able to take down a juvenile desert drake. Those legless snakelike dragons ran amuck in the desert, scavenging for food, terrorizing farming communities. That is when Leto saw me. He was only a captain at the time and patrolling the desert region next to the Wilds. He approached my mother, who almost killed him for getting too close, and asked if he could take me under his wing as his pupil.

My mother's secret was out, and my father was furious and almost amassed a small army to try to stop Leto from taking me away. That is when General Moss, the most influential man in the desert, brokered a deal with my father, securing them financially and providing protection and status higher than most royalty in the desert, with ties to secure trading routes. Because of what my mother did, all other females in the clan were being bargained for to be taken by Arcadia. A small rebellion of lords almost caused a war with my family, but in the end, Arcadia protected us.

Before I left with Leto for my new life, Mother came up to me and said, "My jasmine of the desert, you have been given a chance to regain your freedom. Grasp it with both hands. Do not fear the unknown, for once the light shines on it, an unknown becomes known. You are strong. You are brave.

"Most importantly, you must be smart, smarter than all others, for knowledge is the key to any victory. When all else fails, trust your instincts, for the inner understanding of one's self-preservation will save you. May the winds be as gentle as the morning breeze, and remember that your father and I love you till the end of time."

With tears in my eyes, I left with Leto and became the best soldier.

Remembering this, I ask Laura, "What is this concoction you are handing me?"

"It is a magic repellant. Those creatures are emitting some type of old and powerful magic. I prefer to be protected rather than sorry." She takes her small dosage from a flask.

"Does this concoction have any unwanted side effects?" I ask.

"The crescent moon flower pulp might give you a slight headache, but that is all, and it's safe to mix with what you already have taken," she assures me.

I rub my forehead and say, "Small might be an understatement, Laura." I grasp my shield and get ready to start our attack.

"You are a strong woman. You will survive," she whispers. "Now, please remind me of what we are doing."

I nod, "I will charge and knock down the enemies that are close to the child. Untie her and support me with magic or any concoction that might hinder our enemy." I point out the path to Laura. "And as you say, that stuffed animal is a hellhound. We will leave it trapped there. We do not need the extra stress."

I take a deep breath. Once Laura nods that she is ready, I stand and begin my assault. I sprint, throwing my shield toward the cluster of enemies near Lynn, knocking one down as the shield smashes into their head, splashing blood on the wall. I am upon them before they can react, swinging my mace, injuring another creature and pushing it to two others, knocking them all down.

Four down, six to go, I think as I ready myself to attack the others near Lynn. One of the creatures points at me and screeches, warning the rest of the room. Its eyes are milky white, and now that I am close enough to see them, I fear for Lynn's safety. I quickly tackle another of them, allowing me to retrieve my shield from the floor.

A bolt of lightning stops my momentum as I look to my side to see one of the possessed men chanting spells that I cannot recognize. Lifting my shield and charging at him, feeling my guard blasted to no end with potent magic, I can break through, bashing my enemy with ease. With a loud war cry, I gain all the attention toward me so Laura can sneak around and help Lynn. Two others begin chanting, but I am too quick. I run and slide, swiping their feet, causing them to fall.

I spin on the ground with a quick jerk and get back up on my feet, gracefully shield-bashing the next enemy. I realize I knocked down all the enemies in a moment of panic, but no one kept the small barrier up containing the stuffed doll.

In an eruption with a deathly howl, the beast grows in size and bites one of the downed priests, almost swallowing him whole. I charge at him, only to be swiped and thrown back to where Laura and Lynn are.

"I am finally free from them! Their cursed bind is forever gone, and now I can kill that rat of a child. Consuming her will make me ascend." He growls loudly as he examines the room. "Pity I cannot grow to my normal size, but lucky you, I am as big as a wolf."

I yell at the creature, trying to buy time for Laura, "Get back to your previous form. We have no use for you!"

He sits on the floor, laughing loudly, as if he is mocking me. "I am a prisoner no more. And those holy worshipers took my binds from the girl away." He raises his chin, exposing his neck. "You saved me from being sacrificed to that damn holy. In payment, I will kill you quickly and exact my revenge on him, except for her." He stands on all fours and crouches, ready to pounce on us. "That small bitch is mine for the taking." His gaze turns to Lynn, who is holding onto Laura.

I suddenly move to stand in front of them, giving him a piercing look. "You will have to go through me, beast!"

Baring all of his teeth, he says, "My pleasure!"

Without warning, he opens his mouth, blasting a furnace of heat in our direction. I kneel and place my shield in front of me, protecting myself as Laura and Lynn hide behind the altar. The hellish flames are heating my shield too quickly, and if I do not act soon, I will be reduced to char, leaving Laura and Lynn defenseless at the mercy of the hellhound.

Suddenly, a glass bottle smashes into the back of my armor, instantly relieving me from the heat, cooling down all my armor and helping me withstand the assault. Another bottle hits the back of my shield, splashing me with a few bits of glass and dousing me in a silver-tinted liquid. Laura seems to have broken two bottles of something to save my life, but I was exhausted from the heat.

"Trist! You are safe! I have been preparing for this day. Go get him!" Laura urges me on.

I hear a light chuckle coming from the hellhound and the sound of paws hitting cobblestone flooring. He says, "Oh, how simple was that? I know you all must be alive, good. I like my food to be well done. Sadly, this holy place does greatly nullify my abilities, but they are enough for the lot of you."

I can see him through the blaze, sitting down and scratching the back of his ear, "At least that holy can't get me here."

Before the daemon puts his leg down, I burst from the flames, sprinting, ready to begin my assault on him. Once he sees me, he stands still, motionless in surprise, attempting to understand how I survived his fire blast. Mustering all of my strength, I hit him with my mace, making sure he has no time to counter. Dealing blow after blow, I suddenly feel a surge of pain with a small explosion a second later, knocking me back a few feet. I land, kneeling and trembling, violently confused about what has happened to me.

"Damn you, knight of Arcadia!" he yells at me.

I look up and see the beast bleeding from his mouth and eye, but his fur is crackling with what looks like electricity.

I hear a pop from a bottle and a rush of frigid wind rushing past me, knocking the beast back. I turn to see Laura taking a chug from the bottle and blowing freezing air out of her mouth. Once she finishes the bottle, she drops it and violently begins to shiver. Her lips are blue, and her skin looks almost as if she is freezing, with black spots on her already pale face.

The hound is frozen solid with an enraged face, giving me enough time to regain my footing and stand. With a mighty war cry, I charge the beast, smashing my mace to his face, shattering him out of the ice and pushing him a good few feet away. To my horror, the hound stands, spitting a few teeth out, growling more menacingly than before with bloodlust in his eye.

"You will not win, beast! As long as I draw breath, I will protect everyone and will send you back to the underworld with your tail between your legs!" I yell at him.

"I will drag you down with me!"

After the exchange of words, we battle fiercely. He attempts to bite as I put my shield up, pushing me toward the wall. I use the momentum to backflip away from the wall, landing behind him, only to be met by a strong hind kick. I use my silver chain, attaching it to my mace and creating a whip-like weapon, spinning it and harassing the beast, forcing him to move or get smashed. All I can think about is how I have to win, how I have to go back home to see my mother, how I will make Leto proud, and how my place in this world is more than what others want from me.

After a shield bash, the hellhound seizes his opportunity and pounces on me. With a grin on his bloody face, he whispers to me, "Why do you fight me, mortal? Just let go. I can make you stronger."

The world slows, and I feel a solid tug on my head as the

beast gets near my ear. "I am pride incarnate. I will make you stronger. All I need is for you to submit to me willfully. I can see the desire in your eyes, the need to prove yourself in a harsh world. I can see all. We would become one. I can be your new mentor, your new family, the lover you want, and the pride in your heart," he whispers sweetly.

The world slowly begins to turn pale, as if it is being morphed into marble, with the feeling of something trying to push me out but not succeeding. I look the beast in the eye and see a small glimmer of fear in it. I concentrate and move one of my arms free from underneath his enormous paw. Out of nowhere, an idea pops into my mind. Ruffus always gambled and bluffed his way through everything, so I lie and say, "I am sure you are full of it. You would not make me stronger, but my body would." His eyes widen in curiosity. "As the desert freezes at night, so will the corpses of your enemies be if you work for me." He smiles, showing great interest in my deal.

"Now, let us touch foreheads and seal the deal, and we will see Lynn and Laura burn." I smile as I glare at him.

The hound moves his face in front of me, about to lower his forehead, but I grip his paw with my free hand and bash my head on his snout, instantly returning the dark colors into the room. The hound yelps and falls back, writhing in pain, as I broke his nose. It is sad for me that the impact made me almost lose consciousness, but Laura runs to me and places her hands on my forehead.

"Curse you! Curse your line! I will exact my revenge!" The hound shakes his head in pain and, with its paw, tries to wipe the blood out of his broken nose.

I cannot move at all. The hit took the last of my energy with it. I can see the hellhound trying to get up but failing, groaning in pain and trying to shake off the attack.

"I will not lose to you, mortals! I will ascend like the other daemon running around this forsaken city," he says, whimpering and attempting to stand on his feet. "I cannot breathe well. This damn holy magic around me, it burns!"

Lynn slowly walks toward the wounded hellhound, pointing her index finger at him, saying calmly, "I will stop the burning, puppy."

The hellhound looks up to her, but before he can answer, a ray of blue light erupts from her finger, covering the hound's body entirely in blue light. The hound yelps and whines in pain, pleading with her to stop. The room lights up brightly, with Lynn's magic emitting a powerful aura that makes Laura sit up in awe next to me.

"What is happening, Laura?" I groan in pain.

In turn, she quietly says, "She is avenging her parents. This is powerful, advanced magic. Has she been able to do this all along?"

I remain quiet as pained cries and yelping echo around us.

Even the desert sun is more forgiving than a child's wrath.

A Tortured Spirit

I t feels like hours, running through the darkness of the undercroft, but as we go deeper, we can feel the magic in the air, as if we are running through thin sheets of linen. I can see all the shovels, pickaxes, and buckets filled with dirt around the tunnel walls that surround us. The priests had to be excavating this even before the tragedy of White Wood happened. As we plunge into the depths, I pull out the small scroll that I used in the medical ward to provide me with light. We then reach an open room. A few lights dance around us at the center, but not enough for us to see well.

"Cub! The elf, she is there!" Erol says and points toward the center, where the dancing lights are.

To my front, I can see a man being hit by the lights, casting multiple dancing shadows, and Clover sitting down on a simple wooden chair.

I hear the stranger say in a deep voice, "Welcome to the antechamber."

I draw my sword as I start walking toward them. "Give it up. We have survived this nightmare you forced on us."

"Cease your pitiful squabble, human, for we have no patience for you," he responds in a stern, commanding voice.

"Alexander, it's over. Resist the possession. We can end this now. Your kingdom is in ruin, and your family has been almost wiped out." I stop moving.

He chuckles lightly and says, "Ye of too much faith, your ignorance will be your downfall. He is lost and cannot hear." Seemingly out of nowhere, he produces the three wards, glowing brightly, allowing me to see him.

Prince Alexander of White Wood, a royal, human-looking man with high cheekbones and a pointy nose, would charm the pants off anybody he meets if it wasn't for his devilish smile showing his vampire fangs. His blond hair is short and well-kept, and his eyes are violet with a hint of red in each corner. He is wearing a long set of navy pants with black boots and a white shirt with a few smears of blood near his long neck.

"You have the last ward, Ruffus. I need it. Now, relinquish it or burn in the afterlife," he says as he extends his arms.

I spit on the ground next to me. "Over my dead body," I growl.

With a smirk on his face, Alexander says, "Gladly."

The ground shakes violently as three bright portals open up a few feet above the ground. A strong gust of wind pushes Erol and me back. As I focus on the portal, I can see three humanoid figures walking out of them. They stand around six feet tall, and they have pale and glowing auras with bat-like faces, bull horns, and the bodies of strong beastmen. As they step out of the rift, they all fall to one knee and begin to fade. Quickly, Alexander places one of the wards on each of their backs, making them bellow loudly and stop fading.

"What are these creatures, my cub?" Erol asks as he gets in a defensive position.

I feel an odd pulse from my sword and see it faintly glow. "Holy, and by the looks of them, they are of lesser stature."

Erol growls, baring his teeth at the three creatures that are examining themselves.

"Who are you?" I demand.

"Once you are mine and I control your spirits, you will know. Now relinquish yourself to me!" he yells.

The glowing creatures snap back and bellow loudly again, charging at us as Alexander opens a new portal behind him, taking Clover with him.

"They are quick, Erol, but they carry no weapons. Let us end this quickly!" I say as they charge at us.

We both promptly learn that these creatures are more robust than they seem. Erol successfully blocks two of them with his polearm and backhands them, only to roar in pain as he pushes them back.

"Do not touch them!" he says as his hand smokes.

"Damn ethereal beings!" I say as I dodge a sweep from the other one.

The being relentlessly attacks me, but I can counter and slice one arm off, letting out golden-colored blood the consistency of sludge. The monster falls back, grabbing its bleeding arm, and I take the opportunity to dash behind him and slice where his tendons would be, making him fall to his knees. With a swift kick from me, he falls face-first to the ground, and without hesitation, I impale him through the back, where the heart should be. Coal pulsates, surprising me, causing the creature to shriek and flinch.

Suddenly, the creature loses its odd white glow, as if its life just came to an end. To my surprise, my sword hand feels as if it's engulfed in fire while my sword vibrates violently. The antechamber turns pale white as a figure appears next to me. I look toward Erol, seeing him stuck in midair, deflecting two attacks.

The figure next to me takes the shape of what looks like a bull beastman to me, making me scream, "What now?" as I attempt to let go of Coal's handle.

As far as I can remember, the Bos Taur is a rare species of bestlia that lives in secluded locations. Father used to tell me stories about these fantastic beasts. They were the first beastmen ever to be recorded in history, and they were avid followers of holy. With solid bodies, hooved feet, and sharp horns, they would be a force to be reckoned with on a battlefield.

Then he speaks to me, surprising me with his knowledge of the common language. "Human, you have trapped me in this cursed item! When I died in Laberynthea, I pledged my spirit to become of the holy! Release me. You have robbed me of my destiny!"

Stunned, I try mustering words, but the apparition gets closer, growling and speaking loudly. "Release me back to so I may see a rebirth in the glory of the holy's light!"

"L-L-Laberynthea?" I stutter in awe. "I am sorry, I do not know what I'm doing or how I keep doing this!"

"Release me so I may return to the White Citadel and become a holy!" the spirit demands.

I grind my teeth and try to think of all possible courses of action I can take, but nothing creative comes to mind. I can see the spirit turning red and growing in size as I feel a chill in the back of my spine and a jolt of daemonic energy surging through my sword. The spirit's anger is changing him, making the white aura around him change different colors.

I pull the sword out with all my might and try to cut the spirit, but the blade goes right through him.

A familiar yet faraway voice whispers in my ear, "Have confidence in the spirit, pray for its safe return, and ask what destination it wants."

"Spirit! Please let me help you. Tell me again, where do you desire to go?" I clutch my sword as I feel it burning me.

"I want to return home!" it yells loudly, changing colors to a wine red.

"Now, Ruffus, send it away!" the soft voice urges me.

"Go home, spirit!" I yell at it, but nothing happens. I can feel odd energy rising all around us, and as I look to my side, I see shadowy figures encircling us and approaching us. A jolt of fear makes me swing my sword wildly, but the shadows creep closer to us.

Multiple voices start to whisper in my head in different languages, but I understand all.

"Feed that spirit to us!"

"Let it become one of us!"

"Give him to us!"

"Our Lord knows your name and who you are. He is coming now for you!"

"No, no! Feast on his spirit and become us! Power awaits!"

The shadows creep faster to us, and I look back to the beastman to see his face full of fear as if I had condemned him. "For gods' sake, spirit, leave! Go home! I release you, please!" I yell in a panic, but nothing happens.

The shadows all abruptly stop and fix their different-colored eyes on the beastman. One of the shadows impales the spirit to what looks like a hook, making the spirit bellow in pain. I gasp in surprise, as I can feel its sorrow and pain.

Cheers and laughter erupt as more voices say, "Take his essence, become stronger!"

Others say, "Share it with me!" as other shadows impale the spirit.

"NO!" I yell as I try to stop them by cutting the hooks with my sword. My hand now feels numb as a power surges through me, combined with a massive migraine. As I slash the lines, my sword starts glowing brighter in a white aura.

I close my eyes and yell, "Be gone!" as a bright golden light erupts from my sword. In my mind, I can see a pair of horrible red eyes staring me down and an echo of a chuckle reverberating.

I quickly open my eyes to see that I am still in the antechamber with my sword stuck to the ethereal being as Erol knocks the other two back a few good feet.

"Good job, my cub! Now go through the portal and save the she-elf! I will deal with these weaklings!" Erol tells me in an excited voice as he keeps fighting.

My mind is flooded with questions and fears. *What happened to the spirit? Why was I there again? What madness did I just witness? My sword is tainted with daemonic energies. I've known this ever since I killed Valke for the first time when he possessed that soldier. I knew it but ignored the facts for my own damn sake.*

I pull out the sword from the vanquished enemy, and as I examine it, my hand trembles. Coal's blade has turned into a type of clear crystal that I cannot identify at the moment. "Is it because I have slain a holy?"

"RUFFUS!" Erol's yell snaps me back to reality. "Go now!"

"R-right!" I shout as I make a mad dash to the portal.

The other two ethereal beings see what I am doing and sprint after me. With a mighty jump, they are on their way to pounce on top of me. I glance back and brace myself, thinking, *This can't be my end!*

"I am your opponent! Now die by my hands!" Erol yells loudly as he swings his polearm, knocking the enemies out of the air and regaining their focus. They quickly counter him and begin wailing on him with powerful punches.

"Erol!" I yell as I stop and run back to aid him.

Erol pushes them both back away from him and yells, "Go

now! And prove to me that you are mine and part of my clan! Show me your strength by killing the bastard!"

I can see him steaming and bleeding profusely from a cut on his stomach. The ethereal being knocks his polearm out of his hands, making Erol grab him with his bare hands and smash him on the ground with pure force. In turn, he faces me glaring, not wanting to repeat what he told me a few seconds ago. To me, this is the first time I see him for what he is, a strong warrior standing proud and tall.

"Go!" he commands me.

I glare back at him and quickly shuffle through my pockets, pulling out my father's handkerchief and the lucky knife I have strapped to my boot. I promptly tie them together and throw them at Erol. With pure grace, Erol catches them between his fingers.

"Bring those back to me!" I say, and turn around, sprinting toward the portal.

Just before jumping through, I look back at him and smile.

He examines the item and then looks at me.

I say, "Come find me, Erol, and take my body back home!" I turn around and jump through the portal.

Requiem: Warrior of the Wildlands

I *will find you. You will be mine. I will hunt for you and keep you safe,* I think to myself as I examine the present that my cub gave me.

I attach the dagger to my belt as I take a deep breath of air. I clear my mind and focus on the task at hand. My body bleeds from the wounds these weaklings gave me, and I will make them pay. The anger in me festers, and I let all my frustrations out with a mighty roar, so my enemy knows that I will be their end and will not show any mercy, as my father taught me.

These pathetic creatures look at me and charge. Foolish. I grab my polearm and ready myself, swinging as they get near. One of them takes the total hit and gets thrown back as the other breaches through my offense. I quickly steel myself for the blow. Jumping backward, I absorb most of the impact, but the damage is done. I feel my muscles tense up and use the pain to unleash more of my fury upon it.

Sloppy, you runt, I think to myself. *I could have taken the hit and countered.*

The enemy charges toward me again, not allowing me to recover quickly enough. I can feel the full impact of their attack as I get thrown a few feet back. Even though my body is wracked in pain, I will never show it. I must not show pain. I will not be the runt my kin believe I am. I will not let these nobodies take advantage of me as my siblings did when I was a cub.

I fight to beat them.

I am always the last to eat, the last to receive what little affection my father gives. Not anymore. I will kill these monsters, cut off their heads, and present them as an offering to him. They will see me as the leader of the tribe. Even though I am the twelfth, they will see me how my cub sees me, as his equal.

My eldest sibling, the firstborn, might have taken my first wife and made her his own, but I will not let him take my cub Ruffus. My eldest sister might have killed my second wife in a duel and taken my firstborn away, but I will not let her take Ruffus away. My closest-age brothers, the twins, might have killed my first partner for being weak, but this time, I will not stand aside as they take everything I love. I will be back with my cub and save him from this hell he was put in. I will not be weak now or ever.

As I recover and land, I see my enemy running toward the portal, and I panic. I must stop them!

I run roaring toward them, making it known that I will stop them no matter what. With a substantial leap, I spin and throw my polearm, making it whirl, successfully stopping both of my enemies cold in their tracks as my weapon smashes into them.

He killed one of these with ease. I can do it twice as fast!

Without any remorse, I grab both of their legs and squeeze as hard as I can until I hear a crack and feel their bones shift by my will. They bellow loudly, which is the sound I love to listen to my enemy make—pain.

I swing them to the back of the room, creating more distance from the portal. I realize my hands are steaming, and a sharp pain makes me shiver, but I repeat to myself, Never show pain.

That used to be my weakness: I showed too much emotion. All of the tribesmen and womenfolk knew when I trained, and I showed fatigue when I limped home. They also knew I showed fear when other local tribes captured me and ransomed me back to my father in exchange for land. Then I was shamed when my father presented me with my first weapon, the polearm. It was a weapon used for distance combat because I was weak and showed my enemy that I could not take a hit. At the same time, my siblings were blessed with better weapons, weapons that required courage to wield and the ability to remain fearless in combat.

After blowing on my hands to see if it will stop the pain, I see the two creatures meld together, becoming as tall as my father and eldest brother. I grab my polearm and spin it gracefully in the air to then point it at my enemy. The creature lets out a mighty roar, smashing both its fists on the ground, creating a minor quake, but I am steadfast and hold on. I stay still, glaring at it, showing no fear as a warrior should do when facing greater odds.

With speed, the monster rushes to me, and with conviction, I run at it with the intent to kill. I cock my polearm back and get ready to swing. As we meet in the middle, our forces clash, creating a loud boom that would make any spectator gasp in disbelief. My polearm hits its mark, but I lose the skirmish. My enemy grows spikes and impales me, all of them stabbing my body, burning my insides. I try all I can not to show pain, but a weak cough followed by blood escapes my mouth as I fall to the cold, stone ground.

I look to my side and see the beast slowly recovering, but I cannot do the same. My body is in too much pain, but I will not let it know. I must never let it know how much damage it did to me.

I slowly move my arm and pull the spikes out of my body, each one of them more painful than the last. These spikes will make great presents for my siblings, and I will show them the battle scars they left on me. As I pull out the last spike, I feel the pool of blood forming next to me, wetting my fur and staining my pants red. My hand fumbles to grab a syringe made by the doctor, hoping her medicine will make me be able to stand. Weakly, I inject myself, and slowly, I feel the energy coming back to me.

I regain some strength and pull myself up off the ground, writhing in pain. I heave quietly as I walk toward my polearm. A firm grip stops me and begins to burn my torso slightly, and as I look down, I see the creature has its hand stretched out toward me, grabbing me. As it squeezes the life out of me, I can hear a few snaps coming from inside me, accompanied by an excruciating sensation.

My only free arm digs into the creature's arm, piercing its flesh with my claws. The creature moans and shifts in pain before it smashes me to the ground. All goes dark for a second. As my vision recovers, it crashes me again to the ground. I regain consciousness as it raises its arm once more.

As I open my eyes again, I see them, my kin. All of my brothers and sisters are smiling at me maliciously, their tails wagging side to side, up and down, waiting for me to die. My father stands the tallest on his four legs, for he is feral and ancient. Before the gods of the Wilds blessed us with the ability to walk on two legs, my father was the last beast born with the ability to walk on all fours. It was almost two eons later when he met my mother, a beastwoman, and conceived my first brother. I can hear him say, "That runt is not my spawn. My seed spawned seventeen sons and daughters, strong as the mountain, fierce as fire, fluid like water. You are the twelfth of my seed given life into this world, wasted on you."

"Father, you should have let me kill him!" says my oldest brother.

In a stern voice, my mother says to them, "None of my children will kill their own flesh and blood. I have taught you that. Your greed for power is why you will never become a leader of our tribe."

"Silence!" my father roars, making all of them flinch. "Runt, you will leave the Wilds and find your place amongst nature. Only return when you can kill me or become champion of our arena. Otherwise, never come back, and hope death finds you soon."

"My chieftain, Father!" one of my brothers replies. "You are the strongest in the Wilds. Not even the army of men and elves dare cross our borders to conquer. Please do not banish him with an impossible task!"

My father backhands him, drawing blood and knocking a tooth out. My brother stands still and looks away as my father says, "You always show concern, Ceiba. Learn your place. I will deal with you later."

My father then looks straight at me and says, "Leave now. Show me that you carry my blood with you, and if you die before facing me, know you will not be buried with our warriors of old in the sacred grounds. No," he says menacingly, "you will rot, and the maggots will feast on you."

I close my eyes and open them again, only to be smashed against the ground for the last time. The monster throws me to the side like a ragdoll as if I am trash. My vision blurs as I hold back tears, only to see an odd item on the floor. I squint and focus on it, only to see the dagger and charm that my cub gave me. A small tear escapes my eye as all around me goes dark, and as I weakly open my eyes again, I can see him smiling at me. Ruffus, my cub. He looks hungry and happy. The elf Clover is sitting next to me, and I remember the smell of the mountain ranges, cedar, coal, and deer for hunting.

I hear him say, "I am so bored! Clover, we are so close to my home! Can't we just stop there before we continue our mission?"

"For the love of all the goddesses, we have to stick to the mission! This fire wyvern has been killing people, destroying fauna, and hurting the trade routes," the elf replies bitterly.

"These are wild animals. It's in their nature to hunt!" my cub adds.

"Wyverns are not from the native ecosystem. The druids need it defeated to restore balance to this area. Remember, we can use all the data we gather today for future expeditions and migratory tracks," she responds.

My cub looks at me and winks. "You know, I bet you have not eaten any food from this location! You, a big ol' beastman, would definitely enjoy it!"

I turn my gaze away as my heart pounds in my chest. I remain quiet.

He is the only person who deliberately talks to me, as everyone else anywhere I go avoids me because my type of beastmen have a bad reputation. He does not see me as a threat, but as a curious person to talk to.

Miles and hours pass as we walk through the mountains until we find the wyvern. An enormous, red-scaled drake breathes fire as its wings flap like hurricanes. Even though it was a juvenile, it was a mighty foe to slay. I see my cub fighting bravely against such a foe, and all I can think is, I will not lose to a human.

After a fantastic skirmish, we end up being victorious,

except I was meant to die that day. On its final breath, the beast got up for one last attack. He spewed his fire, and I was too slow to react.

Then suddenly, he was on top of me and hugging me, and with a yell, he said, "Do not move!"

As the hellfire passed through us, I thought, *How did he save me, and why did he save me?*

Ruffus went out of his way to save my life. A weak human, someone I could snap like a twig in the blink of an eye.

After the fire died out, he dropped a piece of parchment and glass. He then fell on the floor next to me, laughing and smiling. "You owe me a ton of food after that, big guy!" He picked up the parchment and said, "Lucky for you, I had this fire ward, saved both our butts!" He stood. "Erm, what was your name again? Oh, right, Erol, how can I forget the name of the man who owes me a drink!" He tapped me on the shoulder.

A tear ran down my face as I grabbed him, hugging him carefully, not too strong so I would not break him, and to my surprise, he hugged me back. I expected him to run away from me. I expected everyone here to let me die, but he was unexpected. "You are stabbing my lucky knife into my body! It will be ironic if it ends up killing me! Now let's leave this grumpy eldar behind and go back home to Bern! I promise you will have a great time!" my Ruffus said as he helped me up and walked next to me, toward the road.

I blink and see his lucky knife on the floor next to me as I feel the monster upon me. My sight turns red, and I can feel heat rushing through my whole body. With the energy I have left, I move and grab my cub's dagger, and with a precise hit, I pierce the creature's chest where its heart should be. My hand dives into its chest, and I smile as I feel the creature's beating heart in my hand.

"You have taken me away from him for too long," I whisper to it as I rip its heart out. The golden blood lands all over me as it falls to its knees. The heart feels warm to the touch, but I do not care. I lick my new trophy smiling over my victory. Two small orbs of light escape its body and explode into a multitude of colors. I stand back and fall backward, landing hard on the cold, cobblestone floor.

"Thank you, my cub," I whisper to myself as the room turns black and I feel my body slowly bleeding out.

I open my eyes again to see my cub lying next to me, caressing my face, and as I weakly blink, he disappears. "I can't die just yet. My cub, I will join you soon. I'm sorry."

My head gently drops to the ground as the antechamber begins to rumble. Still in my hand, the heart of the unnamed holy beats slowly.

My hand twitches and squeezes the heart until it stops beating as I take one more breath, praying to anyone who can hear me, "Save him."

The Highest Point

As I jump into the portal, all I can think about is Michael, Trist, Laura, Lynn, Clover, and Erol. We all have come so far in such little time. This mission was intended to provide aid for the people of White Wood, but it turned out to be a hellish trial of survival. I wonder if we are supposed to be the ones to save this town.

To me, this siege on White Wood makes sense now. These wards were created by holy magic. They were supposed to send the wayward spirits and souls back to where they belong, but if we had made it to Castle Town and activated it, the nobility, which are vampires, would have all either died again or been weak enough to finish off.

Does River Front know about the nobility of these people and their history? Impossible. Lady Helena was here before she must have known. Was this a deliberate attack on White Wood? Yes, they are an old line of vampires, and, yes, they are creatures of magic and chaos, going against natural law and the top predator against common folk, but the ones I met, with the bit of interaction I had, do not match the savages of old tales.

Or were these wards supposed to suppress the magic in White Wood or neutralize the magic in the surrounding forest? Without magic, it would be easier to lay siege to this kingdom, and control of the magical forest would be beneficial to whoever conquers it. This is what Cardinal Ludwig wants, a purge of chaotic magic and creatures in the area.

Then there is the question of all these undead monsters around the city. Usually, these creatures do not cooperate with anything. The only goal for them is to feed, but since we got to this town, all of these creatures have systematically worked together to stop anyone opposing it. I had no idea how powerful a daemon could be. Alexander is a formidable foe if he can amass this army of the undead, but that does not explain why a holy has possessed him and is using him.

As I have understood the laws of chaotic magic and holy magic, a necromancer is the only one who can successfully use a soul, while a holy magic user can only use a spirit. A spirit has a consciousness still, while a soul is a form of energy. A spirit will lose consciousness, becoming a soul, while a soul can regain consciousness, becoming a spirit.

From what I have learned from Jura and my father, once a living thing dies by a non-natural cause, a priest or a necromancer can suppress the spirit to stay in its vessel and only have around two minutes to seal the wound and reattach the spirit back to its body. Still, only a priest can cast the miracle if the spirit is not tainted. Once the body starts to decompose, a spirit will become tainted, allowing the necromancer to revive the body or remove the consciousness and use the soul as a form of energy to control the vessel or tether it to anything else.

As I land on the other side of the portal, a cold gust of wind greets me, making me shiver. My surroundings tell me I am outside on a platform, as the clouds are closer to me and the sky lights up with lightning every few seconds. On the horizon, I can see a glimmer of sunlight trying to rise, but the clouds engulf it as if they were meant to forbid it from the light of day. I walk up to the edges to see that I'm on the cathedral's highest point, and below me, the city is engulfed in flames with red wisps flying around. The moon is slowly falling to the horizon, still shining fully in a crimson-red hue.

"You survived," says an exhausted voice.

I turn to see Alexander lying against a broken wall next to the portal and on his side. Clover is heaving as if she has awakened from a nightmare.

"Clover!" I quickly walk up to them with my sword, ready to impale Alexander, but she raises her hand to stop me.

"Do not," she says weakly, "kill him."

I push Alexander out of the way and kneel next to Clover, caressing her face and inspecting her. Her dagger is melted, her book is almost entirely torn apart, and on her hand, I see three makeshift wards with a white glow surrounding them.

"Ruffus, you do not have time to waste. I am trying to siphon the wards' energy into these, but I can't. You have to stop him from opening more rifts." She groans as she begins to glow in an aura of light.

I administer my last syringe to her, hoping she can be restored with some energy. Throwing the empty needle aside, I can see Alexander attempting to stand but utterly failing. I feel pure rage boiling inside me as I near him with my sword, ready to impale him again, ending his pitiful existence. As I turn to him, I can see the agony in his face. One of his fangs is chipped, and tears run down his face. I grab him by his blond hair and expose his neck to me. He weakly grabs my arm but fails to break my grip.

"Do you know how you kill a vampire, Alexander? All you need to do is decapitate them and rip the heart out, burning them after."

"Please." He coughs weakly. "I am to blame for a lot, but not this." He gasps in pain.

I mock him by stuttering what he said back, and I put the tip of my sword on his neck. "I will give you what you failed to give the people of White Wood: last words. Now, what are they?"

"Ruffus." Clover raises her weak voice to me. "He is telling the truth."

I glance at her, dropping Alexander onto the ground. She points at an area that I overlooked to my side, going away from the cathedral. A flight of stairs heads up to a blue, glowing platform that looks as if it is made of glass, and on it, a dark red wall of light stands, resembling a barrier.

"It is a fully fledged, named holy," Clover says dryly. "He absorbed all the holy magic from the wards, and I have been trying to steal it back, but to no avail. Alexander was possessed by him. It made him summon Valke and the hellhound and commit necromancy, using his vast knowledge of ancient magic. He tricked Alexander's followers into thinking Alexander was giving them orders, and he is the reason corrupted undead are roaming the streets. Alexander was able to entrap him in a chaotic barrier so he would not escape. If Alexander dies, we all die."

I glare at Alexander and say, "Luck is on your side."

I turn back and kneel in front of Clover, asking, "How do you know all of this is true?"

She shifts and says, "I tried killing Alexander a few minutes ago by transferring all the holy magic I had in my body to him. In turn, I empowered the holy, and he was able to escape Alexander's body." She looks at the barrier. "He named himself Ekesi."

"How do I defeat him?"

"Just like you killed Valke, but no aid will come to you from any outside source," Clover says as she turns her gaze on me.

"Great, just like the fight in the arena," I murmur.

Clover attempts to stand up, and with my help, she succeeds. "Alexander and I will do all we can to aid you, but we cannot enter the barrier." She stumbles and weakly kneels in front of Alexander.

"Once I enter the barrier, can I escape?" I ask.

"No," she replies, unable to look me in the eyes.

Doubt engulfs my mind, but before I give Clover my answer, she places her hand on my cheek, saying, "Ruffus of Bern, over my three hundred years of living, I have never met a human more capable of this task. You have shown bravery, willpower, growth, and heart. Now, please, lend us your courage one more time, and try to kill it before Valke arrives."

I look at her. "What happens if a daemon and a holy fight in White Wood?"

She says, "First, we would be dead. Second, whoever wins ascends, and I do not know what would happen next."

I scoff and say, "Great, I'll add it to the list of shit that can go wrong today." I run my hand through Clover's hair and say, "Go through the portal. Erol is there, most likely jumping up and down in victory. Tell him I need him." I kiss her forehead and walk toward the staircase.

"Ruffus," Clover calls out to me, "may the goddess guide your path, and I will see you when this is over."

I blow her a kiss and wink at her. She rolls her eyes and smiles as she walks toward the portal, dragging Alexander with her. As I go up the staircase, I think about everything that has happened here again. We had the fights we had, the enemies we defeated, the crises we found, and the allies I made.

I try to calm my nerves by saying, "I hope Erol takes me out to eat again, and if he does, I hope it is not dragon marrow again. I threw up fire for the next three days after eating that." Each and every step is harder to make as my body shakes in fear, but I go on moving forward to the last task I have before my mission is complete.

The Last Requiem:
A Gambler's Fate

I make it to the top of the staircase, and I can see him, the creature responsible for everything, looking toward the cloud-covered sunrise. He notices me as I walk up to the barrier, turning his body to face me. The holy looks exactly like Valke after he ascended in the arena match, except with smoother edges. His fur is blue, and his eyes are golden. The aura around him is one of peace and tranquility. Beautiful glistening orbs float around him, smashing the far side of the barrier, causing it to crack slightly.

In a deep voice, he says, "Ruffus of Bern, you have been quite the thorn in my side. As it stands, I would have thought my kin would have already disposed of you. Or at least repossessed you."

I place my hand on the barrier and walk through it. The wall feels like I passed under a sheet of water as it touches my skin, making me shiver as I finish traversing through it. "Who might your brother be?" I say with a shake, already knowing the answer.

"Valke, or so the monstrosity calls himself," he says in disgust. "The first fallen holy." He sizes me up and turns his gaze toward the clouded sunrise again. "I am destined to kill him. Did you know? After I pierce his heart, I will ascend to an archangel and join my lords in the eternal battle for this realm's ruling."

"'Ascend.' That damn word escapes your lips as it did with Valke. At this point I might as well get it branded on my body." I unsheathe my sword slowly and notice it glowing faintly in dim golden light. Ekesi glances toward me, eyeing my sword carefully.

"What an interesting artifact you wield. Fine craftsmanship. It seems as if it were supposed to be an ornament to one of the Three's temples," he says curiously. "I might have use of it. It could break this barrier." He gestures to me to come closer. "It glows with stolen power."

"What will you do if I release you? I have personally seen what destruction you have brought to White Wood. You had me thinking a necromancer or a daemon was the cause of this!" I say as I point my blade toward him.

"The only way to ascend to my heavens is to be seen as worthy by my lords through fierce combat and restoring order, and that is what I intend to do. The forest was balanced by the druids who communed in it, but the prince killed most of them. Now only chaotic magic reigns through it. A shame, really, but the shift in magic and his desperation for forgiveness allowed me to possess him fully. Now begins the healing process for White Wood," he says sternly.

"I am sure you were not whispering in his ears to do bad things," I mock him.

I can hear him growl and almost lose his composure. "The vampire named Alexander found me in the chapel dedicated to my kin years ago, a fool to try to study my arts. I could see his corrupted spirit needed guidance, and I provided it," he scoffs.

"The only good deed that he has done was to kill his father and purge his line almost to completion, eliminating some chaos in this town and restoring order to his corrupting spirit. It took every ounce of my power to reach out to others to make Alexander take the necessary steps to be possessed by me."

"The letter from the grande cardinal of River Front, so Alexander would meet the priest of your church," I say bitterly.

"The old follower thought he was helping bring his theology and saving the souls here, which he did. And Alexander's curiosity for power was his downfall."

"As I said, you were behind his madness," I interrupt. "He destroyed this town with your influence! You plunged White Wood into uncontrolled chaos, ruining the balance established by the druids, all for your gain! You are no better than Val—"

With a flash of blinding light and speed, I am suddenly choked by Ekesi's hand, being held eight feet in the air.

"Never compare me to that waste of a spirit," he hisses.

I grab ahold of his hand and try to break loose from his grip, but he will not budge.

"Unfortunately for you, I can smell that you were near him. I pity you—haunting you every step of your way, causing doubt in your mind. This is what I mean to rid the world of: doubt! I mean to create hope through action, harmony through words, and peace through death." He squeezes my neck tighter and looks at my sword. "You wounded him with this blade. I can feel an echo of his presence in it as well. A weapon that slays an ethereal being becomes cursed, and yet your resolve will keep you from losing complete sanity, a feat not easily achieved. Even the young, unnamed holy fell to this accursed item." He raises his claw-like hand and places the tip of his finger on my forehead. "Now, allow me to see your memories so I may judge you correctly. Should you live?"

With a hard tap on my forehead, the area around me turns white, making everything look as if it's made of marble for a moment, but ending quickly as I reject him.

"You have the ability to block me. How?" he asks as he sniffs around me. "No." He examines my eyes, and with the tip of his thick tongue, he licks a small drop of blood from the puncture wound he made on my forehead. "There is something, a serum, running through your veins, blocking a direct path to your mind. Mortals' intuitions and creations are astounding."

I grunt some words out and try to talk, but my windpipe is being crushed. The only sound that comes from my mouth is, "Meep!"

He loosens the grip on my neck.

I cough and say, "This is what I needed, fresh air! And a dressing for my forehead. Can't you be gentler?"

"Speak, pray to your creators!" Ekesi yells at me. "For these will be your last words."

I begin to talk nonsense as quickly as I can manage, trying to buy time for me to search my pockets for anything useful. As I shuffle, I stab my hand with what feels like a long, thick needle.

"I do not understand," Ekesi whispers to himself. "In the face of judgment, you do not plead for your life or ask to make a deal. Instead, you choose to talk about your dislike for a dish that contains dragon marrow."

"You asked me to speak." I cough and smile. "So, I spoke. Now it's your turn to tell me your opinion."

As Ekesi gets ready to berate me, I take the opportunity to stab him with the thick needle on the bottom of his forearm. In surprise, Ekesi loses his grip on me, and I am ready to counter. I quickly grab onto his arm, and as expected, he tries to shake me off. Using the momentum, I launch myself up high enough for my foot to deliver a solid kick to his face and push myself far enough to be away from any of his attacks.

Ekesi staggers, losing his footing as he falls on his back, stunned at what just happened to him.

I land on my butt, putting my hand on my neck, rubbing it as I cough.

"You will pay for that!" he says as he gets up to face me, but to his surprise, he can't see me as I recover and roll away, flanking him from behind.

With a swift slash from Coal, I can cut where I think his tendons should be, hoping to inflict a good deal of damage, but my blade slightly bounces back once it makes contact. I'm able to slice a few hairs and only cut skin-deep. I immediately notice Ekesi's tail is different from Valke's.

Instead of his three bull-like tails, Ekesi's resemble a reptile's, thick on the base and shortening to the tip with a few scales that shimmer even in the darkness. Fascinated by it, I don't anticipate the tail rearing back and smacking me with immense force, smashing me to the barrier.

As I land face-first on the ground, I can hear Ekesi muttering a few words that I recognize because I have heard Michael chant them before. As I rub my forehead and stand back up, I see Ekesi glaring at me as he rubs the area I attacked. His hand glows in dim golden light, illuminating the area, showing me his muscles.

Now I've done it. He is angry, I think to myself.

"A valiant effort on your part, but to no avail," he says, looking at me. I can feel him wanting to rip me to shreds as his finger-like appendages twitch uncontrollably. "My lords and fate smile upon you, for I cannot kill you because I cannot judge you."

"Lucky me," I say as I wobble a bit. "Nice to know that you can't kill the unjudged."

"Although if it were self-defense, I could kill you, human. For I am protecting my own life, and the law allows in that situation." He smiles as he walks to me, slightly shaking his wounded leg.

I give him a weak wink and charge at him. I know I can still fight, even if my whole body is about to shut down from exhaustion, hunger, and all the injuries I've picked up.

Ekesi stops and stands still, almost surprised at my actions. From behind him, a few glowing orbs rush toward me like arrows released from a bow. I dodge one and reach into my coat for a throwing knife, quickly releasing it toward Ekesi. An orb catches the blade, releasing a small splash of liquid from it. Surprised, I stop and observe the orb ripple as my knife aimlessly floats inside of it.

"What in the Three's name?" I murmur as I slowly back away.

Ekesi raises one of his eyebrows and twirls one of his fingerlike appendages, instantly lowering the area's temperature. The orb with my knife in it quickly turns solid and elongates, creating a spear using my knife as the tip, and with a snap of Ekesi's finger, the spear projects toward me.

"You have to be joking!" I yell as I backflip out of the spear's way. "You can manipulate water?" I grunt at Ekesi.

With a smirk that brings a chill to my bone, he begins to walk toward me again, making a weak fist, returning the temperature to what it once was and creating an immense amount of humidity, instantly drenching all of my body, even my undergarments. As he reaches the middle of the platform, he lets a mighty roar out toward the sky, creating a multitude of lightning strikes around the barrier.

Instead of being paralyzed in fear, I take the initiative to attack him as he howls, but my lower body doesn't obey. I glance down only to see my legs encased in ice. I let a gasp out as I smash the ice with the hilt of my sword, only for it to quickly regrow and creep up my legs faster.

Ekesi lets out a small chuckle as he says, "Did you think you were the only one who could cause a distraction?" He glances toward the covered sunrise and says, "I knew someone had to come and attempt to defeat me. You see, I wanted the eldar to be the one. Her body and attuned affinity to magic would serve me the best."

He raises his claw-like hand and snaps his fingers, making liquid rise up to my torso, slowly freezing. I can only yell in agony as the ice begins to burn my body.

"Sadly, you were the one who came through the barrier, and just by looking at you, I can tell you are magically impaired. The only useful thing to come out of you is that sword that is now frozen in your hand." He turns his gaze to me. "I am ready and powerful enough to open rifts. The only thing left for me is to possess you. You see, only mortals from this plane of existence can open a rift to my world. It is rare for one to happen naturally, but then again, here I am. Fate extended her hand to me."

Panic engulfs my thoughts as I smash the ice as quickly as I can, but it regrows, spreading faster and creating a more rigid shell. "You are a fool to kill me, Ekesi! You cannot possess the dead, and the potion I have taken will not allow you to possess me, even if I fall unconscious! I know my potions and tinctures!" I bluff because I have no idea if what I said is true.

He raises his eyebrows, coming up to me. He inspects me with his eyes, wondering if what I said is true. After a brief pause, he grabs my shaking hands and encases them in ice, making me gasp in pain. "I know not if you speak the truth, but I have an idea of how to remedy my predicament with a hypothesis of mine. As you can see, I can manipulate liquids, and since a tincture and blood are liquid—"

My brain begins to quickly think up more lies as I see Ekesi materialize a sharp-looking shard of ice on the tip of his fingernail. "You know, I learned that cutting me into slices won't fix your prob—"

Ekesi cuts the right side of my neck where the jugular is located, quickly placing his hand on it. He whispers to me softly, "The cold should slow down your heart rate enough for me to be able to siphon all the tincture out. Your body contains an unnatural substance, and I must cleanse the blood."

I gasp and twitch in shock as I feel my warm blood run down my neck. Nothing in this world has prepared me for a death like this. I was half expecting to be eaten by a monster, stabbed by a harlot, or even hugged to death by Erol, but I never expected my death would be at the hands of a holy.

"Yes," he says as he licks his lips, "I can feel the difference in your blood, but I can also feel you fading into peace. Do not fret. I won't allow death to cast its warm, caring embrace on your spirit, for it is not your time yet." With his other hand, he softly caresses my head. "Forgive my intrusion, Ruffus of Bern, but this is for the greater good, for a better world."

My body feels colder than it has ever been before, and my skin feels the weak wind calmly touch my cheeks. My heart begins to slow down, and each breath I take feels as if I were back home with my parents and siblings. I feel peace as I have never felt before, and my eyes begin to close as darkness consumes my vision.

A tiny spark of light quickly blinds me as I find myself standing naked next to a small pond. The sky above me shows me a multitude of celestial bodies and stars blanketing the skies as a warm breeze gently touches my body. A cool mist consumes the area as a figure appears from behind me. I quickly turn around and see my sister, Yubia. She is as innocent and beautiful as I remember her, and she looks as if she hasn't aged.

A strong gust of wind abruptly blows toward me, making me cover my eyes, and after it subsides, I slowly put my hands down, opening my eyes, seeing the environment changing around me.

Now I am next to the ocean with my feet deep in the sand. I look at my body that currently has linen clothing on it. Next to me is my sister, wearing the same thing, sitting down on the wet sand. I join her as a weak wave touches both our feet. The warm water brings a smile to my face as I take a deep breath of the salty air.

Yubia turns her head and says in a sweet voice, "Seems you are in trouble, big brother. Fighting a holy this time?"

I chuckle. "You know me, I bite off more than I can chew. This is why I like soup. I don't have to chew much." I turn my gaze toward her to see her smiling at me. "Is this real?" I ask as another wave caresses my feet.

"This is as real as you believe, but you cannot cross to the next realm," she says as she looks up to the starry sky.

"Why?" I ask as I turn my gaze toward the celestial bodies up above.

"The holy is keeping you alive. Its power grows in strength, but death is giving you a moment of respite."

I slowly fall and lie on the warm sand, burying my hands, feeling each grain on my fingers as the warm waves touch my body.

"Hold on for a few more seconds, Ruffus. Fate has other plans for you, and the oracle has spoken to me about the future," she says softly. "Now, big brother, it is time to go back. The holy is beckoning you, and you must go to him."

"An oracle?"

I sit up to look at Yubia, but she disappears before I can say goodbye to her. I look to the horizon and see an enormous wave about to crash on me. I lower my head and look toward my feet, only to be smacked by the water and dragged by the powerful current, restoring all my senses. I can feel freezing water entering my lungs, and with a scream, I return to the horrible reality I was dragged from.

My eyes burst open, only to see Ekesi looking behind me with fury in his eyes as a giant fireball smashes his face, knocking him back a few good feet. I feel the ice encasing me weaken, and with a strong jerking movement, my body breaks the ice, making me fall quickly to the ground next to my sword. I gasp for air, coughing up what looks like a yellow substance out of my mouth. I turn to the side, trying to focus my eyes, only to see Ekesi shaking his head, recovering from the enormous fireball that struck him.

"*Reik men tehmpret!*" a familiar voice yells behind me as multiple fireballs that resemble a herd of horses charge directly at Ekesi, slamming him against the barrier wall.

I weakly staunch my neck and turn to see all of them, battered and bruised, bleeding through their clothes and armor, exhausted like me but with relentless conviction in all of their eyes.

My friends.

Michael is bloodier than usual and looks angry as his hands glow with a dim light to them. Trist wipes dried blood off her mouth with the look of someone who has had enough with this place and is ready to pounce on our enemy. Erol is about to go on a rampage. I can see his body has gone through the meat grinder.

In front of all of them is Clover, standing tall with her

hands engulfed in flames and her eyes showing a collected sense of triumph on her last attack. She has a wooden stick in her hand that reminds me of a tree branch, and with a loud Elvish incantation, another enormous fireball forms in front of her and, with a snap of her fingers, launches like a cannon toward Ekesi.

I wave at them weakly and say softly, "You guys took your sweet-ass time getting here."

"Did he hurt you, my cub?" Erol says in an infuriated, shaky voice as he limps toward Ekesi.

"The holy killed him and brought him back to life, Erol. Also, he's bleeding on the floor," Clover states.

"I sensed it when it happened," Michael added.

Erol lets a mighty roar out and charges at Ekesi as he tries to recover from the immense fireball, followed by a war cry from Trist and a barrage of magical attacks from Clover.

I crawl toward Michael, who quickly runs toward me, and say, "Glad you didn't kick the bucket, Michael."

"I thank the Three for their mighty wisdom that sent Lynn and Laura toward me in my hour of need. They brought me back from the trance I was in. I was as good as dead. I suppose if it was not for both of them, well, it would be a different ending. It seems a revenant was chewing on my shoe," he says as he lays my head on his lap, slowly and softly touching my forehead.

With a tear in my eye, I ask, "Am I undead? I died and saw my sister."

Michael looks into my eyes and smiles at me. "No, by the Three's grace, you are still considered living and not undead. The holy kept your brain and heart intact. You never died—you just had a near-death experience. Any other day, I would ask your opinion on the experience of this miracle," he says as he slowly heals me, restoring my energy.

"It was not something I'd recommend doing," I say weakly.

"Noted," he says with a smile.

Michael looks up and creates a shield in front of us with his free hand, successfully deflecting a gigantic ice shard away from us. He falls back, gasping for air, saying, "Ruffus, I have used up my reserves. I cannot heal or give you any more of my energy without the consequence of my death. Go, finish this fight!"

I weakly stand, feeling slightly rejuvenated as Michael gasps on the floor. I slowly get him up and place him near the staircase. "Here, you are not safe, but if an attack comes your way, you can try to get through the barrier and fall down the stairs quickly to avoid certain death."

Michael lets out a laugh and says, "Yes, because falling down a staircase won't kill me."

I smile as I turn to see the fight behind me. Erol gets smacked across the platform, but Clover catches him with her magic and rejuvenates him a small amount as Trist shield-slams Ekesi and blocks his counter toward her. Elegantly, Trist parries and connects a chain of attacks to Ekesi that makes me wish he would not get up from that onslaught.

Sadly, before the last hit strikes, Ekesi opens his mouth and blows a freezing wind out, encasing Trist in a sheet of ice, trapping her. He quickly rears back and uppercuts her, breaking the ice, sending her up a few feet in the air. With haste, I make my way to him and slide on the floor, attempting to cut his feet, but again, my sword bounces off, directing his attention toward me. To my luck, Coal wounds Ekesi's legs and makes him bleed a golden substance out. Furious, he looks at me, and in return, I wink at him, causing the veins in his head to pop out as he roars and attempts to grapple with me. He misses me by a hair as I slide away from him and throw my last four knives at him, making contact but bouncing off his skin.

"Cub! Swap weapons!" Erol yells as he runs toward me. He

throws his polearm at the beast with grace, hitting him, while Trist runs back, grabbing Ekesi's attention.

I throw Coal at Erol with all my strength, praying he will catch it and not get impaled by it. Erol sidesteps, grabs the hilt of the flying blade, and gives me a quick nod as he charges toward Ekesi. Erol spins the sword in the air with a decisive leap and stabs the holy deep through his chest.

The fight is over.

Ekesi falls to his knees with a gasp, looking down at the impaled sword on his chest. He shakes his head and lets out a deafening howl, creating a strong gust of wind that pushes all of us to the ground, barely allowing us to stand.

"Impossible!" he yells as he raises his hand. A bright blue light shoots up to the sky out of his palm. "You all have been a plague to my plans. I will not allow you, mortals, to stop me from purging White Wood. No, not just this place, but the world, from its chaos! You have all been judged by your actions toward me and are now an enemy of law and order to this realm. May the afterlife show you mercy!"

Violently, he punches the ground down on the platform, causing it to crack and break. With a loud snap, the platform shatters, breaking the barrier around us. We all fall toward the roof of the cathedral.

With a loud yell, Clover summons a potent spell of wind that takes the form of a raven, cushioning the fall to the roof. As I groan and get up, I look at the area and sigh in relief when I see everyone is alive but semi-conscious on the floor. I turn to face the sky, only to see the holy floating down with two eagle-looking wings on his back.

Slowly descending, he admires the new wings and gives a quick nod toward me. "Your companion might have killed me, but my lords have blessed me with time and power to open a rift. I do not need you. After that, this blade will claim my body. Now I am the catalyst that will begin this long-awaited war that started in Laberynthea!"

He begins to flap his wings as if he is learning how to control them, giving me enough time to grab my grappling hook and tie the Knitting Guild rope to it. As Ekesi begins to fly away, I start to spin the grappling hook violently and mutter, "You are not going anywhere."

I release it, landing perfectly on my target, Coal. As he flies away, my feet are ripped from the ground. It surprises me that Ekesi doesn't notice the extra weight, but then again, I am sure he has never flown before in his life.

The cold air and winds are trying to knock me down, but I hold on. Any other time, I would be terrified of my current predicament, but I have experienced so much fear in the last few hours that my mind has nothing left to give.

I climb the thin rope with all my remaining strength. As we fly above the forest, I can see a multitude of lights on the ground as if it was a small army approaching from River Front. We reach incredible heights as Ekesi stops climbing and takes a loud, deep, long breath of air before he starts his loud and powerful incantation. Raising his hand, palm facing up, he unleashes a blue ray of light toward the dark clouds, creating a funnel down to him.

I reach Coal and grab onto Ekesi's chest fur. The tug announces me, turning his view to me. "You are too late. In mere seconds, I will open the portal to my kingdom, and the cleansing will begin."

I grab Coal's handle, and with force, I pull it out of his chest, simultaneously hearing him gasp in pain. With finesse, I swing myself toward his flapping wing, and with a strong yell and a swift cut, Ekesi's wing is no more, and we both plummet to the ground.

As we fall, he grapples with me, but I am able to slash toward his face, giving him a clear cut through, releasing his grip on me. But with a rapid punch, he pushes me away from him. At this moment, we are at a stalemate as we now both plunge to our deaths. The howling wind rushes my ears, and looking toward the horizon, I can see the sky clear, and the sun has fully risen, giving the sky its morning colors.

We did it, I think as the ground closes in. White Wood is safe. I close my eyes as I await the end of my fall, only to feel terrible pain, forcing me to open my eyes, to meet Ekesi's rage as his claw-like hand impales my stomach.

"You will not have a peaceful death, mortal. I will see to it that my body will keep you alive and conscious as all your bones shatter. Know I will not die but reincarnate in a new body," he says, and starts laughing as we both plummet into a lake deep in the forest of White Wood.

As the bones in my body shatter, I see him close his eyes as a white orb the size of my fist leaves his mouth. My lungs fill with water as we slowly fall deeper into the lake. All I can see above me are a few dancing lights as the world goes dark around me, still feeling every single inch of my body in excruciating pain.

The nightmare is over. Everyone is safe.

A warm pair of hands touch my icy, dying body, making me shift my eyes, only to see Yubia once more.

"You did it," she says as she smiles above me. I feel the bottom of the lake hit my back.

"Rest. You deserve it," she says, and caresses my face. I start to close my eyes.

"May the Three guide your way back home, Ruffus," her voice whispers in the darkness as the lights above me begin to fade.

White Wood Sonata

As it has been foretold, the creature and Ruffus fall to the forest from the sky, while the Tenth Regiment of Arcadia reaches the gates of White Wood. They are able to purge the remaining feral undead and put out the fires plaguing the area. All of the people who fled White Wood are safe in an encampment created by Commander Leto's bodyguards with the help of General Moss's army of River Front. In the medical tents, a bishop and his healers can save the injured soldiers and members of the nobility who are not undead.

Soldiers storm the cathedral to find the group of adventurers, alive but severely injured on the cathedral's rooftop. The alchemist known as Laura leads the expedition to rescue these people, and with what little magic and medicine she has left, she can stabilize them from death's embrace. Except she can't find one of them. She looks high and low but is called back as the others need her attention.

The bestlia known as Erol does not speak a word, looking as if he has lost something of immense value to him. All of the soldiers can see how shattered and broken he is as he limps out to the cathedral.

The enforcer known as Michael helps the captain of the Seventh Regiment of Arcadia walk as all of the soldiers go to her aid first, only to be cursed at and ordered to find "him," but none of them know who "he" is.

The archmage known as Clover cries uncontrollably as she sits below her goddess statue in the medical tent, praying and whimpering, "Please tell me where he is. Give me the ability to see what can change his fate, give me the wisdom if I can't, and give me strength and capacity to do what needs to be done." She taps on her earring slowly. "Ruffus, please answer me." Deep down she realizes her prayers are hollow.

The prodigy child of the two most powerful mages of White Wood holds Laura's hand, and in her other, she carries a stuffed black dog that looks ragged and worn. She looks down, acting the calmest of them all, but once she sees Clover, her eyes start to water.

Berserker Alan leads a siege to the castle and is able to entrap a single powerful daemon with the help of his war priests and Locem, the head of the royal guard. The creature is incredibly weakened from a skirmish, but his wounds are not fatal, and it serves as a warning to others of what might have happened in the throne room. The rescue party delves deeper to save the last of the royal family in the catacombs in the castle. To Locem's surprise, he finds his sister amongst the vampires, weak and worn from battle. It seems she defended them from the feral undead and is now viewed as a hero.

The prince of White Wood is taken to the royal tent only to be embraced in a loving hug from his sister, now the queen of White Wood. He tells the story of what happened and how it happened. He is treated as a prisoner of war and taken to a cart guarded by the elite of Arcadia.

As the sun rises high in the sky, tranquility is felt around White Wood, creating hope for the people to find refugees and reclaim what they have lost. Fathers find their sons as children learn of the deaths of their parents. The mixture of emotions felt in White Wood reminds the troops of River Front how quickly life can change.

The animals in the forest begin to chirp, welcoming the morning light and the end of the evil that was cursing it, as druids from around the area leave the safety of their sanctuary and commune with the forest, beginning the restoration of balance.

The morning dew is witness to a beautiful maiden walking in the forest, alone. She is one of the only beings alive who can hear my whispers. I can see her, but she only sees me as a pale figure. As she walks down the beaten path, her elegant dress catches the colors of the fertile ground as small animals look from their burrows curiously in the direction she is heading. The cool fall wind caresses her face, moving her blond hair wildly as she reaches an enormous fallen hollow tree.

A druid bear beastman awakes from his meditation and walks out of the hollow tree, greeting the maiden. "Child of the water goddess, the spirits tell me they sent for you, for there is something lost here that should be found. But first, let me introduce myself. I am Estefan, speaker of the forest and head of the Circle of Druids."

His shaggy brown fur has twigs pointing out. This beastman's body is full of fresh scars with one of his eyes bandaged. His armor is made out of leaves and bark with a staff made out of white wood. Wisps surround him as small animals shuffle around his feet and the tree.

The maiden bows to the druid and says, "I am Helena, head of the College of Magic in River Front. It is good to see you are alive and well." She stands again and asks, "A voice led me here, almost like a murmur. Not from a wisp, but someone asking me to find something lost. What is lost?"

The druid beckons her through the hollow tree. She stands next to him as they walk together through the forest. She can feel the immense spiritual power and wild magic emanating from him, an equal to her. The druid says softly, "This is a forgotten path that my ancestors taught me as a cub. We are near the lake, where a whisper of a pale creature prophesied to me that someone like you would come. What is lost, I do not know. An artifact, perhaps, or a treasure of some sort? I am excited to learn."

They both reach a meadow, and, in the forest, they see a grand white tree that pulsates with extraordinary power at the center. The branches change colors every few seconds as wisps float around, disappearing in its light blue leaves. Helena stops and stares in awe at the majestic tree.

The druid stops, observes the wisps entering the tree, and says, "This is the Pale Tree. It's removed most of the taint of corruption by itself. Nature always finds a way to heal itself. The tragedy of White Wood and its corruption will be siphoned and cleansed."

"Never in my life have I witnessed something as magnificent as this," she whispers as the druid coughs slightly.

He moves a few bushes out of his way with one swipe of his staff. "The lake is this way. If by fate we meet again, I will gladly give you a tour."

They both reach a glimmering lake filled with spirits and wisps floating on the mist above the water's surface.

"Is it there?" she asks.

"It would seem so," he says as a wisp flies to his ear. "Now, I will wait here so you can retrieve whatever needs to be retrieved. The forest is back. I must help restore its power, but I cannot leave you lost here." The druid turns and glances deep toward the forest.

The wind blows lightly through the forest, sending the whispers of trees into the air, calming the area in a peaceful state. Helena walks toward the water and sees how still it is, projecting a perfect reflection of herself. She slowly takes off her jewelry, muttering an old Elvish incantation, then gently places her bare foot on the water, creating a slight ripple.

She stands above the water's surface, observing the wisps around her as she walks to the middle of the lake where all the floating wisps are. As she reaches the center, the wisps and spirits unify and form the silhouette of a young child, stopping Helena in her tracks.

She kneels, looking away from the apparition, saying in Elvish, "I am blessed, I am honored, I am not worthy."

The child who is I, touch Helena's head and smiles. As the wind blows gently on us, my voice speaks in an unknown dialect to Helena that she can understand but not imitate. "It won the favor of the forest. May life always be in balance," I say before disappears, only leaving a small lily pad where I stood.

In Elvish, Helena says, "Thank you, goddess of the forest." She wipes a tear out of her eye, for she has experienced what only a select few have before. She turns to see the druid bowing his head as a transparent figure gently caresses him lovingly.

Back at the camp, Commander Leto walks to the forest's edge, sniffing the air. He can see and hear rustling in the distance, slowly getting closer to him. A werewolf and a human druid child jump out of the bushes playfully. Seeing this, Leto stands tall, observing both of them with detail.

With a sigh of relief, the druid child gives the werewolf a flower. They both run along inside the forest once again, disturbing a few hidden birds. A few seconds later, Leto sees Lady Helena riding on a mighty white elk with large antlers upon his head.

He walks up to them to see a sleeping body encased in tree bark behind her. She carries a sword covered by a blanket that emanates power with a few wisps floating near it.

Leto stretches out his hand, grabbing the hilt of the covered sword. Examining it, he asks, "Is this what you felt?" His hand shakes, dropping the weapon on the ground.

Helena shrugs, "I am not sure."

"Who is that on the elk behind you?" he asks, walking toward him.

"He had this sword in his grip when I found them." She dismounts the elk gently and brushes her hand on its fur. "It took the combined powers of a druid and me to near the body and the weapon.

"I recognize this face. Is this—" he says as he comes to the realization, but Helena is the one to finish his sentence.

"The luckiest man in this realm, Ruffus of Bern."

Leto glances at her as he picks Ruffus up, throwing him on his shoulder, and says, "Let's see what information he has for us. Cardinal Ludwig is blessing everyone as they come out of the city. I don't trust him to examine Ruffus."

"There is no information that we can extract from him." She looks toward the smoky sky. "I will not allow it."

Season Change

I suddenly open my eyes as I gasp for air, startled by the memory of the holy in my mind, impaling me through the stomach. The lights in the room blind me for a few short seconds as my eyes adjust slowly to my surroundings.

I quickly try to move my arms and legs, only to feel a sharp pain over my whole body. My bones feel as if they have been glued back together, while my muscles twitch uncontrollably. My eyes shift directions to see my right leg and my right arm in a cast. I am shirtless, with new bandages covering my torso and a few patches on my thighs. I slowly move my left arm to rub my face and feel more bandages all over my cheeks. The memory of the holy cutting my neck drives my hand to the location. I can feel a few stitches and scarring beginning to appear.

I sigh in relief as I put my hand down to my sides again and slowly move my head left and right. Looking around, I see that I am in a medium-sized room with cozy-looking furniture with a fireplace that has a pot that is bubbling slightly. The smell of chicken soup drives my stomach to gurgle, making me realize that I am starving. My gaze turns to the window, tinted in many different colors. It has a picture of a violet half-moon, reflecting the colors on the walls and furniture in the area.

Slowly, I begin to sit up on my bed. This is not new to me. How long was I out this time?

I look toward my nightstand filled with cards and small baskets of fruits, sweets, and a brand-new stuffed black dog toy with a blue bow laced on its neck. The toy has a small note saying, "Get well soon! This is my favorite toy. He will keep you safe! —Lynn Merr."

I grab it, look at its black, beady eyes, and pray that this is not a trapped hellhound. I put it back where I found it to see a miniature painting of my parents beside a beautiful bouquet of jasmine. I smirk at the picture and grab the note that my father wrote on the flowers, and it reads:

I took your sword to the workshop after the grande cardinal gave it back to us. Do not worry, it is safe to wield. It had a few exciting spells on it, but we will talk about it once you feel better. Your mother has a surprise for you when you come back home to Bern. Know that we love you and are proud of you.

I look toward the door to see Coal wrapped up in brown linen and tied with hemp next to a few boxes marked with the Knitting Guild's seal. They look like clothing and a new pair of shoes or hopefully a new satchel or coat.

As I imagine what goodies there might be in the boxes, I hear a slight snore to the side of my bed, accompanied by the shuffling of clothes. Quickly, I poke my head to the side to see Jura asleep on a small blanket, looking as comfortable as a person sleeping on the floor can be. I can't help but smile as I grab an apple from my basket and drop it on Jura's sleeping face. As expected, he wakes up startled and ready to kill me until reason snaps him back to reality.

He whispers my name in surprise. In his reaction, he hugs me, saying, "I thought we had lost you for the second time this month. Gods, you are reckless!"

With my one good arm, I hug him back and say, "I'm like a weed. You can't get rid of me that easily."

I should have kept quiet because he punches me hard in my shoulder, making me yelp in pain.

"You amazingly lucky buffoon, you idiot of the highest degree! I swear, if you were not injured, I'd make sure to kill you and get someone to revive you back! You had Mother and Father worried sick!" he says with a tear in his eye. "We thought you were slain by the creature plaguing White Wood! You were out for ten days. Father and Mother did not leave your side for three!"

I look around. "Where are they now?"

"I told them to go back home and come back in a week," he replies.

"That holy did a number on me. I don't even know how I survived," I say as I place my hand on my neck, rubbing the scar.

Jura looks confused. "What holy? The Grande Cardinal informed the public that it was a daemon that plunged White Wood into chaos and that the holy wards restored order in the forest. He has a campaign at the moment trying to expel ancient magic users and daemonic scholars from this city. Still, Lady Helena uses her political influence, countering him and saying that the more we know, the better we can combat the unknown. She is a firm believer that it was not a daemon. I do not know what happened, and everyone from the company somehow forgot. I feel foul play. Before they all were questioned, they had to be seen by Cardinal Ludwig. I even took a few of the witnesses to the Grande Library, but no new wisps came out."

"Wait, what?"

"What happened in White Wood, Ruffus?"

I stay silent for a few seconds and ponder. *How could everyone forget? No, they did not forget, that's impossible. At least five of us witnessed it. The only thing I can remember well is that before the creature almost won, it spouted some nonsense about the war at Laberynthea.*

I sigh and look at him and lie. "I don't remember, Jura. Might have been a daemon, not a holy. They all look the same. All I know is I got wounded a few times, and the constant reminder of a place called Laberynthea keeps echoing in my head."

Jura looks me in the eyes for a second and sighs, grabbing a chair and bringing it next to the bed for him to sit on. "It is fine if you don't remember. And if you do, don't tell me. I'm sure the walls in here have ears. As for Laberynthea, that is the lost city of the gods. Remember, Father is on a constant expedition with the archeology society to try to locate it. The place is lost in time. Those echoes might be of our father talking about it at the dinner table when we were kids."

I grab an apple and offer it to Jura, only for him to smile at me and take it from my hand.

"So, how are the others?"

"The enforcer known as Michael returned to the church, giving a full report to the hierophant. He is now under watch for conspiracy under Cardinal Ludwig's orders and recommended by a few important politicians from White Wood to be trained to become a bishop or an inquisitor," Jura says.

"Conspiracy?"

"Yes," he says as he takes a bite out of his apple. "Seems he also thought a holy attacked, but when he was interviewed by the court of the queen of River Front, he could not provide evidence, and no wisps could be extracted from his memory. The Grande Cardinal thinks he is suffering from delusion."

"Where is he now?"

Jura puts the core of the apple on the floor next to him and says, "He comes around every other day to check up on you. He was the one who brought the cauldron filled with clam chowder. It was delicious. Pity you did not taste it."

"Wait, what?"

"What?" he says slyly. "As for Captain Trist, well, now second commander of the sixty-fifth infantry unit. Her leadership skills and tactical decisions granted her major praise in Arcadia. She has had no free time since she got out of the hospital," Jura says in a slightly jealous tone. "She almost lost her ranking after she outright called the Grande Cardinal a liar. It seems a creature resembling a holy was the cause." Jura shrugs. "The cardinal said daemons are known to trick people into thinking they are holies"

"Funny. Well, guess she is playing in the big leagues now." I grab a banana and peel it back carefully.

"As for Clover, I do not know what is going on with her. Meister Helena keeps all of their affairs somewhat secret. The only news is that she is helping with the White Wood restoration program," Jura says as he stands, walking to the sweets basket and snatching a chocolate cookie.

"How's her husband?" I ask.

"Under your debt. You saved Clover. He is the reason why"—he pauses and smiles—"Well, you will find out soon enough."

I raise an eyebrow in curiosity but remain quiet.

Jura grabs three more cookies and sits on the chair next to my bed. After he finishes eating them, he says, "As for the cat, no one knows where he is. After he got out of the hospital, he left abruptly. A friend of mine told me he was seen heading to the Wilds with a bag filled with creatures and animal parts."

"Oh," I say in a sad tone. "Well, what about White Wood?"

"Ah, the question I have been waiting for," Jura says eagerly. "Well, thanks to your efforts, they have become a more vital ally with this kingdom. They allowed an embassy of Arcadia to be built, and more churches will be erected. The alchemist Laura is now head of the town restoration program, and as for the prodigy child, Lynnet Merr is now Meister Helena's private student.

"They have visited multiple times, so I know they will be back soon. As for Alexander of White Wood, he got a full pardon from the queen of White Wood for the act of regicide, but he is not part of the royal family anymore. He relinquished all his titles and prestige. Lady Pryde, his fiancée, was able to use her house name, and witnesses proved an alibi saying that she protected the royal family trapped in the catacombs and the hospital from the daemon."

"I do not trust or like her," I say as a hint of rage escapes my lips.

"I agree. I do not trust her, but she did leave this for you." Jura shuffles his pockets and pulls out a ravishing-looking yellow rose. "She asked to tell you that she will be in contact soon."

"Great."

"Her brother came to visit you twice. The poor man looked so sickly. It surprised me he could even walk. It's like the air of the cathedral made him sick," Jura says as he observes the rose, handing it to me.

I take the rose and give it a quick sniff, "That smells good." I take another sniff. "Really good." I take a longer whiff and sigh in pleasure.

Suddenly my eyes tear up as a foul-smelling scent that reminds me of sewers engulfs the room—Jura coughs and gags, placing both his hands on his face, covering his mouth.

"Gods save us! What is that!" Jura gags as he speaks.

The door to my room slams open, and holding a big, steaming, broken bone is a dirty-looking Erol.

"My cub!" he exclaims as he runs to my side of the bed, throwing the bone toward Jura. Jura catches it by pure reflex, but the dense bone must have been heavy, as the chair rattles and Jura is left breathless.

Erol jumps on the bed, hugging me and smelling me all over. He quickly picks me up and lies on my clean bed to put me on top of him.

He gently rubs my head and says while he purrs, "I will provide better warmth and comfort!"

My angry-looking face hits his chest as my medical IV is ripped out of my hand by his movements, but I have no energy to move and retaliate.

Jura had to run to the bathroom to take off his clothes because the bone dripped a foul-smelling sludge on him. I can hear him coughing and throwing up as he yells Erol's name.

Erol looks toward Jura's direction and says, "What a pathetic welp and weakling of a kin to my cub." He moves his head to give me a quick lick on my hair, only to say, "My cub, you are bleeding! I will fix it!" Seemingly out of nowhere, he pulls out a jar filled with what looks like mud. He pops it open and slaps the salve on my hand, saying, "Better!" in a happy tone as he warmly hugs me, rubbing my back this time.

In that instant, Jura comes out of the bathroom, angry and half naked, with his sword, Quartz, drawn. "Get off him, you pathetic excuse of a bodyguard covered in fleas!"

"I take insult, whelp! I have no fleas!" Erol snarls as he skillfully jumps out of bed, making me spin in the air, landing face-first on my pillow.

As they rumble around in the room, all I can think about is that I cannot move and there is a pillow covering my face. So this is how I actually die, suffocated by my own pillow.

A pair of gentle hands pick me upright, allowing me to

gasp for air. As my eyes focus on my savior, I can clearly see it's Michael. He has a beautiful and expensive-looking set of deep blue robes. His hand carries a new, small, freshly made tattoo that reminds me of the emblem of Arcadia. After he places me correctly on my bed, he inspects the slop on my hand and says, "Earth balm from the Wilds. This must be Erol's handiwork."

I nod as I look toward them. "They keep fighting. It's like they are siblings."

"They will tire themselves out soon enough," Clover says as she walks through the door, wearing a comfortable-looking dress. "Again, your brother is indecent and fighting with an almost nude beastman. Does he have no shame?" she says as she avoids their fight and walks up to us, placing a basket of elven baked goods on my lap. "Goddess, this room is filthy."

I open the basket and grab a loaf of brown bread. "Wow, this looks fancy!"

"Yes, my husband wanted to treat you to good food before I hand you some bad news," she says as she rummages through her handbag.

I take a bite out of the soft loaf and say, "Mffhat fad bews?"

"Glad you asked! Here is your bill for the destruction that you caused in White Wood!" she says as she pulls out a roll of paper that is long enough for it to fall on the floor.

I start to cough violently as Michael gently rubs my back and says, "If it makes you feel a slight bit better, I had to pay an immense amount of gold for all the magic rules I broke."

As Clover begins to read off what's on the list, our attention goes to the door, as Trist accidentally lost grip of her present. Her attention is directed toward Erol and Jura fighting on the floor, and she does not know if she has to help or stay gawking.

As a few more days breeze on by, I am finally released yet again from the hospital wing in the Great Cathedral. The monks joke that I should have a room ready for me at all times. I laugh with them but feel a sense of dread after the thought in my head comes that they may be right.

Slowly, the leaves inside the city begin to turn yellow and orange, as fall is now upon us. The smell of food in the marketplace always reminds me of home, as I see children and adults running around with pumpkins and the last of the summer squashes.

Erol did not visit me on the last day at the hospital but did send a raven with a scroll attached to its leg. It read:

Come to the Old Markets next to canal in Traders' Berth. Find house that has number 11. I have a surprise for you.

—E

Doing as I'm told, I make my way through the broken-down and decrepit neighborhood. A warehouse-looking building containing the number eleven catches my attention, and as I walk next to the canal, I can see a few merchant boats heading to the exits of the city. As I make it to the reinforced double wooden doors, I can hear the noise of metal hitting metal and hissing on the inside.

I open the doors to see an ample empty space. The warehouse is two stories tall and the size of around three relatively big houses combined. I see Erol placing a pretty big piece of meat on an old-looking wooden table in a corner.

His ears move toward my direction, and with a smile, he beckons me in, saying, "Welcome home!"

"Home?"

Erol runs to pick me up and says, "Lord Hearth bought this place for you, so I move in! I knew my cub would be too embarrassed to ask me."

"Does that mean Clover is our landlord?"

Erol shrugs and puts me down on the ground. I spin in place, looking at the high ceiling, noticing all the broken wood panels, cracks in the foundation, and spiderwebs that have caught a pretty big-looking rat. Erol gently grabs my hand and walks me to the table, where the piece of meat is steaming, giving off a foul aroma.

"Dragon marrow," I say as I look at Erol's happy face. It would break his heart if I reminded him again that I detest it. "I made it especially for you, and tonight I will take you to the tavern, and we will feast like never before!" he says as he sits on a crooked chair, placing rusted tableware on the wobbly table.

I walk next to him and hug him, saying, "This is a great homecoming. Thank you."

We sit down as a few rats run around only to be snatched by a terrifyingly big spider. Erol looks uncomfortable. "Big spider. You exterminate, I no want to get near."

"How about this?" I pull out my dice. "Lowest roll has to capture them."

Erol shows his toothy smile as he gets near me. "Deal." He swipes the dice out of my hands and rolls a five in total.

"Damn, Erol, get ready to clean!"

I roll my dice as Erol licks my cheek and whispers in my ear, "Snake eyes."

Epilogue

All the pieces are in place as White Wood's sovereignty is slowly chipped away. The oracle can see a seat of power slowly planning and scheming in the world of mortals. Quiet whispers corrupt the hearts of kings and nobles.

The doors of Laberynthea rattle with excitement as the sealed evil waits for the key unknowingly created. The innocent that has slain the untamed and the sanctimonious is now a pawn to fate, as she has decreed that they are directly bonded. The whispers in the empty stone halls beg the oracle's prediction, but she remains quiet as she stands guard in front of a grand silver gatehouse.

Now, an ominous wind blows toward the castle embedded in the mountains. A power disturbs the minds of the people—a castle in the sky.

Erol

Ruffus